KILL THE LIGHTS

Also by Simon Williams

Talking Oscars

The childhood shows the man
as morning shows the day.

– MILTON, *Paradise Regained*

ACKNOWLEDGEMENTS

I would like to thank the following for their help and co-operation: Warner Chappell the Music Publishers of *My Fair Lady* for allowing my story to revolve around a revival of *My Fair Lady*; Sharon Jones, the Company Manager of *Phantom of the Opera*: Cumnor House School for the memory, the Minority Rights Group for their report Number 47 and Stokenchurch Dog Rescue Centre. My love and thanks also to Dolores Kearney, Amanda Conquy and her daughter, Helena Conquy-Brown, and Lisa Glass for their patience and lunches.

PROLOGUE

Julita Pascal was not going to be a chorus girl for long. No, sir, not if she could help it. There was energy and joy in the way she danced and no matter where they placed her she always stood out among the others in the line. 'Who's that redhead on the left?' 'Ain't she hot, that broad at the back?' She was always the one to be singled out. Julita was going to be a star.

In its third year on Broadway, *Together We Can Can-Can* had lost some of its early lustre. The original cast had left long ago for new revivals and the audience was mostly out-of-towners, even students in Nebraska were wearing the sweatshirt. Such shows can run for years, cruising on their own momentum, and if the performers find it stultifying there are always two things that make the tedium worth while: the applause and the paycheck. It's not unusual for some of the cast some of the time to hold something back, but Julita never did. For her the roar of the greasepaint and the smell of the crowd were still loud and pungent, and at every show, even at matinées, she danced full out and her smile looked for real.

On her dressing table in the interval Julita found an invitation. Nothing unusual in that, of the six girls she shared the room with she generally had the lion's share of the propositions. For the most part they were crude or crazy and were dismissed out of hand, but this one had style and authority, and for once Julita was tempted. A single orchid always carries its own persuasion. Of course her fellow dancers egged her on, she was the youngest among them and they nursed a sneaking disregard for her virtue. A pizza in front of *The Late Show*, they argued, had nothing on dinner at the Waldorf. 'Even allowing for a side order of extra pastrami, kiddo.'

Above one of the mirrors was a printed postcard that read, 'You have to kiss a lot of frogs before you find the prince.' And no one could say the girls weren't diligent in their search. Every evening they shared secrets as easily as hairspray, trading details that would make a sailor blush. Together they scoffed at manhood and its *modus operandi* and giggled at its prowess. At the end of the day, though, Man was the enemy they chose to sleep with. 'For Christ's sakes what's wrong with frogs anyways?'

'Go for it, Jules,' said the honey blonde with herpes. 'Live for today.'

'Take a chance,' said Mo.

'Take a douche,' said Sophie.

'Supposing he's a weirdo,' said Julita, already planning what to wear.

'You wish.'

'He's probably gay.'

'Or rich.'

'Or Puerto Rican.'

'With a name like Mortimer Franklyn Junior? Gimme a break.'

'Eat the lobster and run, girl.'

'You gotta kiss ass to get on, kiddo.'

'So kiss it.'

'Enjoy.'

Over dinner, the invitation suggested, they could discuss Julita's career. 'Your talent is ready and worthy of better things,' wrote her host. He certainly knew the way to a dancer's heart. By the end of the interval ambition had overriden doubt and Julita accepted.

After the curtain-call the company were quick to disgorge from their wigs and frocks, all the paraphernalia of their fictional lives. They had chicken soup and reality to get home to. After a final barrage of homilies on how to handle her host, his wealth and his genitals, the girls left and Julita was left alone in the dressing room.

'If you accept this invitation, my driver will be waiting for you at the stage door,' the note had said. Julita took her time, unhurriedly trading the crude stage make-up for something subtler, something for candlelight rather than limelight. She puckered her lips at the mirror image and squirted Guerlain on her neck. What would her mother say? She scattered the thick curls of her hair, the rich red of a cock pheasant, and swirled in front of the full length mirror to check the flare of her dress, bottle green silk.

'You look terrific, Jules,' said the stage door keeper as she handed in her key. 'Have yourself a nice one.'

At the kerb was a limousine shining clean and black like coal in the street light. An icy wind gusted down 45th Street, a tornado of junk food wrappings.

'Miss Pascal?' the driver asked, holding the door open. They went round the block and headed smoothly east across Times Square. Julita felt wicked and superior in the leathery warmth as she savoured this taste of her Shirley MacLaine fantasy. If this was a by-product of the stardom she craved, she craved it all the more. This was the life. Through the plate glass window the neon frenzy of Broadway was soundless like a dream.

Julita resisted the temptation to ask questions about her host for the driver's courtesy was purely functional and they drove in silence. He parked in 56th Street at the side entrance.

'Suite five-oh-oh-three,' he told her with a token doffing of his cap.

'Thanks,' she said. 'See you later.' It was safe to assume he'd be recalled to take her home.

'Good night, miss,' he answered.

The lift purred upwards and the first flicker of apprehension crossed Julita's mind. For someone who spent her life side-stepping trouble at street level, wasn't it crazy to be walking into a blind date in a private penthouse suite? If he turned out to be a dirty old man, she'd just take the smoked salmon and run.

'I'm so glad you could come,' he greeted her. 'How do you do?'

Julita shook his hand, dry and warm like pitta bread.

'Let me take your coat.' He seemed to remove it from her as if by magic. 'Do you like champagne?' His voice was quiet and coaxing. 'Do sit down.'

The room was dimly lit and its colours had the soothing neutrality of corporate taste, designed perhaps to foster its own anonymity. You're always safe with Regency stripes and chintz. In the fireplace fake flames flickered heartlessly with a telltale regularity and on the walls were hunting prints; red coats galloping in a carousel round the room, their quarry always one picture ahead.

Mortimer Franklyn wore a dark grey suit and a silk tie the colour of rhubarb. 'To you,' he said, raising his glass.

'To me,' Julita answered. The iced champagne gave her that dangerous feeling of control. From speakers out of sight she could hear opera playing faintly. What was it? They talked about the weather in staccato phrases, like two people playing for time. Was it Verdi perhaps? Yes, the summer had been hot. And wasn't the winter cold? Julita felt a gentle panic as if the pauses gave her vertigo.

Mortimer stood with his back to the fireplace like an actor in a play. The silence didn't seem to bother him at all.

'I think it's just too awful about the ozone layer,' Julita said valiantly. Her host nodded, studying her with the cold focus of a man not listening. Which Verdi was it, she wondered as the conversation floundered again. Perhaps he didn't care about the ozone layer.

A waiter glided in behind silver-domed trolleys and with the steely swiftness of a commando raid dinner was served. Julita suddenly had the idea it was all a mistake – the invitation had been meant for some one else.

'You liked the show then?' Julita heaped caviar on to fragile toast.

'No,' he answered lightly. 'I hated the show. I liked you.'

'Oh, thanks,' she said with her mouth full.

'You have talent. A good voice. Personality. You move well. You're very attractive.' He paid the compliment with a detached tone, like a diagnosis. There was no hint of flirtation and Julita wondered if he was gay. Certainly he was neat and tidy with his napkin tucked in.

4

'I have so little to do in the show,' she said modestly.

'Yes, that's right.' Mortimer prepared his next mouthful with great precision. 'But you have a certain quality, Julita, a certain quality. Very special.' He topped his caviar with egg yolk and chopped onion. 'I've got plans for you,' he said and put it in his mouth.

'What plans?' she asked too eagerly.

'We'll come to that later. I'm going to ask you to read something for me.'

'You're a producer?'

'I'm your host for the moment.' He filled her glass with wine. Verdi's music swelled into the room. There was no mistaking the voice of Placido Domingo, soaring like an eagle, nor the opera, Macbeth. Julita shivered at his bloody choice.

They ate the asparagus without speaking, somehow trapped in a synchronised ritual. Their eyes met with each mouthful, his unblinking and alert, hers wary. What was going on? If this was a duel, she was being outwitted. Don't defend, attack, she told herself. Take control, think Shirley MacLaine. Bubble for Christ's sake, bubble.

Over the salmon she forced him into conversation with a barrage of questions. Their common ground was musicals and they traded memories, blow for blow. They were well matched in terms of recollection; hardly a show was left unmentioned from *Oklahoma* to *Cats*, from *The Boyfriend* to *Cages Aux Folles*. With the faked gaiety of a stand-up comic, Julita fended off the pauses, plying him with questions and answering his unasked. As conversations go, it was far from fluent – it had the stilted rhythm of a demonstration film. Anything was better than the menace of silence.

The waiter showed no sign of returning and all the time Julita was aware of his scrutiny of her, his eyes had the alertness of a predator. She wasn't game.

'Relax,' he said. Is any instruction less soothing? There was even something in the measured way he ate his raspberries that increased her malaise. A pizza and *The Late Show* had never seemed more appealing.

'I know so little about you,' she said.

5

'No more you do,' he answered, and his smile went no further than his lips. 'And I know so much about you, you with the red hair.'

'Oh, do you?' The room seemed suddenly warmer. In the dim gold light Mortimer's skin was the colour of parchment. 'Like what?' she challenged.

His eyes were unflinching, sharp as a salamander. He breathed air in through his nose. 'You were born just after midday on Tuesday, the fifth of December 1964, Caesarian section, six pounds, five ounces, in the Des Moines State Infirmary. You are the eldest daughter of Stephen and Maria Pascal, your full name is Julita Maria Agnes, and your family home is one-oh-three-seven Jefferson Avenue, Des Moines, Iowa. Your mother was a teacher, your father a mechanic. Your favourite toy was a Spanish donkey that played music when you pulled his tail. You had chickenpox and measles when you were four, and mumps when you were six. You showed an early enthusiasm for music and won a certificate of excellence at the Des Moines Junior Dance Academy. Your best friend was called Stacey Corent and you had two guinea pigs called Starsky and Hutch. At the age of eight you had your tonsils out. Shall I go on?' Mortimer's voice was as smooth as castor oil.

Julita wondered if she was drunk or dreaming. Was this a surprise party, a joke? What business did this man have with her weight at birth, her mumps, her guinea pigs, for God's sake? And all the time he was sitting opposite her with the faraway look of a statue.

Julita could feel tears of sweat rolling from her armpits, her heart was pounding and her throat was dry. There was danger here; not the usual quick-as-a-flash downtown danger. This was a slow gentle danger; a scheming sneaky danger that she had already let go too far. She stood up, her knees trembling in a bid to be casual.

'Do go on,' she said in Katharine Hepburn's voice. 'You've obviously been to a lot of trouble.' Her legs were like stilts as she wandered the room feigning interest in the huntsmen on the walls.

'Your grades were good,' her host began again like someone

6

who had been interrupted. 'Not exceptional. Three "A"s but a "B" average. You majored in Music and Drama at the Atlanta College of The Arts.'

Julita was behind him now studying the door. No key in sight, no bolt, no chain.

'You left with honours and came to New York where you joined the elite NTA Institute studying under Meg Sjhornson. In your final term you had a – '

Julita ran to the door. She twisted the handle to left and right, she pushed, she pulled. It didn't move.

' – notable success as Sally Bowles in *Cabaret*. Do sit down.'

It wasn't an order but as a reflex she obeyed. Stay calm, she told herself, like with horses. Steady boy.

'It's a wonderful show, *Cabaret*,' she said.

'Yes,' he answered. He was studying her again the way shoppers do merchandise.

'Is that it, then?' she asked. 'My biography, my cv, is that it?' She was sitting within easy reach of the telephone.

'You're five feet six, you weigh one hundred and three pounds. Your first date in High School was Barnaby Wyatt. Your boyfriend in college was Jerome Schiltzer, an English major in the baseball team – '

With her left hand Julita snatched up the receiver and with her right she dialled.

'It's disconnected. Since then you have had three serious affairs – '

Julita hung up.

'And in July last year in the Walter Cohen Clinic you had a pregnancy – '

Julita stood up.

' – terminated.'

'I'm leaving,' she announced.

'Currently you are living alone on West Eighty-ninth Street. In the bank you have a credit balance of just over nine hundred dollars – '

'I don't know who the hell you are or what sort of game this is but I am leaving.' She could not keep the panic out of her voice. Even Shirley would have lost her cool by now. There was no point in trying to clothe this nightmare with

7

normality. 'I am leaving,' she repeated in case he hadn't heard.

'I'm sorry, I'm sorry.' His quiet, measured voice was suddenly overflowing with contrition. 'Forgive me, Julita, forgive me. I didn't mean to frighten you . . . how rude, how silly of me. Please don't be angry, please.' His head was on one side, innocence itself.

'Fetch my coat, open that door. I'm leaving.' Julita was almost shouting to control the fear that tightened her throat.

'I had no idea it would make you angry. I wanted to show you that . . . I had taken trouble. That's all. Please don't be cross.' He turned away and blew his nose. 'I've ruined it all.'

Julita relented. She felt exhausted and confused, manipulated and raw.

'OK, OK. No offence. I'm not angry. OK? Just tired . . . it's really time I went home.'

Without speaking Mortimer went to the fireplace and took from the mantelpiece a thick book. He turned the pages slowly until he found what he was looking for.

'I said earlier I'd like you to read for me.'

'Oh yes.' Julita remembered. He wasn't just a nutcase, he was a producer too and her host, her captor.

'It won't take long. And then, of course, you must go home.' He handed her the book. 'Do you know William Blake?'

'"Tyger Tyger"?' What kind of an audition was this?

'Yes, yes. Read it, please. Take your time.'

Julita sat down. At every turn things were getting crazier, banal and disconnected like in an early morning dream. Her throat was dry and the words on the page in front of her seemed to be offering resistance.

'When you're ready.' Mortimer had his back to her, staring into the fire with its non-combustible coal.

Julita coughed and took a breath.

> 'Tyger! Tyger! burning bright
> In the forests of the night
> What immortal hand or eye
> Could frame thy fearful symmetry?'

From force of habit Julita was projecting her voice, giving the verse no texture.

Like a man deep in prayer Mortimer moved slowly across the room. The wail of a police siren, from somewhere way below in the sweet, safe streets of New York City, cut through the silence. Its faint sound only emphasised her isolation. She was on to the third verse now.

> 'And what shoulder, and what art,
> Could twist the sinews of thy heart?
> And when thy heart began to beat,
> What dread hand? and what dread feet?'

Mortimer was standing behind her now, she could hear the measured inhalation of his breath. With slow fingers he loosened his tie, and as he slid it from his collar, silk on silk, it made a stealthy sound.

The heat of the room was pricking at Julita's skin, her pulse was heavy and fast like on first nights. She was half way through the poem battling with a fear of heights. No turning back. She had the poem to hold on to. Whose side was William Blake on? His or hers? Two verses to go.

> 'When the stars threw down their spears
> And water'd heaven with their tears,
> Did he smile his work to see?
> Did he who made the Lamb make thee?'

A flash in the air, pink in the dim gold light, pink the colour of rhubarb. Silk suddenly against her throat – draped loosely from behind, almost cool against her skin brushing back and forth, back and forth. His breathing was deeper now, faster. But his tie slid slowly back and forth – a gentle sawing against her neck. Julita was in a trance, a rabbit in the headlamps, panic-stricken and spellbound. She was fighting to stay calm, her head spinning with vertigo. And all the time Mortimer's silk tie was softly brushing her throat, rhubarb against her creamy skin. One more verse to go. Stay calm.

'What are you doing?' she asked, as if she didn't know.

'Carry on reading,' he answered. 'Carry on reading, you with the red hair.'

In a whisper she read on.

> 'Tyger! Tyger! burning bright
> In the forests of the night
> What immortal hand or eye
> Dare frame thy fearful symmetry?'

A silence like the sound of the ocean was pulsing in her ears, a silence that went on and on. The rhythm of the silk was slow like a snake against her throat. Mortimer was breathing as if the air smelled good – long and deep. Time passed, seconds and minutes confusing themselves in the silence.

'I must go home.' Julita spoke quietly so as not to cause alarm.

'No.'

'I must go home.'

'No.'

The room was hotter.

'What is going on?' Her voice was sterner now. Game over. 'What is going on?'

The tie was suddenly still. Her host leant forward and whispered in her ear, 'A little death.'

It was confirmation of a truth she already knew. It was beyond doubt. What other outcome could there be? Too late her hands flew up to grab the tie as it tightened round her throat. She screamed. She fought to free herself from the pressure that was pulling her into the chair. Her scream was loud and ugly and her feet were sliding on the carpet going nowhere. She felt giddy and could smell the stale sweetness of his breath.

Suddenly they were on the floor, entwined like new lovers in a ferocious passion. His eyes were shining with frenzy and the veins on his temples stood out under the sheen of his sweaty skin.

For a crazy moment she had the idea that it was him being throttled, not her – his life, not hers, that was in dispute.

10

There was a terrible drumming in her ears and his voice rasping, 'You with the red hair . . . red hair . . . red, red hair.'

She went to scream again, a dry screech that faded as her neck was squeezed in the tourniquet of silk. What was this man, this stranger clasping her on the brink of death? She could feel his body hot and wet against her. She went to scream again. No sound. Her mother's face was flashing in her head. 'I'm wearing clean panties, Mom, like you said, in case anything should happen. Clean panties, Mom, I promise.'

Julita was tumbling, burning, drowning, weightless with just her head and his, sobbing and demented. The world was going from pink to vermilion to maroon then black. There was no air. No air. No air.

Julita Pascal wasn't going to be a chorus girl for long. No, sir. She was going to be a star.

1

Griffith Gallagher walked slowly to church. The cold fog that had slunk in from the sea appeared not to worry him, this solitary figure on the promenade. There was about his movement a ghostly elegance. The truth was he could go no faster; to carry a stick would be to acknowledge his invading enemy, the rheumatism that nestled in his bones. So he chose to give the impression of a man unhurried and free of pain. It was the small vanity of an old actor, a performance for no one's benefit but his own. He had never wanted to be old and these final years seemed endless and without pleasure. Perhaps he prized his dignity too highly. For Griffith this seventh age of man was nothing but a penance. This era of the lean and slippered pantaloon was not to his liking.

'Good morning, Mr Gallagher,' a fellow Christian shouted in the churchyard. Swathed in tweed she was already shining with goodness as she scuttled past him. He wasn't deaf.

'Good morning,' he answered quietly. He did not know her name or even bother to raise his black fedora. For him, communion with the Lord was a private matter as with a bookmaker or a tailor. As for parochial bonhomie, he had deliberately nipped it in the bud. Coffee mornings and whist drives were not his cup of tea. Being brought out of himself was the last thing he wanted. Before you could say 'jumble sale' they'd be asking him to read the lesson. No thank you.

The church was far from full and dank with a week's disuse. Griffith took his seat at the back and sank slowly on to unsupple knees. He closed his eyes and his knuckles shone like ivory as he clasped his hands in prayer. Why was he here? He didn't believe in God and he hated the vicar. His prayers were offered on a sale-or-return basis, he had only returned to the ritual of Christianity as a last resort in the same way he had taken to sleeping pills and malt whisky. All he wanted was a little comfort.

'We have left undone those things we ought to have done. And we have done those things we ought not to have done.' The vicar's voice had the glib geniality of a Bingo caller. 'And there is no health in us.'

Feeble sunlight splintered through the stained glass window, the Last Supper, lending new colour to the flowers of a recent funeral. Griffith studied the grey heads of his fellow worshippers. From what sins, he wondered, did these quiet citizens seek release? Craven images in the day centre? Coveting a neighbour's bus pass?

> 'Breath through the heats of our desire
> Thy coolness and thy balm
> Let sense be dumb, let flesh retire . . .'

If only, thought Griffith, the coolness and the balm had breathed through the heat of his desire, he would not now be quite so keen to let sense be dumb and his flesh retire. And with frail voice the good parishioners of Hove sang on.

> 'Speak through the earthquake, wind and fire
> O, still small voice of calm.'

Like a man firing arrows in the dark he prayed for peace of mind. He had nothing to lose. With the taste of the sweet wine still in his throat he left the church nursing a small illusion of relief and at the corner shop on the way home Griffith filled a carrier bag with all the Sunday papers. Every one of them he bought. It was part of his mission.

Normally on a Sunday his son, Dominic, would come and take him to lunch in a country pub. Over beef that was never pink they would discuss cricket or theatre. On these subjects they could talk for hours without communicating. He did not like to admit it but Griffith missed the company of his daughter-in-law on these occasions. The conversations with Harriet were at least varied, she was always on about

13

something – high fibre or Save the Whale. 'The split' had come as no surprise to Griffith. Dominic had not found the knack of married life. Like father, like son.

But today Griffith ate his lunch alone looking at the sea from his tenth-floor flat. Self-catering was an art he had honed down during his touring days, though now it was mostly a simple transfer of items from freezer to microwave. He ate directly from the tin foil container to avoid the washing up. From his small verandah he threw scraps into the air and the gulls screeched greedily to catch them. The sea was dull and flat, its horizon blurred in to a low sky.

The time had come for his weekly task. Through scratched bifocals he began his scanning of the Sunday papers. He spread them on the table one by one, his index finger coursing back and forth across their pages. Over the years his thoroughness had not diminished, nor had his dread of finding what he sought.

Revolution and famine, scandal and finance were of no interest to Griffith. He skimmed through them, shaking his head from time to time. It was part of a world that no longer affected him. He clicked his tongue at the theatre reviews: who was Ayckbourn after Coward? Branagh beside Olivier? Where was the bravura, the glamour, the respect of verse? (He hadn't actually been to the theatre since Ralph Richardson died.)

On to the tabloids – he was half-way through. Did his memory play him tricks, he wondered, or had bosoms got smaller since the war? The nipples were fine but the tits were not up to par ... He hadn't had a decent erection since 1978 (with that widow in Bognor Regis). This pleasant thought left him quite unprepared for the shock, the urgent pounding of his heart on seeing the small paragraph on an inside page:

BRUTAL MURDER OF BROADWAY DANCER

Flattening the paper with trembling hands Griffith read, 'The body of 24-year-old Julita Pascal has been found in a rubbish tip on the Lower East Side. The vivacious young redhead had been in the chorus of the smash hit show *Together We Can Can-Can*. Reports indicate that she went missing after a mystery dinner date ten days ago. Police sources confirmed that the case was being treated as murder but would not release details. It is believed that the girl's body had been mutilated.'

Griffith cut the item from the page and sat with it in his hand, staring out the window. He read it again and again. '. . . vivacious young redhead . . . mutilated . . .' And then he dialled his son Dominic's telephone number. It was time for Griffith to be unburdened; for too long he had left undone those things he ought to have done. From somewhere in his memory he recalled playing Glendower . . . *Henry IV, Part I* at the Lyceum in Edinburgh and could hear Hotspur shouting in his head, 'Oh while you live, tell truth and shame the devil.' Oh yes, he would shame the devil if he could. He read again the newspaper cutting in his hand, with a sadness not so much for Julita Pascal as for her murderer.

Pressing the receiver to his ear Griffith studied the photographs on the mantelpiece, photographs of his unanswering son, a box Brownie collage of his childhood: in swimming trunks and on horseback scowling into the sun. One of him with sideburns singing with the band, another on his wedding day grinning blithely beside that bitch. The largest photograph was a colour still from his most recent film, his face now older with the wistful eyes of his mother looking into the middle-distance.

No reply.

It rang on and on. It was just as well unanswered. What was the point anyway? What would Dominic make of his feeble confession? What could the poor, dear boy do about it? What comfort could he offer? He would simply take the story as new evidence of senility, but for Griffith it was a dementia altogether too vivid to be endured.

Griffith hung up at last and with unseeing eyes stared out of the window again into the dusk. All he knew for certain was that the God he didn't believe in had not heard his prayers.

Twenty miles away on the other side of the Downs the telephone rang unanswered in Dominic's cottage. Only his

15

dog was there to howl at its persistence. Dominic was driving north following an impulse he knew was crazy. It was twilight and he regretted not spending the afternoon with his father. These days there was a safety in the sameness of their meetings: the lunch, the stroll, the game of chess, the grumbling and the silences. All they really shared was a wish that the other was more amiable. For whose benefit they met was never clear. As he approached Northampton he was already convinced his journey was a mistake. He knew that surprise visits could be boomerangs that curved round and hit you on the back of the head.

So what was he doing sitting uncomfortably in the half dark watching his wife in the arms of another man, this denim-clad lout? What did he feel as she swung the shining weight of her hair to one side to offer her neck for kissing. It was all too familiar, the way she closed her eyes confident of the pleasure she would give and take. He remembered too Harriet's smile as they joined together, the faraway smile of someone remembering a recipe.

It wasn't simple jealousy he felt, that proprietorial worm that feeds on reason. There was more to it: nostalgia, embarrassment, remorse and just a little excitement. He felt too the loneliness of someone whose exclusivity is blown.

'Go on. Go on,' she whispered like someone to a storyteller.

The young Lothario was pummelling her breast with the gusto of a mechanic and his unsubtle hands wrenched at her buttocks as if to split her. His passion was cold and athletic, a mere exhibition, Dominic told himself. He had always known when Harriet was faking it. So why was he holding his breath?

Like drunken dancers the lovers moved towards the bed and fell upon it entwined. Dominic half closed his eyes unsure whether it was to shut out the picture or improve the focus. His wife let out a familiar moan – a deep exhaling of breath, something between a gasp and a chuckle which Dominic found treacherous in its accuracy. He wasn't ready for this. By the dim light he watched the couple writhing earnestly together in a silence broken only by the age-old percussion of the bed. They were tangled in their clothes like presents half

16

unwrapped. He wanted to shout out, 'Stop. Stop.' As if what was happening was for his benefit not their own.

Suddenly the action on the bed was frozen. A still picture of dishevellment as a car door slammed in the distance. Harriet was wide-eyed with alarm, her partner had a stupid look of bewilderment.

'My husband,' she whispered.

'I thought he was in Buenos bloody Aires.'

'So did I.'

'Christ,' he screamed.

'Quick under the bed.'

'Look here, I – '

From off stage a voice called out: 'Hello, darling, I'm home. Where are you?'

'In the bedroom, darling.'

With well-rehearsed frenzy the couple sprang apart like anti-magnets. Coitus interruptus in the style of the Keystone Cops. In double time the scene was transformed. In seconds Harriet was quickly re-shevelled, casually reclining with a book on the bed while underneath it the unhappy swain lay breathless, clutching his motorbike helmet.

Enter the husband in a pinstripe suit, carrying a briefcase. All around him the audience laughed and Dominic sat back, welcoming for a moment the return of unreality to the scene. Only much later did he realise that for the price of his ticket he had learnt two things. Firstly, the play was not that good, and secondly, he was a long way yet from being free of loving his wife.

Immediately after a performance is a delicate time for an actor, a re-entry phase where he has to shed the face and costume of his alter ego and resume his own identity. A visitor into this no man's land must tread warily, for the player feels he has nothing more to offer except a tooth mug of warm white wine, he is at his most vulnerable and his paranoia can run amok. Tell him he was 'terrific, darling, in the final scene', and instantly he wonders what the hell was wrong with the first two acts.

Dominic paused at Harriet's dressing room door before knocking. It was only a studio performance but there was a crowd of people milling about backstage. He wished again he hadn't come. It was over a year since he had seen her face to face.

'I loved it. You were terrific. Great.' He was standing behind Harriet watching her take off her make-up in the mirror. 'Really terrific.' With busy fingers she was smearing her face with great scoops of the cream that wipes the smile off an actor's face. Her eyes were smudged black with mascara.

'It's not your kind of thing.' She glanced at him in the mirror, a wily panda not quite trusting the bamboo shoot he offered. 'You should have let me know you were coming.'

In truth she was quite glad not to have known. Playing a love scene in front of your estranged husband is not every girl's idea of a fun day's work. She offered him a drink by mistake and was glad he declined. 'I'm sorry, I forgot.'

'I really thought you were great.'

Dominic remembered how rare and elusive sincerity can be backstage. He wanted her to believe him. 'Very funny and er . . . touching.' The tables had turned and it was now his performance that was under scrutiny.

'Thank you.' Harriet sounded brittle without meaning to. She tugged her hair brutally back and forth through an elastic band, a switch of ripe wheat flaying the air.

Neither of them could quite be the person they wanted to be with each other. Had that been the trouble all along?

'Do you want to have supper?'

Dominic had not planned to ask her but he wanted time to let the awkwardness between them subside. Harriet studied him in the mirror for a second; she was wrapped in a blood-red towel and his eyes were fixed on the galaxy of moles between her shoulder blades. His hand nearly reached out to stroke her chalk white skin.

'Yes, that'd be lovely,' she said. And they smiled at each other, the smile a kind of truce.

'I'll wait outside,' he said. He couldn't remember the last time he had seen her naked and the idea of her being coy didn't appeal to him.

'I won't be long,' she answered with the shrug of a girl whose coy days were over.

18

Rumour that Dominic Gallagher was around had travelled fast. A group of autograph hunters had assembled at the stage door. Cold hands proffered paper and pens. 'Put with love.' 'Make it to Karen.' 'It's for my aunt.' 'You're taller than I thought.' Harriet hung back. She had almost forgotten the discomfort of bathing in his reflected glory.

'Are you anybody, love?' a woman asked. They were like carol singers clustered in the lamplight.

'No,' she answered, 'I just work here.'

A man in a balaclava nudged her. 'He's great, isn't he?'

'Yes,' she answered. He was once.

'A real star I reckon.'

And one to whom her wagon was no longer hitched, she reflected as they drove off through the town.

'I'm hoping that you'll be finding satisfaction, sir, in our victuals.' The manager of the Taj Mahal Northampton was breathless with solicitude, his teeth gleamed out from a face the colour of consommé. 'It is a delighted honour to be entertaining a thespian of your magnitude, and a lady of such beauty . . .'

He withdrew at last and in the backwash of this hyperbole Dominic and Harriet ate their curry in silence for a time, he a Madras, she a Vindaloo.

When they began to speak it was with the taut formality of characters in a Coward play. Very flat, Northampton. They were taking stock of one another like old adversaries when the war is over. The gap between them had widened and they were neither of them sure if the distance lent enchantment. They discussed the play in general and Harriet's performance in detail.

'You were marvellous,' Dominic said, '. . . intelligent and . . . spontaneous. You've got this extraordinary . . .' he nearly said sexuality, '. . . energy on stage. You were really very good.'

Harriet laughed at his flattery and he studied her face for a moment hoping that his eyes were not registering the hopeless nostalgia he felt for her. 'I was appalled by the idea that it was me who had kept you away from the stage for so long.'

She smiled in acknowledgement. The silence of the restaurant was splintered by the sound of an old sitar tape. With her head on one side the light of the candle caught the sheen of her skin. She had expected to feel threatened by his opinions, diminished by them like before, but she didn't. There was nothing mocking or dismissive in what he said. This quiet, attentive man was not the husband she remembered. This teetotalling Dominic was quite new.

'No notes?' she asked. 'No criticism?'

Dominic thought. 'That dress you wore in the first act.'

'The red one?'

'He nodded. 'It's not good.'

'You don't like it?'

'No.'

'Oh.'

'It looks cheap.'

'It was cheap.'

'It shouldn't be. It should look really classy, a proper grown-up, well-cut dress. That's the kind of girl she is.'

'Yes.' Harriet was instantly disenchanted with the red dress. 'It's the budget. They couldn't afford Karl Lagerfeld. Actually we're desperate to find a producer to bring the play down to London. What do you think?'

'It would be a good part for you to be seen in.' Dominic didn't say that the critics would massacre the play.

'We haven't had any luck. It'd cost a fortune to transfer us to the West End, and producers don't want shows like this without a star name.'

Dominic could smell his wife's cleansing cream across the table, the clean scent of witch hazel. He was shifting broken pieces of poppadom around on his side plate as he remembered the love scene in the play and what he had felt watching it, that dizzy longing of an addict for his bane. What the hell was he doing here on a wet Sunday evening in Northampton inviting in all this pain? He wanted to leave, to escape the sound of the damn sitar. When he looked up he caught Harriet's look of pity unawares.

'What about your mother?' he asked. 'Couldn't she help?'

20

As a theatre owner his mother-in-law seemed the obvious suggestion.

Harriet shook her head to dismiss any idea of nepotism. 'It's not quite her bag. Anyway she's got enough on her plate at the moment.'

Phoebe Brunswick had five years ago inherited the theatre empire of her husband, Austin. It had been Dominic who had encouraged her not to sell up, had persuaded her that there was no big mystique in the running of theatres. 'It just takes common sense and taste,' he had told her. So she had ignored the pressure round her to abdicate and had tentatively begun to follow the instruction of her husband's will to 'carry on as best you can, my darling. It won't be easy but there's no one else I can trust and I know you love the theatres as much as I do.' They had only been married for eight years and there was on his side of the family considerable opposition to her legacy. Gradually she had taken control; what she lacked in authority at the boardroom table she made up for with her beguiling Texan charm and logic. Where Austin had bludgeoned, she coerced, and slowly she was finding her feet.

In the early days of her widowhood Phoebe had spent a lot of time with her daughter and son-in-law. Dominic had been filming in Greece and then in Thailand and the three of them had travelled around together. It was a trio that worked well. The relationship between mother and daughter had not always been harmonious and Dominic had been an unwitting catalyst between them. When Phoebe had first heard that the marriage was being suspended she took it personally and made frantic attempts to mediate. Dominic could remember her shaking her head with its great mane of grey-blonde hair. 'You're a pain in the arse, the pair of you. For God's sake what do you think marriage is, fun or something? It's hard goddam work, I tell you, and I should know.' Her score sheet carried two divorces before Austin. 'Besides who the hell else would want either of you?'

Dominic poured more wine into the glass of the other pain in the arse and filled his own with water. 'How is she? What's she up to?' he asked.

'She's fine. You know what she's like. Actually she's had

21

some lousy luck at the Theatre Royal. They had a small fire in the scene dock and she had to cancel the whole damn season of plays.' The Theatre Royal was the smallest of Phoebe's three theatres, a Victorian playhouse in Marlow. 'She's up in Manchester at the moment. *My Fair Lady* is opening at the Princess next week, her very own production, isn't that great?'

'Yes, that's a big show for her to be doing. Who's in it?'

'She's got Leo Benson playing Higgins.'

'Leo Benson?' Dominic had thought he was dead.

'He's in that sit-com at the Beeb *Don't Bank On It*. And a marvellous girl playing Eliza, Tessa Neal.'

Harriet paused. Behind her, hanging askew on the green flock wallpaper, was a painting of a tiger glaring out of its surreal jungle.

'The really marvellous thing is I think she's got a boy-friend, well an admirer anyway. Actually I'm not sure, he's the guy who's put up most of the backing for *My Fair Lady*, seriously rich . . . Sir Philip Sullivan, one of your heavy-duty City blokes.'

Dominic nodded as if the name was familiar to him, perhaps it was. He wanted to reach out and touch her skin, her throat, her breasts, what a source of pleasure they had been. 'That's good news,' he said. 'What about the Brunswick?'

'Oh, she's still got that ghastly *All Singing, All Dancing* in there. It's not her show of course but it pays the rent each week. It should run for years.'

'Good.' Dominic nodded. He knew that without her flagship theatre doing decent business Phoebe stood no chance of breaking even and her shareholders were forever baying at her heels. 'Good,' he said again.

Over the rim of her glass Harriet smiled at him, the smile of a conqueror.

'It's good to see you,' she said, and from her tone Dominic had the feeling she had quite outgrown him.

'Yes.' He was again shifting the shards of poppadom to avoid her scrutiny. 'I'm sorry not to have been in touch.'

Dominic did not want to look into the reason why he had

22

chosen to isolate himself. He was not ready to admit that he had been sulking at the world for having driven him to drink.

'What about you?' Harriet asked. She was feeling reckless, she wasn't putty in his hands any more. 'What are you up to?'

Dominic half-smiled as though he was too clever for such a trick question, and said nothing.

'Isn't it time you stopped this hibernating, Domo? Mm?'

He lowered his eyes to avoid the gaze of his wife and the tiger on the wall behind her. The poppadom was an impossible jigsaw and he began to eat the pieces one by one. Hibernating was he? She'd be saying next, 'Isn't it time you started to face the world again?'

'Isn't it time you started to face the world again?' Harriet asked. Her eyes were flecked with amber in the candlelight. The restaurant was nearly empty and Dominic looked at her for a moment silently imploring her to shut up.

'I mean you can't go on mouldering away down in Sussex for ever.' She thought there was a warning in his eyes but pressed on anyway. 'You must be bored shitless. I mean, what do you do all day? Why don't you get a job, do a movie, for God's sake? I can't think of anything more boring than being stuck in the middle of a boys' prep school way out in the sticks. I mean you're cured, dry. You're OK, you look terrific. Why not get on . . . isn't it time you got on with your life?' She didn't care if she was on dangerous ground, she was only putting the questions that Phoebe had urged her to ask.

Dominic looked away as if he had not heard. He remembered the voice of his counsellor at the clinic. 'Give up the idea that you can control things. Get real, Dominic. Be honest.' He wanted to make her understand that he liked the school and Sussex, and the long empty days and not having to chase about the world making crap-awful films and he liked the solitude and he did not miss her at all. Not much.

'I've got a dog,' he said.

'Oh yes.' Harriet could think of nothing else to say.

'A sort of cross-bred Border Collie,' he told her.

It was an explanation she seemed not to fully comprehend. They smiled at one another briefly like two people marooned together. The music had stopped at last so Dominic asked for the bill.

'Dare I presume your satisfaction?' asked India's answer to Uriah Heap.

'Certainly, we've had a marvellous evening.' Dominic wrote out two cheques, one for the Taj Mahal with a twenty per cent tip.

'You are most abundantly generous, Mr Gallagher.'

And the other he handed to Harriet.

'For me?'

'No,' he answered, 'for Karl Lagerfeld, a dress for the play. My Christmas present a bit late.'

'Oh Dom ... you are sweet.' Holding her hair from the flame of the candle she leant and kissed him on the cheek. 'Thank you.'

Her skin was soft against his cheek and Dominic could feel his old fear of the future stirring again.

'You are a fine and happy couple.' The manager beamed as he ushered them into the rain. 'Long may your cup be overflowing with happiness.'

In the dim light of his sitting room Griffith sat staring out at the blackness of the sea, a sea that reflected nothing but the inertia of Hove on a Sunday evening. He was heavy-hearted like someone about to make a journey, caught between not being able to leave and not wanting to stay. His head throbbed with indecision. Again and again he read the neatly extracted cutting in his hand.

BRUTAL MURDER OF BROADWAY DANCER

The soft option was of course suicide, a quiet exit that would arouse not much surprise and only a little grief, a death that would go down as a spoiled paper in life's ballot box.

The other option was harder, it was the one he had been on the brink of all these years. It was an obligation long overdue to set the record straight, and the weight of it was oppressive. He stared out of his window and saw only the mutilated body of a redhaired dancer. His mind was made up, he owed it to

24

her, to this girl, this Julita Pascal. He would tell the truth and shame the devil for her sake, and the others.

Griffith reached out his hand for the telephone and from the darket corner of his memory he dialled the number. Was it really his hand? He watched his finger hovering between digits, the knuckles swollen and shiny like pebbles. This was no moment to fall asleep. He blinked and blinked again to find focus, the sound of rushing water filled his ears. The room was spinning round gently and the lights from the promenade were all at once fireworks exploding quietly in his head. His veins were full of sand and his limbs were somehow waterlogged. What was happening? Where had this kaleidoscope come from? Had he been struck by lightning? Or by darkness? He was soaring out over the sea, spinning and dizzy; flying or dying; he felt so heavy it didn't matter.

In his ear a voice was echoing down the telephone. 'Brachameda. Brachameda.' He went to speak but his tongue was just flesh caught in his mouth. He tried to say his name and dropped the receiver. Griffith Gallagher. Griffith Gallagher. Nothing moved. Who was he? Who had he been?

'Hello. Hello. Who is it . . .? Hello.' The voice was shouting down the earpiece on his lap, the lap of a statue of himself. Then all he heard was the sound of disconnection.

2

Harriet and Dominic sat in silence staring at the rain as it landed gently on the windscreen in front of them. They were parked outside the terraced house that she had rented. The bedroom light was on. He wanted to tell his wife that he missed her all the time, night and day, and he could see no point in having cured himself if it wasn't for her sake. He wanted her to know that he felt breathless with wanting to make love to her. He wanted to suggest a new beginning or a rewrite of their old ending. Why else had he come? The time was not right, he told himself as he took the traditional Gallagher option of silence. Harriet was not about to ask him in for coffee, not on a first date.

Dominic looked up at the window. 'Are you having an affair with him?'

'Who?'

'The boy. The boy in the play.'

'Greg,' she said.

'Yes.' What the hell did his name matter?

Harriet never thought he would ask.

'Sort of,' she answered accurately.

Dominic remembered the cock-sure youth with his bandy-legged virility and his noisy kissing. He felt suddenly foolish like the bowler-hatted husband in the play. No doubt the boy was waiting for her sprawled out on the bed. Dominic wished to God he had stayed at home or in Buenos bloody Aires.

'How old is he?' he asked.

'Compared to me you mean?' Harriet knew as she spoke she had given herself away.

'No. I mean compared to when he was born.'

'He's twenty-five,' she announced as if it did not matter.

'I'm sorry . . . I'm sorry.' Dominic cursed himself for having so easily caught her raw nerve. 'I'm sorry . . . it's none of my business, is it?'

The question went unanswered. They listened to the rain on the roof of the car, each wondering how they had arrived at this strange moment. The reasons for their separation had taken on the simplicity of a fable. The lapse of time had stood the truth on its head and the old confusion of cause and effect had set to work.

'Well . . .' she said.

Dominic started the engine.

'Thanks for coming up,' she said. 'And for the curry and for being so sweet . . .' She meant the cheque.

Dominic nodded. 'It's OK.'

'Send my love to your dad.'

'And mine to your mum,' he answered.

She kissed him briefly on the cheek and they remembered for a moment the smell of each other's skin, among other things.

'Good night.'

'Good night.'

She opened the door and was gone. And Dominic was accelerating homeward, the windscreen wipers slicing away at his nostalgia.

The saying is in the theatre that a bad dress rehearsal means a good first performance. Usually it is only quoted as a consolation to actors who find themselves floundering in an unfamiliar costume. The stage, too, is booby-trapped with new hazards. Notorious among these are the gun that won't fire, the telephone that doesn't ring, the door that jams, the wig that goes askew, etc. These rebellious props are not helped by the sweaty and trembling hands of actors who take comfort in such superstition.

But the dress rehearsal of *My Fair Lady* at the Princess Theatre Manchester had run smoothly and the show seemed quite ready for its first audience. There comes a time when the cast need more than just their director's approval – they need paying customers in the Stalls, applause and laughter and all the rest.

In the role of Professor Higgins, Leo Benson had all the easy charm of an actor who had been playing the part for years, the confidence of knowing he was on a winner. As he began the final number he showed no sign of being daunted by those who had sung it before him, he had put Rex Harrison from his mind, it was his part now. Like lovers, actors have to see themselves as the original, the one and only. There are no predecessors.

> 'I'm very grateful she's a woman
> and so easy to forget
> Rather like a habit one can always
> break and yet
> I've grown accustomed to the trace
> of something in the air
> Accustomed to her face.'

Phoebe Brunswick had not been a producer long enough to have become cool or detached about the rehearsal she was watching. Sitting with her chin in her hands at the back of the Royal Circle she was simply enthralled. She watched with pride like a parent, it was her director, her designer, her actors and musicians who were bringing her vision of the show to life, giving it dimension and style. As Professor Higgins tilted his Trilby over his eyes and said, 'Liza, bring me my slippers,' her only worry was that as a dress rehearsal it had been too good.

Behind her, Maurice Loftus of the *Sunday Globe* watched her stand and clap her actors. 'Bravo, my darlings, bravo,' she shouted at the stage. She wore jeans and a silk bomber jacket, her hair was swept back from a face tanned and healthy that had its own exuberance and gave no real clues about its age.

'You must be Maurice Loftus.' She turned to greet him. 'Shall we do the interview here? Why don't you come and sit beside me . . . I'll fetch us something to drink . . . I'm so sorry to keep you waiting but wasn't that fantastic? Isn't it going to be great? How was your journey? Perhaps you'd like a sandwich . . .'

Maurice had not been pleased with his assignment. With a degree in English and Philosophy, the show business page was not where he belonged. He had travelled up from London determined to find a tough angle on Phoebe Brunswick. The cuttings he had read suggested a picture of the brave widow struggling on smiling valiantly in adversity and he saw it as his duty to apply a note of cynicism. He was not coming all this way to write another eulogy. But as he drank the champagne she poured and ate the smoked salmon sandwiches that arrived, he felt his bad intentions evaporating.

'A production of this size,' he said, 'is something of a new departure for you.'

Phoebe exhaled a great plume of smoke towards the chandelier. 'I had no choice. Necessity is the great mother of all production. As a theatre owner you have to have shows. You have to have bums on seats. You have to pay your overheads like any other landlord.'

'So you were forced to produce this show for yourself.' Maurice looked at her through his round gold spectacles.

'Yes. That's the only way to have any quality control. Otherwise you just have to accept whatever is on offer from all those other guys – the producers who are just out to make a buck. There's so much rubbish about, don't you think?'

She asked the question with her faint Texan drawl and he was forced by the sheer blueness of her eyes to agree.

'You know the kind of thing, tatty old whodunits and farces about vicars who have lost their trousers, that kind of stuff.'

'So you'd rather not have a show like *All Singing, All Dancing* in one of your theatres,' Maurice suggested gently.

Phoebe smiled at the trap she'd walked into and filled his glass. Whatever private reservations she had about the show at the Brunswick, she could not afford to tread on the toes of its producer, not for a moment. It was the bread and butter her business needed while she was making jam.

'I didn't say that, now did I, Mr Loftus?' she answered sweetly.

'Please call me Maurice.'

Phoebe snapped her Dunhill lighter at a new cigarette. 'Not just yet if you don't mind.'

'Any reason?'

'Yes.' Phoebe fixed him in her unflinching gaze and exhaled smoke over his head. 'We all know what familiarity breeds, don't we? And that's the last thing I need at the moment, especially from a puppy like you, the WRP whizz-kid of the Trinity College Trotskyites.' There was no rancour in Phoebe's voice. 'The General Secretary, weren't you?'

Maurice studied her for a moment before laughing. 'Point taken, Mrs Brunswick.' He could only respect a woman who had done her research so thoroughly. 'You were saying . . .'

Phoebe gave him the benefit of her broadest smile, a mocking, confidential smile that seals a pact. 'I was saying that sometimes as a theatre manager I'd rather have home cooking than take-away food. It's important not to aim too low, you've got to respect your audience. I don't think the theatre is the place for playing safe. You've got to take risks. Without that vitality the theatre is not worth the candle. You've got to put yourself on the line.' She pointed at the stage where the crew were dismantling Professor Higgins's study. 'And at times like this I think it's worth it, don't you?'

Maurice nodded. He was busy scribbling notes in his spiral pad quite overwhelmed by the elegance and optimism of this woman who was two years older than his mother. He could examine later the unease she caused him with her vitality and the smell of Joie and the steady gaze she gave him under languid eyelids.

'Er, but surely presenting quality plays without subsidy is rather daunting, isn't it?' he asked. She seemed undauntable.

Phoebe took the opportunity of thanking her sponsor in print. Sir Philip Sullivan was virtually her sole investor, she explained, and yes, he had the reputation of being a hard businessman but he was a philanthropist as well. He was backing her production not just with his money but with his enthusiasm. Privately she sensed it was an enthusiasm which carried that promising ambiguity of a man and woman doing business. Publicly though it did no harm to be seen licking the hand that fed her actors.

Maurice had completely abandoned his prepared questions by now. 'It's been nearly two years since your husband died –

30

I wonder how well equipped you felt to take on the administration of his theatres?'

'Not well equipped at all,' she answered, 'but I had no choice.'

'You could have sold up. Wasn't that what was expected?'

'Yes, that's why I never considered it. Anyway I wanted something to do.'

'A challenge?'

'If you like.' She allowed him the cliché. 'Or perhaps just a distraction.'

'You haven't had much success so far?' The question was not unkindly put.

Phoebe needed no reminding. 'No, I haven't, have I?'

Four months ago she had stood in the smouldering workshops of her Marlow theatre, had listened to the faint sounds of an injured building coming to terms with its wounds, and had smelt the acrid smoke. Was it paranoia or had there been also a whiff of arson in the wind?

She stubbed out her cigarette and extinguished too the memory. 'I put it down to bad luck rather than bad management.'

'So there's no truth in the rumours of a take-over of the Brunswick Empire?'

'No,' Phoebe lied casually with her eyebrows raised to belittle the idea. She put from her mind the furious entreaties of her husband's family. 'It's not possible anyway. I have a controlling interest.' From her tone she meant not just on paper. 'We're on the up now, we've turned things round. We're winning.' There was no doubting her determination. 'We'll soon have all three theatres on their feet . . . I mean this production of *My Fair Lady* should run through till Christmas. It'll be a sell-out, a zonking great smasheroo, don't you reckon?' Maurice preferred opera but found himself agreeing. His plan not to write a eulogy had long flown out the window. 'Well, I think that's just about it, Mrs Brunswick . . . Would you mind if our photographer took some shots of you and Leo Benson and maybe the girl?'

'Why not? It'd be a pleasure,' Phoebe answered. It would be good for business anyway.

Maurice was struggling back into his anorak. He thanked her too profusely and was about to leave. 'There is just one more thing I'd like you to know,' he said. 'I actually left the Workers' Revolutionary Party last summer before I joined the *Globe*.'

Phoebe shook his hand. 'I'm glad to hear it.'

'I'm Green now.'

'You certainly are.' She dazzled him with another smile. 'Get out of here.'

The photographer wanted to take his picture outside the front of the Princess Theatre. 'The three of you with your arms linked, OK?' Leo Benson stood in the middle with Phoebe on his left and Tessa Neal on his right. They were a beaming, triumphant-looking trio who chose not to remind themselves of the superstition about good dress rehearsals. The wind blew their hair into chaos as they did their best to pretend it wasn't icy cold.

'Closer together,' the photographer called out. 'Smile ... just one more ... Closer ... Smile ... Hug one another ... Just one more ... Laughing, that's great ... Hold it ... Again ... Just one more ... Marvellous. Thank you.'

As he packed up his cameras he didn't think he'd got much of a picture. He didn't know he'd got a scoop.

Dominic was well out of earshot of the telephone. He had volunteered to help the groundsman and for some time had been waddling slowly up and down pushing the whitewash trough round the junior school football pitch. Like a man in a trance he watched the sluggish wheel spewing out its trail between his legs, brilliant white on the dull grass. It was the end of half-term and, with the back of winter broken, Easter was only six weeks away. Crocuses were out behind the goalpost and the daffodils had begun their slow thrust through the hard ground. Soon estate cars from all over the country would be delivering the inmates back to Chelwood House School. The boys and their parents would hover about in their respective uniforms – red blazers and old Barbours wondering what they had forgotten and when to kiss goodbye. For the moment, though, Dominic was enjoying the comforting distraction of his job, the safety of monotony, and he could not hear his telephone.

The headmaster of the school was a childhood friend, a beaming moon-faced man born to perpetuate the wearing of shapeless corduroy and to instill in little boys some of his own affection for the world, its puzzles and its beauties and its elementary maths. He had been christened Marcus Peter Bagley but the world had always known him as 'Baggers'.

It had so happened that at the exact moment of Dominic's departure from the rehabilitation centre, a small cottage had become available in the school grounds. Baggers had seen it as providential and invited, no insisted, that his old pal should take advantage of it. 'Do you a power of good, keep you out of the way of your thespian cronies. You'll be left well alone. None of the boys know who the hell you are and in any case they wouldn't give a damn.' Dominic had been too feeble to resist and certainly he was not ready to return to his London home.

Reluctantly he had accepted. He told himself a few days would do the trick. A week perhaps. Well just a month. Another term, why not? He had now been in the cottage for over a year and found himself in no hurry to leave.

Gradually he had taken on the ethos of the place, had come to enjoy, maybe even to depend on its regularity; the noisy times and then the quiet. He found contentment in the solitude. From his window he could see the boys busy at their recreation and, beyond, the South Downs on the other side of which his father led his own lugubrious life in Hove. He took occasional meals with Baggers and his wife, he walked for hours with his new dog and reread his favourite books. It had been a time of rediscovery and he had not had a drink for fifteen months, four hundred and fifty-four days actually, each taken one at a time.

Slowly Dominic had allowed the inquisitive boys to seek him out. He took to watching them on the cricket field and had even seen fit to try and improve their bowling. In fact, young Gilchrist had finished the season with a record five for eleven against a neighbouring school, largely due to Dominic's leg-break technique. Gradually he had been persuaded that he

33

could impart some of his knowledge of Shakespeare to the boys. They seemed to like it. It wasn't boring after all. In scruffy pullovers and with bulging pockets, his students took to reciting at the end of term concert. The gentler ones only narrowly missed the point of Hamlet's soliloquies while the more blood-thirsty set about Macbeth with horrible gusto. All in all Dominic had come to feel comfortable at Chelwood House.

Meticulously he traced round the outer touchline of the pitch, his strides were small and slow while in front of him his breath hung briefly in the dusk before dissolving. He seemed to be part of the touchline, balancing on it between the past and the future, afraid to fall. On the drive down from Northampton he had been unable to lose the thought of Harriet from his mind. There she was in front of him, the old Harriet and the new, a Harriet half in the play he'd gone to see and half in the life they'd led together. With his head-lamps stretching into the rain ahead, Dominic could not escape the memory of her from way back, the smell of her skin and the taste of her. He wanted to go back or begin again, to rewind or fast-forward. He wanted to hold her, to kiss her, to stroke her, to tangle her hair and lick her breasts and be coupled with her again like in the good old, sweet old days before things had gone sour.

He didn't regret the journey, it wasn't the skirmish into the past that he had planned, it was more a reconnaissance of what might lie ahead. And she had been right, of course, he could see that now; it was high time he called a halt to his hibernation, it was time he faced the outside world again, that frantic place beyond the school gates. He could feel it somewhere in his own subsoil, the old urge to begin again.

From nowhere in the gloom Baggers was suddenly walking beside him. 'I've got some bad news I'm afraid. It's about your dad,' he was saying. 'I've just had a call from Hove Infirmary. They've been trying to reach you. He's had a stroke.'

As Dominic ran off, the white line he had been trailing fell slightly short of meeting up with where he had begun – he had not quite reached his point of departure.

*

For Leo Benson as he woke there was the memory of applause and celebration and much 'Darling, you were wonderful'. The audience at the Princess Theatre Manchester had stood and cheered and at the party afterwards Phoebe had hugged him with tears in her eyes. But now as he lay on his orthopaedic bed he could feel the dull ache of dehydration about his person, sure proof that he had drunk too much, and as always with a hangover there was a matinée to face that afternoon, a prospect that called for a double dose of Vitamin C. Alone in his fifth floor service flat he gently set about the morning process, the coffee and the shave, the reading of *The Times* and the choosing of shirt and tie. He telephoned his wife in Gerrards Cross and told her again, in the cold light of day, the details of his triumph, gave her the go-ahead for a new patio with a built-in barbeque and blew a kiss down the line to their daughter, the apple of his eye, just off to college. He was pleased to hear that the daffodils were doing well and asked after the neighbours. It was an ordinary conversation between man and wife.

Leo was not in the mood for the financial wisdom of Louise Botting on Radio 4 so he retuned and quite by accident stumbled on the local news on Piccadilly. It was the last item of the bulletin that caught his attention and rather changed his life: 'Following an accident in Preston Road, Moss Side, yesterday, the body of a young man has been identified as that of thirty-one-year-old Peter Trevelyan, a box-office manager from London's Regent Theatre. It appears he was the victim of a hit-and-run driver and the police are appealing for witnesses.'

For a long time Leo stared out of the window without seeing the sharp skyline of Old Trafford, and the coffee went cold in his hand. He thought of the boy, freckled and anxious, and the memory of their encounter put the ache of old age in his bones. The fact of the death and the manner of it were separate in his mind, the one was saddening and the other alarming for it stretched his definition of 'accidental'. The story Peter had told him was made credible now and Leo knew he owed his companion a post-dated apology for not

35

believing him. The least he could do was try and set the record straight, too late.

At his father's bedside Dominic drank his mug of tea two-handed. Green curtains had been drawn round the bed for privacy but they did nothing to shut out the sounds of communal discomfort from the ward. He sat without moving. From time to time he leant forward with a towel to stem the dribbling from the down-turned corner of his father's mouth.

All through his childhood Dominic had watched his father disguising himself for different roles; he was used to seeing him with all kinds of different faces, sometimes swarthy, sometimes pale or florid or hook-nosed or bearded or bald. But this was one he'd never seen, this was not his father, this was his father's shell held together by some residual vitality.

Griffith's face had avalanched to one side and his teeth had been removed. Perhaps the wind had changed the way they said it would. The sound of the old man's breathing was a rapid gentle puffing, too feeble even to flicker a candle. His pale eyes had the far away look of a day-dreamer and even directly in their gaze Dominic was unseen as he sat wondering what to feel.

'You're going to be OK, Pa.' Dominic didn't know whether to shout or whisper.

Like someone peering into the distance, Griffith scowled at his son close at hand. Which one of them was the ghost, he wondered, for Dominic was somehow inaccessible, plate glass separated them. He wanted to say something, he had an urgent message to deliver, or was it a confession? He could not remember what it was. There was a shadow in the fog inside his head – a dense fog, colourless and quiet and then quite suddenly a girl was crying for help, sobbing and terrified, a dancer in a tutu with long red hair. Only for a moment could Griffith see her and then she was gone. He could not hold the thought in focus and his lips felt numb and disobedient. Perhaps he was drunk or had been to the dentist? He could feel spittle running down a chin that surely wasn't his.

Dominic held his father's hand, dry and brittle like a chicken's foot. He stroked it. Studied its history . . . Was it these fingers that had taught him his first chords on the guitar, and how to tie his first bow-tie? In his battle with alcoholism Dominic had learnt to quell sentimentality . . . 'Get real, Gallager – no wanking,' his counsellor had upbraided.

'You're going to be OK, Pa,' he said again.

Inside his head Griffith was shouting, 'No, no, I'm not. I'm not. I'm dead, my darling boy, dead as a dodo.' But no sound emerged, only his Adam's apple twitched in transmission of the thought. And for a fleeting moment the redhaired dancer was screaming at him again begging for help.

After a time staring at each other, Griffith dragged his hand across his chest, pointed briefly to himself and put all his effort into a feeble signal; thumbs down.

'You're going to be OK, Pa.'

But they both knew it wasn't so.

For the elderly ladies in the stalls of the Princess Theatre, this matinée was a rare treat, Leo Benson in *My Fair Lady*, two of their favourites combined. They were nothing like the smart upwardly mobile audience of the previous night, quite the opposite. This was a legion of white-cardiganed aficionados who had planned their excursion with military precision; they had worked out which bus was best and when to spend a penny. They had their boiled sweets at the ready, all set for three blissful hours suspended from reality.

'Ladies and gentlemen,' the announcement began, and they were quite unprepared for the shock, 'I'm afraid I have to tell you that due to circumstances beyond our control we have no choice but to cancel this afternoon's performance of *My Fair Lady* . . .' The disappointment was fourteen-hundredfold, the sound of lamentation filled the theatre. The man on the stage raised his hands for silence and went on . . . 'On behalf of the management, we can only offer our sincere apologies. Full refunds will be made of course at the box office, or you can rebook for another performance . . .'

Backstage the consternation was no less intense as the

actors returned to their dressing rooms; they, each one of them, had a theory about Leo's absence.

'He's had a heart attack.' 'A crash.' 'A breakdown.' 'He's on a bender.' 'He's been arrested . . .' 'It's simply so unprofessional.' 'Do we still get paid?'

In the company office the production manager was speaking to Phoebe at her London office.

'What do you mean he's disappeared?' she asked.

'Just that. He didn't turn up . . . I held the curtain as long as I could. He didn't ring. They checked his flat and there's no sign of his car. He's disappeared.'

'Jesus,' Phoebe whispered. 'Have you called the hospitals, the police?'

'We're doing it now.'

'Have you spoken to his wife?'

'Yes. He called at breakfast, sounded fine apparently, very cheerful. He's just disappeared.'

'What about the understudy?' Phoebe asked.

'Nowhere near ready, I'm afraid, he's hardly had a rehearsal what with having only just opened, I mean you wouldn't expect . . .'

'I understand,' Phoebe interrupted. 'We'll just have to wait and see. Let me know the moment you hear anything, OK, Jason? And for Christ's sake try and keep it out of the papers.'

They hung up.

Phoebe was standing in the office way above the upper circle of the Brunswick Theatre. It was part of the penthouse from which her late husband had run the family business. The windows were double glazed against the soundtrack of all the hurly-burly of central London. Below her in huge neon letters *All Singing, All Dancing* was emblazoned across the front of the building, the lights pulsing in the monochrome of the afternoon. The show was a 'foot-stamping romp', according to the *Chronicle*. 'A laugh a minute bonanza that should pack 'em into the Brunswick thru the nineties.' It was a hope shared devoutly by Phoebe.

She stood with her hands on her hips and stared out at the pewter-coloured clouds rolling in over the rooftops of Bloomsbury. 'What the hell do you reckon is going on, Major?' she asked without turning to face her managing director.

Malcolm Kendal was sitting in the corner of the sofa gazing into the aquarium. He had always been known as the Major, not so much in respect of his rank, he just looked the part. Phoebe had inherited him together with the theatres and their problems. As her right-hand man he could only offer her his loyalty and common sense. He was of a stolid nature, and his fellow members of the Garrick drew straws to avoid his company at lunch.

'He's probably just forgotten there was a matinée. He's probably having a p-u or a bit of crumpet.' The Major's eyes were following the angel fish beside him as they weaved through the water.

'He's not the type for God's sake.'

Phoebe had been drinking champagne with Leo the night before. He had always struck her as a mild man, reliable and professional, and the thought did nothing to relieve her feeling of foreboding. She lit a cigarette and let the comfort of it bite into her throat.

'I can't bear it if anything goes wrong . . . not again.' She had sat in the dress circle watching the show and, hearing the shouts of 'Bravo', had dared to think her troubles might be over. 'How do we stand?' she asked.

'You mean the share price, old girl?'

As company secretary it was the Major's job to monitor and record the fortunes of Brunswick Holdings. The shares had been in decline since Austin's death, and the price had taken a further dip since the fire in Marlow.

'Actually,' he answered, 'the price is holding pretty steady at the moment, it seems to have levelled off around the thirty-five p. mark.'

'Well that's good news,' she said. Phoebe had also inherited her husband's horror of being taken over; the sovereignty of his theatres was beyond question.

'Well, no actually.' The Major cleared his throat. 'It's bad news. You see the broker reckons we're being sopped up.'

'Sopped up?'

'Stalked,' he explained. 'Someone has probably left instructions to buy up every line of stock that comes on to the market. That's why the price has picked up.' Next to the Major the fish looked quite jovial. Someone is after us.'

'Who in the name of fuck is it?' She released the expletive together with a plume of smoke.

Phoebe's ferocity and her language often disquieted the Major, he was a bachelor of the old school who failed to see the vulnerability she hid.

'A shareholder's identity,' he explained, 'need not be revealed until his holding exceeds five per cent. Above that he is obliged to make a declaration to the Stock Exchange.'

'And that hasn't happened? So there's nothing we can do.'

"Fraid not, old girl. We'll just have to sit tight. There's no point in shooting until we can see the whites of their eyes.'

In her dark moments of paranoia, Phoebe had the idea that she was being besieged by an invisible enemy trying to starve her out of her theatres. When the time came though she knew she would not hesitate to pour boiling oil over the battlements. The fire had been an accident, she told herself, and Leo would turn up at the theatre this evening as right as rain, there was no cause for alarm.

As Phoebe turned back to the window she wished she had the courage to call Sir Philip but how could she explain to him that the star of the show he was financing had gone absent without leave, without reason, and without an adequate understudy. Behind her on the sofa the Major was still staring at the fish. He envied them their quiet life pampered and free of sharks. He would be happy as a guppy.

Dominic wasn't sure why he had come to Griffith's flat. Standing in the hall, he picked up his father's black fedora and held it for a while. He ran his finger round the inside of it and stroked the nap of the material. He knew not to put it on but sniffed it before he hung it up again. He had spent the afternoon back at the hospital holding his father's hand and watching him sleep, an old man marooned between life and death. The sister had said he seemed agitated but was 'holding his own'. His own what? He'd never wear this hat again.

40

With unnecessary stealth Dominic moved about the flat. His father seemed quite out of reach among such tidiness. In the waste bin was evidence of convenience food and all the Sunday papers were neatly folded on the table. On the shelf inside the window were Griffith's geranium roots ready for repotting, they were dry and gnarled like artichokes. The promenade looked dismal in the darkening of a day that had, at best, been grey.

Dominic made himself coffee and drank it like a detective at the scene of an accident, a gentle one inside his father's head. There were no clues as to how the thunderbolt had struck its victim and sent him only half way to his death. There was no evidence of tumult or disorder, everything in fact was spick and span in a way that suggested secrecy.

It was time to go home, but Dominic couldn't leave. What did he want to find and what was he supposed to be feeling? To distract himself he browsed through the Sunday papers. He scanned them with no real purpose; wasn't it odd that his father should have so many, everything from the *Independent* to the *Mirror*. On an inside page of the *Sunday Globe* he was surprised to find a neat hole where some item of news had been carefully excised. What was it, Dominic wondered, that had so taken his father's interest? The other papers were perfectly intact. He looked around to find the titbit that Griffith had extracted, and eventually concluded that it must be in his father's pocket.

Before leaving, Dominic turned down the thermostat and switched off the lights. The place would have to guard its secret in the dark and cold. Outside the door he left a note – 'No milk till further notice' – and he took with him his father's fedora as a keepsake.

Randal Morton was cunning, bisexual and good with figures; he was perfectly equipped to be a theatre impresario. As a young producer he had been prolific in his output of fairly low-grade shows. Quantity not quality had been his trademark on the touring circuit. The talent he employed was not always *la crème de la crème*, more the top of the milk; old hacks and stars from bygone soaps. The shows themselves looked skimpy; in a Randal Morton production the sky would wobble when someone shut the door. But over the years he had persevered, and nowadays he smoked cigars and used words like 'charisma' and 'pzazz'. He had come to be accepted by the establishment.

In the fetid quiet of his study Randal was spending a quiet evening at home in his West London mews. Spread in front of him were the weekly returns of his eleven shows. All of them from around the provinces and London showed a healthy profit, a profit to be siphoned off, and concealed. With gold-ringed fingers he punched the information into his computer, sipped a gin and puffed at his cigar. At his feet a young actress keen for a break in musicals was applying herself to his open fly, he saw it as creative accountancy.

The telephone rang, the red one. 'Yes,' Randal answered, then listened for some time. It seemed that Leo Benson had disappeared from the Princess Theatre Manchester leaving poor Phoebe Brunswick's production of *My Fair Lady* in the lurch. Another rotten piece of luck – he had nothing against her personally. He listened carefully to the instructions he was given and when he questioned them the voice said, 'Do it', and the line went dead.

In his stomach Randal had the uneasy feeling of a man who knows he is on the back of a tiger, a powerful tiger racing downhill fast. He zipped up his trousers and poured himself another gin.

3

When she had first split up with Dominic, Harriet had felt restless and incomplete. She had taken no pleasure in the solitude, in doing what she liked and when, and sleeping diagonally in the bed. It had taken time to debunk from her mind the idea that people had to live in pairs and that putting up with another person's shortcomings was a fair price to pay for the dignity of being *à deux*.

She knew and didn't mind that her affair (it had never been a romance) with her young co-star in *Up for Grabs* was already burning itself out. Greg's real pleasure was in his own body and not in hers and anyway his need for fried food and videos had begun to irritate her. At the outset their attraction had been inevitable, almost de rigueur for February in Northampton. 'Oh, my darling, a toy-boy,' her best friend had chuckled. 'How gorgeous, I love a snack between meals.' But she knew that soon she'd be on her own again with no one to keep Dominic from her thoughts.

Earlier in the day she had had her mother on the telephone utterly distraught that her leading man had now been missing for over twenty-four hours. Phoebe was desperate to keep it from the papers and seemed to have the belief that there was a conspiracy against her. Harriet put it down to paranoia or old age, but either way she didn't like it.

When the telephone rang Harriet turned down the music and switched off the iron.

'Hello. Is this Harriet Balfour's number?'

'Yes.'

'This is Randal Morton. Could I speak to her?'

It was a joke of course. Why should Randal Morton be calling her, and in Northampton.'

'Oh yea,' she answered. 'Well this is Glenda Jackson here,

I've just popped in to feed the gerbils and I'm afraid Miss Balfour is in the bath with Tom Cruise.'

Randal laughed, Harriet's response flattered his godlike status among actors. 'Perhaps you could ask her to call me . . .'

'Is that really Randal Morton? I'm so sorry. It's me. I thought it was a joke. I'm Harriet Balfour. Hello.'

'Hello.'

'I'm so sorry.'

Actors and actresses spend their working lives on the wrong end of a buyer's market. Eighty-five per cent of them are out of work at any given time so their deference is inbuilt – producers are idols to be showered with apologies and thanks, flattery, champagne, KY, embalming fluid, anything.

'I'm so sorry,' Harriet repeated. 'How silly of me.'

'It's OK,' Randal answered. 'I'm sorry to be calling you at home. I just wanted to say how much I enjoyed *Up for Grabs*. I thought it was extremely good, very interesting, topical . . . superb.'

'Thank you . . . thank you. How kind.' Harriet was looking at herself in the mirror almost curtsying with disbelief.

'And in particular,' Randal went on, 'I thought you were excellent . . . a finely judged performance . . . very amusing and touching and everything.'

Harriet thanked him again.

'I gather,' he continued, 'that the production in Northampton is rather your own project?'

'Er. Yes. Yes. Well I sort of found the play and kind of got the actors together . . . somehow managed to persuade the theatre to let us have the studio for a few weeks.'

Harriet was too modest to say outright that she had produced it single-handed.

'Well in my opinion the play should be seen down here in London,' the impresario was saying. 'I think there's an audience for it . . . New plays and actors full of commitment, that's the life-blood of the theatre, don't you agree?'

Harriet agreed. She could see herself nodding in the mirror.

'And it's come to my attention that the Fulham Studio

44

Theatre is available. It's just the kind of show they need in there, don't you agree?'

'Absolutely.' She did.

'Well why don't we see if we can't come to some arrangement, you and I?'

'You mean to put it on, in London?' Harriet did not mean to sound stupid.

'Yes. I'm sure we could raise the money somehow. It shouldn't need much and with a few good notices we'll get it back in no time . . . What do you think?' He made it all sound so easy.

'Yes,' was Harriet's answer, 'why not?'

'Well look here, love,' said Randal, 'why don't you and I get together and work out a bit of the nitty-gritty, eh? How about lunch on Thursday?'

'Fine.'

'Why don't you come to my office about one?'

'Fine.'

When Harriet put down the receiver, that dear, sweet, beloved instrument of delight, she turned to grin at herself in the mirror idiotic with triumph. She heard the key turning in the lock and couldn't wait to tell Greg the news. There's only one way to celebrate glad tidings on a wet afternoon in the Midlands.

'Phoebe, old girl, I've got Randal Morton on the line,' the Major told his boss. 'I think you'd better talk to him.'

She had enough on her mind with the problem of her wandering star. He'd been gone for more than twenty-four hours now and they were on the point of cancelling a third performance of *My Fair Lady*. Phoebe could see that the Major was giving her no choice but take the call.

'Put the creep through,' she said placing a new cigarette between her lips.

'Hello, love, how are you?' Randal greeted her.

'I'm fine, Randal, and you?' She could picture him, his mean, slimy features and lank hair. He would be wearing white moccasins as always and his bow-tie would be askew.

'Mustn't grumble, mustn't grumble.'

Why did he have to say it twice?

'Two things, my love. Firstly I was so sorry to hear about Leo doing a bunk. What a shame, I'm told the show was fab . . . Still I'm sure he'll turn up.'

'Thank you.' His sympathy repelled her. 'Yes, I'm sure he will.'

Phoebe was appalled that the news had reached him already.

'He'll be back soon. No problem.' She sucked in menthol smoke to cool her dislike of the man. 'And secondly?'

'Well I'm afraid, my love, I've been looking at the box office returns of *All Singing, All Dancing* and they're not good enough. I'm going to have to take it off.'

'Take it off?' Phoebe sat down.

'That's what I said.'

'You're not serious?' Phoebe knew he was. 'You're crazy.'

'The show has got to close. I'm sorry but there it is.' His tone was unnecessarily jovial. 'The margin is just not there, love, it's not worth my while.'

'Look, Randal, it's a bad time of year.' Phoebe used the cliché in desperation. It can be a bad time of year at any time in show business. 'It'll pick up. It's a great show. It's wonderful. In the summer with all the tourists in town and with the pound way down, it'll sell out. It's a great show for goodness sake.'

Phoebe loathed it. The show was bland and vulgar but as a landlady she could not afford to lose her tenant, she needed the rent.

'I'm sorry, love,' Randal said. 'I'm left with no option, I've got to take it off.'

'Look, Randal, don't let's be too hasty. I'm sure we could come to some arrangement.' Phoebe was clutching at compromises. 'Perhaps we could drop the rent for a while.'

Across the room the Major grimaced with disapproval.

'I'm sorry, Phoebe,' Randal answered like a game show host. 'God knows it's the last thing I want to do, put people out of work and all that. But I've got no choice. It's got to close.'

'OK, Randal, when?' Phoebe was irritated now. 'What notice are you giving?'

'A month.'

It was the minimum, from courtesy he owed her more.

'OK.' Phoebe's voice was crisp.

'I'm sorry.'

'It's OK. Goodbye now.' She hung up. 'Screw you. Screw you, you greasy little sonofabitch. Screw you, you crazy, tasteless little shitbag.'

'I always said he was a common little oik,' the Major said and absently he wrote it on his Asprey's memo pad, 'oik'.

Phoebe turned away from him, her eyes stinging with frustration. The charade of resilient little widow at the helm was crumbling and she did not want to embarrass the Major. Real producers don't cry. Who did she think she was anyway running the theatres on a wing and a prayer? It wasn't like this in *Good Companions*. She watched the pigeons on her window ledge strutting about among the piles of their own droppings. Perhaps they, too, were in show business, she thought.

'There's no use just sitting there, Major,' she said without turning. 'Fix us both a dirty great martini.'

Kitty Benson had been heavily sedated for most of the forty-eight hours since her husband's disappearance so she could not at first grasp the meaning of the message that was delivered together with three dozen red roses. It read:

> 'Haply I think on thee, – and then my state
> Like to the lark at break of day arising
> From sullen earth, sings hymns at heaven's gate.'

> All my love, for ever, Leo.

From high up on Alderley Edge to the south-west of Manchester the views of Cheshire and in the distance Wales are delightful even in February on a sunless afternoon. During the day the car parks are a popular picnic area for families; in the evening it is a classic trysting place, young lovers embrace in old bangers while older couples pair up in company saloons. It was an anonymous call from one of the latter, an adulterer no doubt, that brought the police out to

47

investigate the Jaguar in the corner position and in it the sprawled body of its owner. The hosepipe from the exhaust was not immediately visible.

'It's that bloke off the telly,' the detective inspector said, 'that comedy thing about the financiers and that.'

The smell in the car was still sickly with carbon monoxide as he opened the door to check the pulse that had been long still.

'*Don't Bank On It*,' volunteered the sergeant, 'that's the name of the programme . . . It's Leo Benson is that. He was in *My Fair Lady* at the Princess. He was reported missing, it was on the board. My Gran was going at Easter.'

'Don't touch anything, lad, we'd best get the boys out from HQ.'

'I must say he looks a lot younger on telly.'

'I reckon we all would. Come on.'

With the usual speed of bad news, Leo Benson's death was on the local radio within the hour and at six o'clock it was the final item on the nationwide bulletin. On the screen they showed a photograph of him starting a fun-run in 1989.

Sir Philip Sullivan was heading for home cocooned from the rush hour in the leather-bound solitude of his Rolls-Royce. It was one of the luxuries he allowed himself. He liked a little elbow room in life, a bit of peace and quiet. He had no wish to be part of the crowd, that great surge of umbrellas around South Kensington. It was his custom to listen to the news on Radio 4 and so it was that he heard that Leo Benson's body had been found, a suicide, it was thought, with no suspicion of foul play. He pressed the button to lower the glass partition.

'A change of plan, Cunliffe, take me to the Brunswick Theatre.'

Sir Philip picked up the telephone and dialled Phoebe's private number at the office. 'I just heard the news on the radio. I'm so sorry.'

'Thanks. Isn't it too awful? I tried to reach you.' Phoebe's tone was flat.

'Are you all right?' he asked.

48

'Yes. No.' She was tired of pretending. 'Where are you?'

'I'll pick you up outside the theatre in twenty minutes and take you home.'

There was something in the unobtrusive authority in his voice that reminded Phoebe of her dear late husband.

'That would be nice, thank you. You're a honey,' she said before hanging up.

Sir Philip gazed out the window and wondered what he was doing dabbling in heroics like a swain. What was it about this woman, this chic and witty, scatty and vulnerable and clever woman that made him so eager to share her problems? In financing her again wasn't he pouring good money after bad, a principal he eschewed? On the other hand, he told himself, at his age he could afford to tilt a little at windmills, her gratitude was worth the price.

The car was edging slowly along beside the Natural History Museum. Sir Philip could remember from his schooldays all those miserable relics imprisoned beyond their time. He could picture them with their reassembled bones cordoned off or sealed forlornly behind glass. Perhaps he was a dinosaur himself, an old bachelor wired together with etiquette and good form.

Since childhood he had really known only a kind of loveless formality with women. With no brothers or sisters, he had enjoyed his mother's love unrivalled and could remember still her rough tweed embraces. Nurses, nannies, his governess and his dame at Eton had given him an austere impression of their sex. Later on, of course, there had been dates with sisters of friends, daughters of neighbours, Ascot, Henley, Goodwood, balls. His love of women had become somehow collective, he had turned wary of marriage and the non-negotiable terms of those who sought it. But there was something in the widow of Austin Brunswick that he found invigorating. Why shouldn't he want to help her, this carefree woman with blue-green eyes? Who cared if he was a retarded schoolboy on a rescue mission?

In front of the Brunswick Theatre Phoebe was talking to a small group of journalists by the box office. 'No decisions have been taken. It's too early to decide what should happen to the show. My concern at the moment is for Leo's wife and daughter.'

'You don't think you're jinxed then?'

'No.' She did.

'You're not tempted to give up?'

'No.' She was.

'You wouldn't be tempted to sell out?'

'No.' She would.

'So there's no chance of a take-over at the moment then?'

'No.' There was.

Phoebe could see Sir Philip's car pulling into the kerb.

'If you'll excuse me, gentlemen.'

'Thanks for talking to us, Mrs Brunswick.'

'It was my pleasure.' It wasn't.

Philip was standing by the car waiting for her. They greeted each other cordially without eye contact and he helped her into the car.

'Brandy?'

'Thanks.'

She looked pale and drawn. He poured her a large glass as the car turned south again, back down the Charing Cross Road. They drove for a while without speaking. Phoebe was glad to be away from the office and having to give the impression she was coping. Sir Philip was not exactly a physical kind of companion, especially not by the standards of a girl from southern Texas, but he took her hand in the dark and she was glad of its dry warmth.

'Poor man,' she said, 'the poor wretched man . . . I can't understand it. I mean why? Why for God's sake should he do such a thing?'

Phoebe was remembering the first night of *My Fair Lady*. Three days ago was it? Leo Benson had been so splendid – charming and urbane and elegant and . . . alive. At the end of the show she had stood and cheered with everyone else and had allowed herself the foolish hope that her struggle was going to have a happy ending.

'Why?'

*

When at last the police and her neighbours and her sister-in-law had left, Kitty Benson sat alone at her kitchen table. She felt heavy with the tranquillised weight of her limbs. Her eyes were dry, her thoughts calm in their devastation. In front of her was the complete works of Shakespeare and the Sonnet (number 29) from which Leo's message had been taken.

29

When in disgrace with Fortune and men's eyes
I all alone beweep my outcast state,
And trouble deaf heaven with my bootless cries,
And look upon myself, and curse my fate,
Wishing me like to one more rich in hope,
Featur'd like him, like him with friends possess'd,
Desiring this man's art, and that man's scope,
With what I most enjoy contented least;
Yes in these thoughts myself almost despising,
Haply I think on thee, – and then my state,
Like to the lark at break of day arising
From sullen earth, sings hymns at heaven's gate;
For thy sweet love remember'd such wealth brings
That then I scorn to change my state with kings.

She had read it over and over again until the tears came and the words were blurred. It seemed she had no choice but to accept it, as the police had done, as a suicide note. She could not bear it. Had her poor husband really 'troubled deaf heaven with his bootless cries', she wondered. Had he really been 'in disgrace with Fortune and men's eyes'.

'I have no choice but to fold the show,' Phoebe was saying. 'I've got to take it off. It couldn't possibly survive this kind of tragedy.' She had accepted Sir Philip's invitation to supper at his home and was trying as best she could to explain to him that his investment in her enterprise was lost. 'There's nothing else to be done, I'm afraid. I am so sorry.'

'No, no please.' Sir Philip seemed more embarrassed at receiving her apology than she did at giving it. 'These things are quite outside our control, there's nothing we can do . . .

And the truth is I was not actually expecting a return on my investment.' His smile of reassurance was a back-handed comfort.

'Well, in fact you might well have done . . . the show was wonderful, really marvellous. He was so good in it . . . poor Leo.'

Phoebe fell silent.

They were sitting in his drawing room, a penthouse stadium rather, with spectacular views of the Thames curling darkly away to east and west. The space between the windows was filled with Thai wall-hangings rich and intricate, and in front of it a huge water buffalo carved in jade stood glumly gazing over the river at St Pauls. The room was filled with paintings: Degas, Chagall, a Lowrie over the fireplace, some drawings by Augustus John and a sweet one by Gwen.

'The shame of it is,' Sir Philip was saying, 'I was so looking forward to seeing it. It's one of my favourite shows.'

'Mine too. Oh, Philip, I'm so sorry.'

'Please,' he said, 'no more apology. It's easily written off.' He waved his hand as though it was small change he had lost. 'It's been a pleasure meeting you.'

Phoebe felt flattered that this elegant man was not the sort of person to let lost money come between them. A manservant brought them prosciutto ham and melon on pale green mongrammed plates. She told him about her tenuous hold on power in the board room and how her late husband's family were constantly urging her to sell up. With all three of her theatres empty by the end of the month, she feared a vote of no confidence at the AGM in September. She explained too her fear that there was a predator lurking in the shadows waiting to spring a take-over.

'It seems the shares in Brunswick Theatres are being sopped up. Someone is after me, I tell you, I'm being stalked.' Phoebe ran her hands through the thick mane of her hair and let it fall forward framing her face. It was a gesture of surrender. 'It's all such a ghastly damn mess . . . Poor Leo.'

Sir Philip smiled at her across the table and their eyes met in a fleeting moment of kinship. He was as near perfection as a widow with her back to the wall could hope for. '*Aequam memento rebus in arduis. Servare mentem,*' he said.

Phoebe raised her eyebrows for the translation.

'Remember,' he said, 'when life's path is steep to keep your mind even. My father had a great love of Horace,' he explained.

It was, of course, a sad occasion that they were sharing but unless Phoebe's memory was at fault her host was flirting with her.

The next morning in several of the tabloid newspapers there were headlines of puzzlement and shock at Leo Benson's suicide. They showed, too, the photographs taken by the *Sunday Globe* of the beaming actor two days before he disappeared. What a scoop! In some he was arm in arm with Tessa Neal and Phoebe Brunswick, in some he was kissing one of them, in others they were all pointing at the *My Fair Lady* logo at the front of the Princess Theatre Manchester. In all the photographs he was laughing or smiling victoriously. It had after all been too good a dress rehearsal.

4

Yvette Vallon should have been a ballet dancer. Ever since she could remember her body had come alive to music; even before she was born the pulse of it affected her and in her pram she had rocked to her mother's choice of classics. Suspended in her baby-bouncer in the doorway of the kitchen, she could remember springing up and down, weightless and dizzy, a slave to whatever music was on the radio. When she had first been taken to dance class at the age of five she knew at once that here was happiness. And tears of anguish and pleasure had poured down her face as she watched her first *Giselle* at L'Opéra. She studied hard, her teachers found her diligent and yet creative. She had that rare chance of greatness, for she danced precisely yet with the freedom of a bird. But sadly, along with her mama's love of music she had inherited her papa's height and by the age of twelve she had outgrown her chance of making it as a ballerina.

'*Alors tant pis*. I make studies in modern, I learn everything is possible. All evenings and weekends I am gone to class. Like a mad thing I am wanting all the time to be the best, *la première du monde*,' Yvette giggled raising her arms in triumph. 'Oh I was terrible, terrible . . . tall like this and full of enthusiasm. *Oh la la*. Music always music. Oh how it is I love *la musique* . . .'

Across the table her host smiled back at her as if infected with her zeal. He watched her peeling a peach and filled her glass with champagne.

'I am boring, no?' she asked with her mouth full of fruit.

He shook his head although he knew the details well enough.

'So I am broken the ankle on the *piste* when I have eighteen years and everything has to change. It is always necessary to

54

be optimist, no? It is not so bad to be a dancer at the Lido. Next year perhaps I will go to become *Captaine de la Troup. Pas mal*, huh?'

The room was quiet and full of a pale amber light. Way below in the Avenue Foch an impatient driver was jabbing his klaxon which set off a barrage of answering horns.

'Everything is OK,' Yvette was saying. 'I show them what the giraffe from Neuilly can do. That's what they call me, *La Giraffe de Neuilly.*'

She laughed again, aware of being scrutinised. Why did he have to watch her like that with the stillness of a lizard? Prompted by greed and hunger and curiosity, she had accepted an invitation to dine with a stranger. She had come here against her own better judgement and had begun regretting it as she arrived. The Ritz was not to be sniffed at, she told herself, and there was no situation she could not handle. All the same she would never do it again.

They had eaten caviar and cold salmon alone in a private room on the seventh floor. From the beginning she had done her best to be vivacious but the conversation had been formal, not to say uneasy, and Yvette had found herself struggling to fill the languid pauses with small talk. Her shoulders were beginning to ache with the tension of this uphill battle and her throat was dry with speaking English.

'You speak very well,' he told her.

'So-so only. Not much. I was student in England for three months.'

'Yes,' he answered, 'on the south coast, in Bexhill at the International School of Languages, in the summer of nineteen eighty-five. You got a diploma, a diploma with merit. And quite right too.'

'You understand all about me, *Monsieur.*'

She used the wrong verb but its meaning was clear. This was not the first time he had displayed a knowledge of her that went beyond the bounds of good manners. She chose for the moment to shut her mind to the implications of all his research. Surely he was benign. As she said, it was always necessary to be optimistic.

'Everything of my life you have learnt . . . it is extraordinary, no?'

He shook his head peacefully.

'I know nothing about yourself, *Monsieur*.'

'That is not important.'

Was the room getting warmer she wondered. Why else was the back of her dress clinging to her skin? Again the conversation was floundering, silently waving its hands in the air on the point of drowning. Again her instinct was to save it. Keep talking, come on, she told herself. Speak. Say something, throw the life belt. Anything. *Vas-y. Parle.*

'Do you like animals, *Monsieur*?'

He nodded.

'So do I. I like animals. Dogs. Cats. Horses. Yes, I like them a lot. My mother she had a little bird like that a, how do you say . . .?'

'Budgerigar.'

'Yes, yes, green and yellow . . . *tres jolie*. His name was – '

'Coco.'

'Yes,' she gasped. 'Yes that was his name.' Her heart was thudding. 'Coco. When I am little he was sitting here on my shoulder . . . adorable.' Come on. Keep going. 'But then he died. Also he was talking . . . very intelligent . . . *Vive la France . . . Comment allez-vous? . . . Bonjour . . . Au revoir.* Things like that. Always in French.' As she laughed she could feel the dryness of her teeth. 'The little bird spoke only French.'

'Of course.'

Yvette felt stupid, and then angry, and then afraid in quick succession. She stood up.

'Sit down,' he said quietly.

She sat down and took a breath. '*Ecoutez-moi, Monsieur, ecoutez-moi bien. Je ne sais pas pourquoi je suis là et vraiment je m'en fou.*'

He did not move, not even blink. She was accustomed to the frenzy of hands groping at her in taxis but somehow this inertia across the table was more menacing.

'*Mais franchement, Monsieur, il faut que je m'en aille.* I am going.' She stood up. 'I leave yes.'

56

'No. Sit down.' He smiled and his teeth showed white as snow between thin lips. 'Please. You sound alarmed. I'm sorry, so sorry. Please do not be alarmed.'

'I am tired. I must go home?'

'So soon?'

She was standing by the door now, horrified to find the handle unyielding.

'I don't know why I am coming here.' She tried to sound casual.

'Surely we've had a pleasant evening. Have we not?'

'Yes. Thank you.'

She felt foolish again. There was no need to panic. He was simply a shy man. A shy man, yes? No, he was a stranger who had her locked in a room. Stay calm. Perhaps the telephone too was disconnected. The evening had taken on a timeless confusion. She longed to be in the cool night air of the Place Vendôme, safe in the streets where she could run for cover or scream for help.

'You have such beautiful red hair, lovely red hair,' he said.

Why did the compliment sound like a threat?

'Thank you, *Monsieur*. I have truly had a pleasant evening. Thank you. But it is late. I must go to my home.'

'Of course,' he said.

Yvette watched him move across the room to the fireplace. He moved with the stealth of someone balancing a book on his head. With his back to her he went on. 'Before you go perhaps you would do something for me.' He turned to look at her, with his head lowered he gazed at her, childlike. In his hand was a slim book, leather bound. 'Would you do a small favour for me, Yvette? Would you?' Even his voice was infantile.

'What is it?' she asked. The fact of his insanity was suddenly as clear as day. Stay calm, she thought, trying to keep the sofa between them. 'What favour is it, *Monsieur*?'

He smiled sweetly as he advanced towards her. 'Remember I said earlier I had plans for you?'

She nodded. Dear Mother of God, what plans could he have for her, this lunatic?

'I want you to read something for me.'

'Yes?'

She tried to look him in the eye but shied away. There was ferocity glinting in his smile.

'I want you to read me something from William Blake. Do you know him?'

'No.'

'Never mind.'

'In French, *Monsieur*?'

'No,' he smiled. 'In English for a change.'

'But I am a dancer, *Monsieur*.'

'A dancer with lovely red hair,' he said, handing her the book.

'I try and read, and then I go home.' She swallowed and her throat was tight and dry. 'OK?'

'OK,' he nodded. 'Page thirty-seven, if you please.' His voice was quiet but not without a certain urgency. 'Sit over there, on the sofa . . . That's it. Do not hurry, Yvette. Slowly would be the best . . . Take your time.'

Yvette's heart was beating frantically with something more than the fear of auditioning. Dear Mother of God, help me.

> 'Tyger! Tyger! burning bright
> In the forests of the night . . .'

'Well another couple of weeks and the cricket season will be under way.' Dominic sipped his coffee. It was a typical, nursing home brew, weak and milky with a hint of antiseptic. Griffith clicked his tongue drily and Dominic went on. 'I wonder if Sussex will be able to hold on to the Nat West trophy.' His father hissed a little and looked away, the limited-over game was a constant source of irritation to him. 'It's the West Indies this summer . . . if only we had some players who could turn the ball . . .'

Cricket had always been a link between them, for half a year at least they used it as their common ground. From his schooldays Dominic could remember the Sunday lunches in dismal pubs, the single parent and the only child trying to reach into each other's lives. Cricket had become a safe area between their two worlds, the dressing room and the dormitory. It gave them a metaphor to work with and plenty to discuss; it offered no threat to the privacies they each guarded.

'Remember the days of Lock and Laker ...' Dominic persevered. 'Derek Underwood? The West Indies could never handle him.'

Griffith stared past him out of the window. Over the weeks Dominic had learnt not to heed the traces of irritation and boredom that his father managed to transmit, the short hissing sounds, the clicking and the weary closing of the eyes.

The West Dell Nursing Home in Worthing had been the best that Dominic could find. The care, the food, the rooms were all immaculate – a five star staging post for two dozen people whose mortal coils were not quite ready for shuffling off. Griffith had the coveted corner room with its view of the golf course and the sea beyond. To begin with he had allowed the nurses to sit him in the lounge with the other residents but soon he had learnt to shake his head at the suggestion and now spent his time alone where possible.

The physiotherapist found him uncooperative. 'I'm afraid your father is simply not trying.' The Chaplain proclaimed him a 'troubled man'. And Matron's verdict was, 'I'm afraid we've rather turned our face to the wall.'

That morning Dominic had visited his father's solicitor in Brighton. It had been agreed that the flat in Hove should be put up for sale and the contents put in storage. Ostensibly he had gone to sign the papers giving him power of attorney but had been surprised, no astounded, to discover that his father was quite a wealthy man. For one whose regimen seemed governed by thrift, who took no holidays and whose clothes were old, a hundred and fifty thousand pounds on deposit is a fat sum. It had been sitting in the bank for nearly forty years compounding interest and quite untouched. Griffith had always been a good actor, respected and seldom out of work but never in the league of big earners in his prime. He never had any life insurance and he did not believe in saving. 'No pockets in a shroud' was one of his favourite dicta. So to

Dominic, the discovery of this gargantuan nest egg was a puzzle. Apart from anything else it rather obviated the need for the generous allowance he made his father, not that he ever begrudged it.

For a while they both stared out the window at the golf course. A fat man in vermilion trousers sliced his ball high into the westering sun. Curiosity got the better of Dominic and instead of leaving he squatted again beside his father's chair.

'Daddy.'

Griffith blinked without moving his head.

'I went into Brighton today, to see Bicknell and Vincent.'

Blink.

'To sort things out.' He was close enough to see the patches of feeble beard the nurse had missed that morning. 'To go through all your stuff.'

Blink.

'Get things in order . . .'

Blink.

'You've got a lot of money, Dad . . . I mean over a hundred and fifty thousand pounds. Did you know?'

Griffith closed his eyes, not just a blink. Of course he knew.

'Dad, you've got a lot of money. I had no idea . . .'

Griffith slowly turned his head and opened his eyes. Unblinking he peered into his son's face with a look of deep consternation. There was no affection in his rheumy stare, hardly any recognition, but the focus was suddenly sharp. His breathing seemed to quicken and then he let out one of his hisses long and as loud as he could, the smell on his breath was of slightly curdled milk. It was a statement of great annoyance. He then turned his head away and closed his eyes, the regal ending of an audience.

Dominic studied the lopsided face with its snow white hair askew on the pillow, and wondered how it was that even in his disintegrated state this man still had the power to make him feel so small. Would he never be allowed to grow up? Dominic wanted to say, 'I'm only trying to help', but what was the point? The mystery would solve itself in time.

He stood up. 'I'd better be going.'

His father's gaze was way down the fairway and into space beyond. He didn't seem to give a damn. These visits every other afternoon did nothing it seemed but debilitate both of them and Dominic always left feeling lonelier than he realised.

'I've brought some Tony Hancock tapes for you.' He'd got the entire collection from the BBC. He had memories of his father laughing at them years ago with his head thrown back like someone in pain. 'Shall I put one on for you?'

Nothing.

Dominic selected *The Radio Ham* and put it in the cassette recorder.

'Daddy, I'm off now.'

As he bent to kiss his father's forehead he could smell for a moment the surgical spirit they used to ease his bedsores.

'I'll see you the day after tomorrow.'

Nothing.

'Hello, Tokyo. This is London. Hello, Tokyo,' Hancock's voice was calling.

It suddenly seemed unfair how little his father had to do to deserve the love he felt for him. 'Bye, Dad,' he whispered, 'take care.'

Blink.

'Bye.'

He left without seeing the tear run down his father's face.

'Hello, Tokyo. This is London. Do you read me?'

Monsieur Vallon tried hard to concentrate on the photograph album open in front of him on the table. In the room next door he could hear the muffled moaning of his distraught wife lying on the bed. He tried hard to concetrate on the pictures of his daughter, his little Yvette with her green eyes and lovely red hair. There were photographs of her new born, toddling, laughing, dancing. There she was in nappies, jeans, confirmation dress, Halloween disguise . . . her costume at the Lido. He concentrated hard on her smiling and confident. His little Yvette. Mostly the photographs were in colour which exaggerated the vivid redness of her hair. Against the paleness of her skin the thick curls were like scattered flames around her head. Monsieur Vallon concentrated as hard as he could to obliterate from his mind the photographs he had seen earlier down at the Préfecture de Police. And he half-closed his eyes to unremember the sight of his daughter lifeless on the slab.

Yvette had been missing for five days since her mysterious dinner date in the centre of Paris. Her body had only that morning been found in the basement area of a derelict house in Neuilly. The police photographs showed her sprawled naked among some debris – they showed her from every angle in every detail. Trussed and mutilated, there she was in the harsh focus of the flashlight, unvital and immodest in the open air. In her dead eyes was the puzzled look of someone who has been shortchanged. Yvette Vallon.

'*Quelle bordelle de merde*,' the duty officer had muttered. 'What kind of bastard can do things like that?'

Monsieur Vallon had stood in the morgue, still as granite with the last fragments of Christianity draining from him. The duty officer seemed embarrassed at the lack of reaction. 'He must really be a maniac, a psychopath, *un vrai cochon*.'

Through blurred eyes the father was staring now at the photographs of the daughter long ago happy and alive, safe behind the cellophane pages of the album. From time to time he could hear the mother sobbing, 'Why?' or 'No' into her pillow in the room next door. He concentrated as hard as he could but it was nowhere near hard enough.

'*Le vrai cochon*,' referred to by the duty officer was no longer in Paris. Unnoticed he had travelled to Charles de Gaulle Airport where he had paid cash for a London flight. An ordinary man with hand-baggage only, he spoke to no one and was quite unnoticed. On the airplane he drank champagne, pleased to have exorcised his other self whose dark intermittent commands he was powerless to resist. For the moment he could again be the man the world perceived him to be, functioning genially as one of them.

Occasionally he felt displaced in the guise of a normal man and desolation would come over him but for the most part he was content with who he was, both of him. He was two people

– one natural, one not. Two separate identities infested his mind, quite incompatible and yet perfectly reconciled, one neatly superimposed on the other for most of the time. Over the years, since all the fun and games began, he had grown accustomed to the burden of his *alter ego* and had learnt to cover the tracks of his alias with meticulous care. There was no catching him, especially not now that Griffith Gallagher had been struck dumb in Hove. There was every reason to drink champagne.

Unnoticed he arrived at Heathrow; his passport wasn't even stamped. He took the Underground to central London, an unremarkable man carrying a hold-all that held no clues as to his mission, for who but a fool would have kept the rubber gloves, the scalpel and the rest. And for anyone who searched him, what was the harm in a leather-bound edition of the collected works of William Blake? None at all.

> And did he smile his work to see?
> Did he who made the Lamb make thee?

'Though I speak with the tongues of men and of angels and have not charity . . .' Phoebe spoke slowly to control her native drawl, her throat was dry with tension and she gripped the lectern for support in front of the full church, 'I am become as a sounding brass or a tinkling cymbal.'

It had been three months since Leo Benson's death and six weeks since the inquest that recorded its open verdict. Kitty had taken plenty of time to plan the service, one of thanksgiving for her husband's life. She had lain awake plotting it like a surprise party for him with all his friends, and his favourite music and prose.

Kitty was sitting in the front row holding the hand of her daughter who stared ahead in disbelief, a daddy's girl with no father. All the cast of *My Fair Lady* were there, reassembled in three pews. The Major in his Guard's Club tie was there sobbing through Psalm 23. Sir Philip was there in a dark grey cashmere suit and so, too, was Phoebe's daughter Harriet in a dark blue Burberry. They all shared an affection for Leo and a puzzlement at his suicide.

'Charity rejoiceth not in iniquity but rejoiceth in the truth.'
What truth?

When Phoebe finished Tessa Neal, who had played Eliza Doolittle, stood trembling in the chancel and sang 'When You Walk Through The Storm'. Unaccompanied, her voice rang out clear and sweet, there were not many heads held up high.

Outside the church the congregation stood about in groups not knowing how soon to leave. It was a fine day with a blustering wind that brought down blossom and dislodged hats. Kitty had to hold hers on (roses on sky blue silk, 'not black,' she had said, 'Leo would not have wanted that'), as she kissed those that offered their condolence.

Phoebe was surprised to see her brother-in-law, Maxwell Brunswick, and his son Tristram standing apart from the rest carrying out what looked like an inspection. They greeted one another, the enmity between them veiled for the occasion. Phoebe's marriage to Austin had never been popular with her in-laws and the Will when he died had provoked much gnashing of teeth in the boardroom. Even from beyond the grave Austin had not lost his flair for mischief, he'd left his brother and his nephew a holding only just too small to wield any real power. They had begun by challenging at every opportunity her credentials for running their family empire and were forever suggesting other people and other options. They needed no reminding that she held the reins.

'I didn't know you were a friend of Leo's,' Phoebe was saying.

'I never met him.' Maxwell seemed to have taken the question as an accusation, then added, 'I was just a fan of his you know.'

Phoebe's smile to Tristram went unanswered, there was only insolence in his eyes, an arctic blue. 'I hope your mother's well,' she said.

'Margot's fine,' Maxwell answered for his son. 'She's fine. We must be off.'

'See you soon,' Phoebe raised a hand in farewell.

Tristram turned back, leant towards her and whispered coarsely, 'Oh yes, Auntie, we'll see you at the AGM,' and then he laughed in her face, a mirthless sound on unfresh

64

breath. It was a threat she understood. With three theatres lying fallow and profits down again, she knew which way a vote of confidence would go.

'Hello, Mum.' Harriet kissed her. 'I thought you read beautifully, well done.'

'How sweet of you to come, my darling.' Phoebe studied her daughter's face a moment, she looked tense and pale. 'Are you OK, babe? Is something up?'

'Yes, I'm fine. Fine.' Harriet hated maternal scrutiny, its accuracy unnerved her. She had a confession to make and longed to unburden herself but this pre-emptive strike deterred her. 'Let's have lunch some time,' she said.

'I'd like that, darling. How's the show going?' Phoebe sensed her daughter was in the usual rush to be gone.

'It's going OK . . . So-so.' Harriet shrugged, they both knew that *Up for Grabs* did not have the public queuing round the block at the Fulham Studio. 'Look I must fly,' she said.

Phoebe wondered why as she watched her stride off, her blonde hair billowing behind her.

Kitty had invited close family and friends back to her house for a buffet lunch, 'champagne and a few bits and bobs'. She told Phoebe, 'Do come and join us. Leo was so fond of you, so grateful. He loved working for you . . . He said you were so generous and enthusiastic.'

Kitty had in fact told the coroner that her husband had been unhappy in rehearsal and under considerable pressure. 'He seemed distraught,' she had testified, and then as now Phoebe was puzzled why she lied.

'Thank you, I'd love to.' Phoebe accepted her invitation even though it blew the chance of a lift back with Sir Philip.

'I wish to God I had gone to the first night,' Kitty was saying, 'but Leo said to wait and come with Amanda at half-term.'

'I wish you had come.' Phoebe wondered as she spoke how different things might have been if she had. 'I wish you'd seen him in the part, he was sensational.' His posthumous reviews had said so too.

Sitting with Leo's family in his comfortable mock Tudor house on the outskirts of Gerrards Cross with its neat garden and trees in bloom, Phoebe was no nearer to accepting that this was a man who had taken his own life. Equally she was no nearer to putting a name to the alternative explanation.

When she eventually got back to the office, Phoebe found the Major sitting waiting for her with his face set in a grim warning of bad news.

'Hi, sunshine.' Phoebe kicked off her shoes and kissed him on the head. He wished she wouldn't do that.

'Old girl, I've just had the brokers on,' he told her in his gravest tone. 'It seems that whoever it is that's after us has broken cover at last.'

'What do you mean?' Phoebe hung up her coat.

'Remember I told you that anyone buying up shares in a company has to make a declaration to the Stock Exchange when his holding goes over five per cent?'

'Yes.'

'Well that's what our chappie has done.'

'Who is it?'

'He's got seven per cent.'

'Who is it?' Phoebe's voice was louder.

'Randal Morton.'

'Randal Morton.' She repeated the name as if it were the diagnosis of a bad disease. 'Randal Morton . . . Randal Morton . . .' The symptoms did not seem to please her. 'Randal Morton is after our theatres, is he?'

'There's no way of being certain,' said the Major. He had had a large protion of steak and kidney pie at the Garrick and was in no mood to precipitate. 'We'll have to wait and see.'

Such a course of action did not appeal to Phoebe. She picked up the telephone. 'Georgina, get me Randal Morton would you?'

'He's still at lunch,' the secretary reported a moment later. 'Shall I try him on his portable?'

'Yes please.'

Randal was in San Frediano's taking a late lunch of fettucini with carbonara sauce. His companion was a voluptuous older actress, a verteran of numerous sex comedies. She was hoping to get cast; he to get laid, so the afternoon

66

held promise for both of them. Suddenly from the briefcase under the table came the plaintive bleep of Randal's cellnet – the cry of a wounded curlew. In a crowded room the sound is ostentatious, and like a fart no one is sure if they need to disclaim it. In Randal's case such toys were for flaunting. He took out the cellnet with a flourish.

'Randal Morton,' he announced for all to hear.

'Phoebe Brunswick.' The reply came like a challenge.

'Hello, love, what can I do for you?'

'Cut the crap, creep.' Phoebe's voice was as quiet and sure as steel. 'Perhaps you could tell me what the hell you think you're doing. I've just heard that you are the bum that's been buying my stock.'

'Now listen here . . .'

'No, you listen to me, you little crocodile.' It was a bad line and Randal could only just hear Phoebe's invective above the static. 'If you think,' she went on, 'that you stand a snowball's chance in hell of getting your grubby little hands on my theatres, you are utterly mistaken. Do you understand?'

Randal was grinning lewdly across the table at his date. She seemed to have aged horribly since the hors d'oeuvre . . . at this rate she'd be senile by the time they got to coffee.

'There's no need to get heated, love.' Randal's voice was smooth as baby oil.

At the adjoining tables people were beginning to show a covert interest in the conversation.

'Don't call me love, arsehole, and I am not getting heated,' Phoebe went on. 'I am telling you plain and simple not to mess with me or you'll be in big trouble.' She could not specify the nature of the big trouble but her voice carried maximum conviction.

'Listen, Phoebe, you ain't seen nothin' yet, I tell you I'm in a buying mood, and I'm making no secret of the fact that I want to move into the property game theatre-wise.' His neighbours were openly engrossed. 'I am going to do everything I can to take control of the Brunswick and you are perfectly entitled to do everything you can to prevent me.'

He was aware of his audience now. He lent over to offer his companion a stick of celery, she licked her lips and took it in her mouth biting at it delicately with capped teeth. It was a cliché she had been plying in episodic television since the days of black and white.

Randal went on: 'If I win I would be more than happy to be magnanimous . . . I could involve you. Maybe I'd have you on the board . . . or as a consultant.' There was a small blob of carbonara sauce on his chin. 'The thing is, Phoebe, as I read it, you've got three theatres on your hands all dark at the moment. It's bad luck, God knows, but there it is . . . no dosh coming in, staff to pay . . . overheads, etc, etc, and a whole load of investors all getting their knickers in a twist.'

As he sipped his Frascati, Randal gave the actress his Burt Reynolds look, the am-I-going-to-give-you-a-seeing-to-on-the-water-bed-later look. 'Now,' he went on, 'with an impresario like my good self in charge, those theatres would all have shows on, good all-round entertainment, shows with a bit of glitz, shows that put bums on seats, my love, money in the bank, Frank. That's the name of the game.' Randal overrode Phoebe's interruption. All around him his fellow diners looked on in amazement. This was the kind of thing you only read about in airport books on self-assertiveness . . . 'Who knows, old darling, under the Randal Morton Administration the Brunswick Theatre might even see a revival of *All Singing, All Dancing*. That way I'd be paying rent to myself – keeping it in the family kind of thing. It's logical, isn't it? Let's do a deal huh? How does that grab you.'

'Let me make myself quite clear, Mr Morton. Of all the people who might or might not want to take over my husband's theatres you are by far and away the least suitable.'

Randal wrinkled his nose at his escort to register nonchalance. The glob of sauce was congealing on his chin.

'You have contributed,' Phoebe went on, 'less than nothing to British Theatre . . . You have exploited it with the lowest, tattiest, cheapest rubbish which has ever shamed a stage.' From down the corridor Phoebe's office staff came to listen. When their boss was on form with the verbals, it was a treat not to be missed. 'You are a filthy, greedy, feckless, tasteless crook and I will fight you tooth and nail, Mr Morton. It will be over my dead body that you stake any claim on the Brunswick. Do I make myself clear?'

'Come on love, be reasonable . . .'

'ARSEHOLE,' Phoebe shouted down the line and hung up. And in the doorway of her office a dozen people were clapping.

With the sound of disconnection purring in his ear Randal continued to hold the handset pressed to his ear. His audience was on tenterhooks and he was in danger of losing face.

'Be reasonable, love, I'm sure we can work something out,' he spoke cosily into the dead cellnet. 'You'll come round to my way of thinking soon enough . . . I tell you, baby, I'm going to make you an offer you can't refuse.' He was speaking his monologue in the base tone of a deodorant commercial. 'It would be great to have you join the Randal Morton initiative . . .' He chuckled, confident that the audience round him were enthralled. 'I'll buy you dinner, sweetheart . . . sure . . . sure . . . Look I must go . . . Bye now.'

With hackneyed sensuality the actress lent forward and removed the glob of carbonara sauce from the producer's chin. 'That's how to ride 'em, cowboy.'

When hollandaise sauce curdles you have no choice but to throw it out. Phoebe saw it as a metaphor. She would begin again. You wouldn't see Robert the Bruce reaching for a jar of Hellmann's as a substitute, she felt quite dizzy with determination, her theatres and her sauce were invincible. On impulse she had telephoned Sir Philip and asked him round to supper. 'Just the two of us and a little bit of cold salmon. There's something I want to discuss with you.' With *My Fair Lady* having folded they hadn't seen each other so much lately, although they both knew they were beyond needing an excuse.

It had been a long time since Phoebe had cooked for two and the pleasure of it was coming back to her, the satisfaction of pitting herself against the raw materials, of having all the ingredients on the table fresh and orderly, to do with what she liked: chop, whisk, dice, taste. After three years of widowhood she had grown unadventurous in the kitchen, eating from the fridge more than the oven. Even with Radio

Thee and a good book, dinner for one is a dull date. Into a clean bowl she creamed the butter with the flour. It would be the best hollandaise sauce he had ever had. With the smell of the bay leaves from her court bouillon in her nose she was enjoying the prospect of giving pleasure, the way cooks do, of presenting and serving up something of themselves.

With the elegance of a conjuror she breached the shells of four new eggs, drained off the albumen and slid the yolks, buttercup yellow, into a dish. With an easy rhythm she beat them into shape. In no time they yielded to the frenzied whisk and came up thick and fast. She looked down at her hands, her mother's with different rings on. Thirty years and two marriages ago the Texan matriarch had told her daughter, 'There's only one way to a man's pocket book, Phoebe-Lou and that is through his stomach.' Wasn't she busy enough without this infatuation running through her head? She knew the symptoms from way back: the impatience and the indecision over what to wear. She had eventually settled for black trousers and a silk eau de nil shirt.

Deftly she added the eggs to the butter, slowly mixed in boiling water. With the sauce in a double boiler over a low heat, Phoebe added lemon and cayenne pepper and kept on stirring. Everything was going to be OK . . . her theatres and her sauce. No more curdling.

Sir Philip arrived with an enormous gardenia in full bloom planted in a hand-painted Limoges cache-pot. He mixed them both martinis, dry as a bone, God bless him. The salmon, he said, was delicious, and the sauce the best he had ever had. They laughed a lot and wondered what the other had in mind. With their coffee they drank Poire William. Sir Philip took his jacket off and lay back on the sofa, Phoebe sat on the floor by the hearth so he could see her from behind. The silence between them was unoppressive, mellow even, but with its own agenda. The space between them was the no man's land where men and women capitulate, where the initiative is offered or taken or wasted.

'So we now know who your predator is?' Sir Philip stole the march on her. 'Chap called Randal Morton, I gather.'

'Yes, the creep. How did you know?'

'It came through at the office.' Sir Philip smiled. 'I like to keep tabs on things.'

'I tell you he means business.' Phoebe lit a cigarette to soothe the memory of the man.

'I'm sure he does. A seven per cent stake in Brunswick at the current market price has got to be worth around three million . . .'

'Two and three quarters,' Phoebe interrupted.

'Has he got that kind of money, this creep, or has he got someone behind him?'

'God knows.'

'Well he's got a long way to go yet.' Sir Philip explained the Stock Exchange rule that when someone has a holding in a company of more than twenty-nine point nine per cent they are obliged to make a bid for that company. 'The thing is we've no idea of knowing who he's hunting with. He could be working in cahoots, his money has got to be coming from somewhere.'

'With the AGM coming up at the end of September I'd like to know what kind of ambush he may have in store for me. His plans to keep the theatres busy could look pretty attractive if it came to a vote of confidence.'

'Come here,' Sir Philip patted the sofa beside him.

Phoebe sat down and he produced a memo pad, leather with gold edges. 'Let's see how the scoreboard looks.'

Sir Philip had been born with a dwindling wealth handed down to him from a line of baronets whose grasp of finance was limited to working out the starting price or a tip. The silver spoon had not rested long in Philip's mouth, he had taken what was left of his wealth and doubled and trebled it in his twenties and thirties. The key to his success as far as Phoebe could see was that hardy combination of energy and common sense. Together they compiled a list of the principal shareholders.

'That only accounts for forty-seven per cent together,' she said. 'What about the rest?'

'They're the only ones we need to worry about,' Sir Philip told her. 'The others are what's called "the rump", the professional or abstaining investor. A lot are dead or untraceable. They're not in the game.' With his Mont Blanc pen he put a neat asterisk against the first three names and beside them the total of thirty per cent. Against the others he wrote seventeen per cent. 'You're in no real danger . . . unless there's something even nastier in the woodwork than we know about. We'll keep it monitored.'

Phoebe took the list and studied it like a race card. It read as follows:

Phoebe Brunswick	*	20%		
Hattie Brunswick	*	5%	} =	30%
Major M. Kendal	*	5%		
Maxwell Brunswick		5%		
Tristram Brunswick		5%	} =	17%
Randal Morton		7%		

Phoebe was glad of his optimism, his let-'em-eat-cake attitude about Randal's onslaught and she wondered how best to broach the subject of her planned counter-offensive. She filled his glass and was aware of him watching her with an air of amused patience. His eyes were calm, unflinching, even at their most solemn they had a smile hovering round them, the kind of smile that carries an invitation to share the joke of life.

Phoebe changed the music, a new CD of *Rhapsody in Blue*, and sat down again beside him not so close. 'I've got a proposition to put to you.' She glanced at him from under lowered lids, a trick of modesty she often used.

'Good,' he said and waited.

'It's based on the principle of third time lucky. When the Major first introduced us it was to get you to invest seventy thousand pounds in a production of *The Three Sisters* at the Royal in Marlow, and you lost the lot. Then there was *My Fair Lady* in Manchester and that went down the pan costing you two hundred and twenty grand . . . Right?'

'Right. So what have you got in mind?' Sir Philip spoke almost in a whisper, hardly the tone of a financial wizard.

Phoebe stared into his eyes for a moment and wondered if he had really liked her hollandaise sauce.

72

'Er ... mmm ... Well in a nutshell,' she went on, it was the phrase she used to signal a long preamble, 'what I need is a dirty great grade "A", fool-proof, cast-iron, smash hit show at the Brunswick. The shareholders have got to see that I mean business, good solid business, not the tawdry kind of crap that Randal-screw-you-Morton wants to put on offer. I'm not having that *All Singing, All Dancing* kind of junk in any of my theatres and especially not at the Brunswick ever again.'

Phoebe ran her fingers through her hair, pale gold streaked with grey, and held it for a moment in a loose chignon on her head.

Sir Philip was looking at her neck. 'Go on.'

She smiled and let the hair fall heavily about her face. 'I want to put on *My Fair Lady* at the Brunswick.'

'Oh,' he said. 'Do you?'

'Yup ... Expanded of course, upgraded, rechoreographed ... new designs, maybe we'll get the original Cecil Beaton ones ... a fuller orchestra, bigger chorus. It would be sensational. I mean a complete and utter smasheroo. God knows the show's a winner on its own.'

Sir Philip studied her in silence for some time, her eyes, her mouth, her neck. He nodded intermittently and said at last, 'How much?'

'A million.'

'A million.' He wasn't questioning her figure. 'How about you? What are you putting in?'

'All I can,' she grinned. 'I ain't got that much left. I'm going for shit or bust. I can only afford around a hundred and thirty thousand. As it is, I'm in hock up to here.'

Sir Philip leant forward. 'Where?'

'Here.' She pointed to her mouth.

'Here?' he said and kissed her lips.

It was a long slow kiss, a kiss that lasted well beyond the end of *Rhapsody in Blue*. It was a sweet gentle kiss, tentative at first then surer. It was not a foolhardy tangling of youthful tongues but a kiss that knew its business nonetheless. He stroked her face and ran his finger softly round the contour of her mouth before kissing it again. He held her in his arms and whispered in her ear, 'Count me in.'

'Oh I will,' she answered, 'I will.'

'It'll be my pleasure to cover the rest.'

'Mine too,' she murmured with a thudding heart.

Hand in hand they went upstairs to seal the deal. They turned the lights down low, both eager to conceal how unaccustomed they had become to this manoeuvring. Wasn't it surely a knack, Phoebe told herself, like riding a bicycle? Oh yes, she remembered. And so much nicer.

It was only later as their pulse rates eased with the spent energy of pleasure and they lay staring at the Emma Temple mural on the ceiling that Sir Philip said, 'By the way, you didn't say who you had got in mind for Leo Benson's role.'

'No more I did,' Phoebe answered as she licked the combined sweat from his left nipple. 'Silly me.'

5

It was over a quarter of a century since Dominic had applied himself to a model kit. In those days it had been a Spitfire or a De Haviland but he found the same principles held good even with a Galactic Zoid Buster. The basic rule is to read the instructions. Barnaby Fairchild had decided not to bother. His project was a mess, which is why he decided to trot down to see Dominic during his spare time before prayers.

'It's gone a bit skew-whiff,' he explained.

And it clearly had, for what robot can function properly with his Energy Thrust glued on back to front? Dominic examined the problem carefully, glad of the distraction. Perhaps provoked by spring and all the clutter of rebirth, he had been brooding lately on his own need to begin again and to be seen to begin again. His life had been on hold for long enough, it was time he began to open his mail and answer his telephone. His days at Chelwood House were coming to an end, so too was his affair – or was it really a romance – with the under matron. The interlude was over, time to go forward, on with the motley.

Dominic poured lemonade for Barnaby and, with his mind filled with Airfix nostalgia, he applied himself to the reconstruction of the ailing space warrior, a kind of metallic James Cagney. The little boy looked on in silence as Dominic set to work.

This then was the scene that Phoebe's telephone call interrupted.

'It's Phoebe Brunswick,' she declared when at last he answered.

'Hi.' Dominic hid his surprise.

'Hi,' she answered, her voice too casual. 'How are you, Dom?'

'I'm fine. How nice to hear you.' He almost meant it.

'Thank you so much for your letter,' she said. Dominic had written to say how sorry he was about Leo's death and the closing of her show.

'It must have been awful for you.' He had always loved Phoebe, not just as the mother of the girl he loved but in her own right. In some ways he preferred her.

'Well that's the way it is,' she said. 'Every black cloud has just been turning out to have dirty great black linings. How about you, Dom? How are you these days?'

'Oh fine, fine.' He could feel the glue drying on his fingers and wondered what the point of Phoebe's call might be.

'And your Pa, how is he?'

'No different, I'm afraid. Pretty miserable.'

'Send him my love.' Phoebe paused. 'Harriet tells me you went up to Wolverhampton to see her in that god-awful play a while back.'

'North,' he said.

'It was North not Wolver . . . hampton.'

'Oh yea. She said you were on great form, looking terrific.'

As a mother-in-law Phoebe made no secret of her wish to see them reconciled. 'That play of hers is doing no damn good at the Fulham Studio, I gather, and what she thinks she's doing with that appalling man, I simply can't imagine.'

'That's her business, he seemed OK to me.' He lied on both counts and longed to ask for news of her. 'What about you, Phoeb? What are you up to?'

'That's what I rang to tell you. I want to come down and see you . . .'

'Oh . . . er . . .'

'Tomorrow, after lunch. I've got a proposition to put to you.'

Phoebe had calculated that it would be good to whet his appetite in advance.

'Oh really? What is that?'

'Are you sitting down, Dom? I'm going to put on *My Fair Lady* at the Brunswick.'

'Good idea,' Dominic said and in the pause that followed he

could hear his mother-in-law exhaling her cigarette smoke, could almost smell it down the line.

'And I want you to play Professor Higgins.'

Dominic's fingers were now dried crisp and he sat down holding the telephone in a brittle, alien hand. In his head a three-hour debate was taking place in a split second. His heart was thudding with indecision, the pros and cons each dazzled him in turn. In the end it was his hesitation that took the conviction from his answer. 'No, really, I don't think . . . absolutely not . . . I'm sorry but no, it's . . .'

'I'll see you tomorrow.' Phoebe's voice had in it an imperceptible chuckle.

The envelope had style, hand-laid vellum with a central London postmark. It reeked of intrigue among the lesser mail. 'Ms Norma Kingson, Flat 2, 37 Station Road, London SE22', it read. Norma picked it up, studied it, sniffed it, carried it through to the kitchen. She was tired from a long and unfruitful audition. She kicked off her shoes and put on the kettle, prolonging the pleasure of her letter. Perhaps she had been spotted and her days in the chorus were over. This could be her big break. Carefully she opened it, cutting through the rich paper with a knife. She took out the single sheet crisply folded. Attached to it was a £100 note.

Dear Miss Kingston,

Please come to dinner with me next Wednesday
evening. I have plans for you that may be of
interest. My driver will collect you outside the
river entrance of the Savoy at 8.30. The enclosed
is merely a deposit attaching no obligation. I look
forward to meeting you.

Yours sincerely,
Mortimer Franklyn

Who was she fooling as she drank her tea. She knew the real nature of the invitation and what was wrong with that, if it hurt no one and paid the rent? Mustaffa need never know, she would tell him, yet again, that her sickly aunt in Essex had called for help. Such was the thinking that Norma went through in the cutting of her moral cloth. In her reckoning, the world owed her a living but she never questioned how the debt had been incurred. It was, after all, an invitation that poor Norma could not refuse.

The following day was clear and blustery with clouds high and purposeful sliding in from the south-west. There was in the wind a faint tang of salt from the sea and mixed with it something sweeter from the fields. The crest of the downs was sharp as a whale's back against the sky, its message to the cricketers of Chelwood House was that there would be no rain-stopped play today.

Dominic had spent the morning with the groundsmen stencilling out the creases for the three home matches. He had concentrated hard on his simple task to keep at bay the prospect of Phoebe's visit. It was the concentration of someone counting the seconds between the lightning and the thunder. He needed no reminding how persuasive she could be.

After lunch eager local parents would come to watch their sons in the first eleven, from car rugs or deck chairs they lent support. 'For God's sake keep a straight bat, Orlando.' So it was on the quieter boundary of the second eleven pitch, not quite in the shade of a chestnut tree, that Dominic chose to install himself. With a bag of peppermints in his pocket and *The Times* crossword under his arm he thought perhaps the storm would pass. She might not come.

Time whiled itself away with the slow moving of the sun behind the chestnut. The home team had been set a modest ninety-eight to win. Dominic had all but finished the crossword, an anagram and a quotation from *The Merry Wives of Windsor* and that would be it. As Wodehouse would have had it, contentment was beginning to flow in the Gallagher veins . . . a classic lull before . . .

'Hi.'

Dominic did not have to turn round to identify the speaker. The Texan twang was unmistakable. The storm was overhead.

'Hi,' he answered.

Phoebe moved round to give him a kiss. She took his cheeks firmly in her two hands and gave him a lengthy inspection.

'You've put on weight,' she said, 'and the beard's ghastly.'

The boy at deep third man was watching the reunion with interest.

'But you're looking terrific, kid, terrific.'

'So are you.'

Dominic tried to answer with his face still impounded in her hands. She made a growling noise at him, the kind used to house-train puppies and then let go. All the visiting fielders were now watching the scene avidly.

'Shall we sit down?' Dominic suggested.

'Thanks,' said Phoebe waving to the boys. She was wearing white linen trousers and a pale lavender coat. There was in her hand a large wicker basket.

'Is this the game against Ashdown Grove?' she asked.

Play had mercifully been resumed.

'Yes.'

'The second eleven?'

'Yes.'

'Good.'

'How did you know?'

'Baggers . . . is that his name, told me. Nice man. And here you are.'

'Yes, indeed, here I am . . .'

Dominic gave her the thin smile of a man who has been caught with his trousers down.

'And you haven't finished the crossword yet.'

Dominic felt trespassed upon. What right of access had his ex-mother-in-law to his bench and his crossword and to pinch his cheeks like that.

'OK, who's batting?'

'We are.'

'What's the score?'

'Thirty-seven for three.'

'What do we need?'

'Ninety-eight.'

'Terrific.' Phoebe seemed delighted.

Dominic had forgotten that she had bothered to learn the laws and the love of cricket for her late husband's sake. They watched in silence for a while. Forbes-Murray skied a ball towards the sun and the blinded fielders stood like statues with their hands in the air. An impossible catch.

'I know why you're here.' Dominic was keen to regain some of the initiative.

'Of course you do. But I am the last person to push you into something against your will.' She was casually studying his crossword. 'What is the *Merry Wives* quote?'

'I don't know.'

'"There is divinity in odd numbers, either in nativity – blank – or death." Six letters. I should know it.'

Phoebe's invasion of Dominic's afternoon was meeting with passive resistance. 'I'll look it up later,' he said.

'It's so lovely here.' She tried again after a pause. 'So peaceful.'

'Yes.'

'Hattie tells me that you're completely immersed in school routine and country life. She says you've got a dog called Smirnoff . . . and a girlfriend, is that right?'

'Is that what she said?' Dominic wanted to know more.

'Actually I think she was only guessing and the word she used was "floozy".'

'Well you can tell her from me to MYOB as they say round here.' Dominic was piqued at his wife's accuracy both in the guessing and the phrasing. 'Mind your own business,' he translated the slang.

Phoebe began taking things out her basket. 'I brought us a picnic. How about some home-made sarsaparilla?'

She produced two glasses and filled them from a thermos flask, the ice swirling in the amber-pink liquid. On the space between them she laid out cucumber sandwiches, Gentlemen's Relish too, with crusts cut off, apple tarts and fresh kumquats. She knew the way to a star's agent. The score had crept up to fifty-eight for five. Dominic felt himself thawing, melting hopelessly under Phoebe's radiation.

'Do you know anything about the City?' she asked out of the blue.

'You mean the City?'

'Yea.'

'No.'

'Well I'm being what they call stalked.'

'Stalked?'

'By what's called a predator.' Phoebe grinned at the melodrama. 'There's a take-over afoot, I'm in danger of being overrun, gobbled up.'

Dominic had expected some heavy persuasion in the showbusiness department and was getting instead a crash course in City-speak and wheeler-dealing. Phoebe explained how it had come to light that Randal Morton 'the sonofabitch slimeball' was now in open contention for the Brunswick Theatres.

Phoebe lit a cigarette, drew in the smoke and let it out slowly, its blueness drifting into the green of the chestnut tree. Dominic watched a gangling boy called Chadwick play forward to a short ball and freeze as his wicket fell. Sixty-seven for six.

'And your in-laws are absolutely not on your side?' he asked.

'No. Old Maxwell goes in for the coveting of his brother's wife's share holding in a big way . . . And Tristram can't wait to stab his Auntie in the back.'

Dominic had met them from time to time at family gatherings and had formed no particular impression of them. He thought he had grasped the situation. 'So what kind of threat does the said slimeball pose?' he asked.

'Not much as it stands. He hasn't got the money or the clout but he sounds pretty damn cocky so God knows what he could have up his sleeve.'

Dominic watched the new batsman in pads too large waddle to the crease with his chin in the air. 'What do you mean?' he asked.

'Well on paper it looks as if I've got the upper hand sharewise. The only unforseen danger would be if a group of some of the small shareholders were to club together and start acting in concert with the predator.'

'In concert with the predator.' Dominic had a picture of the

Dagenham girls choir having a sing-along with Jack the Ripper.

'It's illegal, of course,' Phoebe explained, 'but a group or groups of investors can get together and agree to vote en bloc. It's also pretty hard to detect. The law at the Stock Exchange is that the arrangements must be palpably illicit to the reasonable man on the Clapham omnibus.' She grinned at this titbit of legal folklore. Phoebe was not about to give him the darker details of her paranoia. 'I'm not saying it will happen but come the AGM I've got to be prepared. I'm not a girl to be easily ousted.'

'No, I shouldn't think you are,' Dominic said. Surely any idiot on the Clapham omnibus could see she was a lady to be reckoned with.

Phoebe glanced at him and for a moment the angle of the sun caught the flecks of copper in her eyes. She looked at the same time wistful and fierce.

At the wicket young Arkwright was ambling in to bat with the home score on eighty-six for nine. Thirteen runs needed to win but no one seemed to care, it's doughnuts for tea that matter at this stage in the game.

'Let's put it this way,' Phoebe was saying. 'If I was a shareholder at the moment I could quite easily be persuaded not to vote for me. My track record ain't that brilliant and my prospects are on the shitty side of rosy.'

'You've had a lot of lousy luck.' Dominic was grateful that she had not mentioned how improved her stock would be by a successful musical, say *My Fair Lady*, at the Brunswick.

'That's not necessarily how it looks from the grandstand. But I'm not giving up.' She snapped her Dunhill lighter at a new cigarette to stress her determination.

Dominic knew the real price of her defiance, the terror underneath, as he watched her blow smoke at the world. Arkwright scythed his bat at a lobbed ball, a daisy-cutter that missed the dolly-drop.

'You see I know I'm not really up to the job,' Phoebe said. 'How could I be for God's sake, a decrepit old cowgirl from Fort Worth? But I have no choice. Austin, God bless him, has dumped the whole damn shebang in my lap. He really loved this theatres, you know, everything about them . . . their history, their elegance, their moods. I can't explain it.' She wasn't doing badly. 'You know during the Blitz he never left the Brunswick, he never took shelter underground. He said he'd rather be bombed to buggery along with it.'

Phoebe paused, shaking her head at the memory of the husband she had loved. Had she betrayed him, she wondered, in the arms of her new lover? No. She had done the better and the worse, the sickness, the health, the lot, and death had them parted so what the hell? 'I remember once, it was after the last night of some show or other and we were standing on the stage at the Brunswick with that vast auditorium empty in front of us and he said, "No son, that's my problem like poor old Henry the Eighth, no son to hand all this on to, no son to keep it safe . . . all I've got is you, my pet, a goddam doolally Yankee."' Phoebe laughed and her face, freed from tension for a moment, looked a dozen years younger. 'Honestly I could kill him for dying when he did. But the point is, you see, he thought I could cope, he trusted me to run his theatres. Entrusted them to me. And I'm lumbered with them . . . So you see I'm not giving up on him . . . not without one hell of a fight.'

The last two batsmen were scampering for a quick single. Chelwood House needed only three to win.

'It's going to be a close thing.' Dominic knew he had no choice. He was utterly lost. Phoebe had already persuaded him to accept her invitation.

Young Arkwright advanced down the wicket to hit the last ball into the sunset and missed. Beyond the wicket keeper the ball trickled towards the boundary. Two fielders collided in the chase. The batsmen dithered, then took a chance. The throw-in went astray. Again the batsmen dithered. 'Run.' 'Get back.' 'Run.' 'Yes.' 'No.' 'Yes.' For a moment their long shadows tangled half way up the wicket and then the match was won. The moment of victory though was quite lost in the hurly-burly.

Three cheers for the winners, three cheers for the losers. And then the two teams ambled off towards the school buildings for tea. Phoebe and Dominic watched them go and an awkwardness seemed to come between them, as if there was no longer any justification for the two of them to be sitting there on a bench in the shade of a chestnut tree. Phoebe began to pack up her hamper.

'I've got it,' she said.

'What?'

'Chance. It's chance,' she said with an unexplained delight. 'The quote from *Merry Wives* ... "There is divinity in odd numbers, either in nativity, chance or death ..."'

They grinned at each other.

'Chance, eh?' he said. 'That's about it.'

From the playing fields came the faint sound of music practice and Dominic looked over towards the school, ivy-clad and dour with groups of boys messing about on the terrace. He watched the scene with the sadness of someone coming to the end of a pleasant interlude – a school leaver.

'Come and meet my dog,' he said, standing up. 'And I've got a bottle of Veuve Cliquot in the fridge.'

'But ...'

'And some apple juice for me.'

'How gorgeous,' she said as they strolled towards his cottage.

'What are we celebrating?' she asked as he filled her glass.

Dominic smiled. 'Well the second eleven haven't won a home match for two years,' he said. 'And I've never done a musical before.'

'You're blooming weird, you are.' Norma Kingston giggled to conceal her anxiety. 'I mean weird. Are you a clairvoyant or something ...? Why should you know all these details ...? I tell you, Mr Know-All, Mr Nosy Bloody Parker, it's a bloody cheek.'

'I'm so sorry,' answered Mr Nosy Bloody Parker. 'I did not mean to upset you. Please don't be angry with me.'

'Well you keep your nose out of my ovarian cyst – it's none of your business and neither is my Dad having done time for GBH ... I don't know what you think I am.'

'You are my dinner guest.' His smile was like the wince of

84

someone who has trodden on something. 'Please don't be upset.'

'I should like to make it clear that I am not a tart. I'm a dancer. Right?'

'Right. I never suggested . . .'

'I mean, let's get this straight. I don't want anything unorthodox.' Norma used the euphemism with delicacy. 'I don't do oral. It's manual or straight, OK?' Her question hung in the fetid air.

'Normally,' he said, 'I like to plan these things. I was going to keep you for later . . .'

His tone was flat as pond water.

'Got caught short, did you?' Norma giggled but the unease in the air was undiminished. 'What do you want then?'

He was standing behind her now and began slowly stroking her hair. He held the weight of it for a moment, then ran his fingers through it, letting the curls slide across the palm of his hand. His actions were unhurried and unimpassioned. 'Red hair. The loveliest of red, red hair. Wicked and lovely . . . red as red. Red and lovely and long.' His voice was steady as the speaking clock.

She sat in a trance, her panic smothered in slow-footed fatalism. His eyes were closed as if he were trying to hold or perhaps lose an image in his mind.

'Is that it then?' she asked. There was no obvious sign of gratification from her sponsor, no moan or spasm, just this taut stillness.

'No,' he answered, his voice casual again. 'There's something else. I'd like you to read for me.'

'Look. I'm a dancer, not an actress. I don't do readings.'

'You got a commendation in your fourth year at school . . . for recitation.'

'There you go again, you and your flipping details . . . Now you stop it.' She tried to sound severe but she shuddered at the accuracy of his research.

'It's just a poem.'

'A poem?'

'Yes.'

'A poem, that's all.' Norma saw it as money for old rope. 'OK.'

The book was leather-bound and he smiled as she took it from him. Their eyes met for a moment, each of them aware they were part of a ritual, a ritual that was only familiar to one of them. Norma knew the poem and rather liked it. She read it slowly with a childlike respect for the punctuation that killed the meter.

> 'What the hammer? What the chain?
> In what furnace was thy brain?
> What the anvil? what dread grasp
> Dare its deadly terrors clasp.'

It sounded like an interrogation, eerie and monotonous. The last verse she delivered with more confidence, almost a note of triumph which was touching in the circumstances.

> 'Tyger! Tyger! burning bright
> In the forests of the night
> What immortal hand or eye
> Dare frame thy fearful symmetry?'

As she declaimed the final line she felt his hands lifting her hair but this time it was her neck he stroked, not unpleasantly. And then there was the cool smoothness of – his tie was it? – brushing back and forth against her throat. His breathing quickened imperceptibly. The texture of the silk was rougher now. The momentum of its rhythm was mounting and the friction on her neck began to burn. She was caught. Trapped. Why had she not paid attention to her first instinct and fled?

A scream was surging from her stomach at last, and suddenly at its point of issue it was silenced as her throat was clamped. The softness of the silk was now a searing metal band that bit into her skin. Only a rasping sound emerged, an ugly gurgle that lost its impetus for lack of air.

They were struggling now, rolling on the floor bound together by his paisley silk tie. The pressure was tightening

86

round her neck and the lights of the room were spangling capsules of pink and crimson, exploding with blood one by one. Her fingers were tearing at his hands with a failing strength, the weight of his body on top of her was tense and brutal, irresistible.

And all the time he was whispering a simple instruction, 'Die. Die. Die.' It was inevitable. Her heart was thudding, desperate for the fuel it could not get, she was giddy and sad and burning. It was all her fault.

'Die. Die. Die. You red-haired bitch.' The archangel at her throat was relentless. His eyes were bulging and bubbles of sweat blistered his skin. He had no right to take her life. 'Die. Die. Die.' She was tumbling upwards through the roof, could see herself tousled and spreadeagled beneath this frenzied man – her murderer. 'DIE.' It was another invitation Norma could not refuse. Then all at once, way down below, she saw herself go slack and all the light was brilliant white again.

6

The telephone was ringing and as always Harriet's first lie of the day was 'No' to the question 'Did I wake you?' It was Phoebe of course, who paid only lip service to the call of Morpheus and had no understanding of other people's need for eight hours' sleep.

'How are you, my darling?' she asked brightly.

'I'm fine, Ma, fine.'

'How's your show doing?'

'It's doing lousy,' Harriet said, and wished she could explain how lousy. She had elected to keep secret the details of her deal with Randal Morton and her panic worsened daily as the business at the Fulham Studio declined. *Up For Grabs* was dying on its feet and taking Harriet with it. She longed to confess to her mother but couldn't quite . . . not today, not now.

'I can't think why that schmuck Randal Morton keeps it going,' Phoebe was saying, 'and why can't he advertise it properly for God's sake? The man knows nothing.'

Harriet listened as her mother told her about her plans to put on *My Fair Lady* at the Brunswick. Sir Philip was going to finance it, the show was going to be upgraded, revamped glitzed up, expanded, and a lot of the cast would be the same. Wasn't it all thrilling? Harriet was pleased and said so. She had always loved the indomitability of her mother and envied her the ludicrous power of positive thought. Beside her, under the duvet, Greg was stirring.

'Don't you want to know who's going to play the male lead?' Phoebe's voice was full of relish.

'OK. Who?'

'Dom.'

'Dom,' Harriet repeated dumbly.

'Dominic.'

'My Dom . . . I mean Dom?'

'Your Dom exactly.'

'Is going to play Higgins . . . You've asked him and he's agreed. He's going to do *My Fair Lady* at the Brunswick?' Harriet was sitting up in bed, amazed. 'Stone the crows.'

'What's that?' The expression was new to Phoebe.

'It means "I'll be jiggered" or "hornswoggled" in American.' Harriet had been brought up bilingual.

Phoebe told her about the picnic she had shared with Dominic, how well he looked and how keen he was to do the show.

'His cottage is adorable. I stayed quite late and he cooked me supper . . .' Phoebe seemed to be gloating, but there was nothing Harriet could say as she felt her comatose partner beginning to rub himself gently against her thigh, the usual half-waking rigmarole. Any minute now his hands would be fumbling away at her underneath her James Dean T-shirt.

'It's wonderful news, Ma, sensational. It'll be a huge success,' she said. If the smell of the greasepaint had lured him back, there was no saying what other reclamations might be possible. 'You don't think he's a bit too young?'

'That's the whole point,' Phoebe answered. 'Think how perfect he'll be as Higgins with his elegance and his arrogance and his oh-so-British bloody-mindedness.' She listed them as virtues. 'To be quite honest, Leo Benson was a bit too nice . . . too cosy in the role but Dom will be tremendous. He'll pack 'em in at the box office . . .'

Harriet could imagine her husband singing, 'I'll Never Let A Woman In My Life' quite brilliantly. 'Oh, Ma, I am pleased for you,' she said, wishing her own problems would be similarly solved.

'Fingers crossed, my baby,' Phoebe answered. 'I'll send him your love, shall I?'

'Er . . . no don't do that. Thank you, Ma.' There were some things Harriet preferred to do for herself.

As she hung up Greg was pressing himself against her with his eyes not yet open. She was cynic enough not to take his early morning hard-on personally but she accepted him nevertheless. He was not the man on her mind though as James Dean hit the floor.

When eventually Phoebe had left the cottage to return to London, Dominic went to see his old friend Baggers. It was only after lights out that the headmaster allowed himself a smoke – a blissful pipe of St Bruno that filled his study with the smell.

'High time you got back to work,' he said, quite unsurprised by Dominic's news. 'You've been treading water here, old chap, and now it's time to get on. Parable of the talents and all that . . . We'll miss you of course, especially that young matron eh? Melissa . . . You rogue.' He chuckled. 'Anyway it's time you got a move on with producing a son for us to educate. You're getting a bit long in the tooth for the fathers' match as it is . . .'

As he walked back to his cottage Dominic pondered the matter of succession. He had never seen himself as a parent, had always felt unqualified, or disinclined, or was it frightened? Who was he to inflict his genes on some new soul? What did he have to offer? . . . No less than his father, he supposed.

'Jeez it'll be great to see you back in action.' Melissa had been delighted with his news. 'I'm just crazy about *My Fair Lady*. I tell you, Dom, I want front row tickets on opening night.' She knew of course their affair was coming to an end, had sensed for some time that she had been harbouring a fugitive. It was time for him to be returned to his natural habitat, and she to hers, the boy next door in New South Wales.

The liaison between them had begun casually enough, a romance born of convenience and a mild attraction. There were of course no strings attached. Neither of them had anything to lose except the memory of former partners, and their lovemaking was always good, free and greedy the way it is when the stakes are not too high. But strings do not stay unattached for long, they tangle of their own accord and knots get tied. Melissa knew it was time to cut her losses and go home.

As Dominic made love to her that night it had felt like the beginning of a long goodbye, she was as always eager and wet for him, lithe and easy; not at all elusive the way a desperate lover can be. And Dominic found, not for the first time, that his wife was there to haunt him at the moment of his coming, as their bodies danced the horizontal dance he realised with a hollow ache that it was Harriet he was reaching for, her name that was almost on his lips. And that's no way to lay a ghost. While Melissa slept he stayed awake listening to the far-away rutting of deer and to the hooting of his neighbourhood owl and he felt the excitement of someone about to take a journey. Was he going forward or back? Should he pack his overnight bag or a trunk?

In the morning Dominic called his agent with the news of his decision. 'Well stap me vitals,' he said. 'Welcome back to the land of the acting, I'll get you a huge great salary of course.'

Dominic explained that was not what he wanted. 'I'll just take the minimum until the production costs are covered, OK, Kenny?'

'So we're talking discounts for the mother-in-law.' Kenny knew he had no choice. Ten per cent of Dominic over the last ten years had paid for his time-share flat in Tangiers.

Ian Drinkwater, the director, called to say how thrilled he was and to arrange lunch for the following week. 'We're going to put all the awful sadness of Leo behind us. We're going to begin again from scratch. You'll be terrific,' he said, and Dominic felt the first twinge of stage fright at the prospect.

The musical director of the show telephoned soon afterwards. His name was Hamish Speight but he was known as 'the stick' because of the baton he so vigorously waved at the orchestra and also 'because I'm not above beating actors with it either'. They too arranged to meet next week. 'I don't want any of your poncy country and western singing in the show.' He chuckled, 'The sooner we get together to work on the songs the better ... We haven't got long as it is.' Dominic suffered another twinge.

The telephone at the cottage was more in use that day than for the year he'd spent recovering there and by the evening he was tired of it. With the roof down on the Silver Strumpet he had driven west into the sunset to see his father.

'Hi, Dad.' Dominic kissed him.

Griffith blinked without shifting his gaze. His eyes were resolutely fixed on the horizon, way beyond the golf course and across the bay and even beyond Bognor Regis. Dominic stood with his arms full of the shopping he had brought and studied the stubborn profile of his father. Cosily wrapped in his blanket he seemed to be getting smaller day by day, his skin sagging about his bones.

'What a shambles,' he said, 'another complete collapse of the England batting – pathetic, eh?'

Griffith registered nothing.

'There was a cartoon in the paper this morning: two old boys watching the television and one is saying to the other, "In the slow-motion replay you can see the dismissal of five England batsmen . . ." I thought it was quite funny.'

Nothing in his father's expression indicated a sharing of the joke. Dominic began to eat the grapes he had brought. He fed one to Griffith who harboured it in his mouth a while and then let it fall from his lips. Peel me no grapes.

'Dad, I've decided to go back to work.'

Blink.

'I thought it was about time. I'm going to do *My Fair Lady*, I'm going to play Higgins . . . at the Brunswick . . . What do you think?'

Griffith's frail cheeks swelled briefly and then released a sigh, not quite a fully-fledged hiss but it carried no hint of approval. In thirty-seven years Dominic had learnt not to expect it. He persevered with the details of the planned production trying to transmit and receive some enthusiasm.

'Should be fun, don't you think, Dad?'

With the minutest movement Griffith shook his head, perhaps the idea of fun was too distant for him.

From his pocket Dominic pulled out a bag of Scrabble letters. It had been Phoebe's suggestion from the night before. 'I brought these for you.' He spilled them on to the table in front of his father and started turning them all face up. 'I

92

thought you might be able to spell out . . . something . . . anything you wanted.'

Griffith continued to scowl at the horizon without looking down.

'It was just a thought.'

Griffith blinked.

'I mean you've just about got the use of your left hand . . . haven't you . . . a bit?'

Griffith closed his eyes despairingly. His eyelids were like the petals of a dried flower ready to crumble or be blown away.

'I'm going to go and have a word with matron, OK? I'll be back in a minute.'

Dominic left the room.

Sister Pearson was comely and patient and a lot more cyncial than her wholesomeness would suggest. Her cheeks shone with goodness like apples; Bramleys not Granny Smiths.

'He's not an easy man, is he?' She made the statement and then added the question out of courtesy.

'No, he's not,' Dominic answered. 'He never was.'

'He seems so restless sometimes. And angry too. If it weren't for the crossness of the man, he'd make a lot more progress . . .'

Dominic explained to her that he was going to be busy and that his visits might be a little less frequent.

'Oh *My Fair Lady* is one of my favourites,' said Sister Pearson. 'You'll be marvellous. Perfect casting.'

Dominic smiled, unsure if this was a compliment.

'And I'm so glad you're better now,' she went on. 'It is a problem, alcohol, isn't it? I like a drop myself. Now for goodness sake don't worry. We'll look after your dad . . . Ring us whenever you like, I'm always here.'

'Thank you,' he said and touched her hand briefly with a gratitude he couldn't properly express.

'Don't you worry – there's plenty of life in the old boy yet.'

'Is there?' he asked.

'Oh yes,' she nodded. 'He's ever so fond of you.'

'Is he? Do you think?' There was no self-indulgence in Dominic's question.

Sister Pearson seemed a little taken aback. 'Oh yes,' she said seriously, 'he loves you.'

Back in his father's room it appeared to Dominic that Griffith had not moved. There he sat frozen in his sulk or perhaps he was asleep. Perchance dreaming of bygone days, walking and talking days . . . ay there's the rub. Dominic bent to kiss his father's forehead. He felt the pale loose skin under his lips and could smell the aroma of some old embrocation. And as he did, he saw that on the bed-table some of the Scrabble letters had been isolated from the rest. They had been clumsily arranged but their simple message was plain to see. It came as no surprise to Dominic but it did not stop him feeling the sting of salt in his eyes.

I

WANT

TO

DIE

PLEASE

Sir Philip had sent five dozen roses to Phoebe at the Brunswick that morning and when she had rung to tell him 'You're a dear, sweet, darling man and the flowers are simply wildly excessive,' he had sent a single one round by special courier. During the day contracts of all kinds were drawn up and in the evening they had driven down together to Glyndebourne.

With their heads still reeling with the exhilaration of Steven Barlow's *Turandot*, they had checked into Gravetye Manor. They drank pink champagne on the terrace of the Elizabethan manor under a fullish moon, they toasted one another, they toasted the Brunswick, Dominic, Lerner and Loewe, the future. They filled their glasses and toasted the moon. They held hands and stared at the shadow of the cedar that stretched vividly across the lawn. The sweet strains of 'Nessun Dorma' were lingering in their heads, they were just two teenagers with a combined age of 122.

In a low voice Phoebe recited 'The Owl and the Pussycat'

and he was smiling as he watched her mouth. There they were, partners, co-producers, kissing gently in the dark in the land where the Bong Tree grows.

Randal Morton had selected from his vast collection a video of a Roman orgy entitled *I Came. I Saw. I Bonked Her* described as an AC/DC/BC romp. But his pleasure was interrupted by the telephone and he was forced to silence the screaming of the vestal virgins before answering.

'Hello – Randal Morton speaking,' he said in the voice of a man who might have been reading a good book. He listened attentively to the news he was hearing. 'Dominic Gallagher?' he interjected and then, 'The Brunswick?' His disbelief was mounting, 'Playing Higgins?' On the screen the Romans now looked flabby and absurd, silently humping away with their laurel wreaths all askew. 'Of course it'll be a fucking smash hit,' he snapped.

If Phoebe Brunswick's fortunes had turned for the better, Randal supposed they could always turn again for the worse. 'She's quite some lady, isn't she?' he chuckled. 'I mean it's OK fighting with your back to the wall, so long as the wall doesn't collapse.'

Normally an actor playing a part like Professor Higgins in a production on such a scale would have months to prepare – Leo Benson had had six – but Dominic had only three weeks before rehearsals were due to begin. With an energy accumulated over too long an absence from his work, he set about the job in hand. He sang, he researched, he read, he jogged, he went to voice class and movement lessons, he went for fittings at Maurice Angel. He lunched each day with the director or the designer – and from them Dominic began to form a picture of the Higgins he would be. A Higgins that suited him, not a Higgins like Leo Benson or even like Rex Harrison but a Higgins of his own. Most afternoons he worked under the eagle ear of 'the stick', initially he found the songs hard to make his own, he felt at variance with the phrasing they demanded, but slowly they came to him. 'Don't

95

sing so damn much,' the stick kept telling him, 'let the lyrics do the work.'

Baggers had agreed to let him keep the cottage indefinitely and each evening Dominic returned there gratefully from town. He wasn't ready yet for his London house, the home of his drinking days. Perhaps there was still a bottle in the bedside table, for sure the cellar was still full and the Bird in Hand was round the corner. Instead he swam with the boys in the school pool or bowled at them in the nets . . . A child of his own? The idea was absurd. He had only to look at the unhappy picture of fatherhood in the West Dell Nursing Home to see it was absurd.

On the Thursday before the rehearsals began Dominic had a call from Harriet. 'I want to see you,' she had said in her no-nonsense tone. 'I've got to talk to you.'

Being talked to always worried Dominic. 'Anything wrong?' he asked.

'No. No. Well yes. How about tomorrow?' she said.

'I've got the day off,' he said. 'Take the eleven-forty from Victoria and I'll pick you up at Haywards Heath.'

7

From the window of her compartment Harriet gazed out at Battersea, Balham, Streatham, their drabness brightened with the vivid green of early summer. She would rather have met Dominic in London, it would be more comfortable asking his help on neutral ground. Thinking ahead, she tried to plan how best to put her problem to him. Under the inspection of those grey-blue eyes she knew she would gabble and feel foolish.

As the train rattled on through Coulsden South, she reflected that there was a feeling of unfulfilled business between them. At the Taj Mahal in Northampton way back in February he had looked at her in a manner that led her to believe he still wanted her. And yet he had not had the decency to mention it. It was typical of him, he had always had the knack of turning the tables on women so that they had the feeling that the favour being granted was his not theirs. And now if rumour was to be believed, he'd got a girlfriend . . . some floozy down here in Sussex. She vowed to her reflection in the window that she'd keep her cool.

Not that things weren't fine with her onstage-offstage lover. Her affair with Greg had a blissful maddening lack of purpose to it, like a one night stand several days a week. She smiled at the thought that there was between her and Dominic something of a stalemate.

As she arrived she found him waiting for her in the station forecourt. His hair was long and he had grown a beard. Harriet was instantly struck by an irksome picture of contentment. There he was in his beloved Silver Strumpet, the Mercedes 280SE with the roof down, beside him on the passenger seat looking equally happy was a black and white collie bitch.

'How lovely to see you.' He kissed her rather heartily and she could feel his frightful beard like gorse on her cheek. He opened the car door. 'In the back, Smirno. Go on, get in the back.' Reluctantly the dog accepted her demotion. 'So nice to see you,' he said as he drove off. It was the voice he used for old ladies.

Harriet asked him about *My Fair Lady* and was pleased to see how enthusiastic he seemed. She told him briefly how badly *Up for Grabs* was doing at the Fulham Studio, she was keeping the details for later.

It was not in fact warm enough to have the roof down, especially under the trees the air had not lost its morning chill. The Silver Strumpet though had always demanded that any other mistress in Dominic's life be stalwart. Smirnoff was resting her muzzle on the head rest and Harriet could feel the coldness of her nose as they took the left-hand bends. She wished to God she had brought a scarf.

They exchanged inquiries about each other's parents; Dominic was delighted at Phoebe's happiness, Harriet sympathetic to Griffith's misery. After that they drove in silence for a while, of the three of them Smirnoff was the only one not feeling ill at ease.

'I thought we'd eat at the cottage,' Dominic said as they turned in at the school gates. 'The food at the pub is foul.'

Harriet had rather hoped not to see the appeal of Dominic's reclusive home. She had rightly imagined the school as an ivy-clad Georgian building, doleful and crumbling, but she had not allowed for the effect that four score boys can have on such a place. With Smirnoff running beside the car as they drove through the grounds, small boys waved at Dominic and called out the dog's name playfully. Everywhere she looked swarms of blue-corduroyed figures were busy at some activity – swinging on Tarzan ropes, playing French cricket. Not at all what she expected.

And neither was the cottage. She might have guessed he'd spend the morning tidying up, all this neatness did not fool her, it was far too shipshape to be true. Any clues about the life he led without her had been carefully stowed away. There were no signs of disorder and none of the floozie either.

'Oh it's lovely,' she said, 'very cosy.' On the windowsill a stephanotis was in bloom and its smell was thick in the air. She was green-fingered whoever she was.

'Yes, it's nice. I like it . . . it's been a marvellous place to . . . recuperate.' He shrugged rather awkwardly. 'What would you like to drink?'

'What are you having?'

'Camomile.'

'That'd be fine.' She longed for a proper drink, a glass of wine at least to soften the issue of territory. The table was already laid, for goodness sake, with gingham napkins to match the tablecloth, hardly Dominic's style. The evidence was irrefutable.

'What's your flat like?' he asked.

'Super,' she said. The apron on the kitchen door carried the instruction 'Kiss the Cook'.

'Fulham?'

'Putney,' she answered.

'Basement?'

'Ground floor.'

'Of course.'

He had bought it for her without even learning the address.

'It's quite handy,' she said. 'Nice and quiet . . . not like this of course but quiet enough and it's got a garden, well a patio . . . you know me, masses of bulbs and things. Only one bedroom of course.'

'Nice.'

Dominic was busy in the kitchen so Harriet continued her inspection. What was he doing, she wondered, with the model of a battleship half assembled on the floor behind the sofa.

'I thought we'd have salad. I hope you don't mind.'

'Lovely,' Harriet answered.

Smirnoff was forcing her to play a losing game with a rubber bone, almost giving it to her and then snatching it back. She was beginning to regret the whole excursion, her skin prickled with the annoyance she felt at seeing his beard and his stephanotis and his gingham bloody napkins. Even the dog had come to bait her. She gave no thought to his trip to Northampton after Christmas; it never crossed her mind that the boot was now on the other foot.

Dominic brought in the tea and as she sipped the sickly brew, he began to make a French dressing for the salad.

'Shall I do it?' she asked.

'It's OK,' he beamed. He'd even got tarragon vinegar. 'It's all under control.'

And it clearly was. The making of salad dressing was another breach of territory. In the corner by the record player she caught sight of a Paul Simon LP. Who was this girl, she wondered, and who was this man too? He bore not the slightest resemblance to the man she had married eight years ago and even less to the one she had left last year.

'I saw you on the telly the other night, an old movie.'

She stood up and wandered to the window.

'Oh yea, *The Glory Guys*, wasn't it dreadful?' Dominic put the gravad lax on the table and sliced the brown bread razor thin. 'Silly, isn't it, we all thought it was pretty fab at the time.'

He and Melissa had watched it together in bed two nights ago, giggling at the flared trousers and sideburns.

'It wasn't that bad.' Harriet had seen it first at school, had dreamt with the other girls of meeting Dominic Gallagher, the heart throb of the Sixth Form. She had not then known that dreams are best left unrealised – 'Thus have I had thee, as a dream doth flatter. In sleep a king, but, waking, no such matter.'

Through lunch they talked like two actors in a rehearsal, neither of them quite sure of their lines or what they were playing at. Dominic seemed happy at the school and to hear him laughing at the children's peculiarities, their quirks and jargon fuelled still more Harriet's feeling of resentment. Children were another can of worms. She had come on business, she reminded herself. They drank coffee sitting in canvas chairs outside the front door. It was a clear, bright day with small clouds racing in high over the Downs like distant shadows of something from the earth. Dominic was silent for a while wondering when she would come to the point of her visit.

100

'Who is she then?'

Harriet had not intended to ask the question. It came out involuntarily and took them both by surprise. For some time Dominic's eyes followed the house martens swooping over the lawn.

'Melissa,' he announced.

'Oh.' She hated the name, she could only see it emblazoned on the side of a fishing boat.

'Melissa Hamilton,' he went on, 'she's helping out here as Under-Matron. She's from Australia . . . working her way round Europe. She wants to be a dentist and she plays tennis very well.' Dominic paused. 'It's no big deal. Is that why you came?'

'No . . . no . . . I'm so sorry. No it isn't . . . Of course it isn't. I'm so sorry.'

'It's OK.'

Harriet sat brooding for a bit, her own foolishness echoing in her ears. 'The truth is, Dom, I'm in rather a bit of trouble. A God-awful ghastly mess, in fact.'

Dominic studied her for a moment. 'I'll get you a brandy, yea?'

'Thanks,' she smiled. Her gratitude was heartfelt. 'Where to begin . . .? It's about the play, *Up for Grabs*. Remember how keen we all were to bring it down from Northampton, to get a showing in London?'

Dominic nodded He could have guessed it would be a disaster.

'Well the only producer who was at all keen to take us on was Randal Morton.' Harriet sipped her brandy, felt it scorching down inside her. 'Do you know him?'

Again Dominic nodded. 'Your mother is having a lot of trouble with him. A horrible little creep apparently.'

'Yea, he certainly is.' Harriet took a breath.

'Well, he said he'd bring the show into London to the Fulham Studio and we were all thrilled naturally . . . Then he turned round and said he was having difficulty raising the money . . . the capital. And er . . . we, that's him and me, had a meeting . . . and he made this suggestion . . . I mean we all believed, really believed, in the play like mad and he suggested . . .' Harriet watched the brandy swirling round in the glass in her hand and felt giddy with stupidity, '. . . that I should put up the money. I said was he mad, no way did I have it. Then he said didn't I have any shares in the Brunswick Theatres and I said yes and he said how many and I told him and he said he'd buy them from me.'

Harriet was gabbling now as she had known she would, and she longed for Dominic to interrupt or at least stop looking at her like that.

'And I said I couldn't of course. And then he said he could see no other way and we . . . talked some more . . . and in the end he said the answer was for him to put the show on with his own money and in return I would give him an option on the shares, an unofficial option that is – a private arrangement. As it turns out what that means is that he has virtually given me a loan against the price of my share holding . . . a loan that's got to be paid . . . about now. The three month option is up . . . and of course he wants the shares.'

Harriet finished her brandy and Dominic poured her some more.

'Go on,' he said although the end of her story was predictable.

'Of course I had no idea the show would lose money . . . I mean we were all convinced that it would be a success . . . a cult maybe, you know. So I hadn't really thought about the possibility of handing over the shares. I thought I could just repay the bastard somehow but he wants the shares . . . Anyway when I signed this deal with Randal I had no idea that Mum was in such trouble with being taken over and things. I mean she's desperate to hold on and she keeps on about how we've got to weather the storm and how, whatever I do, I mustn't sell my shares because when push comes to shove we're going to need them. They're pretty vital, you see . . . and . . . er . . .'

'You haven't told her?'

'No . . . I mean I can't, she'd kill me. She would never forgive me . . . Christ I'm such a bloody fool . . . I feel I've betrayed her, Austin too, . . . I mean he was only my stepfather . . . but I never thought . . .'

102

Harriet shrugged and fell silent. She felt small and silly and treacherous. There was no reason for Dominic to help her and she wished she hadn't come.

'Poor you,' he said. 'Poor old you.' There was in his voice not the slightest note of censure.

'Stupid. Stupid. Stupid.' She blew her nose on a tissue that fell apart in her hand.

'What do you want me to do?' Dominic asked, the offering of his handkerchief would have been too much in the style of Cary Grant.

'I don't know.' Harriet was uncomfortable in the role of damsel in distress.

Dominic pondered for a moment. 'I'll go and see the bastard.'

'Randal?' she asked.

'Yes.'

'And?'

'And . . . sort something out,' he said.

'How?' she asked, although it is not for the damsel to enquire how the dragon is to be slain.

'I've no idea. I'll talk to him . . . I'll think of something.' Knights on white chargers are supposed to have the knack of improvisation.

'Mummy mustn't know . . . she'd never forgive me.'

'Of course.' Dominic realised that for her to have come to him for help Harriet must be in a desperate state of remorse. Her face was hidden from him by the screen of blonde hair that hung heavily forward. When she was downcast like this he was her slave. She was still his wife, wasn't she, this forlorn figure at the other end of his binoculars, always would be. The vow they had taken all those years ago, naively on their knees, was irrevocable. 'With this ring I thee wed, with my body I thee worship.' The distance between them was temporary, sooner or later their marriage would begin again.

'Don't worry,' he said, 'we'll sort it out.' And he patted her hand, patted her hand like a brother when really he wanted to be stroking it like a lover.

'Thank you. Thanks,' she sniffed. 'Oh God I've been such a

103

silly bitch. I mean it's a golden rule, isn't it, not to back your own horse?'

'How much are we talking about?' Dominic wondered if he could afford to put his money where her mouth was. He rememberd Phoebe saying her daughter had a five per cent holding in the family firm, a holding that gave her the advantage, thirty to seventeen, over Randal's position. With Harriet's mortgaging on her share, the balance would be twenty-five to twenty-two, too close for comfort at the AGM.

'My shares are worth just under two million,' she said, 'around one and three quarters actually . . . Of course there's been no dividend for years, well not since before Austin died.'

Dominic nodded again. He remembered too his pledge to endow her with his worldly goods. *'Up for Grabs* never cost that much to put on, did it? I mean it's a cheap enough show and there's been no advertising or promotion.' It crossed Dominic's mind that Randal Morton had planned its failure for his bigger scheme of things.

'No, of course not,' Harriet answered, 'but that's the deal we agreed, that was my collateral.'

'Leave it to me,' he said, without an idea how. 'Do you feel like a walk?'

And so they strolled through the grounds, each noting the pleasure of being in step. There was a kinship in it such as Mr Darcy might have enjoyed with Elizabeth Bennett in the Royal Crescent.

'The swallows were late this year,' he said.

'I can never tell them from swifts,' she answered.

'No. Neither can I,' he said and as they both laughed their eyes met in one of those fleeting glances of eternity.

Sitting by a rhododendron tree they passed a boy with thick glasses reading P. G. Wodehouse and eating toffees. Sheer Elysium. They stopped and chatted for a while.

'He's so like my dad, miss,' he told Harriet.

'Who?' she asked.

'Gussie Fink-Nottle,' he giggled.

The day had lost its reality, had become timeless and vague like the afternoons of childhood. The sun was almost warm and the bird song was subdued. And they walked on still without talking, beyond the hobbies shed and the lower games field, on and on. They were nearly out of bounds.

Harriet was walking ahead of him now confident that Dominic was studying her. And he was. Her dress was a faded floral original from before the war and when the breeze blew it flatted the soft cotton against her body. And Dominic could see the shape of her for a moment sculpted in cornflowers, bright blue on grey. And when her hair shifted Dominic had a glimpse of the back of her neck. She wore espadrilles and her legs were bare. What with the nape of her neck and the backs of her knees Dominic was senseless to anything but the idea of making love to her.

They stood still and stared out over a gate into a field full of cows. The silence became thicker, on it went doubling and redoubling its own complexity. They dared not look at one another for fear of losing face.

'What are you thinking?' the more generous of them asked.

'I was thinking,' Dominic lied, 'that perhaps in my next life I'd like to be a cow – an orderly productive life chewing and shitting among the buttercups.'

'You could always do pantomime.'

'What about you?' he asked.

'. . . I wouldn't want to be a cow. I'd rather be a . . .'

'What were you thinking?' Dominic interrupted.

'An eagle or a horse perhaps,' she said then paused. 'I was thinking of that poem of Christina Rossetti, "Sudden Light". Do you remember it?'

Dominic nodded, of course he remembered it. He had shown it to her in the first place. 'Yes, I think so,' he said.

Still without looking at him Harriet leant on the gate and in a quiet voice began:

> 'I have been here before,
> But when or how I cannot tell:
> I know the grass beyond the door,
> The sweet keen smell,
> The sighing sound, the lights around the shore.'

Dominic did not know if she had forgotten the second of the three verses or whether she was expecting him to say it. He felt dizzy with the speed of the small clouds. Almost in a whisper he recited:

> You have been mine before,
> How long ago I may not know,
> But just when at that swallow's soar
> Your neck turned so,
> Some veil did fall – I knew it all of yore.'

When he finished Harriet moved round close in front of him. They stared into each other's eyes. Her breath was sweet, Dominic could smell a faint trace of camomile and brandy from lunch. They just stood looking at each other as the distance between them went on narrowing. '"I knew it all of yore",' he repeated. Everything except their want for one another was melting away. Hips or lips, which touched first? With a surreptitious slurring of the initiative their bodies and their faces came together, perhaps simultaneously.

Harriet's arms were round his neck and Dominic's were round her waist. Their lips and then their tongues were reconciled. They seemed to kiss for ever. Without the awkward matter of words they were making themselves quite clear. Their bellies were pressing together as they kissed minute after minute, gently and then fiercely on and on expunging as they did the months of separation. They were at the same time familiar and brand new to one another.

'If you don't take me to bed now,' she said, 'this minute, I think I'll collapse.'

Harriet clearly meant what she whispered, so they turned back in the direction of the cottage, passed the lower games field and the hobbies shed. Without even holding hands they walked slowly, each of them weighted down with molten lava in the pits of their stomachs. They could not talk either for there was too much other matter to be unburdened first and their minds were full of nostalgia – or was it anticipation?

Who was seducing whom Dominic wondered, and did it matter? His resolve had not just crumbled, it had evaporated

106

in her arms. She was the addiction from which he would never be cured. Beside her booze was a piece of cake. He glanced sidelong at Harriet and for a moment she was solemn as a bride and then she let out a laugh, mischievous and apprehensive. He was her slave, a junky.

For her part Harriet felt exalted and triumphant. 'New lamps for old.' She was his genie, a queen, a tart. She was a fruit puffed up and ripe for him – a fig perhaps ready and sweet. The slate was wiped clean, they would have the best of both worlds. They were not old lovers or new, this was a reincarnation. And as they walked along she hoped a wicked hope that Melissa, she of the fishing boat with her stephanotis and her Paul Simon album and her dinky bloody gingham napkins would hear of or see or sense what they were up to and be defeated, utterly scuppered, sunk without a trace. She did not give Greg a thought.

Once in the cottage Mr and Mrs Gallagher had scores to settle, they were on the stairs heading for the bedroom happy at last to be behind closed doors. Harriet went ahead and Dominic was close behind. The backs of her knees were there in front of him, the brown skin wrinkling and tautening with each tread. The pulse was heavy in his crotch, a measured thudding that echoed upwards through his body. There was no stopping his hands from reaching out and taking hold of her thighs. She froze like a dancer on the staircase. Her legs were warm and smooth, he ran his hands from her ankle up her calf, round the shins and along the inside of her thighs. She sighed. It was a sign of approval, of someone pleasantly apprehended on the stairs.

His left hand now travelled lightly across her belly and then was still, holding it in his palm. And his right hand was moving between her legs with the gentle stealth of a poacher. She was a trout to be tickled from the water. And she was wet. The cotton of her pants was drenched already with her pleasure. And as he stroked her she moaned softly and felt incontinent with wanting.

With trembling clumsy hands Dominic and Harriet struggled to shed the clothes that hampered them, zips and clasps and belts and buttons all rebelled against undoing. At last they were as good as naked, and their bodies clung together arching sweatily as they kissed. At their feet the cornflowers lay crumpled by the weight of Dominic's jeans. Their kissing now was slavering and greedy as they stood half way up the stairs with their legs quivering.

Harriet was above him, flat against him so his mouth could reach, could lick, could suck her breasts, one and then the other, and the pleasure of it seared gently through her very core. She moaned softly. He was utterly entwined by her legs, her arms, her hair – he was giddy with the taste of her skin and the faint urgent smell of her wanting him.

Slowly she shifted the burden of her weight to Dominic and as he held her wrapped round him he was a tree and she his trunk, his branches, his leaves unfurling. They were on the brink of one another as she lowered herself on him. Dominic held on to the bannisters with the strength of Hercules as he reached himself towards her. And inch by inch they joined together, scorching each other with their private heat. With a gasp of something like disbelief or ecstasy they were reunited.

Holding her thoroughly pivoted upon him, Dominic staggered on up the stairs and through the bedroom door and all the time she was giggling and murmuring his name, 'Domo . . . Domo . . . Domo,' as he stumbled like a colossus across the room and crushed her mercifully on to the bed at last. They had known it all of yore.

Later that afternoon they drank herb tea together in the garden as if it hadn't happened or they had dreamt it or been mistaken. In silence Dominic drove his visitor back to Haywards Heath station, the silence of two players gambling with funds they couldn't afford to lose. Neither was going to up the ante, neither was ready to fold. And anyway their separate worlds were impatient to reclaim them; he had an under eleven cricket match to umpire, she was due on stage in *Up for Grabs*.

He wanted to say, 'You've no idea how much I've missed you. I don't think I can live without you,' but said instead, 'I'll sort out that Randal Morton business. Don't worry.'

She wanted to say, 'Shall I come back tonight? Will you

call me?' but said instead, 'Thanks . . . and for God's sake not a word to Mum. And get rid of that vile beard, will you.' She gave him a brief kiss and got out of the car.

Dominic watched her striding away from him in her cornflower dress with her hair bouncing imperiously in the sunlight. 'Come back,' he nearly shouted, 'I forgot to say I love you.'

But she was out of sight and Smirnoff had jumped forward into her seat, and he was left trying to remember the last verse of the Rossetti poem.

> 'Has this been thus before?
> And shall not this time's eddying flight
> Still with our lives, our loves restore
> In death's despite,
> And day and night yield one delight once more?'

It does not become a senior police officer to display a queasy disposition, but the truth was that Detective Chief Inspector McCloud was a very squeamish man. Post mortems were not his forte. The sight of a kidney bowl, let alone a scalpel, was enough to quite unman him. So, as Dr Reardon concluded his work on the slab the policeman fixed his gaze on the window, a rectangle of South London twilight. He tried not to hear the detailed account that was being dictated but his nose could not forestall the smell of preserving fluid, sweet and pungent in the too warm air. McCloud closed his eyes and breathed deeply the way his wife recommended: in through the nose, out through the mouth.

'Formaldehyde. It's a ghastly smell, isn't it?' Dr Reardon was peeling off rubber gloves. 'The smell of death.' He turned back to his assistant. 'Cover her up and put her away, Jim.'

Quite by accident McCloud looked and caught a final glimpse of Norma Kingston of Flat 2, 37 Station Road, London SE22 and wished he had not. There she lay pale and shorn staring at the fluorescent light without a care. Splayed out flat with her unbleeding scars she looked like a statue filleted. No trace of a personality was left behind, she was a ghost already, with skin on.

109

'Do you mind if we go outside?' McCloud pretended he was desperate for a cigarette but the pallor of his cheeks fooled no one. They sat on a bench beside the car park. 'Can you give me the rough gist, I'll read your report later . . . in lay language.'

'Well . . . it's as nasty a crime as I would wish to come across . . . I mean what has been done to that girl is really bloody horrible. The chap that did this one is not a nice man. In my book he's already a fully-fledged psychopath. And you'll have trouble catching him . . . He's cool and clever and he's sick.'

'Tell me.'

'She's been dead about five days. She was strangled, from behind with a scarf or a tie or something – Forensic will be able to tell you. She put up a hell of a struggle.' For a moment the doctor looked up at the evening sky or the godless abyss beyond. 'After death she was stripped and shaved . . . from head to toe, there's scarcely a hair left on her, even her eyebrows. It was done with great care. You know, he even cleaned between her legs with surgical spirit . . .' The doctor shook his head with the weariness of a man who had seen enough of man's inhumanity.

McCloud could think of nothing to say, he shook his head in sympathy. 'Go on.'

'Have you ever come across infibulation?' the doctor asked.

'Er no, not . . . directly.' McCloud was not sure and did not want to risk putting his ignorance on the line.

'It's a primitive custom whereby the sex organs are put in some kind of a clamp, predominantly used to ensure the chastity of women in the absence of their partners . . . a tribal thing . . . The labia majora are fastened together, often by means of a thorn which can be broken when the spouse returns from war or hunting or whatever. Together with female circumcision it's one of the more barbaric abuses of women . . . but that's by the by.' The doctor paused. 'Norma Kingston had been infibulated . . . not by a thorn, you understand, she had been quite literally sewn up . . . the lips of her vagina stitched together . . . and a very neat job he made of it. Quite meticulous . . . he used some kind of very fine fishing line I reckon, and a needle.' The two men watched

110

a sparrow in a puddle, each of them appalled at the world and horrified by their sex.

'Of course you'll get the details in my report when it's typed up. She had had a certain amount to drink and a good dinner . . . fish of some kind. She was a dancer, you say?'

McCloud nodded.

'She seemed pretty fit. You have no idea how she met up with her murderer?'

'No.' McCloud cleared his throat. The cigarette was no comfort to him, it tasted dry and bitter. 'She told her boyfriend that she was going to visit her sick aunt in Ongar.'

'And she disappeared en route?'

'Yes and no. She has no aunt in Ongar, in fact no aunt at all.'

'So,' said the doctor, 'that rules out abduction. It was some one she knew?'

'It looks like it,' said McCloud.

'Not the boyfriend?'

'No . . . Horrible little Turkish git, only interested in saving his face. His alibi looks solid enough.'

'But she knew her killer.' The doctor pondered. He, too, was a sleuth, dealing as he did with the less vital clues. 'That's what surprises me. In all probability she had dinner with him.'

'It was possibly a blind date,' said McCloud, grinding out his cigarette.

'You mean . . .?'

'No, no. I'm not saying she was on the game.' The policeman was looking to gather information not impart it. 'So what kind of a bloke do you reckon we're after?'

The doctor chewed his lip in thought. 'In physical terms you've got very little to go on – no obvious trace. Forensic may come up with something but I doubt it. We're dealing with a very thorough, very cool customer. No, not cool. Cold, ice cold, I should say. Normally he would appear perfectly unremarkable, an ordinary man like you or me. I can give you no clue to his age or weight or height, or class or what he does for a living . . . He is probably cunning enough to leave false trails anyway.'

111

'A madman?' McCloud's head had begun to ache with his revulsion, perhaps he would retire and go into private security work. At least there he'd be back in the good old realm of robbery and simple greed.

'A man with an unimaginable psychological disorder. To me it would be less frightening if I had found evidence of a fevered maniac at work. But on the contrary the evidence points to a meticulous operator, a man quite unhurried and very careful . . . A man deranged, beyond cure.' The doctor checked himself. 'I'm sorry I'm banging on a bit . . . let's be practical. What else can I tell you . . .? He's right-handed.'

'Oh really?' McCloud wrote it down in his book.

'Judging from his needle work, I should say definitely right-handed.'

'Unless he had her upside down?'

The doctor thought for a moment. 'No.'

'Anything else?'

'Not yet. We've got to wait for the lab tests. I'll let you know. You'll go through the files, of course, I mean it's a very specific crime.'

'Of course.' McCloud was not seeking instruction on how he should proceed.

'It might be worth checking abroad – in particular the murders of . . . blind dates.'

'We'll check all round, doctor, never fear.' McCloud stood up and was glad to feel the blood staying in his head. 'What do you think about the statement to the press? What should we say? They're putting a lot of pressure on us.'

'Nothing. The minimum.' The doctor sounded adamant. 'Certainly no details . . . no hinting at anything of the nature of the crime. It'll come out later, of course, but in the meantime my advice is to keep shtum, otherwise God knows what it might provoke.'

'I agree,' said McCloud. What had happened, he wondered, to the simple days of *Dixon of Dock Green*, the programme that had been the lynchpin of his vocation. 'I agree. It's best to keep the initiative. We'll just release that she's been raped and murdered, that should . . .'

112

'Oh no, no,' the doctor looked quite surprised. 'She wasn't raped, didn't I mention that?'

'No.'

'That's the strangest aspect of my examination. There's no evidence of any passion. I don't believe that penetration occurred . . . And there's no trace of semen anywhere. As I said, this is not a crime committed out of lust, rather out of hate, a monumental hatred – maybe for this girl in particular but more probably for womankind in general . . .' Dr Reardon looked grim and sad at once. 'She was not raped, she was desecrated. Her murderer has got to be found, McCloud, it's more than possible that he's done this sort of thing before but there's no doubting he'll do it again.'

8

On the first Monday of rehearsal Dominic arrived early at the Brunswick. He was the new boy with his script still freshly marked up. The company were assembled on the bare stage with the auditorium cavernous in front of them. One by one Ian Drinkwater introduced them, his fellow actors, the chorus, the dancers, the understudies and the stage management team. Actors are in no way exempted from the universal shyness at first encounters – unscripted their opening gambits are just as trite and dull as anyone else. Mostly Dominic smiled and listened.

'I worked with your dear father years ago,' said Barnaby Russell who was playing Colonel Pickering. 'So sorry to hear the old boy's not well. Send him my love, won't you?'

'I think we met once before at a charity dinner in Esher,' said Enid Carroll who was playing Mrs Pearce, the housekeeper.

'I think we share a common problem,' said Isla Stewart who was playing Mrs Higgins, Dominic's mother in the play. She leant forward to whisper 'John Barleycorn' with a giggle.

'Are you a golfing man?' asked Teddy Fitzgerald who as the dustman Doolittle apparently did everything except eat the scenery to get his laughs.

'Welcome to the company,' said Martin Carp who, as Freddy Eynsford Hill, had the lovely 'On the Street Where You Live' to sing each night. 'Will you be wearing a wig?' His tone was confidential and Dominic could see the tell-tale glint of spirit gum at the edges of his widow's peak. 'Not that you need one of course . . .'

'This is the bit I hate most,' said Tessa Neal as she shook his hand. 'The read-through . . . who was it said that the only purpose of the first day's rehearsal was to get through to the second?' It was said for his benefit; he realised Eliza Doolittle was seeking to sooth her Professor Higgins. Tessa's face was heart-shaped and her skin shone so that her cheekbones had a look of edibility. As she grinned at him Dominic remembered of old to beware of moist-eyed girls with up-turned noses.

They spent the first two days slowly plotting the moves of the play. Dominic wrote them in his script, the others didn't need to, for them the problem was the persistent echo in their heads of Leo Benson. For them it was a revisiting of old territory that called for patience with their new leader. They could see it was hard enough for Dominic stepping into a dead man's shoes without them telling him how to walk.

*

Monday, 22nd May
'Opening at the Princess in Man, with poor old
Leo B. was frightening enough but arriving at
the Brunswick to start M.F.L. all over again was
SCARY. I mean the WEST END . . . It was good
to see all the familiar faces, dear old Teddy et al.
And as for him, Dominic G., Piero Dimonzi jacket
and jeans . . . he has that look . . . you know as if
he couldn't care less. Actually he seemed rather
distant or perhaps he's shy. He's going to be
quite a different kind of Higgins . . . not at all
uncle-ish like Leo. Dominic is really aloof, sort of
effortless and arrogant the way Higgins should
be. Enid calls it 'filmic' but I suppose we had all
got quite used to Leo who was, let's face it, a bit
. . . well . . . hammy really. R.I.P. . . . When we
did the Hertford Hereford and Hampshire scene
and he feeds me the chocolates, puts them in my
mouth he gave me such a look . . . Oh dear, you
know what I'm like . . .

*

'Ladies and Gentlemen. I'm so glad to see you all. Thank you so much for coming.' Phoebe addressed the thirty showbusiness reporters with her usual drawling charm. Her hair was swept back and she shone with well-being and gold; in primrose yellow silk she looked quite luminous. 'I know how busy you all must be. I think the hand-out gives you all the details about what we're doing and the cast are here to answer any questions. Thank you.'

The entire company had been asked to attend although it was obvious that Dominic would be the focal point. They had come in the cause of team spirit and were sitting in a semi-circle in the foyer of the Brunswick. They drank champagne and listened to Dominic answering the questions. He paused before giving his replies and gave off a calm he didn't feel. He remembered only too well the process of the paparazzi, the voracious grinding up of privacy.

'The rehearsals are going very well' . . . 'Yes I'm certainly daunted'. . . 'Ask the company here, they're being very patient and kind'. . . 'Yes we'll be doing a cast album'. . . 'Too young? Thank you for that but actually I'm not'. . . 'Yes I suppose it is a come-back'. . . 'Yes, I'm scared shitless'. . . 'My wife is fine thank you'. . . 'No comment. I'm here to talk about *My Fair Lady*'. Dominic longed to be out walking with Smirno in Ashdown Forst.

'It says in the press release,' said a reporter at the back, 'that there's going to be a special Sunday night gala at the Princess Theatre, Manchester, before you open at the Brunswick?'

'That's right,' Dominic nodded.

'As a benefit for Leo Benson?'

'Well his family . . . Yes.'

'Did you know him, Leo Benson?'

'Not personally,' Dominic answered. 'He was a marvellous actor . . . he was a good man with many friends. It's not at all easy taking over from him.'

'Is it true then that you have already sent his widow a personal cheque for five thousand pounds?'

'I'm not answering that.' Dominic wondered how they had found out.

A girl in leather put up her hand. 'Are you ready for this?' she asked sweetly. 'I mean are you fully recovered?'

'Oh, I see, you want to know about my drinking.' He smiled then paused. Against his leg he felt a faint pressure from Tessa beside him. It was an infinitesimal gesture of support. He went on, 'Well the bad news is I'm still an alcoholic but

116

the good news is,' he raised his glass, 'I drink my tonic neat these days . . . I'm dry.'

A pale man in corduroy put up his hand.

'Can you tell us then if you'll be going to any more British Film Award Ceremonies?' The cruelty of the question was thinly veiled and put the room to silence.

'I think maybe not,' Dominic answered slowly, his eyes fixed on the reporter, 'not for a while. Even if I was invited . . . which isn't likely, is it?'

Dominic's pulse was thudding at the memory of his drinking Waterloo. He had been over-primed in the name of hospitality, had misjudged his intake by a double or two and overstepped the fine line of the drinker's code. He could remember suddenly standing there in the bright light with a sea of idotic faces in front of him, cameras too, a microphone that had seemed irresistible. It was a minor award anyway for a film he had not enjoyed making so he had let rip.

According to the press the following day his diatribe against the Government's funding of the British Film Industry was impassioned but misplaced. He had pointed his finger in accusation and had become incoherent (tired and emotional the tabloids had sniggered). And worst of all he had caused embarrassment to the Duchess. Two men had helped him from the stage and sent him home. He had walked for some time; lurching along the Embankment, he had leant and stared into the swirling blackness of the Thames. The misery and confusion were still vivid in his mind. Later that night with the hideous award he had won still in his pocket, he had taken a cab to his first meeting with Alcoholics Anonymous.

'Nice question,' he said. Dominic always smiled at his protagonists, a trick he had learnt from his father. 'Good to see you've been at work.'

For a moment there was unease in the room, the reporters cleared their throats and the actors crossed their legs the other way. From the back Phoebe winked at him, giving and showing confidence. 'So let's talk about the show,' he said, 'it's really going to be fabulous, you know . . . terrific.'

'Is there any particular reason why you should have chosen

to work for Phoebe Brunswick?' The question came from a wily-looking Scot.

'Cue for mother-in-law joke,' Dominic answered. 'It's just a part I want to play and she is a great producer.'

'The rumour is,' the Scot went on, 'that she's in trouble. The Brunswick theatres are in line to be taken over . . . You hadn't heard perhaps, Mr Gallagher?'

'Of course I've heard,' Dominic spoke patiently. 'I just don't see it as a threat to be taken seriously.'

'Why is that?' The Scot was coaxing now.

Dominic wanted to toss a caber down his throat. He took a breath. Perhaps this was an opportunity not to be missed. If he was going to achieve anything in the rescue mission for his wife, perhaps now was the moment to take the initiative and come out firing from the hip.

'Because,' he answered, 'any threat from Randal Morton cannot be taken seriously.'

Thirty pens were busy now scrawling across spiral pads. Phoebe lit a cigarette and one or two of the actors drained their glasses. The Brunswick Theatre PR man closed his eyes – he had seen enough own-goals in his time.

'Why not?' The Scot scented blood at last.

'Firstly, I don't think he's got the money or the support to make a serious bid,' Dominic said. His mind was full of his wife's plea for help; he had, too, a brief memory of her blonde head on the pillow beneath him half smiling, half wincing with their pleasure. 'And secondly he hasn't got the know-how or the taste to run a chain of theatres.'

Phoebe blew out a funnel of smoke. 'Attaboy,' she whispered to herself.

'You have something against Randal Morton?' the girl in leather asked.

'Good heavens, no, not personally.' Dominic's sincerity was manifest.

'What's your objection then?'

'He's not the right person to administrate theatres like the Princess, the Brunswick and the Theatre Royal in Marlow.'

'In what way?'

'Have you seen any of his shows?' Dominic asked.

118

Some had, some had not.

'How do you mean?'

'His productions are skimpy and tatty and altogether low grade, they show no love of the theatre and no respect for the paying public. But that's just my opinion.'

The room was silent as ink spewed out, looping and swerving across blank pages. Dominic went on, 'And personally I don't believe that the shareholders would vote in favour of such a man against Phoebe Brunswick. In my opinion it would be foolish for anyone not to endorse her re-election as Chairman of the Board. She's doing a great job . . . as you will see from her production of *My Fair Lady*. . .'

'Well I think that about wraps it up, folks.' The PR man had a flare for knowing when to cut his losses. 'Thank you, everyone, perhaps you'd like to get a few photographs? Outside perhaps?'

As the barrage of cameras flashed and clicked, Dominic smiled and looked and waved as he was told. He hugged Phoebe for them as Leo had done five months before, and kissed Tessa too, catching as he did the smell of baby shampoo. As always the whole procedure of feeding time for the tabloids left him feeling somehow diminished.

Later he reflected that his heroism had been foolhardy. Perhaps he had not been shooting at the enemy after all but merely firing blanks into the air and making a target of himself.

As he slipped out of the stage door that lunchtime, Dominic found himself intercepted by an earnest, hesitant young man with thick, round spectacles. With some uncertainty the boy explained that he was Maurice Loftus of the *Sunday Globe*. Dominic remembered him from the press call, a cub reporter among the wolves. It seemed that he had written an article about Phoebe earlier in the year; he had met her in Manchester on the eve of Leo Benson's death, and had been intrigued by her.

'I mean I think she's just fantastic, you know . . . dynamic, sensational.' The sun glinted on his glasses in admiration. All he wanted was five minutes of Dominic's time. 'I think

119

I've come across something that may interest you.' There was an urgent look on the boy's face and he smelt of peppermints. They sat on a bench in a graveyard round the corner and from inside the church they could hear the faint sound of a lunchtime recital on the organ.

'I'm not really a journalist *au fond*. I've just come down from Cambridge, I'm sort of filling in actually, I want to be a playwright. Showbiz gossip and stuff is not my scene, I'm not very good at that sort of thing.'

It was so obvious that Dominic smiled. 'Go on.'

'You see, I liked what you said about Randal Morton. Exactly right. I spent a bit of time looking into the take-over scenario . . . looking for an angle after my interview with Phoebe. And I rather ruled him out. I mean he's tacky and greedy as you said but he hasn't got that much clout. Would you like a peppermint?' From the pocket of his old linen jacket Maurice produced a bag of loose sweets and Dominic helped himself, they were the ones he liked.

'You see, according to the experts,' Maurice went on, there's no real incentive for Randal to be stalking the Brunswick, not in investment terms. So if there was no profit-based motive I just put it down to some kind of ego trip . . . end of story.' He looked at his watch, he had not yet learnt that five minutes to a journalist is a figure of speech, not a measure of time.

'And then I had a telephone call from a university friend of mine whose flatmate had a girlfriend called Lynette who, it turned out, was working as a temp at Smollet and Todd, a small firm of architects in Horsham. She's quite a clued-up sort of girl and . . . to cut a long story short, quite by chance when she was working late one night she thought she had thrown out some piece of paper she needed and she was looking for it in the waste bin next to the copying machine when she came across . . .' Maurice was taking a folded piece of paper from his pocket, '. . .this.' He handed it to Dominic.

It was a photocopy that had been crumpled and smoothed out again. Dominic could see at once why it had been relegated to the waste bin, it was off centre and quite crooked.

120

In the top left-hand corner it was marked 'STRICTLY PRIVATE', its title read 'PROJECT WEST WIND. V.5'.

The plan itself was of a large building, ten storeys high. The whole structure was of brick and supported in four huge columned arches. On the first and second floor it had rows of arcaded windows, and along the top of the front elevation there was a row of intricate cornices and a looping frieze. At ground level were half a dozen shop fronts with an elegant portico in the middle. In the foreground were set a few ornamental trees and lamp posts decked with hanging baskets of flowers. Whatever it was, it looked harmless enough as new developments go. Dominic studied it for some time.

'Well?' he asked.

'You can't see what it is?' Maurice seemed pleased.

'No.'

Maurice produced a pen from his pocket. 'Look here,' he said, pointing to the background features of the drawing. 'The sort of things architects can't resist putting in for fun, just to show their plan in context.'

Dominic could see no particular significance in the distant skyscraper, the trees and spires, a huge crane faintly silhouetted against the skyline. Maurice put his hand in his pocket again and with a flourish brought out a Polaroid photograph and showed it to Dominic.

The photograph had been taken on a clear sunny day and showed the front of the Brunswick Theatre, there it was, the familiar *My Fair Lady* logo with Dominic's name above it. Even more alarming were the words 'Opening 22 June'. He stared at it for some time, blind to any particular significance. It took Maurice pointing with his pen to widen his understanding; gently he drew Dominic's attention to a distant skyscraper, some trees and spires, a huge crane faintly silhouetted against the skyline. Dominic held up the plan beside the photograph, his heart thudding with comprehension.

'Christ,' he whispered. There was no doubting that the plan was of the Brunswick. It was three storeys higher and all the hallmarks of a theatre had been removed from the façade but there was no mistaking it. 'Christ Almighty.'

'Exactly,' said Maurice, relieved to have made his point.

'What the hell are they going to do with it?' Dominic asked.

'Well the most likely theory is that it'll be a hotel. As you can see there are shops and things on the ground floor and probably the basement, the reception would be on the first floor with the rooms, say two hundred, above. On the roof they would probably have a restaurant or whatever. It's been quite well done.'

'It certainly has.' Dominic felt outrage more than admiration.

'Of course we only have this single elevation to go on. But Lynette reckons they've been quite clever preserving the overall look of the place, its period and so on. They've probably made allowance for a small auditorium of sorts somewhere within the building, as a sop to the Arts lobby.'

'So there you have a pretty obvious profit-based motive for a take-over,' Dominic said.

'Absolutely . . . And there's no saying what else they have in store.' Maurice blinked like an owl.

'They?' Dominic echoed. 'Yes, of course.' From where he sat it was obvious that Randal could not be working single-handed; he was operating in concert for sure on a quite unphilharmonic scale. 'Who the hell are they, these people?'

'I've no idea.' Maurice looked at the sky. 'Lynette thought it best not to ask too many questions about the office.'

'You haven't told anyone else, have you?' Dominic asked.

'No. I thought you might be the right person to talk to.' Maurice did not look like the kind of man accustomed to being alone in the hot seat.

'We must be very careful,' Dominic said. The outside world he had just rejoined was even nastier than he remembered. It looked as though his wife was in hock to something heavier than sharp practice and he had no idea how to proceed. He needed time to think things through. 'Very careful indeed. It's going to take a lot of patience to catch these bastards with their pants down.'

The final notes of the Bach fugue echoed triumphantly from the church behind them and evaporated in the midday sun.

'Project West Wind', Dominic read out the title of the plan. 'V.5 . . . What do you reckon that's all about?'

'Well I wondered,' Maurice began, there was a glimmer of satisfaction in his tone, 'if it might not be Shelley.'

'Shelley as in Percy Bysshe?'

'Yea . . . "Ode to the West Wind" I thought.' Maurice was almost grinning. 'So I looked it up . . .'

'And?'

'Well if it is the codename for the project, I think our property developer is a bit of a wag . . . I took V.5 to mean verse five.' Maurice delicately removed the peppermint from his mouth for the recitation:

'Wild spirit, which art moving everywhere;
Destroyer and preserver; hear, oh, hear.'

9

Phoebe poured herself more coffee and chuckled again. Strewn around her on the bed were all the newspapers with Dominic's photograph smiling up at her in different sizes. His views on Randal Morton were described as 'a tirade' under the headline 'STAR WARS'. The *Daily Post* told how the dried-out actor had lost none of his reputation for being a rebel. Mostly the reports were sympathetic and Phoebe was glad to see that Randal Morton had growled nothing but 'no comment'. The Major had rung to tell her that the box office at the Brunswick had never been busier which only proved again the old adage that there is no such thing as bad publicity.

Beside her Sir Philip was reading the *Financial Times* in his lime green silk pyjamas. 'It says here that Dominic is the *enfant terrible* of the British Theatre,' he laughed.

Again they had spent the night together gently moving the goalposts of their friendship. With the slow shedding of designer nightwear, they had whispered breathlessly to one another of the pleasures of it all. For a moment in each other's arms they were young again, alive to the movement of the earth despite the rheumatism. No mention yet of love between them, but the affection was taken as read.

'Everything is going to be all right.' Phoebe kissed his neck.

'I think it is.' He smiled with pleasure. They each took off their glasses and put them on the bedside table, and as they began to kiss the daily newspapers slid to the floor.

'*Oh noctes cenaeque deum,*' Sir Philip murmured.

'You and your bloody Horace,' Phoebe giggled from under the duvet.

124

Their nights and feasts of the gods though were interrupted by a call from Dominic.

'That was a mighty fine piece of work, kiddo,' she said. 'My pappy always told me that the best form of defence was attack.' Phoebe made it rhyme with 'kayak'. But then she listened to what he had rung to tell her and the feeling of well-being drained from her. She felt ridiculous hearing these machinations with no clothes on.

'What is it?' Sir Philip asked when she put down the receiver.

'He says he's got hold of some very interesting plans. He wouldn't say from where . . . all very secretive. An architects' drawing of the Brunswick if you damn well please, a development plan to turn it into some dirty great hotel or something.' There was flat disbelief in her voice.

'A hotel?' Sir Philip reached for his spectacles. 'It's not possible.'

'He's got a copy of the drawing.'

'Who from?'

'He wouldn't say, some firm in Horsham. He says it's absolute dynamite. If he can trace who's behind it and link the plan to Randal Morton, he'll be able to blow him off the face of the earth. He made me swear not to tell anyone.' Phoebe decided to exempt her lover.

'Dear God in heaven,' he said. 'Who the hell can it be? If it is Randal Morton, he's something quite a lot more than just an ambitious theatrical producer.'

'Exactly.' Phoebe reached for the comfort of her menthol cigarettes. 'It also means he's got a lot more clout behind him than we reckoned, the slimy little sonofabitch.'

'Well we must expose him. Turn him over to the fraud squad.'

'No,' Phoebe interrupted, 'Dominic said not yet. I think he's on to something. He wants to make his own enquiries – he's afraid otherwise it might all go off at half cock.'

'Shouldn't he be learning his lines for goodness sake?' Sir Philip sounded slightly peeved that he had lost the monopoly on heroism. 'What's he playing at?'

Phoebe lit her cigarette and slowly blew out smoke at the

ceiling. 'He made me swear not to do anything. He said to be careful . . . there's no saying who Randal might be in cahoots with or what they might resort to in order to protect Project West Wind.'

'Project West Wind?' Sir Philip queried.

'That's what it's called, this abomination.' Phoebe shivered and moved in closer under Sir Philip's arm. 'It's some quote from "Ode to the West Wind". . . "Wild spirit which art moving everywhere" . . . something, something, something . . .' Phoebe had not taken it all in from Dominic's call.

'Destroyer and preserver, hear oh hear.' Sir Philip completed the couplet from memory. 'We had to learn our Shelley at school as well as our Horace.'

'You know, Philip, I'm really quite scared,' she said.

'Don't be,' he said stroking her shoulder softly. 'Don't be. I'm here.'

Sister Pearson thought that the photograph of Dominic Gallagher hugging his young co-star was unflattering but she saw it as a chance to cheer her grumpiest resident. Griffith Gallagher had not been eating well lately, hardly any solids and precious little fluid either.

'Another lovely day,' she chirped as she entered his room.

As a source of acute irritation to the old actor, her voice came a close second to his bed sores. Her tone had pretensions to youth and joviality, neither of which she had any right to.

'Another cloudless day, Mr Gallagher, always a delight, isn't it?'

Griffith stared ahead. Actually you fat-assed, bow-legged, overbearing, common, patronising lump of lard, actually, I prefer clouds . . . great black, blustering clouds, he might have said had he not been robbed of speech. Instead he thought it to himself and hissed quietly. And now the bitch was rearranging his bedclothes, plumping up his pillows and exuding the smell of her cheap scent; there was no limit to his loathing of her. Not in all his years of touring provincial theatres with innumerable leading ladies had he experienced quite such a purity of hatred.

'I've got something to show you,' she said coyly.

126

As long as it is no part of your hideous anatomy, he wanted to say as he looked resolutely out of the window at the cloudless bloody sky.

Sister Pearson produced the *Daily Post* with a flourish, held it in front of him so that Dominic's smile was six inches from his father's face. Slowly Griffith brought his eyes unblinking from the horizon to confront the photograph. With no visible sign of pleasure he scrutinised it minutely while Sister Pearson stood patiently, waiting for him to read the accompanying paragraph.

Griffith shook his head at what he read. He had always held the belief that it was not good policy for actors to antagonise producers, the biting of the hand that feeds you was best left to an agent. So Dominic's outburst he reckoned was petulant and ill-judged (he was his mother's son). He shook his head again and sucked his teeth. And as for the young girl beside Dominic in the photograph, her with the fulsome smile, there was no doubt in his mind that the two of them would soon be tripping the light fantastic. Huh.

Sister Pearson was about to withdraw the newspaper from the old boy's view when he let out a gasp. There was agitation in his face and his eyes were sharply focused. He breathed more quickly, letting out a volley of hissing sounds. Sister Pearson held up the newspaper in front of him again.

'You must be ever so proud,' she said. 'It's a lovely picture.'

From Griffith's mouth there came a clicking sound that denoted pleasure and at the corner of his lips there was a brief twitching that might have been a smile, a fleeting spasm of pleasure. It was moments like this, Sister Pearson told herself, that made her job worth while.

'I thought you'd be pleased with it,' she said.

Griffith nodded and clicked again. Slowly he raised his left arm up and with the too long nail of his forefinger he tapped the bed table.

'Would you like me to leave it here for you . . . would you? To look at?' she asked.

Griffith nodded. Sister Pearson folded the paper so that the photograph of Dominic faced upward from the table. An angry gurgling sound erupted from Griffith's throat; it was

127

not what he wanted. She moved the table closer. Another gurgle followed by the slow hiss of irritation told her that she had again misunderstood her patient. His eyes looked from her to the newspaper and back. Again his yellowy talon tapped the table.

'What is it?' she asked, raising her eyebrows like a nanny to a child. 'What is it?'

Click. Hiss. Gurgle, gurgle. Sigh.

Sister picked up the newspaper and held it in front of him again. Griffith nodded.

'Do you want me to leave it here or not?' There was perhaps a limit to her patience after all.

Griffith nodded. Sometimes he missed the power of speech with a vivid yearning that made his neck throb. He nodded again and clicked as sweetly as he could. She put the paper down again on the table, this time unfolded. Griffith nodded and closed his eyes with relief – at last she had got it right.

'There we are then,' she said sweetly, 'I'll leave it with you, shall I?'

Griffith nodded. And then at last she left the room, waddling in her sensible shoes. In the distance he could hear the familiar drone of the floor polisher advancing down the corridor. He turned his eyes again to the *Daily Post*, not to the smiling photograph of his son but to the paragraph in the bottom corner of the page. The headline that had caught his attention read 'SHOW GIRL'S BODY FOUND'.

Griffith leant forward as best he could the better to read the smaller print beneath. It had been a while since he had read a newspaper and he did so now with dread.

'The body of 26-year-old Norma Kingston was formally identified yesterday. Norma, a dancer from South East London, went missing last month and her body was discovered four days ago on wasteland in Streatham. A police spokesman confirmed that they were continuing a full-scale murder enquiry but would make no comment on reports that the body had been mutilated. Norma's boyfriend, Mustaffa Ishksa, a croupier from Istanbul, was released after questioning without charge. Outside the home they shared he would only say, "I am distraught. I cannot believe that Norma was

128

two-timing me. She was my ideal woman." According to police sources there is very little evidence to go on.'

Having read it twice Griffith sat back quivering among his pillows. He stared out over the golf course towards the sea and wondered what to do. Unable to speak or write, he was marooned, a shipwrecked witness with no flags or flares. But the problem did not daunt him, he had nothing to lose now with death having so thoroughly lost its sting. Somehow he would find a way of getting his desperate message in a bottle and hurling it forth.

Sister Pearson was pleased to note that Griffith ate a better lunch that day: fricassee and then extra prunes with his semolina.

'I'm as thick as two short bricks,' giggled Margot Brunswick to her dinner guests. 'At least that's what Maxwell always says, isn't it, Max darling?' She grinned through the cande-labra to him at the other end of the table. He scowled back as usual; already there was that lubricious look in his eyes that told her he had drunk too much.

'What was that, Margot?' he growled. 'What are you saying?'

'Mother was saying,' Tristram was giggling stupidly, his teeth bright in the candlelight, 'that she's as thick as two short bricks, Dad.'

'What of it?' Maxwell's bottom lip had an unkindly curl to it.

Margot was not brilliant, it was true, but her wide circle of friends around Bagshot chose to see her as kind and reliable. Over the years she had become accustomed to what she called Maxwell's 'little ways'. He spent so much time these days in London or abroad that she chose not to look for and therefore not to find the lipstick on his collar.

'I say,' said a guest with no hair, 'did you see in the paper the rumpus that actor chap has been kicking up about your jolly old family business?'

'Yes I certainly did.' Maxwell's mouth was full of chocolate.

'Dominic bloody Gallagher,' Tristram muttered, 'back on the juice by the look of it . . . nothing but a piss artist.' He

129

had been laughing vapidly all evening, over-revving. And this was another area in which Margot elected to be blind. She was quite unaware of the tell-tale signs of his addiction, the rapid speaking and the shifts of mood. Had she looked she would have seen that lately the pupils of his sapphire eyes were huge and black, dilated with cocaine.

'Poor Phoebe, she does have rotten luck, doesn't she?' Margot was saying. 'What with the fire at Marlow and poor old Leo Benson doing himself in.'

'All the more reason for her to hand the theatres over to someone who is half way competent.' Tristram's malice was obvious, he ignored his father's look of caution. 'They shouldn't bloody well be hers anyway. She's got no right to them.'

'That's what I was saying,' Margot interrupted. 'You two would be much better in charge ... sell them off or something ...'

'Do be quiet, Margot.' Maxwell's nose shone vermilion in the candlelight, a beacon of his ambition.

'I said at the time,' she went on, 'you should have contested the will. Your brother can't have been in his right mind.'

'Exactly, Mother, Uncle Austin was off his trolley.' Tristram was waving a spoonful of chocolate mousse. 'She's got no right.'

'I mean this chap Randal Morton,' the bald man said. 'He's the man you want in charge. You should have some damn say in the matter, I reckon.'

Father and son exchanged an uneasy look, they were playing a more subtle game than that.

'I must say I don't understand it. It's beyond me,' Margot said, 'but then you've always been a bit backward in coming forward, haven't you, Max dear.' She beamed sweetly, begging to be disabused.

'Anyway,' her husband said, 'it's planks. Not bricks.'

'What, dear?'

'You're as thick as two short *planks*.'

'I beg your pardon.'

'You're as thick as a brick ... *a* brick, one brick, or as thick as two short planks. That's how it is, that is the idiom.'

Margot was bemused. 'There's no need to shout.'

'You can't be as thick as two short bricks.' Maxwell's smile was cruel. 'There's no such thing as a short brick.'

'Oh I see,' said Margot. 'More mousse, anyone?'

Ben Delahay had finished all the stuffed olives by the time Dominic finished explaining the delicate mission he was on regarding the Brunswick Theatre shares. They had become friends at school, had played conkers and squash and country and western together at Christ's Hospital. They had gone their separate ways to stockbroking and film-making but had kept in touch. In fact ever since Dominic's early success, Ben had guided him in the ways of financial cunning. He was the obvious person for Dominic to call upon for help and they had arranged to meet at the Berkley after rehearsals.

'Well, Gallagher,' said the financial whizz-kid, 'you're in deep shit, aren't you?'

'That about sums it up I suppose.' Dominic ordered two more drinks, one soft and one not so soft for his old friend.

'The thing is,' Ben said, 'you've got no positive absolute link between this Randal Morton bloke and the scrap of paper from the waste bin – this West Wind business. So you can't expose him.' Ben spun the ice round his new drink. 'Now apart from his rather dodgy deal with Harriet and her shares, which again you can't expose, his bid for the Brunswick Theatres looks on the surface to be pretty legit.'

'Yea. So what do I do?'

'Well, he's not on his own, is he, this chap?' Ben gave his boy-scout grin. Dib. Dib. Dib. 'So we've got to find out who he's teamed up with, right? And for that we need access to the company register. The company secretary would have a copy which might be better in the circs. Secrecy is vital.'

'What would I be looking for?' Dominic asked.

'A link or linking factor between two or more investors.'

'A link that would be obvious to the average man on the Clapham omnibus?'

'Exactly, Gallagher.' Ben grinned. 'Well done.'

'I'll get the Major on to it.' Dominic made a note.

'Who's he?'

'Malcolm Kendal, Phoebe's right-hand man, . . . also known as the Major.'

'Best not. Do it yourself.'

'For Christ's sake he's one of the good guys.'

'There are no good guys.' Ben was speaking in earnest. 'No good guys. Do you understand?'

'Oh come on . . .'

'I'm serious. The most important thing is for no one, no one to know that you're snooping around. If the predators, whoever they are, get wind of what you're up to, either they'll go to ground or . . . you'll be in serious danger. These people mean business.'

Dominic thought for a moment, daunted by the serious tone of his friend. 'The trouble is we're rather up against the clock,' he said. 'The AGM is only a few weeks away.'

'Yes, but we're only concerned with a very small number of investors, we should be able to track them down, somehow we'll be able to pinpoint them . . . for the most part they're non-voters, passive investors. It's the buggers who turn up with a fist full of proxy votes you've got to watch out for.'

'You'll help me, won't you?'

'Of course.' Ben had now finished the roasted peanuts as well. 'We'll think of something. Obviously it would be a great help if by then your mother-in-law's prospects had improved.'

'You mean if *My Fair Lady* was selling out at the Brunswick?' Dominic asked.

Ben nodded. 'It might even help sort out your marital problems too.'

Dominic studied his friend for a moment, not liking the truth Ben had spotted. 'Mind your own beeswax, Delahay.'

Reluctantly Randal Morton was allowing his feathers to be smoothed, even by his standards though the stress factor was high. With eight shows currently touring the provinces and all the problems of his bid for the Brunswick, he saw himself as a juggler with too many balls in the air. In the face of all the public abuse he had received from Dominic he had been sorely tempted to retaliate. His home and office were beseiged with eager journalists, he could so easily have denounced the

132

actor as a crackpot, a drunk, a has-been, a cuckold desperate to re-ingratiate himself, but he had been persuaded to keep his silence. 'No comment,' he had barked. 'I have nothing to say.' His arteries had fizzed with a dreadful anger. 'The last thing I want is a slanging match with Dominic Gallagher,' he had lied.

As a boy he had sat open-mouthed in the balcony of his local rep. Against the background of all the unhappiness at home, the world he saw under the proscenium arch looked rosy and simple. The plays had French windows and happy endings and he longed to be part of it all. Nowadays what he felt for the theatre was the ambivalent love of a cheating husband.

'Fuck the better part of valour,' he said. As he paced about his office, his white moccasins went gliding through the shag pile. In the two leather armchairs Maxwell Brunswick and his son, the brooding Tristram, were drinking gin and waiting for him to subside. 'As far as Gallagher is concerned, the better part of valour is a short sharp kick in the balls.'

'You'll get your chance. Don't worry.' Maxwell's voice was reassuring.

'He won't know what's bloody well hit him.' Tristram's patience was not the real thing. It was a fake that hid his true nature, the spite and jealousy.

Randal Morton was not to be placated. 'You don't think I should make a statement? I mean, last year, for God's sake, I produced twenty-eight shows across the country, over three hundred weeks of theatre. It's the logical next step for a producer who is that prolific to get himself into bricks and mortar.' Out of modesty Randal transferred to the third person. 'It's crazy for him to be paying rent all the time. People need to realise that with him as a new figurehead, the Brunswick Theatres will be safe, both artistically and economically . . .'

'There'll be plenty of time for that,' interrupted Maxwell. 'Meanwhile the less said the better. Believe me, it's all under control . . sewn up.'

'We'll keep the element of surprise for the AGM,' Tristram giggled. 'Give Auntie Phoebe a nasty shock.'

133

'We'll keep all the PR stuff for afterwards.' Maxwell drained his glass. 'When you're installed at the Brunswick.'

'Trust us, we can't fail.' Tristram tapped the side of his nose.

When they had gone Randal drummed his fingers on the blotter and wondered who to trust. As an ambitious juggler, he ran the risk of balls raining down on his head.

10

Harriet had interpreted Dominic's public salvo against Randal Morton as being auspicious. It was the dust cloud on the horizon that she chose to see as the cavalry on the move. Obviously he had a plan to retrieve her shares and undo her treachery. He had not spoken to her directly since her visit to the school and she was beginning to wonder if their lovemaking that afternoon had been an aberration, a mere hiatus in the status quo. The memory of it was spectacular, illicit and yet familiar in her mind. Surely it was the same for him. He owed her at least some statement of intent – an avowal or an apology.

'I'll get it, babe.' Greg rose to answer the telephone. He was kinder and more attentive now the tables had turned on him. He had even stopped smoking in bed, desperate at finding himself a seller on a buyer's market.

'No. I'll take it.' Harriet snatched it from him. 'It's my phone, for God's sake.' She took the telephone into the bedroom out of earshot.

'Hello, Harriet? It's Randal here.'

'Hello,' she answered. This was not a social call. Perhaps he was going to close the play, write it off.

'I have been reading some fairly unpleasant stuff about myself in the papers lately,' he was saying, 'a lot of shit, in fact, from your ex-husband. I want to know who the fuck he thinks he is coming the great-I-am slandering me to buggery and back . . .'

Harriet wondered if he had yet run out of steam. 'Yea. I read it too,' she said gravely. 'Nothing to do with me.'

'Oh wasn't it?' Randal sneered. 'I was just wondering if perhaps you had been shooting your mouth off about our little deal. I thought that you might have forgotton that our arrangement vis-a-vis the funding of *Up for Grabs* was confidential.'

'I never told him. I haven't even seen him. I don't talk to him.' Harriet was looking out the window not seeing the cloudless day.

'I'm telling you the show is a turkey,' Randal went on. 'It's going down the pan and with it goes our investment, yours and mine. That was the deal. So the best thing for you to do, young lady, is to keep your mouth shut, do you understand?'

Harriet cleared her throat. 'Yes.'

'I understand of course that when our secret comes to light, as it will before long, it'll create a certain tension between you and your mother but that's tough shit.'

Harriet sat on the bed feeling quite nauseous, she knew that in her mother's book disloyalty was the least pardonable of sins.

'And tell Dominic to back off,' Randal went on. 'Tell him to mind his own business, tell him to get off my back or . . .'

'Or what?'

'He'll be in trouble.'

'Is that a threat?' she asked.

'You're fucking right it is.' His laughter crackled down the line. 'I'll have his fucking head kicked in.'

'I'll tell him,' she said before the line went dead. She took a pill to ease the sickness in her stomach.

'Who was that?' Greg asked.

'Just a friend of Mum's,' she said patting his jealous head.

In contrast to the well-ordered routine Dominic had enjoyed at Chelwood House, the first week's rehearsal came as a shock to his system. It was a time of rediscovery. He found himself functioning well with energy and patience, he could barely recognise his previous self, the drinker – miserable and withdrawn with half a bottle of vodka in his pocket. Also, and this surprised him, he was happy to be back at work.

For the second week's rehearsal the company were going to Manchester where they would have the benefit of working on the stage of the Princess Theatre. The new scenery was

136

being built there and the actors were keen to familiarise themselves with it as it was assembled.

Dominic drove up on Sunday evening. He listened to the rehearsal tape of the show and sang his way north with his dog beside him. The lines running through his head were not just Alan Jay Lerner's, there were Shelley's too echoing in his mind. 'Wild spirit, which are moving everywhere; Destroyer and preserver; hear oh hear.'

The office had booked him into a small private hotel to the west of the city which gave him a self-contained annexe, a bungalow with its own patio garden. In terms of décor it fell between baroque and Conran but suited Dominic's purpose well enough. Mrs Daisy Bolt, the manageress, was only too pleased to look after Smirnoff during the day and, as instructed, she had hired a piano. 'I reckoned you'd not be wanting a grand in your room just for practising.'

On the Monday it was a slow stumbling rehearsal that gave Dominic an idea of what work remained to be done. Having worked for so long in films he had grown accustomed to presenting his performance piecemeal, a fragment each day carefully distilled for the camera. He had forgotton there are no retakes in the theatre, no cuts when things go wrong. On the stage an actor is up against that great dark giant that eats live actors. It is a tired or eager or restless giant with fifteen hundred pairs of hands to clap or not. A tricky giant, Dominic remembered, that had to be faced with real courage, not his old familiar courage from a bottle.

His fellow actors were encouraging at the end of the day though privately they nursed the fear that his performance was all too miniature. As a director Ian could see that Dominic was an actor who needed to get the internal mechanism of the character he was playing sorted out before putting it fully on display, he was an actor who worked from the inside out.

After the rehearsal Dominic was taken to the star dressing room for a costume fitting. In the full-length mirror he got a first glimpse of Higgins's outer shell; the tails and opera hat, the tweed suit, the cardigans, the trilby ... slowly it was coming together, the merging of flesh and fiction. When they had gone, the designer and the tailor, there was a knock on the door and a middle-aged woman came in.

'I'm sorry to trouble you. The stage door keeper said you were here. I hope you weren't asleep. You must be exhausted. I did not mean to disturb you. I just came to pick up Leo's things – his make-up case and bits and bobs. I think it's in the cupboard. Please don't get up. I'm sorry, I'm Kitty Benson, Leo's wife. Widow. How do you do?'

'How do you do?' Dominic had recognised her straight away but had not liked to interrupt her monologue, the flow of it seemed so delicately balanced on this side of self control. They shook hands.

'I won't be a minute. It's probably in the cupboard.'

'Oh, yes.' Dominic could think of nothing to say. He had not thought of the room as being Leo's. He felt intrusive and thoughtless. 'I'm so sorry,' he said.

'It's all right, I won't be a moment.' Kitty was kneeling at the cupboard.

'I mean . . .' Dominic had meant to express sympathy. 'I could have sent them on or brought them to you.'

'Actually I wanted to see you.' She stood up again holding a small suitcase and a pile of her husband's first night cards. 'I wanted to thank you for your kindness . . . I mean the cheque for God's sake. It was so . . . generous. You're very kind.' Her voice was brusque with self-restraint. 'I was going to write to you . . . You've no idea how use . . . vital it's going to be with Amanda and everything. It was ludicrously kind of you. I mean . . .'

'Please.' Dominic tried to staunch the flood of gratitude.

'You've got no reason to be bothered with us.' Kitty was awkwardly shuffling the cards in her hand. 'Good luck. Break a leg. Knock 'em for six. I'm so sorry Amanda told one of the newspapers about it. We were just so amazed at your . . . kindness.' Tears were springing from her eyes as she turned away. 'I'm sorry. I'm sorry. I'm sorry.'

Dominic stood like a useless bystander unable even to offer a clean handkerchief.

'I'm sorry,' she kept repeating as if her lapse of control was inexcusable.

138

What comfort could he offer her, this desolate woman in her Jaeger skirt and blouse, Dominic wondered, and found himself hopelessly patting her shoulders. She was holding a framed photograph from among Leo's things – it showed her family as it had been: father, mother, daughter on the beach, sunburnt and squinting at the sun. She polished the glass with her wet handkerchief, not knowing that the blur was in her eyes.

'He was a good man,' she said, and then, with no trace of sentiment, she dropped the pile of greetings cards into the wastepaper basket. 'I'd better be going, it's a long drive.'

'You drove up?' Dominic could only stand in the middle of the room feeling inadequate.

'Yes. Well I've got to collect his things from the flat he had as well . . . He'd taken it for four months anyway you see and I couldn't really face it before.'

'You're going to his flat . . . on your own.'

'Yes,' she nodded. 'The police finished with it weeks ago. I'm taking most of his stuff to the Oxfam Shop in Gerrards Cross . . . It's got to be done.'

'I'll come with you,' Dominic offered without premeditation, 'you might need a hand.'

She smiled her acceptance and they left the theatre together carrying Leo's things.

The flat was immaculate, clean and bland. Its colours and style bore all the hallmarks of a letting unit rather than a home. Nothing the police had found there had contradicted the theory of suicide and the apartment itself gave no reflection of any drama, barely of any life.

Dominic followed her from room to room as she busied herself with the dismal chore of packing away her husband's things. He poured her some wine from the fridge and let her talk.

'OK. I know people must have thought we were an odd couple, incompatible . . . with me being a teacher and him being who he was. But he always said it was my not being in the business that kept him sane. He needed his feet keeping on the ground . . . And then when this big break came with *Don't Bank on It* on telly . . . oh it was wonderful. Amanda was just a baby and Gerrards Cross was a blessing after Clapham. I remember when we were first together and he was in rep and we had no money he promised we'd have a house in the country one day. "You'll see, my squirrel," he used to say, "with roses at the door and fruit trees . . . and a proper compost heap."' Kitty laughed, 'He always had this thing about having a proper compost heap . . . oh dear.' She stopped abruptly, the memory too vivid for her. The tears ran down her face and neither of them spoke for a time. The silence between them was unoppressive and Dom let it ride.

Kitty paused for a moment, running her hand down the lapel of her husband's raincoat. Dominic filled her glass again. It was twilight. Kitty stood by the window with its high view of Manchester and shook her head in the manner of a mild rebuke. 'Poor old Leo,' she said quietly.

A modest sensible woman, Dominic thought, such as his mother might have been. Harriet was certainly not like this, he could not imagine her sorting out his sponge bag when he was dead.

For a time Kitty ambled about the flat without speaking, it was a final inspection, perhaps a search for some memento that the police had missed. And then she came to rest among the suitcases and carrier bags grouped together in the sitting room.

'Perhaps you'd like to have dinner with me.' Dominic was miserable on her behalf, he wanted to comfort her and be comforted.

'Yes,' she smiled, 'why not? I'd like that. Amanda is staying with friends and I'm in no fit state to drive. Why not?'

'Well let's get out of here.' Dominic sensed that her strength of will was at breaking point.

'I'll just call home and leave a message.' Kitty put down her empty glass on the table by the telelphone, and froze. Her eyes were fixed on the digital dial. 'L.R. ?' she said quietly. 'L.R., is that what you press to reconnect with the last number you dialled?'

'Yes. I . . .'

Before he could finish Kitty had picked up the receiver and

140

pressed the button in question. 'It'll probably be our number at home, or something. The police must have checked it.'

As it began to ring she seemed suddenly frightened. This dialling out beyond the grave was perhaps a trespass. She was on the point of hanging up when a voice answered. 'Hello,' it snapped.

In a panic Kitty clamped her hand over the mouthpiece and thrust the receiver at Dominic. And there he was confronted with his two least favourite things: improvisation and the telephone.

'Hello.' The voice was impatient in his ear.

'Hello,' he answered calmly. 'To whom am I speaking?'

Dominic found himself using a rather plummy voice, something between Derek Nimmo and Robert Morley.

'Who is this?' L.R. sounded testy now. 'Who is this?'

'I asked first,' Dominic insisted.

'Who are you?' L.R. was without doubt a grumpy type. 'Who is this?'

'I am a friend of Leo Benson's.' Dominic fired his arrow quietly into the dark.

'Oh.' The tone of voice was suddenly different, meeker. 'Did he give you this number?'

'Yes.' Dominic's voice was quieter now and deeper, along the lines of Orson Welles. 'He said you might be able to help me.'

'With what?' L.R. was getting ratty again. 'Who are you?'

Dominic had no idea. He certainly did not want to be himself. 'That's not your concern,' he said. 'Leo spoke to you didn't he . . . the day he died?'

There was a long pause. L.R. was clearly putting in some thought on the matter. Dominic felt he had retrieved the initiative. Kitty stood with two fists clenched to her mouth like a child watching a fight.

'Yes, yes he did.' The answer came with reluctance. 'We spoke briefly.'

'He told me.' Dominic sensed he had the upper hand but over whom and about what he had no idea. 'He told me everything.'

'Did he?' L.R. was being cryptic.

141

'Yes. I don't think it's a conversation that the police know about, yet.' Dominic was following his instinct.

'For Christ's sake I didn't know he was going to top himself.' L.R. was on the defensive.

'Maybe, but the police would still like to know.'

'Who the hell are you? One of his little bum-boys?'

'Mind your own business.' Dominic's brain was reeling.

There was another pause. L.R. was putting in a bit more thought. 'What do you want?' he asked.

'What do you think?' Dominic answered. The last thing he wanted was the ball in his court.

'Money?'

'Right.' Dominic was worried now. The two of them were leading each other down a criminal path.

'How much?' L.R. was keen to do a deal – what deal?

Dominic had no idea. What price should he put on this unknown asset he had stumbled upon? If he answered too high or too low his bluff could easily be called.

'Twenty thousand,' he said.

'Fuck you,' said the man with no name.

'Take it or leave it.' Dominic was veering towards Michael Caine.

'Ten.'

'Twenty.' Dominic could see no reason for lenience.

'For God's sake . . .' L.R. pleaded.

'Twenty.' Dominic looked towards Kitty who was standing transfixed with bewilderment and curiosity.

'OK, OK,' L.R. relented. 'I'll meet you tomorrow.'

'Where?' Dominic knew a rendezvous was impossible.

'I'll have to think.' L.R. sounded as if he too had an identity crisis. 'Listen, you frig me about on this and there'll be trouble, do you understand?'

'As if I would.' Dominic allowed himself a note of flippancy. Mae West possibly.

'Call me at the same time tomorrow,' L.R. sounded in charge again, 'I'll tell you then . . .'

'Yes, but . . .' The line had gone dead.

Kitty and Dominic stared at each other like two people in

shock. They were each seeking enlightenment from the other, none came.

'Who the hell was that?' she asked.

'I've no idea.'

For Dominic the problem was that at the same time tomorrow the flat, together with the telephone and its memory of L.R. would no longer be at their disposal. He paced about in puzzlement.

'For goodness sake what was he saying . . . what's going on?' Kitty was impatient for explanation.

'I'll tell you in a minute.'

He was rummaging in his leather hold-all. He brought out the pocket tape-recorder he used for rehearsal purposes and a blank tape. He loaded it and pressed again the L.R. button on the telphone, this time holding the receiver to the built-in microphone for it to record the sound of each digit making its connection. Later he would have the problem of deciphering it.

'Hello.' The testy voice was on the line again.

'It's me again,' said Dominic. 'Er . . . you wouldn't prefer me to call you at the office?'

'No, definitely not. Here will be fine,' was L.R.'s hasty answer.

'All right, then. Cheerio.' This time it was Dominic who had the last word. And having hung up he then dialled each number in turn and recorded its audio signal for future cross-reference. After years of wondering how it was that he so often got wrong numbers, Dominic now had to apply himself to the problem in earnest.

On the way to the restaurant Dominic gave her an edited report of his conversation with L.R. They ordered sea bream with mangetout and new potatoes. Kitty drank Frascati and Dominic Aqua Libra. Their thoughts and conversation were never far from the problem of L.R., who it was and what was the secret he valued at twenty thousand pounds? Towards the end of the meal Dominic sensed she was weighing him up. She went to speak and then didn't.

'I think Leo was being blackmailed,' she said at last without looking at him.

'Blackmailed?' Dominic showed surprise. Had he perhaps underestimated her. 'For what . . .? By whom?' he asked.

Again Kitty took her time. Dominic did nothing to hurry her, he poured the last of the Frascati into her glass. She took a sip and then a deep breath.

'You see I knew when I married Leo that he was . . . er . . . a bit the other way. Gay, queer . . . whatever you like.' She shrugged at him across the table and went on. 'I've never really thought it mattered . . . You see I've always been rather . . . er, shy of men . . . or rather of masculinity. Maybe I'm frigid or something.' She took a sip of wine, avoiding his eye with the awkwardness of this self-analysis. 'And anyway . . . Leo was very kind to me and . . . gentle. He wanted to settle down and have children . . . he liked ordinariness and routine and I suppose he got them from me. He was – I've got used to saying that now – a marvellous husband and father . . . wonderful.' She paused a moment. 'And if, when he was away he felt a need . . . to go a little wild, so what? It never bothered me . . . it was nothing to do with us. We didn't talk about it of course . . . I just turned a blind eye. I mean it didn't threaten me or anything . . . I mean we all have our different little needs, don't we?'

Dominic nodded at this simple truth, he too had his little needs.

'Well, as I say we never discussed it but I always knew . . . It's funny, isn't it, but I couldn't have borne it if he had been with another woman. I mean I know I'm no great shakes . . .' This was not false modesty, it was the real thing.

'Was there someone here in Manchester then, do you think?' Dominic asked.

Kitty nodded. 'I'm pretty sure.' Again she paused and took another sip of her wine. 'Yes. I reckon he had a boyfriend up here . . .'

A bum-boy as L.R. had called it, Dominic recalled.

'And I suppose,' she went on, 'that someone was making trouble about it . . . threatening to expose him or tell the newspapers or something. He couldn't have stood that . . . he was a very proud man, set a lot of store by his dignity. I mean he'd rather . . . I nearly said die . . . than have it all out in the

144

open. It was his secret thing . . . If only he could have told me, we could have, we could have . . .'

'Weathered it?'

'Yes.' She was glad of his prompt. 'I would have stood by him.'

Dominic pondered the plight of the wretched man hounded by the threat of being forced out of the closet. An ordinary man who loved his family and his compost heap and had opted for a lonely death rather than wreck his image. A man who valued dignity and had taken his own life to save it. A man who had underestimated the compassion of his wife.

'And you mentioned none of this to the police?' he asked.

'Oh no.' The idea was appalling to her. 'That would have been unthinkable. If he died to keep it secret, it would have been a betrayal. I couldn't have done that to him . . . the poor, dear, silly man. We could have weathered it, together.' She shook her head. 'But it's best left like this now, a mystery . . . I can't think why I'm telling you really.' Her cheeks looked quite flushed in the candlelight.

'And you think that whoever it was on the telephone earlier was blackmailing him?' Dominic asked.

'Yes.'

'And now we're blackmailing him, whoever he is.'

'I suppose we are,' she said with surprise. 'There's irony for you, there's no point really is there? I'd like to know who it was though, that did that to Leo. I'm rather tipsy. I am sorry.'

Dominic managed to persuade her to drive home in the morning and stay the night at his place. He made up a bed for himself on the sofa before taking her in some hot chocolate.

'You're a very nice man,' she said, 'you should find yourself a new wife.'

'No. I don't think so.' Dominic was standing beside the bed.

'Why not?'

'Because I'm still in love with the old one.' Dominic surprised himself with the admission.

'Oh good,' she said. They smiled at each other briefly in acknowledgement of this common bond.

Kitty had hiccoughs now as she sipped the chocolate. 'The

145

only funny thing is,' she said, 'about a week before Leo died he rang and said he wanted Amanda to have a treat for finishing her mocks and why didn't I get tickets for the show at the Regent – the rock musical about Cromwell. Amanda loved the idea but I didn't fancy it. I told him I'd rather see that revival of *West Side Story* at the Forum. They're side by side anyway. So I managed to get tickets one for the Regent, one for the Forum. My God, what a price I had to pay. What a rip-off.'

She looked altogether calmer now sitting in the middle of Dominic's bed wearing his old blue shirt. She took another sip. 'And we were just about to set out, Amanda and me, when Daddy, Leo, rang us from Manchester. He said he hoped we would enjoy ourselves and could we do something for him. He wanted us to count the exact number of seats in each theatre. I said whatever for, and he said it was important. He just wanted to know.' She put her mug down. 'Don't you think it's odd though?'

Dominic thought it was. What significance could there be in such information? Kitty shrugged drowsily, her hair barely dishevelled on the pillow.

'You're a very nice man,' she said.

And Dominic wondered if perhaps he was. He switched out the light and left the room. It had been a busy day that had yielded plenty to keep his mind from sleep. All those hobgoblins who lurk on the edge of consciousness were waiting for him. He lay awake in the small hours allowing them to uncork themselves while his feet were pinioned by the weight of Smirnoff sleeping soundly.

At last he heard a blackbird singing and got up to make coffee. He had work to do before going to rehearse. With his pocket recorder and the telephone on the table in front of him, Dominic set about tracking down whoever it was Leo had last called on the day of his death. With each number in turn he dialled and listened, then dialled again and doubled checked his findings. It was not a London number. After more than an hour he was gaining confidence, and to make sure of his information he walked across the park to a telephone box where the tone of each digit matched his findings. He had got

146

it. Triumphantly he returned home with Smirnoff cantering round him, her coat glossy in the new sunlight. He began to feel light-hearted and optimistic, there was no dragon he could not slay. With fresh coffee and his script he sat on the patio and went through his lines, muttering them out loud into the morning air, repeating them over and over until he utterly possessed them.

The process of learning lines is more than just a trick of memory, it is an intricate mechanism that links thought and speech, brain and tongue. The spontaneity and effortlessness are not easily achieved. As a point of focus Dominic had Smirnoff gazing at him from beside the geraniums, a canine Liza Doolittle. 'I've grown accustomed to her face . . . Like breathing out and breathing in, she seems to make the day begin.' He recited the final lyric to her. For her part she watched him with an alertness that is often labelled love.

Unlike Dominic, Kitty had eventually slept quite soundly and as she woke Dominic could see her mild face being reclaimed by unhappiness. Over breakfast her main concern was that she had betrayed her husband.

'You will be careful, won't you?' she said. 'Perhaps it's best to leave well alone.'

'I think we've got to find out who it is we are blackmailing, don't you?'

Kitty nodded. From memory Dominic dialled the number he had decoded. It began ringing. Kitty was beside him leaning over his shoulder to listen.

'Hello . . . two-three-eight-five-nine.' A woman's voice.

'Mornin' miss, engineer.' Dominic used a fat rough voice with the lisp of a dullard. 'What seems to be the trouble then?'

'I beg your pardon?'

'There's been a fault reported on this number.'

'Er, no, I don't think so. Well actually it's my husband's business line. I wouldn't normally be answering it, the machine should be on.'

'Subscriber's name?' Dominic was beginning to give up hope.

'The same,' she answered.

'Same as what?' Dominic's engineer was at his most stupid.
'As ours.'

'Do what?' Dominic was getting desperate. 'What hours?'

'The subscriber's name on this line is the same as on our other line.'

'Oh . . . right.' Dominic was projecting weary bemusement down the line. 'Gotcha . . . name of Higgins, is that it?'

'No, no, it's Brunswick.'

'Brunswick?'

'Yes. Honestly, you people . . .'

Margot's rebuke was gentle, in the sphere of quickwittedness she was not a pot to call the kettle black.

'Oh. Right . . . Brunswick.' Dominic's stupefaction was more genuine now. Kitty and he exchanged looks of puzzlement. 'So you're Mrs Brunswick then?'

'Yes.'

'Not Higgins.'

'No. Mrs Maxwell Brunswick. Really . . .'

'Oh . . . Right. . . And you've no problems?' Dominic asked, apart from your husband being blackmailed. 'No trouble on the line?'

'No I don't think so . . . Actually come to think of it I've got a little crackling in the bedroom.' Margot was trying to help.

'I'll have it checked out,' Dominic answered. 'Sorry to bother you. Cheerio.'

'Cheerio.'

Dominic hung up. 'Did Leo know him?'

'Not as far as I know.' Kitty sipped her coffee. 'He never said anything.'

'I'll check it out with Phoebe,' Dominic said. His list of unanswered questions was growing all the time.

With a further salvo of embarrassed gratitude and apology, Kitty prepared to leave.

'Drive carefully.' He kissed her briefly on the cheek. 'I'll be in touch.'

Dominic could not define his sympathy for her, this brave, simple woman resolutely guarding the door of her dead husband's closet. She was somehow of a different age, stoic and appealing – the kind of character Celia Johnson played

148

in wartime movies. She was even wearing a headscarf as she drove off with the back of her car piled high with Leo's belongings. Dominic watched her go and then set off for work himself. With the show at least he had some idea of what was going on. But with regard to the other matters on his mind, he was groping in the dark.

The Major was seated in front of his Amstrad computer with his eyes dismally scanning the details on the screen. It had taken him many long hours of tuition to master the technology. 'User bloody hostile,' he had growled at the instructor, but now he had dominion over it. He had stored away not only full details of the Company Register of the Brunswick but also, on Phoebe's suggestion he had added certain local information to the disk – details of the buyers and sellers, volume of trading and dates. The program was his exclusive territory and he guarded it zealously.

'Howdy, Major.' Phoebe had breezed into his office. She bent over and kissed him. He wished she wouldn't do that. The smell of Dior overwhelmed him. 'How's tricks?'

'Well I've just had the stockbroker on the telephone, old girl,' he said. 'Trading in Brunswick is pretty brisk – as you'd expect on the back of all that brouhaha from your damn son-in-law. I tell you, old girl, the AGM is going to be a bit of a bunfight.'

'But the box office has never been busier' – Phoebe had her hands on his shoulders – 'so we'll just have to batten down the hatches.' She used the cliché specially for him. 'Weather the storm and all that.' And she was gone.

The Major took an antacid tablet, his third that day, and reflected on his feelings. Their name was jealousy but it never crossed his mind. He often boasted that he had never been in love but the symptoms looked pretty nauseating in others. And this courtship of his employer and Sir Philip seemed to bear all the hallmarks of the full-blown complaint. He felt nettled by it, a little excluded perhaps, he was after all the one who had introduced them – not for any romantic purpose, it had been a business proposition at the start.

149

Flowers and hampers arrived for her each day. She had her hair shorter and her lunches longer. It all looked pretty grim to the Major. In the words of his bewhiskered old nanny, 'It would all end in tears before bedtime.'

11

Dominic and Tessa spent the morning working with the director on their scenes together. In particular Ian Drinkwater had been coaxing her towards a tougher view of Eliza. With her new Higgins she needed to adjust. Whereas Leo had played the professor with a misplaced warmth, Dominic was an actor not afraid to portray him as aloof and selfish as Shaw intended, a proper Pygmalion to bring her Galatea to life.

'I don't want cosy exasperation,' Ian had told her. 'I want you to be furious. When you throw the slippers you really mean it. The romance of these two people is impossible, it can never work, it is the wishful thinking of the audience, and the less you play it up the more they'll want it, right? It's a battle, not a romance. OK?'

Dominic had rightly imagined that Tessa was in need of reassurance and asked her to lunch. They were sitting in the corner of a small Italian restaurant. As always Tessa found herself talking too much, relentlessly laying her cards on the table and there he was looking at her with that look of casual curiosity that promised no reciprocal revelations.

'I'm not really an actress. I'm a singer,' she was saying. 'I just love to sing, actually I'd rather sing than talk.' Not at the moment it seemed. 'My mother took me to voice lessons when I was about ten, not because she wanted me to be a singer, I had this stammer. I still do sometimes. The singing was supposed to be a kind of therapy. You see, I had been through this rather difficult . . . rather difficult time and she thought it would help. She's wonderful, my mum. And it did . . . My teacher used to get me to sing the things I couldn't say. 'Please, Mum,' Tessa sang in the style of Gilbert and Sullivan, 'get me a sick note for today, I can't face the idea of

151

netball in this weather.' She laughed, coiling her fork into the pasta.

Dominic smiled in sympathy, not quite sure what type of pain he had glimpsed in her. What raw nerve was it that suddenly had taken the merriment from her face?

'You sing like a bird,' he said. 'You make it look so effortless.'

'You too.' She grinned at him as a tail of spaghetti snaked between her lips.

'Well in my case it's not real singing, it's talking to music, isn't it?'

'My mum's got all your records from the seventies,' Tessa said and kicked herself. It was not the kind of remark that bridges an age gap.

Dominic shrugged. For a moment he recalled his singing days, the concerts and the recording sessions, the adoration and the drugs. Flower power or was it the grass? He saw that time as a kind of holiday, a detour that took him away from and then led him back to the acting career he had always wanted.

'We wore our flares with pride.' He smiled, that was all she was going to get from him on a nostalgia level. 'What was it that made you stammer then?' he asked.

Sometime later she recognised that although she wanted him to know the answer she could not give it to him, not in spoken words, out loud. 'It was a childhood thing.' She wished it was.

Over the coffee they discussed the show; as Henry Higgins and Eliza Doolittle they were on much firmer ground. At least there they had some idea of how the story ends: 'Liza, fetch me my slippers.'

*

May 25

'Lunched with D. G. I practically forced him into taking me. He was *so* sweet and attentive. I made a complete PRAT of myself. I wish I could tell him that the gap in our ages doesn't matter. Mandy says she reckons he wants his wife back . . . Hey-ho. He's going to be brill. as Higgins. We did a lot of work today on our scenes. . . . He's great to act with and Ian D. said this afternoon that our scenes were much better, getting quite meaty he said.'

*

When rehearsals finished Dominic sat in his dressing room for some time, deep in thought. He had spent the working day puzzling over the nature of Professor Higgins but now his thoughts turned towards his predecessor in the role, Leo Benson. He thought of Kitty, his widow and the fierce loyalty with which she defended her husband's secret. He thought of the angry voice he had heard on the telephone the night before offering him money for information he did not have. And the more he thought the more inquisitive he became.

'What's the best gay club in town?' he asked the stage door man.

'Gay, lad?' Albert was of the old school. 'You mean queer?'

'Yes.' Dominic conceded. Both words had lost their way in life.

Albert chewed his tongue for a moment scrutinising his daughter's heart-throb with curiosity. 'I hadn't reckoned on you being a shirt-lifter – you're not, are you?'

Dominic couldn't explain he was asking for a friend. 'I was just wondering.'

'Oh aye,' Albert nodded. 'Well I believe there's a club called the Hole in the Wall over in Kirby Street run by a lady by the name of Gwen Quatro . . .'

In the corner of the basement bar a pianist played tunes from old musicals, distorting them with his sloppy style. As yet there were only a dozen or so assorted members drinking in the reddish light while the manageress polished glasses behind the counter. Gwen wore gold lamé trousers and lipstick in a shape that used to be her mouth. With the light behind her some said she looked like Judy Garland.

As he entered Dominic was unworried by the casual acknowledgement of his fellow men.

'What an honour to be sure,' Gwen greeted her new guest. Dominic ordered an orange juice and asked her if she could spare him a few minutes. 'I used to be in showbiz myself,' she told him as she sipped her tequila. 'I used to do a contortionist act, you know, fire-eating and that in the halls.'

Judging from the difficulty she had crossing one fat leg over the other, Dominic reckoned her contorting days were long past. They sat in a corner weighing each other up as they talked. She was a woman well accustomed to all the foibles of the human condition, of her customers in particular, these sad men in cashmere and the boys in leather.

'So why are you here?' she asked at last and when Dominic told her she sighed, 'Poor old Leo. Bless his soul . . .' She studied him, balancing his discretion against hers. 'Yes, he was here. He must have come in about ten days before he died.'

'Alone?'

'He arrived alone.' She waved across the room and called out, 'Ta-ra, Eric love.' A tape of Frank Sinatra was playing. 'Look, this is confidential, isn't it?'

Dominic nodded. 'Of course.'

'I mean, I was in a terrible state. I didn't know whether or not I ought to tell the police or anything. He was married was Leo, you know. I mean it might have had some bearing on . . . why he did it . . . But there again it might not have done and then where would I have been? I mean I've got my reputation to consider, people here trust me. So I thought, sod it, leave well alone, let the poor soul be buried in peace . . . or in dignity at any rate. Think of his poor wife.'

'I'm sure you did the right thing,' he assured her.

'Well as I say he arrived alone and I signed him in. He was drinking whisky I remember, sat right here in this corner. Poor lamb, he didn't look that comfortable.' She paused savouring her drink. 'And after a while he was joined by a bloke . . . What was his name . . .? Peter Trevelyan that's it, drank spritzer. Then after an hour or so they left.'

'Together?' Dominic asked. 'Leo left with him?'

Gwen nodded and her great gold earrings swung back and forth. 'He was a nice lad . . . from Preston I think it was originally. What a tragedy . . .'

'What?'

'He had this accident you see about a week later . . . He was run over.'

'The boy? Dead?' Dominic could not help sounding stupid.

154

Again Gwen nodded. 'Hit and run driver over towards the university somewhere. It was in the paper. Imagine . . . he was only thirty-one. From Preston and all. A pale-looking kind of lad . . . yes, Peter Trevelyan, that was his name. It seemed he had been working down in London in one of the big West End theatres. He was a box office manager, it said in the *Evening News*, at the Regent, I think it was . . . And whoever it was never even stopped . . .'

Dominic ordered more drinks.

'And I reckon,' Gwen went on, 'that poor old Leo must have been quite choked up . . . I mean I'm not saying that's why he did himself in, but it can't have helped, can it – not if he was fond of the boy?' Gwen took no pleasure in the telling of this news nor was she maudlin. She only applied drama to trivial things and vice versa. 'Anyway in the end I said nowt. His poor wife had enough on her plate without me putting my oar in.'

Old Blue Eyes was singing 'Mountain Greenery' and a man in a yellow shirt was singing along to it at the bar using a tonic bottle as a microphone. Dominic was overwhelmed by a desire to be gone from the Hole in the Wall Club.

'Call me,' he said, 'if anyone else comes asking questions, will you?'

He thanked Gwen and promised her tickets for the Gala at the Princess before leaving. Outside, the evening air was sweet with early summer and he drove home with the roof down wondering why he gave a damn.

'Margot I'm not interested in Avril's bloody barbeque, I couldn't give a flying toss,' Maxwell interrupted his wife. 'What I'm asking is if you took any calls, any messages on the phone in my study – not yours. Do you understand?'

'Yes dear. No.' Margot had grown used to the wrath of her husband over the years, it was one of the few elements of him that had always been exclusively hers and as such it had a value.

'No, dear, I took no messages, no one rang, not a soul, not on your phone.' The conversation with the idiot engineer that morning she saw no point in passing on – he had obviously

155

got more important matters on his mind, poor man. 'I'm going back to my garden,' she said and left, trug in hand, for the paradise of her vegetable patch.

Maxwell poured himself a drink and watched the telephone. With regard to the wretched little poof who was seeking to blackmail him, there was no form of retribution he did not contemplate, if only he could lay hands on him.

'Oh how awful . . . A hit and run driver,' Kitty said when Dominic told her what he had discovered. 'Poor boy, only thirty-one you say . . . Poor Leo too.'

'You don't think it's curious,' Dominic suggested, 'that he worked at the Regent Theatre . . . Wasn't it there and at the Forum that Leo asked you and Amanda to count the exact seat numbers?'

'Oh yes, it was,' she said. 'What do you think it means?'

'I don't know,' he answered. 'Perhaps Maxwell Brunswick can explain.'

'Have you spoken to him?' Kitty asked.

'No. I thought I'd let him stew for a bit.' Dominic could see no way of pursuing the man without exposing himself. Anyone prepared to buy back a secret for twenty thousand pounds has to be counted as dangerous. 'Did you do as Leo asked by the way?' he asked.

'You mean count the seats? Oh yes, certainly we did, and I telephoned the next day to give him the numbers . . . I thought it must have been a game or something but he said was I sure we'd got them right, it was important, and not to tell anyone.'

Dominic asked her if she still had the figures and wrote them down when she at last found them.

'Oh by the way,' she said before hanging up, 'do you play golf?'

'Yes . . . a bit,' he answered, 'not for quite a while . . . Do you want a game?'

'No . . . I just thought you might like to have Leo's clubs . . . They're a new set, Zanussi, I think they're quite good.'

Dominic was silenced, not with gratitude for the offer so much as affection for the donor. He thanked her as best he

156

could and said goodbye. On reflection though Leo owed him a little peace and quiet on the links.

As he was going to bed the telephone rang. It was his old school friend, Ben Delahay.

'Gallagher, you damn shaver, it's taken me yonks to track you down. How's things up there in the land of the chip-butty?' Ben saw the world through rose-tinted bifocals. They talked for a while before the whizz-kid came to the point. 'Look here, I've had rather a good wheeze, seeing as you seem to be in the business of drawing the enemy flak.'

'What is it?' Dominic asked, then listened for some time, grappling with the difficulties of City-speak. At school the two of them had been avid readers of John Buchan and the plan proposed bore all the hallmarks of a Hannay exploit, an adventure that Ben could enjoy by proxy while Dominic sat in the firing line.

'Don't you think it might be rather a nifty stunt, Gallagher?'

'Yes, it has a certain prep school lunacy, if we can make anyone believe it.'

'It's a cinch, I tell you,' Ben assured him, 'but it's vital not to let on to anyone – not your mother-out-law, not anyone, OK?'

Dominic agreed.

'I'll arrange to have it leaked through into the bottom end of the City press over the weekend then. OK, Gallagher?'

Dominic supposed it was.

'That should make your Randal Morton chappie choke on his porridge, don't you reckon?'

Dominic reckoned it would. As a 'nifty stunt' it was a perfect spectator sport.

'And having lit the blue touch paper, old chap . . . stand back,' chortled the old dorm captain. 'Better still, scurry off down to Moss Bros and get yourself a bulletproof vest . . . Ha Ha.'

Maurice was late leaving the *Sunday Globe*; by chance he had found a flyer sent in from the Brighton *Evening Argus*, a short paragraph in the stop press of no interest to his paper.

157

It read: 'A fire broke out today in the offices of Horsham Architects, Smollet and Todd. The blaze, which started in the lunch hour, was quickly brought under control but a spokesman for the firm said that office equipment had been damaged and some files destroyed. The cause of the fire has not yet been established.'

A large vodka in the pub on the way home did nothing to settle the unease in Maurice's stomach and as he grilled his two lamb chops with a sprig of stolen rosemary he tried to believe that the news of the fire did not overstretch the long arm of coincidence. He tried telephoning his original contact who had unearthed the photocopy of Project West Wind and found that she had left not just the firm but also her flat and the country. There was no forwarding address either – he was not meant to find her. As a cub reporter all this evidence of intrigue should have made his blood run hot with zeal, but it ran cold instead, with fear.

12

The following afternoon it had been agreed that the company should attempt a run-through with full lights and microphones. Dominic knew it was a manoeuvre designed to make him commit himself. There could be no more mumbling in the half-dark now his bluff was to be called.

'I'm Ron, the sound engineer,' said the moon-faced visitor to Dominic's dressing room, 'known as Ron-Ron ... a Supremes fan ... Ron-Ron as in "Da-Do-Ron-Ron"' He shook Dominic's hand. 'Have you worked with a body mike before?' From his kitbag Ron-Ron produced a transmitter pack off which dangled the short aerial wire.

'Normally, of course, it'd go under your costume but for this afternoon it's just for you to get the feel of it, before we have a full orchestra call next week. I usually come round in the interval to change batteries, to be on the safe side.'

'What about the microphone?' Dominic asked. 'Where does it go, on my lapel or something?'

'No, not any more. We get too much rustling from the clothing.' Ron produced a yard's length of very thin wire on the end of which was the microphone, no bigger than the head of a matchstick. 'Where possible we like to put them on your head, right at the hairline or in some cases where the wig joins. It gives a much better sound quality.' From his box of equipment he took a loop of thin elastic. 'Now put that round your barnet so that it's comfortable.'

Dominic fiddled about with it for a while and eventually settled for having it run just behind his hair line in the front and smoothed into the nape of his neck at the back. Ron then ran the wire through the hair on top of his head and wound the microphone round the elastic in the front, so that it was resting just in his hairline. Dominic brushed his hair back

159

into place and was surprised to find that the microphone was pretty well invisible and he could hardly feel it on his head.

'Now all we have to do is plug you in at the back here and Bob's your uncle. What you have to remember is that you are now effectively bugged. I can tune into you at any time. In the normal run of things I won't bring you up on the speakers until you walk out on stage. And with the amplifiers we've got I can even get your voice to follow you about the stage. And of course I fade you out when you exit.' Ron-Ron was packing up his box of tricks. 'Go easy on the expletives though, these things have an effective range of about a quarter of a mile and we don't want to offend the local mini-cabs.' Ron-Ron chuckled, he was obviously a man who enjoyed his work, a sound man.

Dominic went to the stage to join the company for a vocal warm-up. The empty auditorium was ringing with arpeggios of each vowel sound in turn – somehow it sounded triumphant and ludicrous at the same time. The little musical director beamed at him across the orchestra pit. The stick was a man that Dominic had come to trust like a lifeguard or a nurse.

'Just take it easy, Dom,' the stick told him, 'feel your way, sing *through* the mike. Enjoy it. Ignore it.'

The rehearsal that afternoon was exciting. The pianist made no attempt to push the tempo as Dominic began to find his feet. The amplified feedback slowly gave him confidence and he began to enjoy the artificial power of his voice as it rang out across the empty seats. And all the actors followed his lead taking a collective courage, they were subtle and sharp and gave the play a new energy and wit. Such rehearsals have a feeling of combustion about them, utterly free and perfectly controlled.

Under the glare of the full stage lighting, and without benefit of costumes, wigs or make-up, the company looked at odds with the play but it didn't seem to bother them. Teddy Fitzgerald was none the less Doolittle the dustman for his azure golfing trousers, and Enid Carroll defied the very pinkness of her track suit to represent the temperate house-

160

keeper Mrs Pearce. Tessa wore jeans cut off above the knee and a halter top. When she sang she sweated so that the hair at the nape of her neck became wet and her skin shone. The main purpose of the afternoon was to give Dominic a foretaste of performance conditions, in terms of sound and light at least. For no amount of rehearsal can lessen the impact of the audience, the great giant that has paid perhaps twenty thousand pounds to fill the seats and waits eagerly for value.

From the first to last Dominic felt in command; he had earned the right of access to the character. Higgins and he had found their common ground. This is the moment of triumph, conquest almost, that makes the job worthwhile. It is the moment of transmogrification when after weeks of courting, the role yields itself to the actor, comes off the page and gives custody of its being to him. Of course Dominic was still a week away from being ready for an audience; he took prompts and missed cues but he knew, and all the company did too, that he had the part within his grasp.

The scenes with Tessa in particular took on a new dimension – tough and subtle and real. Their relationship became a contest, a dance of stubborn people resisting the obvious magnetism. Tessa, too, was finding new facets of her character to play, an ambitious woman not just an eager waif. So that at the end (the one of happily-ever-aftering not prescribed by G. B. Shaw) when she made her final ultimatum to be treated not as a flower girl but as a woman, there was a defiance in her blue-green eyes that made her irresistible.

By the time Dominic reached his final song he had found not only the right emotional charge but also a voice unafraid to hold the occasional note and let it float in the air effortless and sweet.

> 'I'm very grateful she's a woman
>   and so easy to forget,
> Rather like a habit one can always
>   break and yet
> I've grown accustomed to the trace
>   of something in the air
> Accustomed to her face.'

There was silence when he finished. The entire company had assembled in the wings to watch and as one they began to applaud him, all smiling and clapping their hands above their head. In the back of the stalls there was celebration too. Phoebe and Sir Philip had slipped in beside Ian Drinkwater and the three of them were now grinning at one another – their new leading man was going to be exactly as good as they had imagined.

'Everyone on stage, please. Full company on stage for notes,' Ian called out. 'Kill the lights, let's have tea.' And when they had assembled round him clutching plastic cups he passed out his verdict and his ideas for further improvements.

'Overall it was fantastic – electric – not just from Dom and Tessa but from all of you. The play has got a whole new life. You're all playing to one another and off one another. We must hold on to that. It really is beginning to look like not just another cosy, provincial revival of an old favourite, but a good, really good, story retold, relevant and unsentimental. Dom, you've done brilliantly, it's really getting there. And Tessa, darling, that is exactly what I meant yesterday. Eliza is really every bit as tough as that – a girl of today. Well done . . . Teddy, you're still overselling a bit. Less is more with Doolittle I think.' Directors are always trying to find new euphemisms for the old instruction not to overact. What he meant was 'cut the ham'.

'Well done, everybody – an excellent afternoon. Thank you.'

In his dressing room Dominic poured tea for his visitors, Phoebe and Sir Philip. They were both full of praise in the proprietorial way race-horse owners are in the unsaddling enclosure. He was their chestnut colt, a thoroughbred who might go the distance in their colours.

'I'd forgotton what a great show it is,' Sir Philip was saying, 'so true to the original, you're an absolutely perfect Higgins.'

Dominic thanked him. It was their first meeting and he liked Sir Philip's casual good manners; he could understand Phoebe's attraction to him with his square-cut good looks and easy charm. It crossed his mind that he could be talking to

162

his future step-father-in-law and wondered if he might be called upon to give his mother-in-law away.

'You're going to be fan-bloody-tastic.' Phoebe grinned her broadest Texan smile. 'Which is just as well considering we've taken over a million quid already at the box office.'

'Christ,' muttered Dominic. A giant who pays that kind of money would take some satisfying.

'A hit at the Brunswick would sure as hell help if push comes to shove in the boardroom,' she said.

'Well it's going to,' Dominic said.

'What?'

'Push is going to come to shove,' Dominic pulled out the copy he had duplicated of Project West Wind and spread it on the dressing room table for them to see. In horror Phoebe and Sir Philip studied the transformation of the Brunswick.

'Isn't that disgusting?' she said with contempt. 'Isn't that the pits? Look at it, it's nothing short of blasphemy.'

'The point is,' Sir Philip tapped the plan, 'it looks like a thoroughly professional job. That's the worry. I really think it's time to pull the rug from under Randal's feet.'

'Not if we want to catch him with his pants down,' Dominic argued. 'If we can tie him to this project, without any question of doubt we can roast him once and for all. If we can't, he'll live to fight another AGM.'

'OK.' Phoebe was holding Sir Philip's hand. 'We'll leave it with you for the weekend, after that I think we really ought to bring in the boys in blue don't you?'

'We don't want you getting your hands dirty,' Sir Philip smiled, 'so close to opening night.'

Dominic decided that this was perhaps not the moment to warn them about 'the nifty stunt' of his friend Ben Delahay. Sufficient unto the day is the evil thereof. 'Tell me,' he said instead, 'do you have any idea if Leo Benson was ever a friend of your brother-in-law? Did he know Maxwell or Tristram at all?'

Phoebe shook her head. 'I don't think they even met, why?'

Dominic poured more tea and told them what he had discovered about Leo and the young box office manager from the Regent Theatre. 'Did you know he was gay?'

Phoebe shrugged. 'Well he wasn't really, I mean I think he just helped out at weekends, or when he was lonely or whatever. I don't see what difference it makes.'

'He seemed as normal as the next man.' Sir Philip's view was naïve for an old Etonian of his age. 'Still, poor chap.'

'You have been a busy boy,' said Phoebe when Dominic had explained. 'Funny voices down the telephone and things, you're a right little Bulldog Drummond.'

'The thing is I've no idea what it is that Maxwell is so keen to cover up,' Dominic said.

'But whatever it is,' Sir Philip turned over the loose change in his pocket, 'the silence is worth twenty thousand pounds.'

'And cost poor Leo his life.' Phoebe spoke almost to herself. 'What in the name of sweet Jesus is going on?'

The answer was a lot more than she knew, for even her daughter, at least on paper, was ranked against her, and her prospect of survival was more delicately balanced than she realised.

After rehearsals on Friday afternoon Dominic collected Smirnoff from the hotel and set out for home. Shouldn't it have been his house in Islington, he ruminated, where all his paraphernalia was in residence, his paintings, books, music, clothes . . . all the debris of his life to date? Instead he was heading for the cottage at Chelwood House, the cloistered bolt-hole where his hat had hung itself.

The motorway was busy with its weekend migration, single drivers mostly with their jackets hung behind them, breadwinners returning home to families. Families . . . Dominic knew that before long, when all the mayhem around him was sorted out, there was some thinking to be done on the subject, some long, hard stocktaking of the soul.

He dialled the nursing home in Worthing to hear Sister Pearson's daily bulletin on his father and told her he would be there in the morning. 'Oh good,' she said, 'he's ever so keen to see you. He's that chuffed with your picture in the paper.' The old boy had been tapping it with his finger all week, tapping and hissing with what she took to be pride. He telephoned ahead to the school and left a message for Melissa; he'd be home later, could she make some soup?

For sanity's sake he tuned into *The Archers* and had just found that he was badly out of touch when his listening was interrupted by the rarity of an incoming call – it was his ally at the *Sunday Globe*, Maurice Loftus, with news of a small fire at the offices of Smollet and Todd in Horsham ... Doubtless any further evidence of Project West Wind had perished, was their conclusion, and neither of them, of course, had confided the information to anyone else. When Dominic disconnected *The Archers* was over and his thoughts were elsewhere, on an everyday story of theatre crooks.

The school was in darkness as Dominic arrived and he put Smirnoff out to canter beside the car as he drove round to the cottage. He had not come directly home, he had taken a detour through London via the Fulham Studio. Sitting at the back of the small auditorium he had watched the last act of *Up for Grabs*. There was his wife acting out this other farce, torn between lover and husband, and he had known his scrutiny of her was the fruitless indulgence of a cuckold. However hard he looked though, he couldn't see the join between fact and fiction; Harriet and the character she played both shared her face and voice, her hair and hands and legs, her bright blue eyes, her energy and her grace.

There was confusion in his mind as to why they had ever parted company; he realised that his fear of going back to her was really just a fear of the future, of facing the two new people that they were now. What was he resisting or hiding from? Perhaps his father held the answer locked in with all the others. In any event he recognised that the legend of their marriage needed re-examining in the cold light of day.

With the thudding heart of a voyeur he had watched the stage-door from across the street and after a while Harriet and Greg came out together. Both of them wore jeans and T-shirts that showed bare flesh above the belt, two midriffs going home together, to smack together in the darkness. Under their arms they carried crash helmets, and from low in his seat Dominic could see them talking and laughing as they walked up the street towards Greg's bike. He watched

165

them swing their legs over the saddle. 'Er ... hang on a minute, my darling, could I have a quick word with you about love and death and pain and the whole damn thing.' He was a window-shopper without a penny in his pocket. After they had gone he drove on home feeling old and lonely in his big car with his shirt tucked in.

As he approached Chelwood House he consoled himself with the prospect of Melissa, he was hungry for the soup that would be waiting and the welcome. Melissa, dear sweet compliant Melissa would soon wipe the gloom from him. She would rub his shoulders stiff from driving and later as they coupled together in the darkness upstairs the thoughts inside his head would be nobody's business but his own.

A swift disabusal of this plan was waiting for him in the note on the kitchen table:

> 'Dom. Have gone to Tunbridge Wells with
> Geoff Partridge for the weekend. I'm off in ten
> days at the end of the term, moving on, so I
> suppose I won't see you again. We had some good
> times. Good luck with the show. All the best.
> Melissa ... P.S. Go back to your wife ... P.P.S.
> Sorry, no soup either.

Dominic ate a bowl of cereal with Long Life milk, he didn't blame her but the thought of her being in Tunbridge Wells with the head of Geography did nothing for his ego. He went to bed hungry and depressed. A confusion of women, a collage of Tessa and Melissa and his wife, sang a wildly amplified 'Just You Wait Henry Higgins' in his dreams.

The golf course within Griffith's view was busy with its Technicolour players, the Saturday sportsman of West Sussex unwinding under a clear sky. The old actor watched them with a loathing distilled against all mankind. It was a loathing fuelled with envy for their blameless lives; he envied them their unimpeded speech, the fluid swing of their clubs. He envied them not dribbling constantly or peeing in a cardboard bottle or being fed tapioca on a spoon by Sister Pearson or having their pillows needlessly plumped up. Mostly though he envied them the cleanness of their conscience.

On the table in front of him was Sister Pearson's *Daily Post* as it had been all week with its large photograph of his son Dominic whom he had failed so badly. He stared at it wondering why it was that all the love he had ever been party to had been contaminated. It looked so easy in others but to him the mere expression of it was a kind of ransom to be paid or bought. So he had eschewed it, this love business, like a club that didn't want him as a member.

But today he had pledged to be as sweet as pie, it was the only hope he had of unburdening himself. Dominic was stroking his hand and patting it like a dog, he was chatting on about his play and the cricket and all the usual claptrap. Griffith wanted to say, 'Please, my darling boy, don't be hearty and please, please don't shout,' but instead he did his best to look attentive.

For his part Dominic thought he saw a gleam of warmth somewhere in the phosphorous blue of his father's eyes, and was that flickering spasm in his jowl perhaps the intention of a smile? When the silence settled between them, Griffith pointed to the bed table and beckoned it forward. Dominic moved it nearer so that the old man brought his hand down on the newspaper photograph of his son, his fingernail like a bird's beak pecking at the paper. Again Griffith pointed, this time to the bag of Scrabble letters. Dominic spilled them onto the table and turned them each right side up, half dreading what the message would be. Slowly Griffith began to nudge the letters about the table, clucking and hissing as he did. When he had finished there was a feeble look of triumph on his face and Dominic came from the window to see what it was his father wanted. Two words had been assembled, one above the other, a bit askew.

REDHEAD
STITCHED

Dominic read them out loud. Griffith clicked noisily to encourage him. He repeated the two words, their significance was not yet within his grasp. 'Redhead? Stitched?'

With the stealth of a ghost the old man raised his hand and brought it down gently on the newspaper, not this time on the photograph of his son but very deliberately on a paragraph beneath it. 'SHOW GIRL'S BODY FOUND.' Dominic read aloud as directed and then leaning forward he took in the story of Norma's body having been formally identified . . . a full-scale murder enquiry. . . no comment on the rumour that the body had been mutilated . . . Turkish boyfriend released without charge . . . very little evidence to go on.

'How ghastly,' he said.

Griffith's finger was again referring him to the Scrabble letters, tapping alternately at the two words.

'Redhead?' Dominic queried.

Griffith clicked.

'Stitched?'

Again the clicking, louder now and faster. The old man was working himself into a state of agitation. Dominic could see that this was no ordinary message of self-indulgence, not the usual request for Bovril or to be left alone. This was something else – crucial and urgent.

'Redhead. Stitched.' He repeated the words again. 'What are you saying?'

Griffith's clicking became more frantic, his finger danced back and forth between the newspaper and the scrabble letters. His breathing was a shallow rapid wheezing and his eyes moved from the table to Dominic and back, over and over again, blinking with a tired vehemence. There was exasperation in him now, palpable anger. His resolve to be affectionate and patient had evaporated in his zeal to make himself understood. What kind of idiot was this son of his? Griffith could feel the blood pumping furiously through narrow veins, he was hot with the need to be unburdened of his secret, filled with a loathing and a loving – *why can't you understand*? His lips were pulled slightly back and through his long teeth he sucked in the air, a frenzied hissing in and out, in and out . . . 'Oh Dominic, my darling, dear, kind, maddening son – don't look at me like that, I don't know what it is you want from me . . . But whatever it is I haven't got it. Sorry. Sorry. Sorry. But please pay attention, there's

168

something . . . something you have to understand. Pay attention, my dear, sweet, forlorn boy, just think, guess, ask . . . *under-bloody-stand* . . . Oh Christ. Why must this bright morning be turning mauve . . .?

With a bemusement that was as old as himself Dominic watched his father getting angrier. Ever since childhood he had found the rage unfathomable. Was he the target of it or just a spectator? Either way he had the same old feeling of hopeless inadequacy. His father's hand was clawing at the letters in a random way, scooping them up and clenching them in his hand. The hissing was nearer to being a growl and the focus of the old man's eyes seemed wayward now.

Griffith was running out of strength and he felt giddy. In his hand (was that his hand?) he held five more letters that he had picked up, their meaning had escaped him. He scratched at the newspaper tearing at it with his finger. The letters and the newspaper . . . together. The letters and the newspaper. The golf course was avalanching towards him – a great mighty greenness. Sunbeams were crashing through the window, a great tidal wave of sound and light. This is it, he thought, at last . . . speak through the earthquake, wind and fire . . . Come on Father Time, come and get me. Please Dominic, understand . . . that's all I ask. Yes. Yes, hold me if you want, stroke my head if you must. Oh God.

'Dad. Dad. Dad.' Above the noise of running water he could hear Dominic's voice shouting, 'Dad. Dad. Dad.' Shouting from the school gates as he drove away.

13

Dominic poured himself more coffee and sat at the kitchen table staring out the window. He could not drive from his mind the memory of his father, the frenzy and then the stillness. By rights a second major stroke should have easily snuffed out the light that the first had only dimmed. But by some quirk of fate the mechanism of his pulse was still intact holding him in the extreme outskirts of life.

Without emotion Dominic had looked on as the nurses attended his father's body or was it a corpse? Griffith's eyes were open but unseeing and his other senses, it seemed, had likewise shut up shop. Only the deep slow breathing gave any sign of life, the gentle pumping of a bellows at a fire quite extinguished.

'There's nothing much we can do for him now,' Sister Pearson had said in her kindly voice. So for some time Dominic had sat alone with his father passive in front of him. He looked more peaceful now and the skin on his forehead was cool and brittle like tissue paper, his left hand was still clenched beneath the bedspread. Gently Dominic prised open the fingers, stiff with rigor, not quite mortis, and had found in the palm of his hand a torn fragment of Sister Pearson's newspaper and five more Scrabble letters, Griffith's last message.

Y. S. M. O. N. – the letters were in front of him now on the table. The scrap of the *Daily Post* carried the story of Norma Kingston's murder. Dominic could make no sense of it; like so much else it was quite beyond him at the moment. He slid the letters about the table and let out a long sigh at the only message they held: MY SON. Yes, Dad, of course.

To distil his thoughts he wrote down a list of questions to which he had no answer. It was a long list. He doodled for some time with a chain of interlocking question marks. Perhaps the answers, too, were linked. Somehow he had to make a start. Where to begin?

Chief Inspector McCloud was supposed to be spending that Saturday playing badminton with his wife and their friends, the Waites, in Hounslow. Instead he was sititing in his office hot and tired – even the cricket on the radio had failed to divert him. He, too, had in front of him a long list of questions – all unanswered.

'Excuse me, sir,' Detective Sergeant Miller addressed him on the intercom, 'we've got a caller on the line I think you should talk to . . . he wants to discuss the Kingston case. Sounds a bit funny.'

'A nutter?' McCloud asked.

'Not the usual type at any rate. He says he wants to talk to the man in charge . . . he was quite adamant.'

'Put him through.' McCloud lit another cigarette. If he had better things to do than talk to cranks, he couldn't for the moment think of one. He had no leads to go on, not even a healthy hunch – a needle in a haystack would be a piece of cake next to finding this particular psychopath in London.

'Chief Inspector McCloud here,' he announced into the telephone.

'Are you the man in charge of investigating the murder of Norma Kingston?' The voice had none of the usual traits of a weirdo.

'Yes I am.' He wished he wasn't. 'And who am I speaking to?'

'Er . . .' There was a moment of indecision. 'I'm sorry I'm not going to tell you. It's not important.'

McCloud had no choice but concede the point. If he was a crank at least he was a well-spoken one. 'What can I do for you?'

'I want to ask you a couple of questions about the murdered girl.'

'Oh yes?' McCloud exhaled a column of smoke towards the Venetian blind. Was this perhaps the press again trying to unearth further details? 'Go on.'

'Did she have red hair, Norma Kingston?' The question was that simple.

'Red hair?' McCloud repeated. It had been agreed at the highest level that absolutely no further information should be released. With the rumours of the girl's corpse having been mutilated still rife among the crime reporters, the switchboard had been instructed that no such questions should be answered. The colour of the victim's hair was hardly in this category, it was after all information readily available from any friend or neighbour of the deceased. It could have no significance. 'Yes,' he answered, 'Miss Kingston had red hair. Is that all?'

Again there was a hesitation from the caller. 'No,' he answered, 'that's not all . . .'

'Well?' McCloud was a patient man, the way things were, his time was there for the wasting.

'Er . . . According to the papers there are rumours of mutilation, or so I believe.' The caller spoke with more delicacy than the average journalist. 'And you have no comment to make on that. Am I right?'

'Yes. That is correct.'

'What would you say then if I said the word "stitched"?'

What the hell would he say? McCloud was on his feet with his hand over the mouthpiece waving at the sergeant through the glass partition, silently ordering him to pick up the extension and mouthing 'trace it'. 'Excuse me, what was that again?' he asked the caller in his casual voice.

'I wanted to know if the . . . er, victim . . . if there was any relevance to the word "stitched"?'

'Stitched?' McCloud attempted to sound bemused but his repugnance of the memory was genuine enough. 'Why do you ask?'

'I want to know.'

'Who are you?' McCloud knew he had put the question too forcefully.

'I can't tell you.'

'I think you should.'

'I'm afraid I won't.'

'Very well then.' In the outer office McCloud could see signs

172

of activity. His subordinates were busy trying to trace the call and it was his time-honoured task to prolong the conversation. 'I can't personally see the need for such secrecy. If you have information concerning the case of Miss Norma Kingston I can only assure you that I personally would be prepared to respect your privacy ... We should discuss things on whatever terms you deemed ...'

'You haven't answered my question.' The caller's voice was clipped now, irritated at being stalled.

'I have confirmed that the victim, as you suggested, had red hair,' McCloud was trying to sound less formal, 'but I'm curious to know how you came by this other idea?'

'You won't answer?'

Was there a note of alarm now in the caller's voice?

'I'm afraid I'm not really in a position to comment on any ...'

The telephone went dead before he could finish his cliché and with it went any hope of tracing the caller's location or identity. Whoever it was had unwarranted access to information about the fate of Norma Kingston, and for a moment McCloud could do nothing to put from his mind that picture of her, an alabaster figure dissected and shorn at the morgue. It was a memory unsuitable to be shared with any innocent member of the public who chose to call.

The innocent member of the public was looking out of the window of his cottage. A dozen boys in swimming trunks were running towards the pool, cantering with their towels held high like banners unfurled. Dominic did not know on what impulse he had hidden his identity, he just sensed that his public profile lately had become too high for comfort ... REDHEAD ... STITCHED ... How had his father come by such information? What were these two facts of Norma's death doing within his ken? Dominic had only the darkest imagining at the secret that was hibernating in his father's head.

Harriet called from the theatre to tell him about Randal Morton's vicious threats. It came as no surprise. Dominic wished he had some news for her, some evidence that he was

173

trying to help. He wanted to be the swashbuckling hero of her distress.

'I think everything is going to be all right,' he said. His mind was full of thoughts of her, naked and grateful and milky white. 'I've got a plan,' he said but couldn't begin to explain it.

In the background he could hear the audience of her show laughing as he told her about his father's second stroke. Harriet knew better than anyone about the thwarted love between father and son, had lived under its shadow as his wife. Her sympathy, though, seemed only to aggravate his loneliness.

Now there was silence on the line between them. Each of them was remembering the afternoon they had spent together at Chelwood House, reciting Rossetti and kissing one another. Had they imagined it all perhaps? Were they simply two old ships that had collided in the daylight or did they have a future? Their conversation became a fencing match as they brandished the names of each other's lovers, and they were both struck by how inadequate talking is as a means of communication. Perhaps Jonson was right about remarriage being the triumph of hope over experience.

'Someone told me you were in the theatre last night,' she said.

'No,' he answered, 'I wasn't.' Why couldn't he tell the truth, that life was pointless without her? Another pause was blooming between them.

'You know what the trouble with you is?' she said.

'What?' Dominic waited and then repeated, 'What?'

'You're just a cold fish,' she said, 'a cold damn fish.'

So that was the trouble. 'Oh yea. Fine,' he answered.

And so it ended between them with experience floundering over hope.

The Major poured fresh gin over the ice cubes in his glass and walked slowly back down the corridor of his flat. He paused to tap the barometer and watched the needle edge further towards stormy, it was clammy enough. He had just returned from a visit to Phoebe Brunswick and his hands

174

were still trembling with the implications of what she had told him. His intention had been to urge his boss to take a conciliatory line with Randal. 'Softly, softly catchee monkey, old girl,' he had said, 'no harm in having a pow-pow with the man . . . try and find a . . .'

'Compromise,' Phoebe had prompted.

'Yes old girl. I mean I'm not as young as I was and I reckon we've got our backs to the wall a bit.' He had also wanted to protest about the call he had had that morning from Dominic Gallagher . . . 'Calls me up at bloody breakfast time on a Sunday morning, wants to borrow the Company Register if you please, wants to take the ruddy disk round to some friend of his. Says he wants to see who we're up against, who's in concert with whom . . . It's a lot of damn hoo-ha. He's not going to find anything. There's nothing sinister to find, for God's sake. We're being stalked, plain and simple, we have to accept it. There's no reds under the bed or any of that kind of lark. I don't know what your son-in-law thinks he's going to find . . . It's a damn cheek apart from anything else. I mean he's just an actor for goodness sake.'

Phoebe had gently patted his knee. 'Suppose I tell you Malcky,' she had said, 'that Dominic has seen, has got a copy of plans to develop the Brunswick . . . an architect's drawing of it as a hotel and shopping mall – a project called West Wind.'

'I don't believe it,' he had answered flatly. 'I just don't believe it.'

Deep in his stomach though he had already begun to. Randal Morton had set an ambush. 'The bastard,' he had muttered. 'Excuse my French, old girl, but what a little bastard.' But this new treachery ran deeper than she realised and he had left heavy hearted with a promise to 'keep his powder dry'.

The Major sat by the telephone drinking his gin. Like Nelson he had been holding the telescope to his bad eye hoping not to see the betrayal in progress. But now with his good eye he could see it all clearly and he picked up the telephone and began to dial . . . the Battle of Copenhagen was on.

14

For the most part Dominic spent the day sitting by his father's bed watching the faint movement of his papery cheeks as the air came and went from his body. His skin was the colour of pearl and the weight of him barely dented the pillow. He was shrinking gently into death taking his secrets with him. Dominic sat and pondered, he bathed his father's temples with cologne and stroked his head. He made a few telephone calls and stared out of the window trying to make sense of what he knew. In the late afternoon he drove to London to see Phoebe.

She was glad of his company as she found herself alone that Sunday. 'Philip's had to go up to see his mother in Scotland, poor darling. She's got Parkinson's disease – apparently she's not got long to live ... I don't think Philip and she have ever been that close so I guess he sort of wants to make his peace. The family have got this magnificent great estate up in Argyllshire ... grouse and salmon and stags and all the whole shebang ...'

She cooked him an omelette and watched him eat it. His keen square-cut face had the distracted look of a man in need of consolation, she knew that things between father and son had never been easy.

When he had finished Dominic asked, 'Can we get into the theatre?'

'The Brunswick?' Phoebe asked. 'Now?'

'Yes.'

'I've got keys to the office.'

'Let's go and take a look. Do you know where the Major keeps his precious disk?' Dominic stood up.

'Yes, I think so ...' Phoebe sounded hesitant, her loyalty

was under strain. 'You mean you want to look at it . . . without him knowing, behind his back?'

Dominic nodded.

'He regards it as private, you know. He doesn't like anyone to see it . . . especially you.' Phoebe drained her martini.

'Exactly,' Dominic said. 'Look, Phoebe, we'll never crack this unless we can find out who the hell Randal's working with.'

'I'm not sure I want to know,' Phoebe said. 'Let's go.'

London was in its mellow Sunday-evening mode and the park was full of people baring themselves to the last of the sun. There was a stillness in the air that forewarns of thunder and the skyline to the east had that sharpness that precedes a storm. It was the kind of evening when birds don't sing. Dominic drove and Phoebe sat beside him wondering if perhaps this was the moment she had been waiting for.

'So what's to stop you and Harriet getting back together again?' she asked. There was no point in pussyfooting about with these things. 'And don't tell me to mind my own business. I want to know what's going on.'

So did Dominic. 'Well, she's got Greg,' he suggested.

'Greg is a slob,' she said, 'a stop-gap, a waste of skin, we can discount him. Now what about this floozie of yours at Chelwood House?'

'Er . . . She's gone . . .' Dominic said, 'to Tunbridge Wells.'

'Quite right,' she said as though it were a verb and not a town. 'So what's to stop you doing the sensible thing and going back to Harriet? Oh I know she's a pain in the arse, but then so are you. Both of you are self-willed and stubborn and bloody-minded but it was a good marriage in a lot of ways. It's worth saving, especially now you're dried out. You've both grown up a bit . . . Take her back for God's sake.'

'Just like that?'

'Yup . . . I dare say it'd take a bit of negotiating,' she grinned, 'a bit of give and take . . .'

'Go on,' he said.

Phoebe needed no invitation. 'Well she's got to accept that you're a . . . that you're a . . .' what the hell, she thought, 'a cold, moody, private kind of a sonofabitch who goes through

177

life dodging commitment, terrified of letting go, terrified of connecting with people, terrified of being let down or stood up or whatever . . . The truth is that's the name of the game, you have to go for it – shit or bust.' She sucked on her cigarette, wondering if she'd gone too far. She didn't care. 'I'll tell you what you are; you're an actor . . . a speaker of other people's thoughts, a taker of other people's feelings. You're a hell of an actor, a fabulous actor, a star – you've got the whole gamut of emotions from A to Z.' She prounounced it 'zed' instead of 'zee' especially for him. 'But you're no damn good at reality, because you won't take the risk, the risk of saying things out loud. Love is something that needs a bit of attention, you know . . . it needs airing from time to time, it needs daylight, and exercise, and *saying* for God's sake.'

Phoebe should have known better than to expect a reaction from Dominic. He seemed intent on the Knightsbridge traffic, so she went on. 'And it's no good this argument about your lousy upbringing . . . What's the point in going through life sulking about a lousy childhood . . . Mother Teresa had a lousy childhood for God's sake. I mean you can't lay all the blame at your father's door . . . He must have done his best, and anyway were you God's gift to the single parent. . .? How adorable were you, how angelic and sweet on a scale of one to two? You and he are two of a kind, I tell you. Well you're your own man now.' Phoebe stubbed out her cigarette and sat wondering by just how much she had overstepped the mark.

Dominic confronted himself fleetingly in the mirror and saw the hollow-eyed unhappiness he had seen in photographs of his mother. He felt the indignation that only the truth provokes, he felt old too and beyond redemption. Without speaking they drove round Trafalgar Square where tourists and pigeons shared the sultry heat. Groups of happy, denimed students were sitting on the steps of the National Gallery, perhaps they all had the knack of it, this loving. Dominic turned up past St Martin-in-the-Fields.

'You're quite right,' he said quietly, 'quite right . . . the thing is where to begin.' It was a rhetorical question that gave Phoebe no licence to reply. Dominic was deep in

178

thought, looking for the truth . . . So he and his father were two of a kind, two of a moody, private, sonofabitch kind.

Without the gentle blur of alcohol he had grown accustomed to a more brutal appraisal of his life. Like someone flying low over familiar country, he could see the landmarks more clearly, the detours, the double bends, the dead ends that from the ground were not so obvious. He had always blamed the flaws in his character on genetics or his Zodiac sign . . . he had been the passenger of his own personality. Had he left it too late for emotional reform, he wondered? Are new leaves that easily turned over in books as old as him? 'Where to begin?' he repeated.

'Have a baby.' Phoebe had sworn herself to silence on the matter (rather as her daughter had done) but she could not help herself. When the answer to a problem is as clear as the nose on your face, it has to be stated. She didn't care if hellfire and damnation consumed her for the breaking of her oath. She lit another cigarette, trying to lend the suggestion a spontaneity it didn't have.

'A baby?' Dominic was on the Charing Cross not the Damascus Road. He turned to look at his mother-in-law and she shrugged as if the idea had come through and not from her. 'A baby?' It was the novelty of the universe. In terms of revelation, the discovery of the wheel, and the splitting of the atom were nothing next to this.

'I mean . . .' Phoebe could see that she had disturbed him. '. . . I mean I don't care about you guys but I kind of want to get to play granny.' She was trying to be facetious now to cover up her trespass. It was not her mission to remind him of the discussion that in the past had met only his veto. She laughed, 'I'd make a wonderful grandmother, doting and batty.'

'Yes, you would,' Dominic answered, 'and yes, you are.'

'Doting and batty. Sounds like a firm of solicitors . . . I'm sorry. I know it's none of my goddam business . . . I'm sorry, I'm sorry. Why can't I keep my mouth shut? I just can't help myself sometimes.'

'None of us can,' he answered. They smiled at one another,

179

the signal of a ceasefire. The subject was closed but Phoebe knew the seeds were sown.

'I think we're in for a storm.'

'Looks like it,' she answered.

In front of them was the Brunswick Theatre and attached to the steel trellis-work that covered the front of the marquee was the *My Fair Lady* logo, the puppeteer of Henry Higgins holding the strings of the flower girl. Above it in huge neon letters was his own name – the name of a man, he pondered, who didn't know how to love his wife.

They parked in Soho and walked round to the side of the Brunswick to a small recessed door that was cluttered with litter and clearly seldom used.

'This is my private entrance. I have an apartment at the very top of the building above the offices. I usually go in through the front of the house where there's a lift . . . but it's all locked up so we'll have to walk. It's quite a climb.' She unlocked the door and the cool dank air came at them from inside. 'Actually it's an escape route. When the theatre was built in the eighteen eighties, it was called The Gala, a variety house. The old rogue who ran it was an actor manager called Jasper Partridge and he had these stairs put in so that when the bailiffs or his staff or the poor unpaid actors came trudging up the front way through the Upper Circle and the offices to beard him, he could do a bunk through his secret door.' They had begun climbing the deep spiral stairs. Such light as there was came from an occasional narrow lancet window. The turret walls were cool, almost damp to touch, and the air was rank.

'When my husband took over the theatre in the thirties he used to come up this way with young chorus girls, I gather. He was a bit of a lad was Austin in his early days.' Phoebe was getting a little breathless as they climbed on endlessly upwards in a tight spiral.

At last they reached the top, the equivalent of seven floors up. There was another door, again Phoebe produced a key and unlocked it. 'Here we are,' she said as they entered a huge drawing room from behind a curtain. It was a long and beautiful room decorated in blue and gold; it had a row of sash windows on two walls. The ceiling was gabled at one end and the moulding carefully defined. There were armchairs and a sofa round a marble coffee table in front of the fireplace, a Georgian desk and a baby grand. At the other end was a dining table and chairs.

The place was comfortable and elegant, in an uninhabited way. There were no flowers or greenery, no untidiness. 'I don't often come here now,' Phoebe said as if to excuse the mustiness. 'When Austin was alive, if he was working late or we were going to a show we'd use it. He called it "The Eyrie". Living over the shop wasn't really his bag.'

The views were spectacular to the east, the rooftops of Bloomsbury were sharply etched in angled sunlight and to the south dark clouds were rolling in ominously from beyond Blackfriars. Considering where it stood, the room had the quietness of a vicarage.

'The offices are one flight down through the front door at the bottom of the stairs. I sometimes come here in the lunch hour for a picnic or a rest. There's a kitchen and bathroom and a bedroom through the back.' She pointed vaguely. 'Would you like a drink . . . coffee or a Coke?'

'No thanks.' Dominic was looking at a photograph of Harriet on the sideboard. She was wearing a baseball cap and grinning a mouthful of metal, this tomboy who had called him 'a cold damn fish' only yesterday. Was she to be the mother of the baby Phoebe had just commissioned, he wondered? He wasn't quite in the mood for investigating fraud any more.

'Do you happen to know,' he asked, 'how many seats there are here in the Brunswick?'

'Yes, of course,' she answered without hesitating, one thousand three hundred and seventy-five.'

'Are you sure?'

'Yea. I see it all the time on the seating plan. Seven hundred and twenty in the stalls, four hundred and thirty-five in the Royal Circle and two hundred and twenty in the gallery. One thousand three hundred and seventy-five in all.'

'And what about say, the Regent or the Forum?' he asked. 'What's their capacity?'

'I'll look it up for you. But I can't see what interest it is.' She thumbed through the official directory and gave him the figures. 'Come on, let's get on with the Company Register.'

Phoebe fetched ice and poured herself a drink. They went downstairs to the front door, then on down again to the offices. The walls were covered in the framed posters and photographs and designs of bygone shows – hits and flops side by side along the corridor, all equal now with the passage of time. The work area was divided into cubicles, each with a desk strewn with abandoned weekday matters. The VDU screens were blank for their day of rest, some of them neatly covered like birdcages. Without the ringing of telephones and the tapping of typists, the place was gloomy.

Phoebe led him into a corner room that smelt of old cigar smoke. The walls were unadorned except for two military prints and a calendar.

'I'm afraid it might take me a while to suss out the Major's programme,' she said, switching on the Amstrad. 'You want the whole damn list printed out, right?'

Dominic nodded. 'In particular any local information he had put together about the investors.' No doubt Ben Delahay would know what to look for in the quest for predators. 'Do you mind if I take a look round the theatre?'

'Sure,' she said. 'You go down the stairs outside the office and you'll come to the bar at the back of the Upper Circle; from there you follow the signs down to the Royal Circle and the Stalls, OK. There's a torch on my desk in the end office. The switches aren't that easy to find.'

'Thanks,' Dominic said and left. The world of desktop computers was alien to him.

There are two kinds of empty theatre. The first is the one the actors have to face when they're in a flop doing a matinee on a rainy day when there's a rail strike. The other emptiness of theatres is less transitory. With no show on its stage and its doors locked, a theatre is a mere warehouse of unused air and seats. Phantoms can easily be conjured up: the echoes of a declaiming, hammy Lear or the dying notes of a diva. The rapturous applause of a glittering audience, too, is readily there for the fanciful visitor. There are ghosts in theatres of

182

course – for what is a ghost but a restless soul with a prank to play or an axe to grind and where better is there for both? For the most part though the spirits of the theatre take their leave at curtain down.

For sure a wind can sneak in backstage bringing with it an animation of its own that is not unghostly. It may make the scenery groan on its ropes and old backcloths bang together in the flies but this is far from being unearthly, it's mere theatrics.

The Brunswick Theatre, though, had only a heavy silence to offer Dominic as he stood at the back of the Upper Circle. In the beam of his torch the stage was a far-off chasm with no scenery to give it dimension. The walls of the auditorium were terracotta and gilt, the light shone across the panels of veined marble and briefly brought the chandelier to life. Dominic took it all in and shuddered, not with a fear of the paranormal but simply at the prospect of his first night in ten days' time.

He moved down to the front of the Upper Circle and with his back to the stage began his task. Twice he counted the number of seats and wrote it down. Then as directed he followed the signs to the Royal Circle and did the same, his torch passing each seat in turn, row after row of bottle green velvet. He slowly descended the great broad staircase to the foyer through the bevelled glass door and into the back of the stalls. The darkness in the auditorium was thorough and oppressive. He stood quite still and listened to the buffered silence, a silence which even as he waited was underscored with a new sound, a faint purring from above, the rain had come.

Slowly he walked down the side of the Stalls and stood with his back to the orchestra pit facing the empty seats. 'Peter Piper picked a peck of pickled pepper,' he whispered, for no actor can resist testing the acoustics of a theatre. Like tailors with a new cloth they like to get its feel. He let the sound float out into the air and fade. He repeated the phrase louder this time and heard the auditorium return it to him enhanced. 'How now brown cow,' he boomed and enjoyed the echo in the darkness. He switched on the torch again and

183

turned it into the gaping orchestra pit with its neatly stacked music stands and chairs. He swung the beam round again and up the centre aisle, then stopped.

A third of the way up the pale strip of carpet in front of him something caught the light, something with a dark glint to it, a patch of wetness was it? Even at a distance whatever it was had a freshness that stood out in its stale environment. Dominic advanced, his torch focused on the object of his curiosity. He crouched to examine it. Before his eyes could translate what they saw, his nose had done the job.

The wetness on the carpet and the shallow formation of khaki sludge that was at its centre was unmistakably dung. The smell of it was immediately vivid and foul and recent. The stain of this loose excrement was circular and had, in the way it had fallen, a symmetry about it. Clearly it was not the stool of an animal but of a man. And as Dominic stared in horror at this stalagmite of excreta it grew, not from within but from above with the almost soundless landing of a further instalment.

Dominic recoiled, stumbling back towards the orchestra pit; he felt sick and afraid and wanted to cry out. His throat was dry with the taste of bile and any sound he might have made was utterly overwhelmed by the first great clap of thunder. It was a fearsome, angry clash of timpani – not the distant rolling sound that allows a count of five or ten, this was a savage shattering noise directly overhead.

The impact of the thunder was such that it hung quivering in the theatre, reverberating in the emptiness. As Dominic went to steady himself, his torch swung upwards and fleetingly caught in its beam – a pair of shoes. They were black and highly polished, neatly laced to feet that hung free, quite unsupported. With two hands to steady it, Dominic panned the thin ray of light upwards to see the socks and then a stretch of shin uncovered. The trousers seemed foreshortened like a schoolboy's but their owner was not growing any more. The jacket and waistcoat of the man hanging in front of him were hardly disturbed, the club tie and watch chain were perfectly in place. The braces, though, were straining at the waistband.

Around the dead man's neck deep in the flesh beneath his jaw was a thin white rope that stretched upward to the front of the Royal Circle where it was attached to the steel mounting to which the stage lights were fixed. His head twisted to one side and his eyes reaching from their sockets gazed blindly at the Royal Box.

Another great explosion of thunder ricocheted across Soho. Dominic stepped back breathing in shallow gasps as though the fetid air might bring him sanity. In the beam of his flashlight he studied all the bloated, dribbling indignity of this recent death. There was no mistaking who it was for he still had about him the bearing of a military man: Major Malcolm Kendal.

15

With Smirnoff asleep beside him on the passenger
seat, Dominic was driving north too fast, as if speed could
separate him from the events he'd left behind. The motorway
was empty and his thoughts were reaching ahead of him
along the beam of his headlamps. He had the window down
for much of the time and could smell the dry earth's gratitude
for rain. He would be in Manchester by dawn, and somehow
ready for work by ten.

As the storm had raged overhead, Dominic had left the
Major hanging lifeless in the Stalls and gone to call the
police. He found Phoebe in the Major's office puzzling the
other half of the day's crime: the disk was missing.

'Oh Malcky . . . oh my poor Malcky,' she murmured as they
stood in the corner of the auditorium. 'Oh Malcky . . . Malcky,
why?' But they knew the answer. She stared in disbelief at
her right-hand man suspended in front of her, his toe-caps
polished, and his eyes fixed for ever on the Royal Box.
Dominic comforted her and while she sobbed he found himself
finishing his interrupted task. Meticulously he counted the
seats in the Stalls. In all the theatre held 1,385, Phoebe had
underestimated it by ten. As the thunder subsided to the
north, they at last heard the wail of police sirens
approaching.

The police spent hours taking statements, photographs,
fingerprints and the rest. 'We're definitely looking at a
murder here,' the superintendent told them, and it was
obvious he was right for the stepladder hidden between rows
Q and R 'didn't get there of its own accord'. In his interview
Dominic gave a simple, accurate account of what had happened, he offered no information or opinion beyond the events

186

of the evening. An instinct for self-preservation told him to keep whatever cards he held close to his chest.

Dominic had driven Phoebe home in an astonished silence. He fetched her valium and poured her brandy and some time later Sir Philip arrived exhausted from his mother's house in the Highlands. The three of them sat round the kitchen table sporadically shaking their heads in shock at the Major's death and each nursing private misgivings abouts its implications. Sir Philip held Phoebe's hand. 'He was a dear, dear man,' the two of them agreed as they mourned their mutual friend. Dominic recalled his conversation with the Major that morning. The dear departed had been brusque and unhelpful in answer to his request and Dominic was now left with a nagging belief that he had been hiding something. RIP. As soon as possible he took his leave, the two of them had each other for consolation and he wanted to be alone to review the situation.

Away to his right he could see the first pale wedge of dawn. He was tired and hungry but on impulse he turned off the motorway and took the road to Chapel-en-le-Frith, went through it and on up to the Peak District, the territory of his childhood holidays. As the sky began to pinken in the east, he parked the Silver Strumpet high above the Ladybower Reservoir and walked his dog. The morning air cleared his lungs, if not his head, and as the sun came up he sat on the side of a steep hill and studied the length of his shadow. He scratched his head with an arm nearly ten feet long and pondered the day's business of life and death; the unsightly death of a man who had known too much and the new life of a baby as recommended by his mother-in-law. The two thoughts were not that far apart in his mind, they both seemed to be part of a scheme too big to be taken in, even at such moments of clarity. He shivered at the size of the conspiracy he'd stumbled on, and with the cold. The world had looked much simpler in his drinking days. Beside him Smirnoff was gazing at the sheep below, panting, her ears cocked. Perhaps she too was puzzling over her real purpose in life.

*

Maxwell Brunswick, it was established, had spent a quiet Sunday with Margot his wife and their son Tristram in the family home outside Bagshot. In the evening they played croquet with their neighbours, Liz and David Cartridge, while Tristram watched a video. They had all eaten a risotto together on the terrace of the house next door before retiring for an early night.

Major Kendal's death was 'the most ghastly shock' to them all.

'We had our differences, of course,' conceded Maxwell. 'But I mean we always exchanged Christmas cards.'

The view of the police was that although the news of the Major's death was not exactly unwelcome, the three Brunswicks of Bagshot had no part in it. As Inspector Hales had muttered, 'Nobody in the home counties murders someone they've sent a Christmas card to.'

'I'll make no secret of the fact that we were not friends, Major Kendal and myself – ' Randal Morton spoke slowly for the benefit of the sergeant taking notes ' – but I respected him deeply.'

On the previous evening, it was established, he had been in the company of a couple of girls eager to be in his production of *Goldilocks* in Birmingham. 'Great bear potential,' he chuckled.

Again the police view was that although Randal was not overly sad at the Major's death, he was not part of it. The two dancers, it seemed, could confirm that it was they who had slept in his bed that night.

The Monday morning papers carried two items of news that directly concerned Dominic. Firstly, there was the prominent story of Major Kendal's murder. Beneath an old photograph of him unsmiling there was various speculation about the motive and the enquiry. His 'showbiz friends' were described as 'appalled', the Brunswick was 'beleaguered', Phoebe 'devastated' and Dominic 'ashen-faced'.

Secondly, what caught Dominic's attention with even more impact was a small paragraph elsewhere in all the daily

188

papers. It announced that Detective Chief Inspector Denis McCloud who was heading the murder enquiry into the recent death of Norma Kingston had received an anonymous telephone call the previous day from a man whom he believed could be of help to the investigation. The caller was said to have been well-spoken and of a hesitant disposition. The police were most anxious to make further contact, his privacy would be respected and so forth.

With his mind still reeling and his stomach tight with apprehension, Dominic arrived at the Princess Theatre stage door. He would be making no further contact with Detective Chief Inspector McCloud. With the two words spelled out by his father, he had told all he knew. He hurried past the group of reporters gathered there without comment.

'You've done it again, lad,' said Albert as he handed him his dressing room key. 'You're a right bugger for putting cat amongst pigeons – all over the papers again.'

Dominic went down to the stage troubled with the thought of what disturbed pigeons do to people under them.

The final week of rehearsal is a crucial time for an actor; it is a time when everything except the play is put on hold. After the opening night personal or parochial matters will resume their rightful place in his priorities, but for the last few days of rehearsal he is inextricable from his purpose. Not so for Dominic that week, quite the reverse. Only briefly during his hours on stage could he excise the heavier and more complex drama that was going on around him.

The theatre of course had been buzzing with the news of the Major's death. Most of the company had met him, some of them liked him, some did not.Tessa thought 'he was rather a sweet old poppet, sort of shy and crusty . . .' 'Used to see him at the Garrick,' Fitzgerald said. 'Between you and me he was a crashing old bore . . .' 'Poor Phoebe,' they all agreed. 'Better get down to work,' Ian had suggested.

The rehearsal was inevitably heavy-footed, the actors were too distracted with reality. Dominic in particular lacked lustre and in the lunch break he arranged the charter of a private plane to fly him down to Worthing that evening, and

189

back again in the morning. At the hotel Betty agreed to look after Smirnoff for the night.

Griffith seemed not to have moved, only his pale stubble had increased and Dominic sat studying him in this passive state. Gone was the old threat of censure, no more hissing and clucking, no more weary rolling of the eyes. He stroked his father's hair without fear, almost hypnotised by the rhythm of his shallow breathing.

Sister Pearson made him up a bed in the room next door. She brought him some soup and a shepherd's pie microwaved to life. 'He's holding his own,' she said. Later he spoke to Phoebe on the telephone. She had spent most of the day with her accountants and the police trying to establish a motive for the murder or at least a link between it and the missing disk. According to the Major's will his shares in Brunswick Theatres reverted to Phoebe which came as a relief. It had also been revealed that the Major's bank account was very much in credit.

'By the way?' Dominic asked her. 'Are you sure about the number of seats at the Brunswick?'

'Yes of course,' there was no doubt in her voice, 'one thousand three hundred and seventy-five. Why?'

'Nothing,' he said. There was no doubting the discrepancy either. 'I never had a chance to thank you for yesterday.'

'Oh you mean my little sermon,' she said, '. . . I'm sorry. I was way out of order. Take no notice.'

He already had. 'Perhaps you wouldn't mention it to Hattie that we talked.'

'Sure thing,' she said, a good go-between never seeks to take credit. 'How's your pa?'

'The same . . . holding his own.' He passed on the meaningless phrase without thinking. He wanted to tell her to be careful but his warning could not have been specific. He just knew that she was in more danger than she realised.

He sat again beside his father's bed and studied the figures that he had got from Phoebe and from Kitty Benson, the official and unofficial, with a margin of ten between them. 'So, Dad, why should three theatres – the Forum, the Regent, and now the Brunswick – all turn out to have more seats

190

than they are supposed to?' He spoke quietly to the softly puffing silhouette of his father in the gloaming. 'What use are they? And who knows about them ...? Leo Benson's boyfriend Peter Trevelyan was a box office manager ... did he know? Did he tell Leo? Is that anything to do with why they are both dead? Is this the secret that Maxwell Brunswick wants to buy back for twenty thousand pounds? If it is I'm in rather a dodgy situation, don't you think? Perhaps I'll get to the pearly gates before you, after all.' Any alarm that Griffith felt was not on display ... 'And what about the Major ... had he perhaps found out about these seats or something? And is it connected with Randal's bid to take over the Brunswick Empire ...? Who commissioned Project West Wind, I wonder. "Wild spirit which art moving everywhere ... Destroyer and Preserver"... Isn't it strange that the architects in Horsham should have an office fire? What the hell is it all about, Dad?'

Dominic had no trouble in finding questions to ask but answers came there none.

'And what about you, Dad? Um? What do you know? How come you've got a hundred and fifty thousand in the bank? And what were you trying to tell me? What busines is it of yours if some murdered girl in south London has red hair, for God's sake? And what has "stitched" to do with it that the police should suddenly come so curious? Why should they be so keen for me "to help them with their enquiries", eh? What is it with Norma Kingston? Eh? Dad, what is it?'

Nothing. No reply. Out to lunch. Gone fishing. Business in liquidation. Closed. Dominic stroked his father's head for a while then turned back towards the open window. He stared out at the golf course, the fairways were silvery in the moonlight stretching towards the sea. He was tired and lonely. Why, he wondered, had he chosen to ask his questions not of the police as would be correct and sensible but of his unconscious father who neither heard nor heeded.

Dominic took the five Scrabble letters from his pocket, they would be his talisman for ever, an anagram of paternal pride. M. Y. S. O. N.

16

For the next two days Dominic applied himself to his work – at least in the framework of the show he knew where he stood. Having got the essence of his performance established, Dominic was now working on it technically – polishing and refining. As with all the other arts, acting is about contrast: light against dark, quick after slow, laughter on the back of tears, and so on. In an actor the skill is half instinctive, half aquired. The element of surprise, this holding of the audience in the palm of the hand, depends on the actor's speed of thought, his ability to turn himself round on an emotional sixpence. It needs hard work and endless practice but come the moment it takes courage. Energy, too, is vital, for that's what gives the written word its life force. To be properly creative, rehearsals need to be in earnest, of course, but also to have a sense of fun, a secret understanding that it's all a hoax. This was not the case of the Princess Theatre for the company could see that the production was clearly blighted.

Late on the second night Dominic telephoned Harriet. Greg answered and in the background of the hopeless conversation with his wife he could hear the sound of violence on the television. He tried without success to persuade her to confess, to tell her mother of the ghastly deal she had struck with Randal Morton. He wanted to suggest a meeting between them, a meal perhaps or a weekend or a baby but he didn't. Harriet sounded impatient as if he had interrupted something, cooking or copulation. He stared at the telephone when they had finished, as always it caused more trouble than it cured.

During the lunch break the following day Dominic invited the box office manager of the Princess for a drink in the pub on the corner. He was a robust Mancunian who loved the theatre, cricket, his pigeons, his whippet and his wife in roughly that order. 'You'll be glad to hear that we're packed to the rafters for your gala on Sunday. We could have sold the seats five times over . . . Mind you at those prices you'd best be good, lad.' Dominic needed no reminding.

'I wanted to pick your brains, Harold,' he said.

'Feel free.'

'In the strictest confidence.'

'Goes without saying.' Harold swigged his Guinness then removed the froth from his moustache. 'Fire away.'

Dominic explained the curious information he had come by, the disparity between the actual and the official seat numbers in three West End theatres.

'That's a rum do,' Harold growled. 'That would be in contravention of the fire regulations apart from owt else.'

'But what would be the point of it?' Dominic put his tonic water next to the pint mug of stout.

'To make money as like as not.' Harold puffed out his cheeks.

'How could it be done?' Dominic asked.

'It'd be no problem scattering an extra ten seats about the auditorium – on the end of each row, or in the aisle or at the back. No one would notice in the normal course of things . . . mind you you'd need to have the theatre carpenter on your side . . . to put these here seats in and whip 'em out again p.d.q. when there's an inspection due.' Harold was deep in thought as he took another swig. 'But they don't have them that often.'

'So what would you do with these seats?' Dominic asked.

'Well . . . it would be easy enough in the box office to print up these extra seats as tickets that didn't show on the official plan. You'd have to understand the computer of course. You could then sell them or get someone to sell them for you and pocket the money . . .'

'Touts?'

Harold nodded. 'Aye and the cowboy agencies.' He sucked his lip like a gamekeeper pondering the vagaries of poaching. 'That would make a handsome profit that would – for the big shows there's no price the punters won't pay when they're sold out. Well over a hundred pound a ticket, I'm told, with the Japanese and Americans.' He let out a soft whistle. '. . . Ten tickets like that'd make you a thousand pounds a night . . . eight grand in your hip pocket at the end of the week . . . it's that simple it makes you wonder . . .'

'Do you reckon a box office manager could keep it all to himself?' Dominic asked.

'I don't see why not. It'd be easy enough to do . . . he'd have to give the carpenter or whoever a few backhanders to keep him sweet.'

'If there were a number of theatres doing it, the chances are it was being organised centrally?'

'I reckon so.' Harold shook his head gravely. 'Sounds more than hypothetical to me, lad, you'd best tell the police.'

'Yea,' Dominic had to agree. 'Not till I've had a chance to see Phoebe Brunswick. So keep it under your hat.'

'She's a good lass is Phoebe,' said Harold. 'She's had a right basinful since her old man handed in his dinner plate. The rumour is she'll be ousted before long.'

'Not if I can help it.' Dominic bought him another pint and they lamented the state of English cricket.

'I remember when your dad was at the Princess . . . way back . . . cricket mad he was, he'd be off down Old Trafford all day . . . Is he still with us?'

'Sort of.' Dominic explained Griffith's condition.

'I'm sorry,' said Harold. 'He was a good man . . . Kept himself to himself mind. There was nowt stuck up about him, he'd always buy you a drink but he was a private kind of man. You wouldn't think it, though, to see him on stage . . . He had that "touch" you know.'

Dominic knew what he meant, could remember the school holidays when he had sat in the wings of provincial theatres watching his father in different plays – farces, thrillers, melodramas. Through gaps in the scenery he had watched the ease with which he took the stage. With beards or cloaks or plus fours, Dominic had seen Griffith make the transformation from the weary, disgruntled man he knew into the characters that the audience loved. He could remember, too,

194

feeling a kind of jealousy – why should the paying public have such access to all his good humour? Griffith had had that 'touch' all right – for theatre use only.

'He should have been one of the big names, I reckon,' Harold was saying, 'but he must be that proud of you, eh?'

Dominic shrugged, smiling. 'Yea, I suppose so.'

'Of course he is.' Harold raised his pint of Guinness so that it touched against Dominic's glass of tonic water. 'You're a chip off the old block, that's what you are.'

So that was the trouble.

That evening Dominic flew down again to Worthing. He sat beside his father's bed with the gloom that is born of tiredness. It had been a slow, thankless day's rehearsal followed by the final fitting of his costumes. He had stood in front of the full-length mirror not really wondering about the clothes but about the man inside them, pale and hollow-eyed at the epicentre of so much vile scheming.

Sister Pearson brought him tea and apologised for not having had time to shave Griffith's face that morning. Dominic did not mind, the faint white stubble on his father's chin was the only sign of any life within.

'It's a beautiful evening,' he told him when they were alone, 'a really lovely summer evening.' Here in the world of living that is. What's it like with you? 'We lost the test match of course . . . by an innings, would you believe?' His voice was light and chatty like a ventriloquist waiting for the answer from his dummy. 'We had another run-through today . . . pretty sluggish . . . you know one of those days when you can't quite get there . . . an uphill slog . . . then a costume fitting.'

He was a schoolboy writing home – a catalogue of events instead of mentioning the homesickness . . . 'I went for a lovely walk last night on Howden Moors . . . Toside Reservoir . . . Do you remember we went fishing once, on the Derwent?' It was useless, who was he fooling with his small talk.

From idle (and then not so idle) curiosity Dominic opened the drawer of the bedside table and took out his father's personal effects: diary, wallet, watch and address book . . . Surely at this point their privacy was beyond invasion. The pages of the address book were flimsy with age and scarred with the deletion of the dead. No entry under 'K' for Kingston nor under 'N' for Norma either. The wallet contained a kidney donor card, a photograph of Dominic, a gangling adolescent in cricket whites, a book of stamps and the visiting cards of several Brighton widows.

The diary told the story of an anti-social man of a fixed routine. Each week carried several mentions of himself – D.G. phoned. D.G. to lunch. D.G. cancelled. From 27 February it was blank save for the chiropodist on the Ides of March. The stubs of the cheque book showed no signs of extravagance or irregularity and certainly no evidence that he had £150,000 in the bank. The watch was an hour behind, poor Griffith had not made it to daylight saving.

Dominic put the things away, their simple secrets were not what he was looking for. The light was fading as he stood gazing at his father, a mollusc that barely dented the pillow. He saw him as a miser . . . of money and love and information. Leaning forward he whispered, 'Dad, Dad, can you hear me?' There was a smell about his father of old bananas, sweet and rotten. 'Dad, for God's sake what is it you wanted to tell me about this girl . . . this Norma Kingston? What is it? So what if she does have red hair? How did you know? And what does it mean . . . And stitched? Stitched . . . You mean tricked as in "stitched up"? Or "stitched" as in sewn?'

The room was warm with the lingering heat of the day and the silence had the heaviness of dusk. Dominic peered closely at the old man, could feel the faint stale breath that issued from him. Quite loudly he repeated, 'What is it about Norma Kingston?'

Was it a trick of the light or did the eyelids flicker? It seemed they did, dry and pale as petals. And was there an imperceptible variation in the rhythm of his breathing as Dominic shouted, 'Norma Kingston.' He was holding his father's shoulders like drumsticks in his hands, 'Norma Kingston. Red hair. Stitched.'

Suddenly Dominic was on his feet staring out of the window, following a random memory that had no point of origin. He had a recollection of an afternoon some time ago, a winter month, a room not unfamiliar . . . high up and too tidy – Griffith's flat, in Hove. Dominic remembered his visit there the day after the stroke. He saw himself standing in the hall holding his father's black fedora. The flat had been pristine, the washing up for one had been done, the rubbish bins emptied, bed made . . . and the Sunday papers, every one of them, neatly folded and . . . the *Globe*. That was it. The connection. This was where his memory was leading him. the *Globe* had had a paragraph missing from one of its middle pages . . . a small article neatly extracted for what possible purpose?

In a moment Dominic had called Maurice Loftus at home.

'It's me, Dominic,' he said when the journalist answered.

'I'm glad you called, I've been trying to reach you.'

Maurice was sucking a sweet. 'I wanted to ask you if you thought there was any connection between the Major's murder and Project West Wind . . . Have you told the police?'

'No I don't think there's a connection,' he lied, 'none. It's more likely something to do with his private life . . . And I haven't mentioned anything about the project to the police. There's no point yet . . . The whole situation is very delicate, Maurice, not to say dangerous. Don't you agree?'

Dominic could hear the sound of a peppermint being extracted before Maurice answered, 'Yes, absolutely.'

'I think we should proceed with extreme caution.' Dominic used his gravest voice. 'Listen I need your help on another matter. I want a back issue of the *Sunday Globe*. Is that possible?'

Maurice said it was and Dominic gave him the date. 'February twenty-seventh. The journalist sounded eager again. 'Any particular reason?'

Any particular reason? Dominic stared out of the window, the sun was almost out of sight, exploding pinkness along the flat edge of the sea . . . The particular reason did not bear thinking about. 'No,' he said, 'it's a personal thing.' And he hoped to God it wasn't.

'I'll have it sent to the theatre tomorrow,' Maurice promised. 'Are you OK?'

'Yea, I'm fine.' Dominic could not put into words how much

he missed the balm of alcohol sometimes. 'I'll call you tomorrow.'

He hung up and immediately dialled Ben Delahay's home number. In the confusion of the last few days he had forgotten 'the nifty stunt' the whizz-kid had devised. With the way things now stood, it would surely be disaster, this was no time for charades, it must be cancelled.

'Too late, old cock. It should be rolling off the press tomorrow morning.' Ben chuckled. 'It should stir things up a bit, especially with old Major what's it having been pushed off his perch like that . . . Rum business, Gallagher, murky waters and all that. *Cave* is what I say. *Cave*, old thing . . . Look, I must fly, taking the memsahib for a spot of dinner. Speak tomorrow. Byee.'

Dominic hung up with a terrible dread of what dividends his old dorm captain's plan might yield. It was too late now for the bolting of the stable door, all he could do was sit back and watch the runaway horse. 'Oh, Dad,' he said, 'what the hell is going on?' But Griffith was lost in the far reaches of oblivion. Dominic picked up the telephone again and dialled Phoebe's number.

On hearing the false information he gave her, she showed disbelief and then rapture and triumph. It was a rapture and triumph, Dominic told himself, that could only succeed by being genuine. But he wasn't happy about holding this bogus light at the end of her tunnel.

'Oh my darling, darling boy – this is simply brilliant news . . . I can hardly believe we're out of the woods,' she said.

'I can't wait to tell Philip . . . We've been feeling so low. You're a wonderful boy.'

In the dining room of their pleasant house outside Bagshot Maxwell Brunswick was having breakfast with his son Tristram. The sun was shining and outside the open window there was bird song. Margot had left early to help with a local jumble sale. Maxwell found himself glancing through her copy of the *Daily Press*.

'Dear God in Heaven,' he said as he came across:

The troubled fortunes of the Brunswick
Theatre group took an upturn late last night
with the confirmation that a substantial number
of bearer shares had come into the possession of
actor Dominic Gallagher. The star's stockbroker,
Mr Ben Delahay, of Hicks Birch and Co.,
explained that the shares had been offered by an
anonymous individual in the aftermath of press
reports that the company was under threat of
take-over. It was not clear what price, if any,
Dominic Gallagher would have to pay for them.
'Bearer shares,' Mr Delahay told us, 'are like
currency, their value is whatever the price of the
share is at the time – they are non-negotiable
and easily traded. We have not yet been able to
check the original Articles of Association or any
amendments to ascertain how many of these
shares exist, and I can only tell you that my
client has a considerable number'. It also appears
that these shares have the added virtue of
carrying a quadruple voting power. This could
make a significant impact on the recent struggle
to power in the Brunswick boardroom. Phoebe
Brunswick, whose company director was found
dead at the theatre on Sunday, said she was
'utterly thrilled, over the moon'. Dominic
Gallagher was busy rehearsing *My Fair Lady* in
Manchester and would make no comment except
that he was delighted. Randal Morton, the
impresario who has been at the forefront of the
take-over struggle, told our reporter that he
knew 'nothing about these shares and that the
whole thing was a load of cobblers'.

Maxwell passed the tabloid journal across to his son who
read it with his mouth full.'What the bejesus is this? Bearer
shares? Quadruple bloody voting rights?' As he spoke small
particles of Crunchy Nut Cornflakes spewed into a beam of
sunlight. 'What the hell does it mean?'
Maxwell sipped his coffee which now tasted less good. 'He's
a pain in the neck that Dominic is . . . he's getting too damn

cocky.' He had the scowl of a man whose best laid scheme had gang a-gley. 'Dominic needs dealing with.'

'Smug bastard,' muttered Tristram.

'And apart from anything bloody else, I still haven't heard from this wretched little poof friend of Leo's . . .'

'Supposing he's taken it into his head to go elsewhere?' Tristram's eyes had the questing look of a ferret.

'We must discount him as anything more than a nuisance to be dealt with later . . . a minor problem . . . our major one for the moment is Dominic bloody Gallagher.' He spoke in ignorance of how close they were, major and minor.

'I've got an idea.' Tristram was on his feet smiling his thin smile. He had always had a flair for finding someone's Achilles heel.

Dominic read the article with a mixture of pleasure and apprehension, the bait was cast, all he had to do was sit back and see what fish would rise to take it. Maurice Loftus of the *Sunday Globe* was first to call him with congratulations.

'Quite a surprise,' he said without rancour. Dominic apologised for not telling him in advance. 'Any chance of doing a follow-up story?'

'Not just for the moment.' Dominic did not want to see egg on his ally's face. 'Actually there are one or two things I'd like you to do for me, Maurice, enquiries. Have you got time?'

'Sure.' Maurice listened carefully to what he was told and made notes of what he was to do. 'Got it.'

'I'll see you this evening,' Dominic said. 'I'm driving down after rehearsals. I'll call you at home. Not a word to anyone, OK?'

Dominic's fellow actors were full of congratulations. 'Looks as though you've saved the old girl's bacon.' Fitzgerald patted his shoulder. 'Sir Gallagher to the rescue,' Tessa grinned. She was wearing a T-shirt of linden green with scarlet shorts and sneakers. It was a good rehearsal that gave Dominic the confidence to think he was ready for the giant on Sunday. A dangerous confidence as it turned out.

As he passed the stage door at lunch time Albert handed Dominic two packages that had arrived for him. The first contained the copy of the *Sunday Globe* from 27 February. Dominic stood outside in the sunlight and turned the pages not wanting to find what he was looking for. And there it was, just as he dreaded, the small paragraph that had been excised from his father's copy months ago.

BRUTAL MURDER OF BROADWAY DANCER
The body of 24-year-old Julita Pascal has been found in a rubbish tip on the Lower East Side. The vivacious young redhead had been in the chorus of the smash hit show, *Together We Can Can-Can'*. Reports indicate that she went missing after a mystery dinner date ten days ago. Police sources confirmed that the case was being treated as murder but would not release details. It is believed that the girl's body had been mutilated.'

Dominic read it through twice with the growing fear of recognition, 'vivacious young redhead . . . mutilated'. Redhead. Mutilated . . . like Norma Kingston.

'Dear Christ,' he whispered to himself. What further links might these two girls, Norma and Julita, both dancers, have? Stitched . . .? And what was Griffith's interest in the matter? How ghastly must his secret be? Dominic walked on down the street. Aimlessly he wandered through the busy lunch time crowds, oblivious of their recognition. He sat on a bench and read again the account of Julita Pascal's death. Only then did he realise he had not yet opened the second envelope.

The message was written in the ungraceful hand of an eleven-plus drop-out – the contents, too, lacked elegance. 'This is to tell you, Gallagher, to mind your own business and keep your mouth shut or your dog will have more than fleas. Watch out.' From the package Dominic pulled out a strip of well-worn leather. It had a small buckle and a name tag, 'Smirnoff'.

17

June 3rd
'Great excitement in the theatre this morning.
D.G. has come by some pile of shares that are
going to put Phoebe in the clear from Randal the
Groper Morton . . . I don't understand the ins and
outs but after all the gloom we've had it bucked
us all up . . . Dom very friendly this morning, full
of beans, our scenes together just get better and
better. This afternoon though he was all over the
place . . . and he took all the numbers at a hell of
a lick. Oh I do wish he'd open up a bit.'

*

With the sun in his eyes Dominic was driving south. In terms
of rehearsal the afternoon had been a waste of time. He had
spoken to Betty at the hotel, she was distraught. According
to her, 'two dirty great buggers . . . twins I reckon, like as
two peas in a pod,' had come to collect Smirno about eleven
o'clock in a big red car, 'a Capri maybe, they all look the
same to me.' The twins had said they worked at the theatre
and that Dominic wanted his dog for a photo-opportunity in
the lunch break . . . 'Oh I feel that awful . . . I am sorry.'
Dominic could hear the plump woman's distress and tried to
reassure her. He gave both her and Albert at the stage door
the numbers where he could be reached.

'I'm sorry – rather an off day. Be OK tomorrow,' he
apologised to Ian without giving any explanation.

He drove in silence, he was in no mood for music or *The
Archers*. He was remembering those bleak days in the clinic.
'Alcohol won't help you control things. Give up the idea that
you can control things.' Dr Silver had kept repeating, 'Get
real. Be yourself.' A horrible instruction to any actor. Who

202

was he anyway or who had he been? 'Be honest . . . it's all *you* – there's no such thing as other people, Gallagher.'

It had certainly felt like it. He had walked for hours in the grounds of the great Georgian house that was his prison. He had sat under the huge cypress tree and tried to see some pleasure or at least some point in the dry world he was joining. To him it looked bleached and too sharply focused.

He remembered the day he had met his dog, that inspired day when he found himself walking downwind of a nearby dog rescue centre. He heard the endless barking of the inmates and had asked to be shown round. It was no more than a warehouse partitioned into small pens, each one the territory of a dog. The air was heavy with the smell and the sound of the animals, all desperate to be claimed.

Dogs sprang at him as he walked by, their muzzles pressing briefly against the mesh of their cages. Christmas puppies past their first flush of adorability, furious terriers, grey-hounds off form . . . Man's best friend, every Jack Russell of them. All of them were barking for remission, it seemed, a terrible noise under the corrugated iron roof. At first Dominic hardly noticed the Border Collie, she had been lying at the back of her pen, but he turned back to take a look at her.

'That's Peggy,' the girl attendant told him. 'A right misery guts brought in by a pensioner who was being rehoused. She's only two but there's no fun in her, is there, Peggy?'

Peggy didn't move. Dominic bent to see her better. 'Peggy, Peggy, come on.' He crouched on the floor. 'Come on, Peggy.'

She approached him with suspicion, she inspected him slowly and seemed to find him wanting. She did not need to be patronised. 'Peggy.' He repeated her name and put out his hand. She sniffed it through the wire and stared at him unblinking with her doleful eyes. 'How long has she been here?' he asked.

'About four months.'

Man and collie eyed each other for some time, neither of them wanting to commit themselves. They were two cynics in separate cages and neither was ready to act on impulse. Her coat was mostly black but half her face was white giving her the look of a harlequin. She seemed healthy, world-weary like himself but alert and dignified. She understood the need to play hard to get, this wallflower of the kennel.

'Why don't you take her for a little walk?' the girl had suggested, sensing a match.

So with Peggy on a borrowed lead the two of them set off on a path through the woods. She walked to heel as good as gold and Dominic enjoyed the companionship. He let her off the leash and watched her begin to run about, sniffing and circling – a piebald seal weaving through the undergrowth. He called her back and she hurried to him, low on the ground, elegant and swift. He gave her chocolate and she lay beside him panting, with her tongue pink as salmon on her black chin.

That's how it had begun, this kinship. The following day Dominic had got permission to have her with him at the clinic. She slept on his coat and he fed her on steak. Her new name had begun as a joke but in it Dr Silver had detected a useful therapy. It was clear for all to see that the arrival of Smirnoff in Dominic's life was a major breakthrough. In fact the doctor made notes on the benefit of such a relationship for a future thesis: 'Going Cold Turkey With a Dog'

Beside him now on the passenger seat was Smirnoff's collar to remind him that she was hostage to his silence . . . a silence about what? He was only too keen to mind his own business. Dominic dialled the nursing home on his carphone and Sister Pearson answered.

'He's much the same, I'm afraid,' she told him, 'very poorly.'

'I'm sorry I can't be there to see him tonight,' he said.

'Well to be quite frank, there's really not a lot of point,' she said, 'is there?'

'I suppose not,' Dominic answered. 'I'll see him at the weekend. Send him my love, won't you?' What use would it be, he wondered as he pressed the end button.

Five minutes further south the telephone rang. Dominic pulled into the nearside lane and answered.

'Is that Dominic Gallagher?' a heavy voice enquired.

'Yes, yes it is . . . Who is – ?'

'Never mind. Now listen . . . You are causing a lot of problems, do you understand? So I'm telling you if you want to see your doggie again you've got to shut the fuck up. Do you understand?' The voice was full of coarse aggression. 'You've got to do as you're told . . . no more smart-arse tricks, no more snooping. You've got to mind your own fucking business, is that clear . . .? Or we're talking dead dogs.'

'Yes, yes absolutely . . . I won't say a word . . . I won't do anything. Where is she? Is she all right?' Dominic did not care how feeble he sounded.

'She's fine . . . And she'll stay fine as long as you do as you're told.'

'Yes. Yes. Do you want money? I'll do anything. Perhaps we could meet, talk it over . . .'

'We'll let you know.' The caller hung up and there was nothing except the static on the line.

Dominic squinted into the sunlight as he drove on south. The anger was warm in his veins. Dr Silver would be proud of him, he *had* given up the idea that he could 'control things' but *if* anything happened to his dog, someone would pay the price.

Maurice's flat smelt of frying. Dominic had called ahead for directions, and was now sitting in a room furnished in wicker, the walls hung with batik cloths. Either side of the mock coal fireplace was a Habitat bean bag.

'I've had quite a busy afternoon.' Maurice poured him a cup of rose hip tea.

'How did you get on?' Dominic asked.

The journalist fetched his spiral notepad. 'Well,' he began, 'I managed to get into the theatres you mentioned and the number of seats in two of the four was higher than the official record. The Wardour and the Rotunda each had ten too many. At both theatres they were very wary – I gave them some story about doing a catalogue of theatrical architecture . . .'

'Very good,' said Dominic, 'so that's five we know of: the Brunswick, the Forum, the Regent, the Wardour, and the Rotunda.'

'I've also got the names of the box office managers.' Maurice handed Dominic a list. 'I think the chap at the Regent is new . . . he was pretty nervous anyway.'

Dominic nodded. It would be the replacement for the late Peter Trevelyan who had taken refuge at the Hole in the

Wall Club with Leo Benson. 'You've done well, Maurice,' he said.

'Then I began enquiries about the ticket agencies as you suggested. I made a short list of the less reputable ones and went down to Companies House to check them out ...' Maurice paused for effect sitting in his yellow tracksuit on the bean bag. 'And Bingo. There was one owned by a company called A Piece of Cake Ltd that has two directors ...' he paused again.

'Well?'

'Maxwell and Tristram Brunswick.'

Dominic whistled softly. 'Yes,' he said, 'that makes sense.'

It explained why Dominic had been offered twenty thousand to keep quiet. Was this the information that Leo Benson had died for? Was this the reason why Peter Trevelyan was run down in the street?

'You have done very well.'

Maurice beamed, an Ariel to Dominic's Prospero. 'So it's obvious that's where the funding is coming from for Project West Wind.'

Dominic agreed. 'It's ironic, isn't it?'

'The trouble is,' Maurice went on, 'we can't prove a definite link. There's no certain evidence that Randal is being backed by A Piece of Cake ...'

Dominic stared into the leaves of Maurice's aspidistra and tried not to equate all this information with the safety of his dog.

'However much money Randal has behind him, he still has not – as far as we can see – got anything like the shares he needs to oust Phoebe from the Brunswick ...' Maurice was eating sunflower seeds from a Chinese bowl. 'Especially now you've come by these bearer shares.'

Dominic nodded ambiguously. 'And we can't see any evidence that he's working in concert with anyone,' he said. It struck him that if he was indeed as ignorant as the average man on a Clapham omnibus, there was no need for the abduction of his dog? Perhaps he knew more than he realised.

'You don't think we should go to the police?' Maurice invited the negative and got it.

'No . . . not yet.' Dominic remembered again the threat to Smirnoff. 'There's no point until we've got a clearer picture; let's see what else we can find out about Project West Wind.'

Maurice agreed. He knew that sooner or later he'd have a scoop to his credit. 'Would you like some stir fry?' he said. 'I've got enough for two.'

The idea appalled Dominic. 'No thanks, I've got to go.' He thanked his eager lieutenant for all his work and left him to his wok.

It was dark now and as he drove through the West End the theatres were disgorging their patrons wide-eyed and beaming with make-believe. The streets were filled with unhurried groups of people for whom the night was young. Dominic drove on westwards. It was young for him too but not with pleasure.

His first port of call was Ben Delahay who hid his surprise and gave a fairly convincing impersonation of a man who had not already put the cat out. 'Didn't we do well,' he chuckled, 'with our little bearer share stunt, eh?' He invited his friend in and gave him the lunch his wife had made for the next day, chocolate mousse and all.

'Delicious,' Dominic said. 'Are you sure Vereena won't mind?'

'No, no, she's sound asleep,' Ben answered with a grin that had not changed in thirty years.

The two old school friends faced one another across the table – one of them ebullient with malt whisky, the other mellow on Malvern water. They could come up with no answers, could barely set the questions. 'We're pretty well snookered until we can tie it all up . . . with something concrete.' Behind Ben was a child's painting Blutacked to the wall. 'I'll tell you what . . . leave that list of box office chappies with me. I'll see if I can come up with something.'

Dominic handed over Maurice's findings. He was restless to be getting on with his night's real business, he felt estranged by all the evidence of domestic bliss: the magnetic alphabet on the fridge, the washing piled on the Aga.

'I want to show you something,' Ben said before he let him go. Dominic followed him upstairs into a dimly lit room, a

207

nursery by the smell of talc. 'There,' he whispered with breath seventy per cent proof, 'look at her.'

Dominic bent forward to see this new young Delahay. She looked quite harmless, prostrate among her stuffed animals.

'We'd like you to be godfather,' Ben said. What he meant was his wife had agreed to the toss of a coin and lost.

Dominic reached into the cot and touched the downy head. 'I'd be delighted.'

And as he drove off to meet his enemy, he began to wonder about the pre-ordination of things.

18

Sylvia Bell was desperate for a pantomime; once she had played Cinderella in London but nowadays she was relegated to wicked fairies in far-flung towns. It was for a Christmas in Doncaster that she found herself obliging Randal Morton on his waterbed. He took her from behind, holding her roughly and banging her head against the leather-studded headboard. 'Hallelujah,' he cried out as he achieved his solitary pleasure. Sylvia wondered if Doncaster was worth it as the post-coital calm was broken by the prolonged ringing of the front door bell.

'What in the name of Sodom and Gomorrah is that?' he growled as he pulled on his black kimono. 'You've got a bloody nerve,' he said as he opened the door. 'Do you know what time it is?'

'Around midnight. It's time we had a talk, you and I. Sorted things out.' Dominic pushed past him. Randal followed him into the sitting room, nonplussed and trouserless.

Upstairs Sylvia pressed her ear to the bedroom door but sadly the conversation was a little out of range. Randal poured himself a drink and stood with his back to the fireplace. 'Well?' He wrapped his kimono more firmly round his body. 'Well?'

Dominic studied the impresario in silence for a while. 'I know about A Piece of Cake and I've got a copy of Project West Wind in my pocket.' Dominic laid his trump cards on the table.

Randal walked about the room in silence, his bare feet noiseless on the parquet. 'What are you talking about?' he asked, unsure if it was his interests or his ignorance that needed shielding.

'I know that your bid to take over the Brunswick is backed

by Maxwell and Tristram with funds from the sale of fraud-
ulent theatre tickets through a company called A Piece of
Cake.'

Randal was at sea. 'OK, then,' he said, 'tell me more wise-
arse.'

Dominic took him through the details of the swindle, the
surplus seats and the illicit profit creamed off with the help
of the box office managers . . . 'When business is good that's
around forty thousand a week. Five theatres, each flogging
ten extra seats a night . . . sometimes at a hundred quid a
piece.'

Randal nodded.

'Maxwell and Tristram Brunswick are your partners,
aren't they?' Dominic was sitting now in Randal's favourite
chair. 'They're backing you. Right?'

'I've made no secret of it.' Randal drank his gin with
attempted unconcern. 'Go on.'

'And once you've got control of the theatres what you plan
to do is develop the Brunswick into a hotel and shopping
centre.' Dominic pulled from his pocket the copy of Project
West Wind. Randal took it from him, studied it for a long
time under the light, and then went to fill his glass.

'It's nothing but a load of bollocks,' he said at last. 'Project
West Wind V.5. What's that supposed to mean anyway.'

Dominic explained.

'It's bollocks,' he said, dismissing Shelley at a stroke. Here
was the man he hated reciting poetry at him in the middle of
the night. 'Look, mate,' he went on, 'this isn't my bag. I'm a
producer, I put on shows, that's what I do – popular shows
that put bums on seats and make a profit. All this other
business . . . hotels and Shelley what's-his-name is just a load
of . . . of . . .'

'Bollocks?' Dominic offered.

'Yes, it bloody well is, mate.' He was pacing about around
the leather three-piece suite.

'I don't think it is,' Dominic answered. 'I think I've got you
sussed which is why I've come to offer you a deal.'

'A deal? Oh yea.' Randal was not good at irony. 'What kind
of fucking deal?'

210

'I want you to give my wife her shares back. Tear up the option.' Dominic's voice was flat like the sea before a storm.

'Just like that?' Randal's fingers failed to snap. 'I tell you *Up for Grabs* lost every penny of its investment.'

'As you knew it would.'

Randal smiled, his lips cruel like Bette Davis. 'That's not the point. She and I have a binding agreement . . .'

'Crap.' Dominic was holding his anger on a tight leash. He looked around the room. The modern paintings on the wall were like diagrams of pain. 'Anyway, with the advantage of these bearer shares I now have,' he went on 'you don't stand a chance in hell. Why don't you give up?'

'You're pathetic, Gallagher, do you know that?' Randal was leaning against the mantelpiece. 'Why should you bail your wife out? She's dumped you. She's shacked up with her toy-boy . . . Why bother? She's not your responsibiltity?'

Dominic stood up and moved towards Randal slowly. 'Oh yes she is, she is my responsibility. Do you understand? She's my wife.' His loathing for the impresario filled his chest and his stomach, it was in his legs and arms, fizzing in his veins.

Randal shifted his position. He didn't like the look in his visitor's eyes. 'I think it's time you went home, Gallagher.' He spoke imperiously despite his unease. 'There's nothing more to say.'

Very quietly Dominic gathered the lapels of Randal's kimono in his hands. 'Listen to me, you bastard. You give up that option or I'll blow your whole stinking game sky high. The whole lot . . . the blackmail, the murder, the fraud. Do you understand?' He peered into Randal's greasy face and smelt the gin and fornication.

'OK, OK, steady on.' Randal felt himself being danced backwards across the room. 'Keep your hair on.' His coccyx was being forced up against the newel post.

'Where's my dog? Where's my dog?' Dominic was shouting so that even upstairs Sylvia trembled. 'Where is she?' he screamed, his hands were gripping at the plump flesh of Randal's neck. 'Where is she?'

'Your dog?' Randal croaked. His face was at once gormless and terrified. 'What fucking dog? You're mad.' Dominic was demented with these ideas, Piece of Cake ... Project West Wind ... What dog? The situation seemed beyond negotiating. 'Get out of here. I don't know what you're talking about.'

Dominic was deaf to the ignorance in his voice, it didn't matter if he was targeting the wrong man with all his frustration. This was the revenge that had been cooking inside him for too long. His fingers tightened on Randal's throat. 'You little runt, you turd, you bastard,' he rasped. Dominic shook his victim. He *could* control things, Dr Silver had got it wrong, he'd prove it. He was in action now, spoiling for a fight.

Randal brought his knee up into Dominic's groin with all the force he could muster. Dominic cried out and fell back dizzy with the pain that exploded through his body. Randal was scampering for the drinks tray. Dominic got to his feet, retreated round the sofa as Randal advanced with a bottle brandished in his hand – Bailey's Irish Cream.

'What fucking dog? You're crazy, Gallagher, off the wall. You're a crazy alcoholic idiot. You know nothing. You're pathetic ... pathetic. Get out of here. Get the fuck out of here.'

He hurled the bottle at his guest. Dominic ducked and dived forward as the glass shattered on the coffee table. Punching wildly he lurched at Randal, they grappled and fell to the floor. They rolled back and forth, their arms and legs flaying the air for purchase. Standard lamps and occasional tables crashed about them as they struggled for the upper hand.

Sylvia was halfway down the stairs wrapped in an outsize towelling dressing gown. She watched the two men entwined in the half darkness. She could just discern the buttocks of her lover, seemingly smeared with her favourite aperitif. Ever eager to play a part in anything that was going, she picked up an alabaster bust from a shelf beside her on the staircase. It was of Lionel Blair and the inscription read, 'For Randy with Love and Thanks. Robinson Crusoe 1979'. She advanced towards the mêlée. She raised the bust, hollow but heavy, above her head; it teetered for a moment as she took aim at the intruder's head. Then gravity, with a little help from Sylvia, took its course and the likeness of Lionel Blair swung through the air. That it struck home was not in doubt, fragments of plaster flew across the floor room and the fighting stopped. A silence fell upon the room. Neither body moved for a moment and then there was an unheaval as the two men went to disentangle themselves. The one on top was inert and the one beneath was saying in a voice that wasn't Randal's, 'Nice one, Lionel.'

There was further movement as Randal's weight was shifted. 'I don't know who you are, but thanks.'

Whoever it was turned on the lights and Sylvia saw to her amazement that it was Dominic Gallagher she had saved. His fine straight nose was trickling blood and he looked a little dazed standing in front of her.

'Oh,' she said, 'it's you.' This wasn't the moment to announce she'd got the wrong man, anyway she hadn't. 'I think we did a charity together once in Sutton Coldfield. Sylvia.'

'Dominic Gallagher. Nice to meet you again,' he said dabbing at his nose.

She fetched him a glass of water which he drank.

'Poor old Randal,' she said.

Dominic followed her gaze and there was the impresario, unconscious on an ethnic rug. His kimono was rucked up about his waist – his genitals looked like the left-overs from a picnic.

'Should I get a doctor do you think?'

'No, he'll he all right.' Dominic felt his pulse. 'I think I'd better be going.'

Randal groaned from the floor.

'Me too,' Sylvia said. 'Could you give me a lift to Earl's Court?' She'd blown her chances of Wicked Fairy in Doncaster anyway.

Before leaving Dominic placed a dented lampshade on his enemy's crotch. He dropped Sylvia at her flat and turned back north for the motorway and Manchester. His head and balls were aching, he was tired but calmer. The road was empty and he drove too fast. Without the adrenalin distorting his vision he began to wonder if he had misjudged his man.

Perhaps after all Randal was merely the front runner, the fall guy who had borne the brunt of his misdirected energy.

The dawn was poking it rosy fingers through the tenement buildings of Moss Side as Dominic arrived in Manchester. He soaked in a hot bath, puzzled and aching, then went briefly to bed. Dear diary, another busy day.

When Randal awoke it was mid-morning, he felt sick and there was dried blood on his face. His sitting room was wrecked too, strewn with broken glass and plaster. Lionel Blair was beyond putting together again. Slowly he struggled for a memory of the night before . . . Hadn't Sylvia Bell come round? There was no trace of her now apart from the used condom in the ashtray . . . and then Dominic Gallagher had been there. As Randal's brain revisited the conversation they had had, he began to feel apprehensive. In the warm light of day the wild accusations took on a plausibility. He swept up the debris on his floor, it was rare for him to be on the receiving end of a double-cross. As he mopped up the Bailey's Irish Cream his mind was full of cunning, he knew that you can only meet betrayal with betrayal.

'Good afternoon, ladies and gentleman, the full dress rehearsal will start in half an hour, half an hour please.' The stage manageress's voice had the crisp bonhomie of an air hostess. It is statutory for actors to be in the theatre half an hour before the performance – if they're late, understudies are alerted and the word 'professionalism' gets bandied about. This half-hour is mainly a time of preparation, for the warming up of the voice, the fixing of wigs, the application of make-up, the donning of costumes, the attaching of body-mikes, etc.

It is also an opportunity for the actor to put from his mind the humdrum problems of his life – the shopping, the VAT, the alimony, the girlfriend's herpes. He must summon up the energy it takes to lift his character from the page and from the coat hanger.

Dominic was sitting in his white tie and tails gently applying make-up to his bruised face. Professor Higgins and he would just have to share his slightly blackened eye and swollen lip for the afternoon, also the dull pain in his testicles. Tessa had brought him a hot honey drink and bathed his face with witch hazel – she studied his wounds with a childlike intensity in her eyes and dabbed gently at them with her cotton wool. She showed hardly any disbelief at his hackneyed account of what had happened – she said she understood how aggressive lamp posts were getting these days.

Don't think about your dad or your dog or any of the other hurly-burly, Dominic told his alter ego in the mirror. Just be Higgins, Henry Higgins of Wimpole Street eighty years ago . . .

'An ordinary man who desired nothing more than just the ordinary chance to live exactly as he likes and do precisely what he wants . . .

> An average man am I
> Of no eccentric whim
> Who wants to live his life
> Free from strife
> Doing whatever he thinks is
> Best for him . . .'

Throughout the dress rehearsal Phoebe sat at the back of the Royal Circle clutching Sir Philip's hand and watching entralled as the production took off. The new costumes and orchestrations gave the show a panache it had not had before and at its centre Dominic had an effortless control, an elegance and a wit that was at the same time all his own and yet completely Higgins. Tessa, too, had bloomed to match her new leading man, had lost the saccharin quality she had before and gained a reality.

'Bravo. Bravo,' the co-producers shouted at the end. On stage the entire company drank champagne and glowed with Phoebe's flattery. She clapped her hands for silence. 'You are all quite simply the very best company I could hope for, all of you. I know it's been difficult, we've had some horrible bad times and sad times, but we're putting all that behind us now

215

... And we are going to have, without any question, the smash hit of the year ... See you on Sunday. God bless. Good luck.'

The company made no secret of their affection for their employer as they cheered and clapped. Dominic drank Diet Coke leaning against the proscenium arch, he, too, knew the rehearsal had been good, had enjoyed the brief escape from reality. It was a short-lived elation. Sir Philip came over to join him, as always there was an air of well-tailored composure about him.

'How's your father?' he asked, his voice quiet with concern.

'He's what the doctors call very poorly,' Dominic answered.

Sir Philip paused for a moment. 'Look, I don't want to interfere or anything but don't you think maybe it's time for you to go to the police?'

At close range Dominic knew the bruising on his face was obvious and could sense Sir Philip studying it as he spoke. 'This development scheme that Randal Morton seems to have got up his sleeve is serious stuff ... You'd be better off handing it over to the boys in blue. Don't you think?'

Dominic nodded, he was right of course. Without consideration for his dog it would be the only sensible thing to do.

'Especially,' Sir Philip went on, 'since you had that little windfall of the bearer shares. How many did you say you'd come by?'

'I didn't,' Dominic answered. 'Quite a few if I can raise the money.'

'Good,' Sir Philip smiled. 'Well let me know if you need any help. And take care. Remember we start previews at the Brunswick in six days. We can't afford anything to happen to you.' He patted Dominic's arm and for a moment their eyes met as if they shared a secret ... 'Oh and by the way, you're bloody marvellous in the show. Bloody marvellous.'

Phoebe came over to join them at the corner of the stage. She embraced Dominic, engulfing him with her optimism and the scent of Armani. 'Who's a clever boy then,' she said squeezing his face so it hurt. 'You were terrific.'

Dominic thanked her and declined her invitation to supper.

He was still holding Professor Higgins's much vaunted slippers when they went to leave.

'No more arguing with lamp posts,' Phoebe said, 'for my sake please.'

'And don't forget,' Sir Philip said, 'call me if you need any help. . . I'd be only too happy.'

In his dressing room the telephone was ringing.

'Gallagher, you've been shooting your mouth off again, haven't you?' The voice this time was more refined, quiet with anger. 'The deal was that your dog would be in trouble if you didn't keep your trap shut.'

'I'm sorry. I'm sorry. I haven't said a word. Honestly. Not to anyone . . . ' Except Randal Morton . . . 'Look, I'll do anything . . . I'll buy her back from you, my dog. How much would you want to bring her back?' In the full length mirror Dominic saw himself still in the tweed suit and trilby hat of Higgins, a dismal figure begging for his dog.

'You stupid bastard. You need to be taught a lesson, you stupid nosey bastard.' The voice was menacing and cold and somehow familiar. 'You've got to learn to mind you own fucking business.'

'I will. I will,' Dominic said. 'Please don't hurt her . . . Hello . . . Hello . . . I'll do anything . . . I won't say a word . . . she likes Pedigree Chum by the way . . . Beef, chicken, heart. Please give her back . . . Hello . . . Hello.'

There was laughter on the line, a cruel sniggering rather, then, 'You fuck off, you wimp.' And Dominic was left with the dialling tone thundering in his ears.

In her dressing room upstairs Tessa ate a fruit yoghurt and listened to Barbara Cook on her headphones. With her legs tucked under her in the red dralon armchair, she unlocked her diary, and wrote:

> 'He is driving me CRAZY. I know he likes me,
> I'm sure of it – I can sense it in the way he looks
> at me sometimes. But then there's this barrier.
> Why won't he talk to me . . .? The dress rehearsal
> was fab. He was so good and so was I actually . . .

Before the show I went to his dressing room to
put something on his bruises (why couldn't he
tell me what sort of fight he'd been in for God's
sake?) and I was bathing his face with witch
hazel . . . I so nearly kissed him. I just want him
to acknowledge that it exists . . . this whatever it
is between us. It does. I know it does. But it's not
just an acting together thing . . . Damn and blast
him. I'm never sure if he's flirting or not and he
makes me feel so silly and obvious. Thank God
Ian has given us a day off tomororw. Bought a
fantastic dress for the party after the gala. It cost
a fortune. It had better be worth it.'

*

Dominic arrived at the nursing home aching from the five-
hour drive and could see at once that his father's retreat from
life had crept on apace. He had bought a great armful of roses
and placed them round the room. He put on an Elgar tape,
the Cello Concerto in E Minor. He sat in the twilight and
took in the sadness of the music and the smell of the roses,
and found them soothing as if it was his own death that was
at hand.

'They've taken Smirno,' he said. 'They've taken my dog.'

Dominic stroked his father's hand again and again. The
skin was dry and cool and the nails had grown too long. He
heard the squeak of Sister Pearson's shoes.

'I don't think he'll be long now,' she said quietly. Death
had lost its sting for her years ago – the mystery of it had
been debunked by familiarity. It meant getting tea and
undertakers and reletting the bed. She handed Dominic a
letter addressed to Griffith. It was a letter from Vernon and
Fairfax, the estate agents in Hove, and enclosed details of
the two bedroom flat with sea views that had been his father's
home. What took his interest was the mention of a garage in
the basement of the block. He had forgotten about that.

'Would you like some soup?' Sister Pearson asked. 'Will
you be spending the night?'

'I don't know,' he said. 'I'll be back later.'

The road along the coast was busy with cars, all pleasure-
bound – surf-boards on roof-racks, students six to a 2CV.

218

Outside the pubs groups of boys and girls in party clothes were laughing and drinking in the street while music played. But Dominic was from a planet where Friday night was no big deal.

Griffith's cleaning woman had been diligent in his absence. The flat was spotless, sterile almost with lack of habitation, the air stale with disuse. In the window box the geraniums were vivid red against the blackening sea. Dominic browsed through his father's books, photographs, papers; he looked through the pockets of his suits and the medicine chest. Whatever secrets they held were well guarded . . . Like the *Marie Celeste* the flat gave no clues, all hands missing.

In the basement at the back Dominic found the garage, unlocked the door and turned on the light. His father's Volkswagen Polo was clean but dusty. Nothing in the boot, nothing in the compartments. As he sat in the driver's seat trying on his father's gloves his eyes fell upon a suitcase on a shelf ahead of him. It was leather with the initials G.G. between the clasps. Resting it on the bonnet Dominic opened the lid and found the sum total of an actor's life: piles of theatre programmes and posters, old scripts and photographs and a Gladstone bag marked make-up. Dominic remembered well the ritual unpacking of this hallowed bag at each new theatre. The methodical spreading of the cloth and the opening of the little drawers of the make-up box itself. From it his father would lay out the sticks of Leichner neatly in rows, the spirit gum, the powder, the mascara, the pencil, the flannel, the tooth mug and the half dozen talismen that stood sentinel in front of the mirror.

Dominic remembered how each new dressing table soon looked the same. It was his father's territory: nothing must be touched, do you hear? It was the forbidden altar. It had been the custom in the school holidays for him to travel with his father, and every evening he would watch him transform himself with grease paint and bits of hair, rosy cheeks and whiskers, or a moustache and dark-ringed eyes. Some weeks he would be old and pale, others young and bright, he would put on a mole for restoration comedy and sideburns for Victorian drama; sometimes he wore gloves and for farce he used a monocle . . . It hadn't seemed like a lousy childhood at the time.

There was no question that Dominic would take the bag – it was his inheritance, he thought, taken a little ahead of time. The idea of following his father's ritual in his own dressing room seemed logical. He sensed too that he would find it comforting before long.

Dominic put the suitcase, together with the Gladstone bag, in the boot of his car and drove back to Worthing for a bowl of Sister Pearson's minestrone. With the prospect of the following day empty ahead of him and the gala on Sunday, he wondered how best to spend the time. Overriding all his other worries was the safety of his dog. It eclipsed even the terror of his first performance. With Smirnoff back and the show open he would be in a better position to confront the other corners of his nightmare, to expose Maxwell Brunswick and his son and blow their stinking rotten enterprise sky high. Randal Morton too. For the moment though he was too friendless and confused to do anything but brood. On the car radio Noël Coward was singing 'Don't put your daughter on the stage Mrs Worthington'. I won't, I won't.

Chelwood House was nearing the end of term, exams were over and everyone was preparing for sports day and the open air production of *As You Like It*. The boys seemed carefree and excited; maybe after all they were aware that these were the best days of their lives. Dominic had lain in late and was now talking to a group of them on the terrace. He drank coffee while they ate their biscuits and chatted.

'You've been in the papers a lot.' 'Are you actually a star?' 'My mum says she's got us tickets to see you in a play.' 'You're not really going to sing are you?' 'Where's Smirnoff?' 'We beat Birch Grove by two runs on Wednesday.' 'The newt pond has been put out of bounds.' 'Hoylake broke his arm on the Tarzan rope.' 'I've got to stay with a Belgian boy in the hols.' 'I've got to play a girl in the school play . . . a Shepherdess.' 'We had the "leavers talk" from Baggers last night . . . Smoking and bonking . . . boring . . . Ugh.' 'Did you hear that Matron's done a bunk . . .?'

It had been late by the time he had got home the night

before. He had scrambled some eggs and taken a bath. The glaring absence of his dog was impossible to ignore – the cottage was the territory they shared and there was evidence of Smirnoff everywhere. He missed her terribly and her namesake not a little.

Dogs . . . children . . . fathers . . . wives. Dominic went back to the cottage where the telephone was ringing.

'Well, my old fruit . . .' Ben Delahay was always at his most jovial after golf. 'I rather think we've hit the jackpot . . . I tried to call you last night.'

'Tell me.'

'Zee plot sickens, mein commandant . . .'

'It's not possible.' Dominic poured himself coffee. 'Go on.'

'Well you know that list you gave me of the box office chappies, the ones doing business with the touts; Piece of Cake and all that?'

'Yea.' Dominic could hear the tell-tale clink of ice as his friend sipped at maybe his second drink of the day.

'Well just for a lark I trolled down to take a shufti at the Company Register. There's the best part of twenty-five thousand shareholders listed in Brunswick Theatres so it was a bit of a-needle-in-the-proverbial. But guess what?'

'I give up.' Dominic was not in the mood to play Digby to his friend's Dan Dare.

'Rather a curious coincidence, Gallagher, but every one of these chappies appears to be the owner of a fair number of shares . . .'

'What?'

'All of them have been buying up Brunswick stock . . . each of them has a holding of between three per cent and four per cent. Between them they've got about an eighteen per cent stake . . . How about that?'

'Eighteen per cent . . . Are you sure?'

'What do you think, that I can't add? . . . They're all in it. The box office managers are blatantly operating in concert. It's barefaced fraud . . . I mean why they didn't use a nominee or something I can't imagine. I suppose they thought that nobody would be seeking to link them together. It's that

221

bloody simple – they are operating in concert to oust your mother-in-law. I wish someone would do the same to mine.'

It took Dominic a few moments to summon up the basic intelligence of the average man on the Clapham omnibus. The plot had not just thickened, it had utterly congealed. 'Christ Almighty,' he said. The implications were great boulders avalanching towards him. 'So what do we do?'

'It's a fraud squad job, old man; this is big stuff . . .' Ben's voice was never short of relish.

'You think it's all set up by Maxwell Brunswick?' Dominic asked.

'Oh I should coco. I tell you it's time to pass it over to the prefects.'

'Yes, of course.' Through the fog of his understanding Dominic could only think of the threat it posed to Smirnoff. 'Yes. I suppose so. Ben, you're brilliant . . .'

'Look I must dash I'm playing in the fathers' match at Dickon's school this afternoon . . . call me tomorrow. Toodle pip.'

'OK and thanks, Ben.' Dominic took his coffee out into the sunlight. He felt utterly beaten.

'Come round, straight away,' Sir Philip suggested. 'We'll have some lunch.'

In his search for an ally Dominic found that the list of candidates was short. Sir Philip seemed an obvious choice – he understood the machinations of high finance and he shared Dominic's concern for Phoebe's survival. The drive from Sussex had taken him under an hour and Dominic was now pressing the entryphone of Sir Philip's penthouse on the South Bank.

'Come on up, old boy,' the speaker invited. Sir Philip was casually dressed and had the clean look of a wealthy man, groomed and fit. His grey hair was swept back so that his widow's peak was a sharp line against his suntanned forehead. He welcomed his guest with a warm handshake and brought him into the vast drawing room where the air was light and cool.

'What would you like to drink? I've just made some fresh orange juice.'

222

'That'd be fine, thanks.' Dominic looked out of the huge window at the great brown glide of the Thames, sluggish under the sun, and the skyline of the city blurred with heat.

'I'm so glad you came. I only hope I can be of help.' Sir Philip handed a glass of orange juice to Dominic, the one he kept for himself was paler – diluted as it was with champagne. 'I was so impressed with the rehearsal yesterday. I thought it was first rate, splendid. And of course Phoebe was over the moon.' Sir Philip smiled. 'Let's just hope the critics are kind to us, eh?'

It's common knowledge that asking actors what they think about critics is like asking lamp posts what they feel about dogs.

'Oh yes,' Dominic agreed, 'fingers crossed.'

They sat in armchairs opposite one another in the centre of the room.

'To *My Fair Lady*,' Sir Philip raised his glass.

'To the Brunswick,' Dominic answered.

'Now then – ' Sir Philip was an instinctive chairman of meetings ' – you said you're in something of an awkward situation. I imagine it has to do with this business of the bearer shares.'

'Well not directly.' Dominic paused feeling unprepared under scrunity; Sir Philip's eyes had the intense focus of a marksman. Dominic was aware again of the power of the man and found in it a quality that was not unfamiliar. A subconscious reassurance? Slowly he explained his findings while Sir Philip listened expressionless like someone at a recital.

'Let's get this straight,' he said finally, 'you're saying that Leo Benson had discovered all about this box office business and Project West Wind and that he challenged Maxwell with it . . .? Dear God,' Sir Philip spoke quietly. 'You're not saying he was murdered.'

'Yes.'

Dominic surprised himself by the certainty of his reply. 'We'll come back to that. Anyway, as you know, for an underhand bid like this to succeed, a predator has to have support – he has to find a way of operating in concert with other shareholders.'

Sir Philip nodded. 'It's not easy to prove.'

'Exactly,' Dominic agreed. 'But I had rather a stroke of luck . . . I gave a list of the names of the box office managers who were part of the cartel to a friend of mine in the City. And he thought he would check it against the Company Register of shareholders . . .'

'And?' Sir Philip showed no sign of impatience.

'All five of them turned out to be shareholders to the tune of – eighteen per cent.'

'Is that right?' Sir Philip allowed himself a half smile. 'Eighteen per cent, that would represent quite an ambush.'

'I don't think there could be any question,' Dominic said, 'that they were operating in concert with the Messrs Brunswick, could there?'

Sir Philip finished his drink. 'None, I should think.' He rose to replenish his glass. 'You've been very clever.'

'Lucky more than clever.' It was true that he had only stumbled upon most of the information by chance. Did that make him lucky? 'I'm afraid it also gives us a motive for the Major's murder.'

'What do you mean?' Sir Philip poured more juice into Dominic's glass.

'I think he'd found out what was going on – that was why the disk was missing. I think he must have made the mistake of challenging the Piece of Cake crowd.'

'I see.' Sir Philip walked slowly back across the room. 'This is very serious.' It sounded it. 'Large-scale fraud and a double murder.'

'Yes.' Dominic could only agree.

'And what about Randal Morton then?' Sir Philip sat down again, one leg casually crossed over the other.

'As a front man he was just about plausible.' Dominic gave an outline of his visit to the greasy impresario.

'Hence the bruising.' Sir Philip shook his head. 'My dear fellow, I wish you'd come to me sooner. Anyway he must have realised you had him snookered with all these bearer shares.'

'Oh yes.' Dominic looked out of the window at a long barge

224

edging slowly up river. He sighed. 'They're bogus, I'm afraid, those bearer shares.'

'Bogus?' Sir Philip's query was only slightly quizzical.

'They don't exist. They never existed,' Dominic confessed. 'They were just a decoy.'

Sir Philip showed no surprise, only a faint admiration as Dominic explained the 'nifty stunt'.

'So you thought you'd make yourself something of a stalking horse, did you?' Sir Philip chuckled.

'Yes. I suppose it was idiotic. I mean I should perhaps have let you and Phoebe in on it.'

'I can see why you didn't.' Sir Philip shook his head as he reviewed the situation. 'Who else knows about all this?'

Dom thought for a moment. 'A chap called Maurice Loftus on the *Globe* – and a friend of mine in the city called Ben Delahay.'

'I see.'

There was a pause.

'On top of it all, they've taken my dog.'

'Your dog?' Sir Philip echoed.

Dominic explained. 'I know it sounds stupid but I'm rather . . . fond of her.'

'I understand.' Sir Philip was no stranger to the stiff upper lip. 'You poor fellow, you're in one hell of a position, aren't you?'

Dominic nodded. It was beyond dispute.

Sir Philip walked thoughtfully about the room. 'It's got to be handed over to the police. I mean we're dealing with very serious crimes here, very serious. Now there's an old pal of mine, Andy Naylor, at the serious crime squad, top man. We could hand the whole shebang over to him . . . With your father being so ill and the first night tomorrow, perhaps you'd like me to handle it?'

Wasn't that why Dominic had come to see him? 'Yes,' he said, 'I think that would be for the best.'

'Leave it to me, old boy,' Sir Philip rested his hand on Dominic's shoulder. 'Not a word to anyone, OK? . . . Of course you'll have to be involved later as part of an investigation but for the moment I think it's a good idea to keep you out of

225

trouble. I'll get on to Andy Naylor and you get some rest, you look knackered, all right?'

In the doorway Dominic shook the hand of his new ally, he was glad to have handed over control of the denouement to a man of such natural authority. They smiled at one another, and their eyes met in a split second of recognition.

'Get back to your father,' Sir Philip said. 'I'll be in touch.'

Driving back to the nursing home, Dominic was in no doubt he had done the right thing. As a stalking horse the time had come for him to be unsaddled and he did his best to put from his mind the idea that he had betrayed his dog.

'Is that Maurice Loftus of the *Sunday Globe*?'

'Yes.' Maurice did not sound sure. At home he was his own man, Maurice Loftus, would-be playwright.

'I understand you're interested in information concerning a certain project, Mr Loftus.' The voice on the telephone was confidential to the point of being inaudible.

'Er, yes.' Maurice was straining to hear. 'What project is that?'

'West Wind, Mr Loftus. West Wind.' Again the voice was quiet but with an edge of irony.

'Who are you?' Maurice asked.

'Never mind. I have information that will be of interest . . . Dominic Gallagher said to call you.' The voice now sounded urgent, almost anxious. 'Can we meet?'

'What information?' Maurice's curiosity was already over-ruling his prudence.

'I can't tell you on the telephone. Meet me at the Five Bells, in Baron's Court. Left out of the station and then second right at the end of Victoria Terrace . . . in half an hour, OK?'

'Hold on . . . I . . .'

'Be there.' The line went dead.

Maurice detected a note of desperation in the invitation that he could not ignore. Pinned on the cork tiles next to his desk was the printed message: 'A WISE MAN MAKES MORE OPPORTUNITIES THAN HE FINDS.'

It was nearly dark as he emerged from Baron's Court station, armed with only a pen and spiral pad. He followed

226

his directions: left then second right and the street in which he found himself was quiet and empty. The pub at the far end looked uninviting. Two men were ambling towards him on the narrow pavement. They seemed unhurried and as they approached Maurice could see that they were both huge and similar in build, a double creation of bone and gristle, a pair of gargoyles, alike as two peas in a pod. They separated to give Maurice passage between them, and he felt quite suddenly the sickening certainty of malevolence. This was the mugging that he knew one day would happen. Not today, please. To run or not? Forward or back? To scream or just hand over his wallet? What would a wise man do now?

As he passed between the twins, they stopped in unison and said his name. 'Mr Loftus.' It was barely a question and never had his name sounded less appealing. This was no random mugging, this was a personal matter. 'Maurice Loftus?' He had no time to deny it, and was only half turned to face the trap when the first fist swung into his midriff. The second struck his chin. Then two more dispatching, as they landed, wind and thought from body and mind. Before oblivion came, he had only a fleeting notion that the sky was puce and that perhaps he had done something wrong.

It was not obvious that Griffith was dead until Sister Pearson confirmed it. 'He's gone I'm afraid,' she said quietly.

Dominic was holding his father to his chest, could feel his body warm and limp with its new freedom. The soft wheeze of his breathing had subsided so gently that Dominic had been unaware of its ceasing . . . yes of course he was dead. He looked at his watch. 11.12 p.m. So this was it, the moment of his earliest dread. It was a moment for which he should have been prepared and wasn't. The shock was quite uncushioned by its own slow process.

'Shall I get you some tea?' Sister Pearson's voice was quiet and seemed too loud.

'No, thank you, no tea,' he said and she withdrew from the darkened room.

He could smell the sweet musty aroma of the old man in his arms and through the faded Viyella he could feel the ribs

227

brittle as cane. As he cradled his father's head he felt it gradually grow cooler. 'Fear no more the heat of the sun,' he whispered, 'nor the furious winter's rages.'

Much later he laid Griffith back on the pillow and stroked the white hair into place. Wet with tears it lay flat on his head. He stood back and turned the light on. With all the worry and anger gone, his father's face looked much gentler now.

The last night party of *Up for Grabs* was not a lavish affair. The cast had clubbed together and bought cheap wine and quiche, beer and pizzas. A Glenn Miller tape filled the small auditorium with the big band sound and the actors joked about unemployment and swapped addresses. Harriet and Greg danced together cheek to cheek, each of them wondering which of them would be first to admit the party was over.

'Harriet, love,' the stage manager was shouting, 'there's someone on the backstage phone. I'll put it through to my office for you.'

'Hi, Domo.' She could not hide her surprise. 'Thanks for ringing, I've been trying to reach you.'

'I got your message.'

'Oh good. Where are you?'

Dominic was driving home across country, he had the roof down to lose the smell of the nursing home – ripening barley in the place of antiseptic. 'Sussex,' he said under a yellowy moon.

'I just wanted to tell you that you're utterly brilliant. Fantastic, wonderful,' Harriet said.

'What do you mean?'

'You know,' she said. In the background Dominic could hear 'Chattanooga Choo Choo'. 'We're in the middle of the wrap party. *Up for Grabs* finally bites the dust . . . Randal came to see me . . . That's what . . . he told me.'

'What?' Dominic pulled into a lay-by to hear better. 'Told you what?'

'He's given me back the option on my shares, he said he'd come to an arrangement with you.'

'Oh really?'

228

'As if you didn't know. He said you'd been very persuasive and that the pair of you had done a deal. Is that right?'

Why should he deny it? 'Yes it is,' he said.

'Well you're fantastic. I can't thank you enough,' Harriet was saying. 'It's a pity we can't celebrate. I mean I can't even tell Greg.'

'No, I suppose not . . . some other time perhaps.' Dominic was parked next to a field full of cows. Friesians with only their white patches showing in the dark. 'Randal didn't say anything else?' he asked. 'About my dog?'

'No . . . he said to make sure and tell you though. You are brill.'

Dominic did not speak. He was the dazed knight who had unwittingly won the joust, a hero dumbstruck with his heroine. He stared at the cows and wondered what had prompted Randal's change of attitude, something more than a coup de Lionel Blair.

'Are you still there?' she asked.

'Yea.' He could faintly hear 'Pennsylvania 65000'. 'Well I just wanted to wish you luck or whatever.'

'That's very sweet of you,' Harriet answered. 'I'm just glad it's all over, all the hassle and aggro . . . I mean it's not much of a play, is it? Let's face it.'

Dominic paused, there were tears of all different kinds running down his face. 'No, maybe not,' he said, his voice perfectly controlled, 'but it was worth doing – you were so good in it.'

'Was I?'

'Yes.' This was not the moment for him to tell her how he missed her all the time, night and day. 'You're a very good actress.'

It was her favourite compliment. 'Well, how about you?' she said. This was not the moment for her to tell him her other news. 'Are you OK?'

'Yes . . . No . . . Dad died.'

'Oh, Dom . . .' She was barely audible. 'When?'

'About an hour ago.'

'Oh, Dom. I'm so sorry.' Harriet was speechless. It was typical of him that he had not told her earlier.

'It's OK. It's OK,' he said. 'I just wanted to tell you.'

It was up to him to say he needed her but there was only a pause in which he didn't. Someone had turned the music up as they shouted their goodbyes and the floundering conversation was drowned by Glen Miller 'In the Mood'.

Rosa had never seen two men so huge as the pair of twins that were now standing in the porch. Identical black suits bulged with identical muscles.

'This is Mr Delahay's house?' one asked.

'Yes, sir.' Rosa had no intention of releasing the safety chain. 'All gone away – back tomorrow.'

'We have some very urgent news for him,' said the other.

'We must contact him.'

'Where are you from, love?'

'I'm Filipino.' Rosa knew the question was unkindly meant. 'Mr Ben gone away.' Her hands were trembling.

'We must find him.' No matter which one spoke, they shared a deep, angry voice.

'Immediately.'

'Where is he?'

'It's urgent.'

The twins took turns in their persuasion.

'I'll give him a message, sir.' She eyed them through the narrow opening. It was past midnight. 'He come back tomorrow.'

'We want to see him now.'

'Not possible, sir.'

'Urgent.'

'I do not know where he is, sir.'

'You do.'

'No.' She was trembling but determined. 'You leave message or go.'

One of the twins leant forward so she could smell the beer and batter on his breath. 'I'll give you money – Where is Mr Delahay?'

'Not here.' She was confused and frightened. 'I don't want money. I go to bed.' She closed the door and locked it.

They shouted at her through the letter box, 'Stupid little

foreign bitch – why don't you fuck off back where you came from.'

Wasn't that all she dreamed of?

Dominic drove home deep in thought. Harriet's gratitude for the deal he had supposedly struck with Randal was still ringing in his ears and he could only wonder what price he'd have to pay. It was too late for clemency, Sir Philip would have already contacted his friend at the serious crime squad. The school was in darkness as he parked outside the cottage. He listened to the engine cooling and stared up at the sky, a great black cosmos that never convinced him of an afterlife.

The cottage showed no signed of intrusion, not that Dominic would have noticed. He drew the curtains and made tea, he walked about studying familiar objects as if they held the clue to what he should be feeling. He sat with pen and paper and wrote out an announcement for *The Times* . . . 'Peacefully in Worthing' hardly told the story. On Monday it would be one death in a column of many others. He turned out the lights and went upstairs. He cleaned his teeth and took his clothes off. He lifted back the duvet and stood frozen.

For some time he didn't move – the air came and went from his lungs. His head was spinning and his throat let out a small dry sound – a gasp, a choke, some kind of plea that his eyes deceived him – but they didn't. He knelt down and gathered up the stiffened body of his dog.

'Oh no. Oh no. Oh no,' he whispered to this second corpse of the evening in his arms. Her tongue was lolling and her teeth were slightly barred as if her death was a joke almost. She bore no signs of violence and her coat was still glossy.

Dominic held her to him, his old companion, and walked about the room. He stroked her, he patted her, he rocked her in his arms, unsure and uncaring if his tears were those of grief or rage. It was only as he wrapped her in an old shirt of his that he saw the note, a neatly folded sheet of paper with his name upon it. 'Next time,' it read, 'it won't be just a little doggy you'll be burying, it'll be one of the boys at the school.'

19

Dominic was unaware of the journey north the following morning, Sunday. The car itself, the motorway, the fields either side bright with sunlight made no impression on him. It was time cushioned with numbness. Children were playing football against the back of the Princess as he arrived. 'Look, it's what's his name.'

'I'm that sorry,' said Albert as he handed Dominic his dressing room key, 'about your father.'

Griffith's death had made the stop press of the Sunday papers: 'Veteran actor, Griffith Gallagher, father of superstar Dominic, was reported to have died peacefully in a Worthing nursing home last . . .'

Before the final dress rehearsal the company all expressed their sympathy, they muttered condolences with their eyes lowered, they gave him flowers, notes, kisses and he thanked them as best he could. Tessa hugged him silently. With her arms around his neck and the smell and feel of her so close Dominic was comforted and a little confused.

'The show must go on, eh?' she said with no respect for the cliché. Her face was young and open, her eyes, an indigo blue, were serious on his account but untroubled. What did she know about death or even middle-age?

There is no quantifying grief (or pleasure either), no apportioning of it, or rationing. It was pointless for Dominic to try and separate the two bereavements in his mind or give one preference. They were utterly different and self-contained, their only common ground was him. He told himself that the sympathy for one was not misappropriated on the other. As he put on his make-up, he could barely look himself in the eye for all the sadness inside his head.

The dress rehearsal lacked lustre; as planned, it was a

232

technical exercise, nothing more. The cast were conserving their energy for the evening – the adrenalin was on hold. Dominic took his performance slowly, observed it from without and marked the pitfalls, a jockey walking the course. He watched his fellow actors too and felt for them a great admiration and kinship.

Ian Drinkwater called them all on stage at the end. The suggestions he made were nothing major, his notes were all a matter of degree: louder here, softer there, darker, brighter, quicker. At this point in the process a good director knows that his work is really done, it's time for the paying public to take over his role of audience, it's their reaction and approval that the actors will be guided by. 'Don't rush it, darlings. You know what galas are like. They won't be that quick off the mark, they'll be bogged down with gin and glitter, expecially on a Sunday evening. Give it energy but don't push it, let them come to you. Trust the show, well done, Dom, you're going to be fantastic. You're all terrific. Terrific. Good luck.'

With two hours to go before the show, Dominic lay on the bed in his dressing room, not really with any hope of sleep. The repose an actor seeks before the first performance is that of a soldier before going into battle. He must allow himself no thoughts of before or after, no thoughts of home. He was interrupted by Albert on the telephone.

'I'm sorry to disturb you, Mr Gallagher, but I've got a chap on the line by the name of Loftus. Says it's urgent – '

'Put him through . . . Is that you, Maurice? Are you OK?'

'I'm in hospital,' Maurice croaked. 'The Charing Cross. I've been rather beaten up.'

Maurice had in fact been lucky – passers-by had called for help as his attackers had shown a clean pair of identical heels. Bleeding inside and out he had remained unconscious until morning. He had spent the day in a swirling hinterland of awareness; his teeth, his nose, his ribs were all in need of repair and his urine was the colour of Campari. Yes, he was lucky, for they had meant to kill him.

As Maurice related the events to Dominic in a painful, dry mumble, the details and the chronology went a bit awry but Dominic got the picture. 'Twins, you say they were twins?'

233

'Yes,' Maurice lisped, 'dirty great buggers.'

'What did they take?'

'Nothing, that's what's odd.' Maurice sounded more urgent now. 'They didn't take anything . . . The point is they said my name.'

'Your name?'

'Yes. They knew who I was.' Maurice was impatient. 'It was *me* they were after.'

'You mean . . .' Dominic was at last cottoning on. 'It was you, deliberately you. You were set up. The telephone call was a set-up.'

'I think so.'

'Christ.' Dominic looked at himself ashen in the dressing room mirror.

'What I'm trying to say . . .' Maurice seemed to have drifted for a moment, 'is, you'd better watch out yourself.'

'Me?' The threat was obvious. 'Yes, of course.'

'Be careful,' Maurice said, 'someone knows we know, you know.'

'Yes,' he answered, he knew the someone who knew. 'Will you be safe there? Is there anything I can get you? Is there anything you need?'

'Apart from a new body?' Maurice croaked. 'I'll be OK. . . Take care.'

As Dominic hung up he felt appalled at all the damage round him. He sat with his head in his hands, deep in thought. All reality had been sucked out of the day and his heart was thudding with a danger he did not recognise. He picked up the telephone and dialled Sir Philip's number. Eventually he reached his ally who listened intently to this latest news.

'I'll get the police on to it right away,' he said. 'The poor man will need protection. . . As for you, dear boy, for God's sake take care.' There was a pause. 'And I'm sorry about your father. Horrid.' They both understood the language of understatement. 'And of course your dog . . . dreadful.' Sir Philip cleared his throat. 'Look, I'll see you later. Just you try and put all this from your mind, leave it to me . . . Good luck with the show.'

234

Dominic hung up with a feeling of reassurance. For a moment he pondered his new friendship and the echo it carried. Then he dialled his old dormitory captain.

Vereena Delahay had never really approved of her husband's best man. Any association with Dominic seemed to reduce her husband to adolescent foolhardiness.

'Wotcha cock?' she heard him greet the actor. 'What's afoot?'

Ben was silent for a while as he listened with a frown on his face. For once he made no jokes, only grunted in agreement from time to time. 'Yes. Yes. Absolutely. I'll call you tomorrow,' he concluded. 'Bye.'

'Well?' said Vereena, standing in the doorway with her arms folded in parody of middle-aged patience.

'Er, listen old thing,' Ben knew when to be tactful, 'no time for questions. We're off for a few days. Immediately. My sister's perhaps. You like Dorset.'

'Now?' she said. 'We only got back from the country half an hour ago?'

'Can't be helped. We're leaving a.s.a.p. ... I'm serious Vee ...'

She could see he was. 'Is this to do with those men who came round last night and were so rude to poor Rosa ...'

'Yes ... possibly.' Ben had not taken in the detail of the Filipino's garbled account. 'It may well be. We must get packed and be off.'

'But what about Charlotte's prizegiving?'

'Doesn't matter.'

'And the Peaks are coming to dinner tomorrow.'

'Never mind.'

'Jason's got a dentist ...'

'Cancel it.'

'You can't be serious,' she said.

'I am, my darling, we're leaving. Now pack.'

'Why for God's sake?' she asked in her not-in-front-of-the-children growl.

'Just for once, do as I say. Go and pack, we're leaving in ten minutes.'

Vereena studied her husband's face for a moment then went upstairs shouting the children's names. They were out of the house in twelve minutes.

With an hour to go before curtain up, Dominic sat at his dressing table like someone waiting for execution. The eyes that stared back at him reminded him of his father – attentive and aloof. They reflected nothing. His skin was pale and in the bright light his cheeks looked hollow, gone was the robust look of good health he had had a month ago. His mind was full of suspicions and he could not lose the feeling of alarm, a danger signal flashing undeciphered in his head. Next to the fears he had in life, the prospect of the gala audience that was beginning to arrive was as nothing.

By an effort of will, he began to prepare himself for the performance. He showered and shaved, went through his exercises, physical then vocal. 'The tip of the tongue touching the top of the teeth,' and 'Red leather, yellow leather,' again and again, followed by scales chanted and then hummed so that his lips tickled. He breathed deeply – in through the nose and out through the mouth. All an actor can hope to achieve at this time is a simulated calm that might just fool the enemy in the stalls. The real thing is out of the question.

His dresser and the ASM called in to check his costume and his props. Flowers and cards were delivered by Albert, grumbling at the rigmarole of a gala when Lancashire were chasing over two hundred and fifty in the Sunday league. Dominic pulled on evening trousers, adjusted the braces, and with trembling fingers pressed in the studs on the stiff front of his shirt.

'It's Ron-Ron,' a voice called through the door. 'Are you ready for me?'

Dominic said he was and stood in the middle of the room while the sound engineer rigged him up. 'I'll be back to check you later. If you start fiddling with the damn thing now, you'll give me GBH of the ear hole at the control desk.'

236

When he had gone Dominic combed his hair to hide the tiny microphone in the middle of his widow's peak.

Ian had suggested he needed to wear more make-up and, looking at himself, Dominic could see he was right. He took his father's Gladstone bag from the cupboard, lifted out the metal make-up box and placed it on the dressing table in front of him. He wondered what memories it might hold, and what comfort there might be in following in his father's footsteps. He opened it.

On the top shelf were ten or so sticks of greasepaint, all numbered and neatly in a row, powder and puff, mascara, eyebrow pencil – the tools of the trade precisely in their place. In the little drawers beneath would be a selection of moustaches and whiskers, spirit gum, an eye glass for playing buffoons, a false nose for Shylock or Cyrano, tooth black for villians – he could examine all that later at his leisure, for now his business was simply to take the pallor from his cheeks.

'Half an hour, please, ladies and gentlemen. This is your half hour call, thank you.'

The tannoy announcement added to the weight of fear in Dominic's stomach. Gently he rubbed into his face a mixture of Leichner numbers 5 and 9. There was no knock and no bidding to herald in the visitors to his dressing room, and Dominic saw them first in the mirror, a trio of men in dinner jackets all holding large bouquets of flowers. He spun round to face them as they stood with their back to the door.

'We just thought we'd pop in to wish you all the best, duckie.'

Tristram was positioned between the other two who towered either side of him. He wore a wing collar and a red bow tie that clashed with the dahlias he was holding, his smile was cold as charity.

'Yea, we just came to say break a leg.' The man on the left giggled.

'Yea, break a leg.' The one on the right was an exact facsimile of the one on the left. Their size, their suits, their smile, their sunglasses all had an awful symmetry. Dominic could feel his heart thumping in his chest – twins. 'Dirty great buggers,' Maurice had said.

'Get out.' Dominic's mouth was dry as sand. None of them moved. 'Get out of here,' he spoke louder and sounded only petulant.

'Sit down,' Tristram ordered.

Dominic sat. 'What do you want? Why are you here?'

'We've come to wish you luck, to celebrate your comeback.' Tristram's voice was quiet and sweet with menace. Both twins put down their bouquets. One of them locked the door. 'And how better to celebrate,' Tristram went on, 'than with a little drinky-winky,eh?'

The three of them were standing over him, unsmiling now and too close for any kind of comfort. Tristram was holding a bottle of vodka displaying for Dominic the familiar logo – Smirnoff. He held it like a weapon, which it was. 'With Smirnoff, anything can happen.' The twins giggled obediently.

'No, thanks.' Dominic wanted to beg them to go away. 'No, really not for me thanks.'

'It's what you need,' Tristram said, 'with all the stress you've had. And sadness too. Diddums . . . A little drink to settle your nerves, help you through the show. Help you face all those people out there . . . it's quite understandable, once an alcoholic always an alcoholic . . . How else could you face an audience like that, all those people who have come to see you, Mr Clever Dick, Mr Fucking Smart-Arse . . .'

It quite alarmed Dominic to see and hear the hatred so vivid in Tristram's face and voice. They had come to sabotage him, to give him vodka and send him reeling on to the stage for a public humiliation. The bottle was being held in front of him, it was the arrow aimed at his Achilles heel. He turned his head, not wishing to look his old enemy in the eye. He wanted to beg, to reason, to entreat, to scream for help . . . no, not scream – no need to scream . . . What was it Ron-Ron had said about 'GBH of the ear hole'. He was wired for sound. Tristram was still pouring out invective . . . 'Thought you'd go poking your frigging nose into other people's business did you. Dominic the big I-am, the lofty goody-goody, the star . . .

238

You just don't know what the hell you're messing with.'
Dominic could hazard a fairly chilling guess. 'Well you're not
fucking well messing with me.'

Dominic leant forward and in a gesture of despair put his
head in hands. There it was, the tiny microphone just behind
his hairline. Gently he flicked it with his thumb, masking
one hand with the other he tapped out a cry for help, a
desperate SOS 'Oh Ron-Ron, save our souls . . . sorry about
the GBH of the ear hole Ron. But hear me, Ron, switch on,
Ron. For God's sake.

On a signal from Tristram, the twins moved round behind
Dominic and took hold of his shoulders and arms. This was
not going to be a voluntary drink. In the mirror he could see
himself – pinioned between the two great gargoyles. Their
hair was dark and tightly curled about their skulls like
shavings of lacquered ebony, and their faces were shining
and pallid either side of his own with its sheen of cosmetic
good health.

'You won't get away with this, you know.' Dominic spoke
louder than was necessary for the benefit of Ron-Ron. 'You
won't get away with any of it. You can't just barge in here
like this, uninvited, and hold me like this against my will.'
Was he being too obvious? 'Just get the hell out of here, you
and your moronic-looking henchmen. Leave me alone.'

They did not leave him alone; with one accord the two
moronic-looking henchmen wrenched his arms up behind his
back, two half-Nelsons, making a whole. Dominic cried out
with the pain. 'Get out of here. Get out. You bastards . . .'

Tristram reached out his hand and took hold of Dominic's
hair then pulled his head backwards with a vicious jerk. Out
of the corner of his eye Dominic could see him produce a
narrow funnel and a length of transparent plastic tubing.
'Just in case you're not feeling that thirsty,' Tristram
grinned.

'Quarter of an hour please, ladies and gentlemen, this is
your quarter of an hour call. Thank you.' Lucinda's voice on
the tannoy brought Dominic back to the lesser challenge of
his return to the live theatre after twelve years. With his
neck craning backwards over the back of the chair his power

239

of speech was restricted and his scalp ached with the pressure on his hair. 'You bastards. You bastards,' he tried to mutter through clenched teeth. He shook his head as best he could from side to side as Tristram leant over him with the tubing in his hand.

'Keep still,' he growled and the flat of his hand endorsed the instruction as it swung into the side of Dominic's face. For a moment he was dazed, could hear nothing except a whistling in his head, then he was being bent back further in his seat and his mouth was being invaded. His tongue was fighting against the plastic tubing in a kind of frantic kissing that made him retch. And as he did he thought his throat was breaking open. Struggling to breathe and gagging wildly with the intrusion, he could only see the straining faces above him. Elbows and hands clamped his head and he was powerless to move as the funnel was held in place. He was choking and dizzy and the tube was now out of sight inside him.

At close range Tristram's breath was foul with old food and wine and the faint pockmarking of his skin gave it the viscid texture of a frog's belly. 'Some people,' he was saying through tight pale lips, 'just can't hold their drink, can they, boys?' The twins laughed. Dominic could see the bottle now poised above the funnel and could hear the sound of pouring. Again he tried to shake his head and again he felt a savage tightening of the grip.

'Sit fucking still.'

Then there was a burning somewhere high up in his chest as the alcohol scorched home and he knew he'd lost his battle. He was drowning in his old weakness and the faces of his visitors were swirling out of focus and they were chuckling in his ear. His trachea was aching with the effort of his retching and his innards were filled with a great white heat. If ever there was aversion therapy, this was it. He was on the point of fainting, the edge of a great welcoming abyss. Relax, he told himself, relax, it'll soon be over. He was spinning now, free falling with the flames behind him . . . it'll soon be over.

The door burst open, the lock shattered by the weight of

two huge stage hands and suddenly the room was full of sound and confusion. Ron-Ron was shouting at the intruders and there was the noise of scuffling. As Dominic fell to the floor the plastic tubing slid from his mouth and he lay on the ground choking for air. Above him the rescue party now outnumbered his visitors who were keen to leave.

'Come on, boys ... We don't want to miss the show.' Tristram was adjusting his tie and added as an explanation, 'We just called by to wish Dominic good luck.' The funnel and tubing were stowed in his pocket. 'He started choking ... it was quite disturbing, wasn't it?'

'Yes,' said the twins.

'Cheerio, Dom,' Tristram smiled, 'we'll see you later.'

'Yes,' said the twins.

'Get out,' Dominic whispered on his knees.

'You heard him,' said Ron-Ron as he ushered them into the corridor. The stage hands dispersed. 'Are you OK?' he asked, helping Dominic to the basin.

'Yea,' he answered, holding the taps for support, 'yea, I'm fine.' He vomited dryly, his gullet was on fire. 'Thanks for coming.'

'It was only by chance I tuned into your channel.' Ron-Ron was patting him on the back, 'but I got your message loud and clear so I got the lads together and came on round.'

'Thanks,' Dominic repeated. 'Perhaps you could get some-one to bring me some coffee.'

'Sure.' Ron-Ron left at once.

On the tannoy he could hear the audience assembling, a sound like starlings at dusk, twittering with anticipation.

'Five minutes please, ladies and gentlemen, five minutes. Thank you.'

Dominic stood in the middle of the room, swaying in his stiff-fronted shirt. He was on deck in a rough sea. The horizon rose and sank, no sign of shore. He estimated he had between twelve and fifteen minutes, allowing for a late start and the overture, fifteen minutes to get himself together and walk out on stage.

His throat was sore and his head was swirling in that old familiar dance, rocking and rolling with aggression and then composure. Oh yes, he knew the feeling, the phoney bravura and then the self-loathing that would follow. And there on the table was the bottle, one third gone. Dominic picked it up, then holding it at arm's length he poured it down the basin and threw it in the bin. He poked his finger down his throat and leant over again, spewing and coughing. His stomach ached and his balance was gone – he'd never make it, not in ten minutes. He sank his face into cold water and stayed there as long as he could. 'Oh, Dad, oh, Dad, Smirno, Smirno . . . Oh dear God . . . ' He dried his face. 'Come on, Come on, Come on,' he said out loud. He saw himself swaying in the full length mirror, he leant his forehead against it and watched himself sobbing

Opinions as to what exactly had happened in Dominic's dressing room varied among the company, but for the moment it did not matter. The overture was coming to an end and the show was about to begin. Dominic was sitting beside the stage in his opera cloak and hat drinking his coffee double-handed. He held the mug in white-gloved hands and stared straight ahead, unblinking like a man in prayer. His fellow actors gave him a wide berth as they paced back and forth in the wings. For any performer it is a private moment, this final galvanising of self, this summoning of courage, this defiance of the bladder . . .

The curtain had risen, and the audience were applauding the scene: the shadowy portico of St Paul's, Covent Garden. The show had begun. Dominic took a deep breath and stood up. He felt sick and unsteady; calm and unreal.

Tessa had arrived in his dressing room with glucose, ginseng, gargle, smelling salts, tiger balm. She made him eat a pile of biscuits and drink his coffee. She helped him with his costume, touched up his make-up – and didn't even ask a single question. In the quiet voice of a nanny she had told him what to do and he obeyed muttering 'the bastards' from time to time. He paced up and down in his small dressing room, trying to clear his head and get his balance. At the beginner's call Tessa had suggested that they should try and run through some of the lines. Standing beside him in the urchin clothes of the flower girl with her face covered in grime, she played the early dialogue with him. They hummed a scale or two and Dominic sang some of his lyrics.

'Terrific. You'll be fine,' she said. 'It's only a stupid show, for God's sake.'

'Thank you, Tessa,' he grinned. 'Thank you very much . . . Finger's crossed.'

She had put her arms around him and held him swaying against her for a moment. The gentle invitation in this gesture of comfort was quite lost on him – only later did the memory of this fragile eager girl come back to disturb him.

'Good luck,' she whispered. 'Let's knock them for six.'

From the side of the stage Dominic stood and viewed the scene in front of him. What kind of a giant would it be he wondered, and then like someone going to his death he moved forward to make his entrance. He was quite unprepared for the overwhelming sound of fourteen hundred people clapping. 'An entrance round' is often thought disruptive to the play but in some cases it carries a message to the actor – a welcome to an old friend. The volume of the applause disorientated Dominic for a moment, it was a torrent of running water in his ears. Then he understood it and felt its warmth. And soon he found himself singing his first number, and his voice gathered strength and confidence. As he came to the end of 'Why can't the English teach their children how to speak', he looked out at the audience applauding and saw only a glittering, beaming mass – a friendly giant.

A charity audience that has paid over the odds for their seats can be notoriously hard to please. The notion of value for money can colour their view and spoil the evening. They will sit in their diamanté and DJs resisting stone-faced the enthralment. But not the Mancunians at the Princess Theatre that warm July evening; they were there to enjoy themselves. They clapped and shouted out 'Bravo' quite happily, and soon they were eating from the hand of the star they had read so much about.

In the Royal Circle Phoebe had her arm linked through Sir Philip's and was watching the show with a pounding heart. She knew nothing of the trauma Dominic had been put

243

through. She saw only his dazzling, leisurely technique and his casual elegance and she had a faint hope that her troubles might soon be over. The show could hardly fail. Beside her Sir Philip watched with half-closed eyes and his hand, when she took it, was cool and dry – hers clammy. 'Attaboy,' she whispered as her son-in-law went on from strength to strength.

Elsewhere round the auditorium Dominic's performance was being viewed with less enthusiasm. At the back of the Stalls Tristram watched alone, his jaw clenched with loathing. No one thwarted him for long. The twins stood lolling at the side of the Royal Circle. One picked his nose, the other his teeth. They were not that much into musical comedy, a video nasty was much more up their Elm Street. Their sympathy was with Eliza anyway, there was nothing wrong with her vowel sounds that they could notice. At the end of 'The Rain in Spain' when Dominic declared 'By George she's got it,' one leant towards his brother and whispered, 'He's going to get it hisself later and all.'

To begin with Maxwell sat patiently waiting for Dominic to stumble as arranged, but as the interval approached he grew angry with the idea that his son had disobeyed or failed him. The whole enterprise was getting out of hand. 'Just you wait, 'enry 'iggins, just you wait.' Beside him, Margot in her mustard-coloured satin dress sat beaming with pleasure at the stage. Her ignorance at what was going on looked blissful as she munched away at the lion's share of the chocolates – all the soft centres.

In the interval, while the audience drank champagne in the foyer, the cast took coffee in plastic cups in the green room. If anything, the backstage gathering had more elegance with the girls in their dresses for the ball at the Transylvanian Embassy, and the men in tails. The general verdict on the show so far was one of cautious excitement – all of them were agreed that they had under estimated the impact that Dominic would have on the audience.

'I tell you,' said Fitzgerald with largesse, 'I reckon he's got something of the charisma of Wolfit in his prime.'

Dominic sat alone in his dressing room. He did not mean

to be unsociable, he just wanted to hold on to his concentration and rest his legs.

'You are doing fab,' Ian had told him in the wings, 'hang in there.'

And that's exactly what he was doing – hanging in there, with his head still reeling and a sickness in his stomach. Don't think of before or after. Just think of now. He pulled the make-up box towards him and began neatly replacing the sticks of greasepaint he had used. Then out of curiosity he opened the other three tiny drawers beneath the top tray. The first two contained all the paraphernalia he had expected – bits of hair, a pince-nez, some throat lonzenges – the ruby ring his father had worn in *Murder in the Cathedral*, all carefully stowed away for their next new purpose. Actors never retire, they just play older parts.

The third drawer was harder to open than the others, filled as it was with a bundle of letters. Dominic took them out and held them in his hand. They were addressed to Griffith Gallagher Esq., c/o Lyceum Theatre, Edinburgh. The letters were in two piles each bound together with an elastic band. The handwriting was small but fluent in style, its loops unflamboyant and controlled. Dominic had no recognition of it, nor did he know the postmark which read: Bridge of Orchy, Scotland, Nov. 1923.

Surely now they were beyond the respect of privacy. Dominic took off the elastic band and slipped the first letter from its envelope. After so long folded the paper seemed reluctant to be opened. The heading was engraved in royal blue.
BRACHAMEDA. FORT WILLIAM.

It did not feel like prying as Dominic began to read.

'My darling, I had hoped that in returning here
I would find my sanity and perhaps some sense of
shame but I feel instead quite glorious. I find
myself alive and glowing and longing for you
again. Oh my dear, I am a wanton trollop, a
fallen women, an adulteress, a school girl. My
virtue has been blown to the wind and I don't
give a damn. You have lit a fire in me that is
burning up my sense of duty, my morality, even

245

my appetite. I cannot read or ride or think even half way straight for the memory of you . . . Of all the seven sins, adultery must surely be the least deadly, the most divinely irresistible . . . Dear Griff, can our love be wrong feeling so right? I waiver between utter despair and such total joy at the thought of you . . . of us. Us together, joined. I want so much to be in your arms and to feel your warmth and strength inside me . . . Oh my God. I think I must be going mad . . .

Archie returns tomorrow from his week's shooting in Shropshire, and I have no idea how I'm going to face him. You haven't merely turned my head, you've sent it spinning towards the moon, my darling sweet Griff . . . To my dying day I'll remember sitting in the Stalls of the Lyceum watching you play Glendower with all that power and passion and knowing all the while that we would be dining together later in your rooms . . . Oh my darling, "what spirits have you called from the vasty deep". . . What future can we possibly have, my dear sweet wicked lover? I am so utterly confused and so desperate to see you. Don't call me here now. . . Oh poor, poor Archie, what am I doing? I will reach you at the theatre. My love. My love. My love. I long to see you again. May God forgive me. Charlotte.'

Dominic smiled at the skeletons in his father's cupboard. It was comforting to think of him as a young actor romancing provincial wives. Hadn't he, too, in early days enjoyed the touring benefits of fringe theatre . . . Perhaps this was the beginning of a new posthumous kinship with his father.

In the great Victorian foyer of the Princess Theatre, front of house, the happy patrons were unhurried. Champagne flowed freely in the name of charity and the interval was easily prolonged. Dominic read on, gently unfolding the brittle pages from long ago. The letters from the first pile, about half a dozen in all, were all in a similar style, swinging between guilt and pleasure, wielding the two-edged moral sword whichever way. Their dates spanned the three following years and were addressed to different theatres – Huddersfield, Swansea, Eastbourne, Crewe.

'My darling, I am in the very depth of remorse. I
am utterly damned, I'm sure Archie suspects. Oh
what am I to do? My darling I ache for you. I long
for your touch, I'm dead without you . . . Can't
wait for Fyfe. Have told A. that I'm going to an
old girl's golf tournament so will have to bring
my clubs!!! We can't go on. When can I see you,
soon, sooner, soonest . . . I am undone, ruined . . .
I must be sensible . . . and remember my duty . . .
What would my mother say? Could I make you
happy? I am your slave . . . I am after all his wife
. . . in blackest desolation . . . in eager
anticipation.'

The letters told a sad story of an impossible love, the age-old conflict between head and heart. Dominic read them with much compassion and wondered what kind of reading the other half of the correspondence would make. He was just on the point of reading the last letter of the first bundle when the call for the beginners of Act II came over the tannoy. It was dated April 1925 and addressed to the Kings Theatre, Portsmouth. He began reading it standing up and then sat down again. Oblivious of the sound of the audience returning to their seats and the orchestra tuning up again, he read:

'Oh my darling. I don't know how to write this
letter, but write it I must. I am going to have a
baby. Our baby. I am both thrilled and appalled.
Thrilled because it is what I wanted so much and
had not thought possible (as you know). And
appalled at the deception it involves to poor, dear
Archie. As the saying goes, I shall be putting a
cuckoo in his nest and will no doubt suffer
eternal damnation. Dear Griff, I have prayed
long and hard in the chapel for guidance and
strength, and have made two resolutions.
    You must solemnly swear on anything you
hold sacred that this will remain our abiding

secret. Archie must never know the truth, I
couldn't face the dishonour. Secondly, and this
pains me to the very core of my being to write,
we must not meet again. Not ever. My misery on
this point is no less certain than my resolve . . .
Please know that I shall miss you and love you
for ever in my secret heart, a heart that is aching
unbearably even as our child is growing inside
me. Please, though, respect my decision and let it
stand . . . Oh my dear Griff, the memories of you
and our times together, your gentleness and your
clever sweet ways with me, your good humour
and your understanding and your utter brilliance
will haunt me for all time. Perhaps after all
Dowson was right (oh how I remember you
reading him to me for that first time in Bolton
was it?): "They are not long the days of wine and
roses . . ." Dear Griff I wish you all the happiness
that I know will elude me and all the success you
deserve. Goodbye. C.'

Sitting in his white tie and tails, Dominic gently returned
the letter to its envelope and replaced the elastic band. What
could the second bundle have to reveal? By proxy he felt a
terrible sadness for this poor Highland lady whose heart had
lost the battle with her conscience. For a moment he was
Griffith too, an actor in a dressing room in 1925 waiting to
do a show and reading the letter when it was fresh. Had he
felt the hollow pang of lost love, he wondered, or had he
merely shrugged and carried on? Dominic hoped it was the
former.

'Mr Gallagher. This is your call please. Mr Gallagher on
stage immediately please.' The stage manager's voice had an
edge of urgency. The other letters would have to wait.
Dominic stood up, his head ached sharply and he still felt
giddy and nauseous. He was a million miles from home, out
of orbit spinning in the dark. As he made his way to the stage
he forced his mind to address the job in hand, to enter the
lighter world of Lerner & Loewe where the happy ending had
already been rehearsed.

Only just before he made his entrance, as he stood pulling

on his white kid gloves, did it strike him that somewhere out there in the great stinking outside world he had a brother or a sister.

After the triumphant return from the ball at the Embassy, the second act of *My Fair Lady* allows the actor playing Higgins a period of respite while Eliza returns to the flower market and her fellow costermongers in Covent Garden. So, having fooled 'that hairy hound from Budapest', Dominic changed his costume and with yet another cup of coffee sat in the wings watching the action on stage. In profile he saw Tessa sing her big number, 'Show me', with Freddy Eynsford Hill. She sang it beautifully with a simple intensity . . .

> 'Here we are together in the middle of the night
> Don't talk of love, just hold me tight.'

The invitation was irrestible flowing from her as it did clear and unstrained echoing round the theatre. With the vodka now almost subsided in his veins and his head still aching Dominic took stock of the situation.

The immediate threat of public humiliation was passed, for the moment Tristram had been foiled. But soon the show and whatever protection it offered would be over and he would find himself still in the dangerous position of a man who knows too much. Such a man has to remain a target as long as he comes between the villains and their safety. 'We'll see you later,' Tristram had said. When the show was over he would again be hunted by his trio of visitors, perhaps even with reinforcements. The prospect held no appeal for Dominic at all. He must escape from the theatre, he needed a bolt-hole and an ally. With Maurice in hospital and Ben lying low in Dorset, he did not have a lot of choice.

Tessa was finishing her reprise of 'Wouldn't it be loverly'. All she wanted was a room somewhere. . . She could sing that again. As she came off stage Dominic was waiting for her.

'How are we doing? Isn't it going well?' she said. Her eyes were bright and there was sweat on her upper lip.

'Yes it is. It's going great. You're marvellous,' he said. 'Listen I need your help.'

'Sure,' she nodded.

Dominic whispered the outline of his situation to her, not the whole story, just enough to convey the urgency and told her what he wanted her to do. She listened carefully, watching his mouth intently.

'Right. I've got it,' she said when he finished. 'There's never a dull moment with you, is there, Gallagher?' she grinned before leaving.

On stage Teddy Fitzgerald was belting out 'Get me to the church on time' – a number that only stopped the show for a while, soon it would be over and the company would assemble on stage for the finale. In her dressing room Tessa changed, ready for the end of the show, and was frantically putting together what luggage she thought she might need. On the tannoy she could hear Dominic singing a reprise of 'Why can't a woman be more like a man' and pondered not for the first time, the reverse. As she put her diary into the hold-all she wondered what tomorrow's page would have to tell.

With everything in readiness, she waited in the wings and as she made her last entrance Dominic was sprawled on the chaise longue centre stage. 'Liza,' he said from beneath his trilby, 'bring me my slippers.' The curtain fell. There was a pause and then the applause began, erupting as the cast lined up and took their bow. It was a happy giant that clapped and listened as the company sang again the choruses of the big numbers. They finished with 'A little bit of luck' and the giant rose to its feet shouting 'more' and 'bravo'.

Tessa and Dominic stepped forward separately and then together. The giant seemed to like them, roaring its approval. Dominic took Tessa's hand and as he did he felt her press into his palm a set of keys. He smiled at her as he took them and she smiled back. They were accomplices now, not just leading man and lady.

Dominic took a step forward, raised his hands for silence and when it came at last began to speak. 'Mr Mayor, Ladies and Gentlemen. I just want to thank you on behalf of all the company for coming here tonight, to this gala performance. You seemed to enjoy it. And so have we.'

The audience applauded its agreement.

250

'You've been quite wonderful . . . As you know this event was by way of being a benefit evening for the widow and daughter of my predecessor in the role of Higgins – Leo Benson – a lovely man and a fine, fine actor. Thanks to your generosity we hope to be sending Kitty Benson a cheque for just over thirty-five thousand pounds, enough, it is hoped, to finish paying for Amanda's education.'

Again Dominic paused while the audience applauded its own bounty.

Phoebe in particular was amazed at her son-in-law's decision to make a speech. When she had asked him to do so, he had been quite adamant in his refusal. 'I couldn't possibly do it,' he had said. 'Surely we don't need to say anything. I'm useless at that sort of thing. Sorry but no.' Yet there he was, bless him, doing the job perfectly with great good grace and sincerity. She smiled in the half darkness and squeezed the arm of her escort. Sir Philip too watched Dominic keenly.

At this point in his speech Dominic should have been bidding the giant goodnight and a safe journey home but instead he paused, like a man on a high diving board. To dive or not? He had no choice and so he began. 'Before the champagne supper in the foyer begins, I would like to thank so many people for making this evening possible . . . the front of house staff, the crew, the stage management, the orchestra, the organisers and of course all the cast. But there is one special word of gratitude that I would like to make to a very special person without whom none of it would have been possible. His contribution to this gala has been nothing short of stupendous . . . I know he's somewhere out there among you, probably wishing to remain anonymous in his modest way. But I'd like to ask him to stand up so that all of us can show him some token of our appreciation. Ladies and Gentlemen, please give a warm round of applause to Tristram Brunswick.' He repeated the name like a call to prayer, 'Tristram Brunswick.'

An audience is a most compliant animal, obedient to a fault. It hisses villains and shouts out its belief in fairies. It laughs when the vicar loses his trousers and cries when Juliet dies. And when it is told to applaud an unknown

251

benefactor, it does so without hesitation. The glittering assembly of Mancunians clapped loud and warmly and as they did they looked round eagerly for a glimpse of the man in question.

Tristram was standing at the back of the Stalls with the twins. He had been on the point of leaving to ensure another meeting with his quarry, either at the stage door or at his car. The last thing he wanted was to be the centre of attention, in the circumstances a low profile was essential but the odds were stacked against him 1400–1.

'Tristram Brunswick.' Dominic was calling out his name again and all round him heads were turning. He felt hot and cold; hot with embarrassment, cold with anger. 'Tristram – come on down here.'

Under the pressure of this unexpected acclaim Tristram was left with no choice. 'Shitting hell,' he muttered to the twins, 'wait here.' With what looked like modesty he made his way down the centre aisle to the front of the orchestra pit. He turned awkwardly and perhaps for the first time in his life he found himself faced with an overwhelming show of approbation. All round him in the auditorium and on stage people were applauding him – he smiled thinly and half-bowed.

'Tristram Brunswick', Dominic announced his name again, 'Without whose tireless efforts this evening could never have been possible – Ladies and Gentlemen I would like to suggest . . . ' Dominic was now holding three hats in his hand – one opera and two bowlers . . . 'that Tristram and his pals, the ever-jovial twins back there, should make a further collection of any change you might feel inclined to put towards the support of the family of Leo Benson, a man we all loved.'

The audience applauded the suggestion and Dominic tossed the hats down to Tristram. For a moment their eyes met in a manner unfitting for a charity event. The twins at last came lumbering to join their furious leader and were allocated the lesser hats.

'It only remains,' Dominic went on, 'for us all to thank you once again for coming and for your generosity. Many of you of course we'll be seeing at the champagne supper, but to all of you . . . take care and have a safe journey home. God bless.' He stood back in line with the rest of the cast, they bowed, the giant clapped yet again long and warmly, and at last the curtain was finally lowered.

Tristram found himself entrapped by a throng of people eager to heap money and praise upon him. He could do nothing but accept both with dignity. The scene provided for his mother one of the proudest moments of her life – and for his father one of the most perplexing.

'He's always been a one to hide his light under a bush,' she beamed.

'El . . . ' Maxwell growled.

'What dear?'

'Bush*el*. It's bushel, not bush. You don't hide your light under a bush – it's a bushel.'

Margot patted his arm. 'He's a wonderful boy, isn't he?'

At the back of the Stalls and Circle the twins likewise had no choice and, immobilised by goodwill, they stood dumb-founded and cap in hand.

Backstage now the curtain was finally down, the cast were indulging in the ritual of self-congratulation: 'Darling, you were simply super.' 'You too, poppet.' 'Wasn't it great?' 'Didn't it go like a bomb?' 'We're going to be a smash at the Brunswick.' 'We'll run for years.' Around them the scenery was already being dismantled for its journey down to London. 'What a triumph,' they all agreed. 'And wasn't Dominic just sensational?' 'Brilliant.' 'Fabulous.' 'Perfect'. 'Fancy him making that extraordinary speech . . .' 'He's gorgeous.' 'I wonder where he is?'

As they dispersed from the stage to change for the party, no one could later recall having seen the leading man. From the moment the curtain had come down it seemed that Dominic had disappeared. Albert at his usual post certainly had no recollection of seeing him leave.

Only the two hefty-looking stage hands who carried Dominic from the theatre in a large wicker skip together with other impedimenta knew how it was he left. As they carried him past his Mercedes they informed him that he had got a flat tyre, which came as no surprise. They deposited him

253

round the corner beside a royal blue Citroën. He tipped them both generously and thanked them for their help.

'You want to watch out,' one of them said. 'The place looks to be swarming with hefty looking villains and it's not autographs they're after either.'

The foyer of the Princess Theatre was filled with people eating and drinking in a good cause. The brows of the men and the shoulders of the women shone with the heat. The entire cast of *My Fair Lady* was there graciously receiving champagne and compliments; they signed autographs and explained how they learnt their lines – all of them except Dominic Gallagher.

'Where is the little shit?' Maxwell rasped to his son. His face was florid with urgency and small bubbles of sweat rolled down his temples. 'We've got to get hold of him.'

'Relax, Dad, we've got men all round the place.'

Tristram was tired of being the nice guy. 'The boys are here.'

There they were, a twin at the top of each great staircase, loitering in their cheap dinner jackets with their eyes alert, watching for their man.

Phoebe and Sir Philip were celebrating with the Mayor. 'It were a grand evening – truly grand,' he told them.

'Well fingers crossed for the Brunswick,' Phoebe was saying. 'I only hope the previews go as well there as it did here tonight . . . don't you, darling?'

Sir Philip did not hear her question, he was looking about the party smiling and observing. Cameras were flashing as Tessa made her way through the crowd. Her hair was up and she wore a sky-blue strapless mini-dress. She was smiling and drinking champagne. 'I've no idea,' she answered the enquiries about Dominic. 'He'll be here in a minute I expect.'

The dangers he had described seemed not at all in evidence and she could see no harm in the assembled guests. For twenty minutes or so she kept on the move spreading herself quite thin among the crowd, she was not planning to stay long; who would with such as assignation pending?

'I thought you were quite brilliant.' Tristram was standing

254

too close in front of her addressing his compliment to her bosom, not her face.

'Thank you,' she answered. 'I gather you didn't do too badly yourself. Over four hundred pounds was it, in your hat? Marvellous of you.'

'Yes,' Tristram answered. 'I can't think why dear Dominic should have done that . . . I did nothing really. Have you seen him by the way?'

'No, no I haven't,' she said sweetly. 'He likes to keep himself to himself I think – he's a very private sort of a man.'

'I wonder where he can be?'

'I've no idea,' Tessa answered. She could smell the breath of the man eager and stale. 'Actually I've got to be going . . .'

'So soon?' he mocked.

'Er yes. . . I'm going down to London tomorrow morning. We start previews at the Brunswick next week.'

'Yes, of course.' Tristram was leering at her. His eyes were close neighbours separated by a thin nose. 'Perhaps I could give you a lift home?'

'Thanks all the same. I've got my car.' She was uneasy now.

'I'll walk you to it then,' he said and the suggestion held only a hint of a threat.

Having said her goodbyes and collected her things, Tessa was forced to allow Tristram to escort her from the theatre. The twins they passed in the doorway were every bit as grisly and huge as Dominic had described. She sensed that Tristram had guessed at her complicity and she chatted brightly to cover her guilt.

'Isn't it just marvellous for your aunt,' she said, 'that after all the problems she's had things are turning out all right?'

'Yes it is. Marvellous.'

Tristram took her arm as they walked down the street.

'I think the show's going to be great, don't you? Dominic is so good in it – he's just pulled it all together, don't you think?'

'Yes. Yes he has,' Tristram agreed. They were standing now beside her royal blue Citroën with only an awkward good night to be said.

'Silly me,' Tessa said. 'Look where I left my keys.' They

were on the driver's seat. 'Honestly I am an idiot,' she giggled. The door was open. She squeezed past him and got in.

'You should be more careful,' he said, leaning into the car.

'I should, shouldn't I?' she said, keen for him to leave.

'And you've no idea where Dominic is?'

'No. I told you,' she said. Again she could smell his breath too close. 'Perhaps he's at his hotel.'

'Well, if you see him, tell him I'll be in touch, will you?'

'If,' she said. 'Thank you and good night.'

Tristram nodded, then slammed her car door and walked off down the street as if he had more important business to attend to. Opposite the stage door he stopped to talk to a thick-set man who was leaning against a lamp post. 'He must be in there somewhere – the bugger's not come out, that's for sure.'

Tristram grunted. 'He'd better not have done,' and went back to rejoin the party where Dominic's absence was much regretted among the guests, not least of all by Maxwell and the twins.

'I wanted to ask him if he'd send something for the charity auction we're having at the Bagshot WI,' Margot said. 'Will you ask him if you see him.'

The noise her husband made before walking off was unintelligible.

Tessa had watched in relief as Tristram left her. As she started her engine she heard a muffled voice coming through the back seat. 'Drive on. Get away from here and let me out, for God's sake.'

She was not quick on the uptake; it had been a while since she had had an international film star in her boot. But she obeyed and drove away to the west of the city in silence. After a couple of miles, when she reckoned it was safe, she pulled in and let Dominic out. The poor man had been shut in with all her dirty washing. He was still wearing the trousers and waiscoat of Professor Higgins and took some time to loosen himself from the cramp.

'Thanks,' he said. 'Didn't that work like clockwork? What did that creep think he was doing?'

'Tristram? I don't know. He seemed pretty suspicious. I couldn't stop him coming. Just as well you weren't in the front seat. I couldn't think where you were. Are you OK?'

'Yea. Fine.' Dominic got in the car beside her. 'You look terrific,' he said.

'Thanks. Where are we going?' she asked.

They were on the run together, doing a remake of *The Thirty-Nine Steps*. As Madeleine Carroll to his Robert Donat, she'd be as good as gold.

'Let's just get out of here,' he said. 'Go north . . . no, south . . . no, east . . . go east.' Dominic had obviously not planned this part of the escape. 'We can't go back to my hotel.'

'Nor mine,' Tessa answered. 'There was a pretty fishy look on Tristram's face. Here . . .' she passed him a couple of books: a road map and a hotel guide. 'See what you can find.' They smiled at one another in the darkness.

In fact they headed north-east towards Halifax, turned off the motorway and took a minor road to Hebden Bridge. As they drove Dominic gave her an abridged outline of the situation she was now part of, and within an hour they were pulling in to a driveway lined with poplars and found themselves in the forecourt of a medium-sized Georgian manor house. It was heavily clad in ivy and unprepossessing. Most of the lights were out but as promised on the car-telephone the hall porter was on duty to let them in. He was old and vague and Irish and showed no curiosity in them as they registered. He led them upstairs and along a panelled corridor to a corner room.

'We didn't have a twin I'm afraid,' he said as he turned on the lights to show them the enormous hand-carved four poster that dominated the room.

'This'll do fine, won't it darling?' Tessa answered. 'Is there any chance you could fix us something to eat?'

'Sandwiches . . . or sandwiches,' he offered.

'That'd be lovely, wouldn't it, darling?' She was enjoying her part. Dominic said that would be fine without turning round, he had a long list of reasons for not wanting to be recognised.

'And a bottle of champagne,' Tessa added.

257

'And one of Malvern water.'

'Right you are,' the porter said. He hadn't read a paper or seen a film in twenty years. Dominic was no celebrity to him, just another shifty, middle-aged adulterer with a floozie.

Alone in the room the two of them moved about self-consciously as if the prints on the walls were actually interesting.

'I'm sorry about all this.' Dominic was referring to the mess he was getting her into.

'I'm sure we'll manage.' Tessa was referring to the bed he was going to get her into. 'I'm going to have a bath.' She spoke like someone quite accustomed to the fugitive life.

Dominic stared out of the window at the silhouette of the moors against a low moon and wondered how safe he was. His head was clearer now and he felt less sick; it was time to inspect the reality and review options. He argued with himself about how to proceed and where and when. Here he was, holed up on the edge of the moors in the middle of the night with a pretty girl. The showdown with the bad guys would have to wait until tomorrow. This surely was the love scene.

The bath was long and deep, Victorian with claw-feet. It stood like a mausoleum in the middle of the room and was lit by three candles on the shelf behind the taps. In it Tessa looked small and elfin with her wet hair slicked back flat on her head. As Dominic came in she folded her arms to hide her breasts and drew up her knees, an urchin vulnerable and shiny.

'Well?' she said. It was not so much a query as a challenge. She too had been contemplating the sweet uses of adversity.

'Well,' Dominic answered. He was leaning against the door still dressed as Henry Higgins. 'Are you OK?'

'I'm fine . . . Are you going to get in?'

Dominic smiled. 'Yea . . . why not?' He unbuttoned his waistcoat, slipped off his braces, unlaced his shoes. She watched him in silence from just above the water line. 'I suppose I'll have to go the tap end,' he asked.

She grinned and nodded at him naked in front of her. There was a knock at the door and Dominic, wrapped in a

258

towel, fetched the tray with their supper from the porter. He pulled up a stool beside the bath and placed it within easy reach. He took off his towel and got into the hot water opposite his leading lady.

With three feet of water between them they eyed one another for some time like chess players. In the reflected light from behind him she looked apprehensive; perhaps she had made a mistake. Dominic reached out both hands and took hers, slowly they slid together easing forward. Over the mountain of their knees they craned their necks and began to kiss. With her face between his hands he kissed her forehead, eyes, cheeks, mouth. She pulled him closer so their lips could meet more easily. They tasted sweet to one another as their tongues came together gently circling and thrusting.

Above the water their arms embraced each other, and beneath it their legs did too. They were entwined so that their lower bellies came together, softly brushing as they rocked in their kissing. She could feel him against her but not inside her. They were on the threshold of one another, aware only of a readiness between them and a heat. She kissed his ear and stroked his hair, she sighed and arched her neck smooth like bone china for kissing.

'Why don't you pour me some champagne,' she whispered to the ceiling.

He opened the bottle, filled her glass, and watched her drink it enviously. Face to face they ate their sandwiches – smoked salmon and rare roast beef – and all the time their bodies were nudging one another below the water, loitering about their pleasure.

'There is just one thing,' she said, 'that I sort of ought to explain.'

'What's that?'

Tessa pulled back a little, scowling slightly as she finished her mouthful. 'I don't want you to be angry or anything . . .'

'No, no . . . Of course not,' he said quietly, suddenly aware of the difficulty she was having.

'Well . . . I've never done this before,' she said simply.

'This?'

She nodded.

'What?'

'I'm a virgin.'

'Christ.'

'At least I am on paper . . .'

'I . . . er.'

'No, no don't say anything. I want to explain, please. I mean I'm not retarded or anything. There's nothing wrong with me.' She wasn't looking at him directly; she half-giggled and went on. 'It's just that I've never been able to . . . allow no, not allow: I've never quite been able to let go – you know.'

Dominic nodded.

She shook her head in an effort to find articulation. 'I suppose it's all . . . rather difficult to explain.'

'You don't have to,' Dominic said.

'I do, really. I want to. I mean I don't want to be heavy or anything but you see I had a . . . a . . .' she paused, looking at him directly. 'I was what they call . . . abused as a child . . . Abused.' She repeated the word as if it were new to her.

Dominic said nothing. He refilled her glass and passed it to her.

'I mean it wasn't that big a deal . . .' she shrugged. 'You don't want to hear . . .'

'I do.' Dominic knew she needed to be heard.

She leant forward and touched his mouth with her forefinger, studied him for a while. 'I was eleven . . . eleven and a half . . . It was with Uncle Ted. He wasn't an uncle really . . . Poor old Uncle Ted.'

Dominic could see her reflection in the water remembering.

'. . . I mean I just thought that's what uncles did . . . you know, fumbling and poking about . . . I knew it was wrong or dirty. I mean he didn't hurt me but it was all somehow strange . . . and he made me promise not to tell anyone. "Cross your heart, Tessa, and hope to die."' She shook her head. 'I mean it seems silly really . . . it was in our living room for goodness sake . . . with our canaries in the cage and everything.' She sipped at her champagne. 'Anyway Mum found out . . . I had stopped eating you see and the teachers said I had sort of given up . . . so I was sent to this shrink . . . to straighten me out. I still go to see him from time to time. . .

260

I quite fancy him actually.' She smiled down the bath at
Dominic. 'I mean obviously we've sorted out the guilt thing
. . . but there are what he calls the "knock-on" effects; i.e. I
haven't yet done *it* properly. . . I mean I'm not scared or
screwed up or anything. I've just never quite got round to *it* –
you know the whole hog.' She was trying to be frivolous now
to lighten the weight of what she described. 'You see, all the
boys of my age are either too serious or not serious enough,
do you know what I mean? It's either the old wham-bam-
thank-you-Mam or it's all too earnest and heavy . . . Anyway
I just thought I should tell you . . . explain. I'm just a dreary
old maid at heart . . . Do you understand?'

Dominic stroked her cheek. 'Not dreary or old . . . Poor
you,' he said very quietly. 'Look . . . we don't have to . . . do
anything. I mean . . .'

'Hush your mouth,' she said. 'No skiving. . . I want you to
make love to me, please. I've been planning it for weeks . . .'

'Oh yea.'

'As if you didn't know,' she said. 'You knew.'

She spoke the truth. Dominic could remember now the
moment that he had known they would be lovers. Their eyes
had met across Professor Higgins's desk as she attempted 'in
'ertford, 'ereford, and 'ampshire 'urricanes 'ardly hever 'appen.'
There had been an instant then, as there always is fleeting but
positive, in which signals are sent and the die is cast.

He nodded. Yes he had known.

'Oh, I wanted you to kiss me,' she sighed, 'and you knew
this would happen sooner or later.'

Dominic studied her for a moment. 'I suppose I did.'

'And I had this idea that you'd understand about me
because . . . because you're . . .'

'So much older?'

She laughed. 'Well, yes that too. I thought you'd understand my predicament.'

'It's not a predicament,' he said.

'Yea . . .' Tessa was determined to finish her explanation.
'Well anyway I'm not looking for the great romance or anything. I mean everyone knows that you love your wife and
want her back . . . the silly cow. That's OK. Good luck to you

'. . . In the meantime I thought . . . and so did you . . . that we would just . . . you know . . . do it a bit . . . I'm not being very subtle, am I? What I am saying is that I won't pester you or behave badly . . . or get heavy or start sobbing and things . . .'

Dominic was gazing into the flat dark water about his knees. He felt appalled for his sex, the brutal maleness of a world that injured women for its pleasure, at the same time the invitation she was making was irresistible.

'Who knows,' he said. With a naked virgin sipping champagne in the candlelight who was he to worry about polemics. Soon the water would get cold.

'I should have kept my trap shut,' she said. 'but I thought you might be expecting me to be one of your swinging-from-the-chandelier type of nymphos . . . or something.' She raised her hands in the gesture of fair trading. 'Anyway I'm fully guaranteed . . . on the pill . . . no strings . . . no problems. A once in a lifetime offer. Hurry while stocks last.'

Dominic smiled at her. 'It's not that difficult you know.'

'What?'

'Making love.'

'Is that so?' She flicked water at him. 'Show me.'

'Tessa . . .' he began.

But she didn't hear him. Holding her nose she slid down under the water so that her hair floated free around her head and her breasts swayed above the surface. She blew bubbles and then came up gleaming like a seal and grinning.

'Get on with it.' She sank her teeth into a peach and offered it to him. They advanced towards one another, sliding forward on their buttocks grinning like conspirators. In the flickering light she looked wicked and moist, dribbling peach juice from her mouth. He licked it from her chin and softly kissed her throat and as they pushed together he could feel himself hard against the crevice of her. She kissed his eyes and then his cheeks and then his mouth quite fiercely with a champagne-flavoured intensity. Dominic held her breasts in his hand, round and firm. He lathered them gently and teased the nipples with his fingers. Tessa moaned quietly into his mouth and said his name several times as if it was the answer to a question. He soaped her back and ran his

262

hands down the smoothness of her spine enjoying the shape of her and the feel of her skin. He held her buttocks in his hands and raised her gently upwards, kissing her all the time. Their tongues were playing out the prelude of their bodies' future business.

Her hands were reaching for him, handling and guiding him to her so that she was pivoted above him. And still they kissed, seeking and giving access to each other. Then slowly she lowered herself upon him. Her nails dug into the flesh of his shoulders and the great exhalation of her breath carried with it a cry of victory and release, of pleasure and surprise. No pain and no remorse. Neither of them noticed the faint swirling pinkness in the water as they locked together.

With what great splashing and unheaval they adjusted themselves to reach their goal was lost to memory. They were aware only of the pleasure, the burning and the rhythm it demanded. 'Don't stop . . . don't stop,' she gasped, shuddering and waterlogged. Then later as he dried her gently on the bed . . . 'Do it again, do it again, please, please do it again,' she giggled.

Splayed across the linen sheets, her body had the silky texture of a Botticelli, a smooth pale amber broken only by a triangle of auburn hair. He kissed her from head to toe and back again; the taste of her was clean and earthy and she moaned freely like someone in a dream. There they were the flower girl and the Professor with their bodies joined again arching this way and that, convex and then concave for one another, staving off reality.

'You're right,' Tessa said as they watched the ceiling turn pink with the dawn. 'It's not that difficult. Now what, clever-clogs?'

Dominic could see the pulse still fluttering in her neck and the sweat on her belly was not yet dry. 'Well let's see . . .' he murmured and soon their blood was up again. Not even to her diary would Tessa give the details of what they did, of how they licked and stroked each other, how they kissed and swayed and moaned together and how at last they fell asleep together in the musty smell of enjoyment.

20

At first Phoebe had been distraught that Dominic had not shown up at the gala supper, later she became quite angry, but lastly she was worried. No one at the theatre or his hotel had any recollection of having seen him since the end of the show. His dressing room had not been cleared nor his car moved. Sir Philip suggested they stay the night in Manchester and they checked in together to the Manchester Palace Hotel. Phoebe lay awake most of the night with a dull but familiar feeling of foreboding – she might have known that the gala had gone too well for her luck to last. Throughout the morning they telephoned round to every possible point of contact and Dominic was nowhere to be found. They drank their coffee in silence, each afraid to voice the fears they had about their leading man, the dried out hero.

By midday Phoebe had become restless with the vigil and decided to go and check out his hotel and look in at the theatre. Sir Philip agreed to stay behind to take any calls that might come through.

'I'll be back later. I'll see you for lunch,' she said, kissing him lightly on the mouth. 'Oh God, I hope he's all right.'

'He will be. He will be.' Sir Philip held her in his arms and stroked her hair. 'Everything will be fine . . . poor old chap, needs a breather I expect; what with all this nonsense about theatre tickets and so on, he's probably feeling a bit of a charlie. . . I've had it all thoroughly checked out. It's a load of bunkum. I mean actors are all a bit prone to paranoia I reckon but where he got that idiotic drawing of the Brunswick converted from . . .' Sir Philip chuckled and shook his head in a parental fashion.

Phoebe found his strength comforting. She was hungry for the reassurance he offered, she had forgotten in her Roman spring that love is deaf as well as blind. She stroked his head and kissed him again. 'You know something,' she said, 'I'm getting far too fond of you.'

He smiled. 'And I you. See you later.'

After Phoebe had gone he poured himself more coffee, which was tasteless, and then unblinking like a Buddha he stared out of the window for some time. Or rather not out of the window, not at the views of west Manchester hazy in the summer heat, but at his own faint reflection in the tinted plate glass. His face had never afforded him any real pleasure, his vanities lay elsewhere. As far as he could see it bore no resemblance to his forebears, whose portraits hung round the hall of the family home. Over the years he had come to know their faces pretty well; had grown accustomed to the row of sombre eyes staring dolefully into the middle distance, generation after generation. A long line of Sullivans, with his father recently immortalised at the foot of the stairs, the paint still fresh it seemed. Even at mid-morning when the sun shone through the high window his face still had that look of florid disdain. One day Philip knew he'd be stuck up there too, his mild sallow face at odds with his predecessors and it amused him to think that hanging next to his father on the wall they would be closer on the canvas than they had been in the flesh. With very little sadness he realised that in the space after him the National Trust would have to hang a landscape or a still life. There would be no sixteenth baronet.

When the telephone rang he answered it without hurry as if he had willed it.

'My dear Dominic – are you all right?'

'Yea. I had some trouble last night . . .'

'Trouble?' Sir Philip sounded shocked.

Dominic told him briefly what had happened.

Poor old you. We've been so worried about you, especially Phoebe of course.'

'Was she furious about the reception party?'

'She was a little upset, worried mostly. Where are you?'

'A little hotel on the edge of the moors.'

'Alone?'

'Yes.' Dominic could see no point in implicating Tessa. 'How are things with the serious crime people?'

'I spent most of yesterday with my friend Andy Naylor, the chief inspector, and his people. They've got to carry out their own investigation and get the warrants out . . . The whole thing is in their hands, have no fear. Andy reckons he should have the lot of them rounded up before the end of the week. They'll need to talk to you as soon as poss.' Sir Philip's voice was calm as always. 'Meanwhile, the whole operation is being handled very much on the quiet, for obvious reasons.'

'I tell you, Philip,' said Dominic, 'I seriously think Tristram is unhinged, I mean a real maniac.'

'Of course,' said his ally. 'Listen, here's what to do. I'll get your car fixed up and all your stuff from the theatre brought round. We'll meet here this evening and drive down to London together. I could hire a couple of private men if you liked . . . to look after us, how about that?' Sir Philip's invitation was irresistible.

'Yea . . . OK. That sounds terrific.'

'We've got to look after you – previews start in London in three days.' Sir Philip was in charge now. 'I thought you were absolutely splended last night, by the way.'

'Thank you.' Dominic sounded tired. 'I'll see you this evening then?'

'Here at the hotel about eight?' Sir Philip suggested. 'Phoebe will be so pleased and relieved.'

'Send her my love and apologies,' Phoebe said.

'Of course. Look, old boy,' Sir Philip's voice had a note of urgency now, 'just lie low for the rest of the day . . . don't talk to anyone. Do you understand? No one.'

'Sure. See you later.'

Sir Philip hung up and poured himself more coffee. This time as he stared out of the window he allowed himself a faint smile – a smile that shows a man's pleasure in the neat and symmetrical conclusion of things. The coffee tasted better now.

When Phoebe returned a little later, she asked eagerly if there was any news. 'Has Dominic called?'

'No my darling,' Sir Philip took her in his arms. 'I'm afraid no one rang.'

Housework was not one of Harriet's obsessions in life. Normally it needed either ignoring or delegating. What she was undertaking now was not so much a spring clean as a purging of her territory. She was reclaiming it with the Hoover and the duster. She was not washing Greg out of her hair – she was scrubbing him off her floor, scouring him out of her bath. This was housework as therapy, for she was now alone.

Harriet had given him her news as a matter of plain fact with no apology, no sentiment, no preconditions.

'A baby?' he had sounded outraged. 'You're going to have a baby . . .? You're pregnant . . .? Christ Almighty. Are you sure?'

Of course she was sure, the certainty was ten days old. Greg opened another lager and paced about the room drinking from the can.

'We'll go halves,' he said at last.

'Halves?'

'On the abortion. I'll pay half.' He sounded charitable.

'I'm going to have the baby. I don't want your money, Greg,' she said. 'I'm not having an abortion.'

'Come on, Hat . . .' He cajoled her as if she had lost her reason.

'Don't touch me,' she shouted. 'Anyway it's not your problem?'

'Says who?'

'Says me that's who. It's not yours.' 'What?' he roared.

'You're not the father.'

'Well who the fuck is?' he roared, his expletive not inappropriate for once.

'Dominic,' she said.

'Dominic Gallagher . . . your husband?' Greg's face was a study in righteous indignation. 'Are you sure?'

Harriet nodded. 'Yes.' Her certainty was sired by wishing.

'How?' he asked with his eyebrows raised.

'We had lunch together at the school.'

'Lunch,' he growled. 'Lunch . . .'

'Yes,' she answered just before the flat of his hand struck her head. The impact knocked her to the kitchen floor but the pain had not been great. She lay there for a while and took stock. She felt no shame, single parenthood could not be worse than this.

Greg had apologised, of course, fetched aspirins and glasses of water, patted her head and muttered, 'Oh God, I'm so sorry . . . Oh God, Hat, what are we going to do?'

Harriet had got to her feet. 'I think you'd better go.'

'Look, Hat . . .'

'There's nothing more to be said.'

She watched him pack in the manner of a martyr. They said their goodbyes with dignity and no regret. In the doorway he turned. 'If . . . er . . .' he began.

'If your agent rings I'll tell him you're with your mother.'

'Thanks,' he smiled. 'All the best.' And as always he slammed the door.

She hoovered the pelmets, she wiped all the paintwork, she turned the mattress, she polished the letter box, the taps, the door knobs. She exhausted herself and sat drinking her herbal tea. For the first time in four months she played a record of her choice . . . Mozart had never sounded so good.

Phoebe rang to tell her the news of Dominic's disappearance and Harriet told her that Greg had gone at last. As she hung up she felt lonely for the first time; God had closed the door and the window too for good measure.

She never seriously doubted that Dominic would be all right, to her there was about him an imperishable factor but she began to remember their early days together, wistfully like a widow, and with all the affection of hindsight. In particular she recalled a picnic they had had when they were first lovers. Under the shade of an old oak in the corner of a barley field they ate lobster and and loganberries in their fingers and listened to the Pastoral Symphony. Through the leaves of the tree the sky was the colour of gentians and they had made love for hours on end. Even from the beginning his knowledge of her body had been surprising and spectacular as if by instinct he knew the secrets of her. Like a kestrel

268

above its prey he would always keep her hovering blissfully on the brink of climax and then what a mighty swooping followed. Oh yes. She had fond memories of her husband and expectations too.

With the prospect of Sir Philip taking charge of his safety, Dominic began to feel better. Earlier, he had spent some time suffering his uninvited hangover. The bathroom where he had sat that Monday morning, incarcerated with an aching head and rebellious stomach, was quite different from the night before – the bath was empty and the candles gutted. On the picnic tray the empty bottle and the peach stones and the crusts of bread showed little of their earlier glamour. The room was filled with sunshine as he tried to expunge from his body the poison that had been funnelled into him the night before.

Tessa ate a huge breakfast, had done exercises and gone out shopping. She had come back with an armful of red roses; the message read 'For services so sweetly rendered'. She brought, too, liver salts and aspirin to put his body to order. They had soup for lunch and walked for a while on the moors – it was time in limbo, the beginning and the end of a love affair, all in one. There was friendship and consideration between them, more thoughts unspoken than not. They were fellow castaways for the day – one of them hoping for a ship to come, the other not.

They made love and dozed and took tea and made love again. And as they did, Dominic began to feel for her that disconcerting pity that only life's victims can solicit. He experienced, too, a most perfidious mirage – in the body of one lover his mind was with another. The ghost of his wife was there again to haunt him even as the girl beneath him was there in the flesh. And as he murmured, 'Oh my darling,' it was Harriet who had him at the crucial moment.

They checked out in the early evening and drove back towards Manchester. Tessa wore her round, thirties sunglasses to keep the sunlight out and the look of desperation in. She chatted easily on the journey with a flippancy she did not feel. If she could be casual, all would be well, she reckoned, but in her diary at the end of the day she knew she'd be recording a different story. For his part Dominic felt a tenderness born of guilt. She had only served to remind him of who he was and what he wanted.

They drove slowly down the street towards the Palace Hotel and pulled in. Dominic looked about for signs of the twins or any other threat.

'See you at the Brunswick then,' Tessa said. 'Don't forget, we've got a technical run-through on Wednesday evening.'

'Oh yes, of course.' Dominic wished he could feel something other than embarrassment and a desire to be gone. 'You going home?'

'Yes, to my mum. I still live at home.' She smiled, 'Perhaps I am retarded after all.'

'No, no not a bit. You're lovely,' he said. And she was. 'Lovely . . . sweet and kind and funny and very sexy.'

'What about you?'

'I'm not so lovely or sweet or kind . . .'

'Where are you going?'

'I don't know . . . home . . . south. . . I don't know.'

He had no idea where the hero is supposed to go during the closing credits . . . into the sunset.

'At any rate you think you're safe now?' Her tone offered the possibility that he had been deluding himself.

'Yes,' he said. 'Pretty well. It's all under control I think. All over bar the shouting. We've just got the show to worry about.'

He looked at her, young and anxious, too easy for him. And he wondered how she would remember him when she was his age.

'I'll call you tomorrow.'

'You don't have to say that.' There was no point in playing hard to get, it was too late in the game for that. 'Give me a kiss anyway.'

He did, a gentle meandering kiss that was going nowhere. They held each other for a while uncomfortably across the handbrake – each of them staring at a different side of the street.

'Drive carefully,' he said and got out of the car.

'You too.' She reached and touched his mouth. A mouth, she reflected as she drove off, that had done so many delicious things except speak what she wanted to hear.

Dominic watched her leaving in the twilight and then turned into the hotel.

'Dominic Gallagher,' he told the receptionist. 'Sir Philip Sullivan is expecting me.' She picked up the house telephone and confirmed that he was.

'Ten-thirty-seven on the top floor,' she said.

On the way up in the mirror of the lift Dominic saw that he looked even older than he thought. His face looked haggard and doleful with all the worry and excess. He knocked on Sir Philip's door and was admitted. Wrong room? Wrong guest? Right room. Wrong guest. He turned too late to leave again.

'Don't move.' The room was in semi-darkness. 'Close the door.'

Dominic obeyed. The voice was unmistakable as was the silhouette of Tristram Brunswick. He advanced to switch on the light. 'You're an elusive little fucker, aren't you?'

Dominic said nothing. Having walked so blithely into such a trap, he needed time to reassess his position. The closing credits weren't rolling quite as smoothly now. Tristram's look of triumph seemed fully justified by the neat black revolver in his hand.

'So, Mr Gallagher,' he said, 'we meet again. No rescue party waiting in the wings this time.'

'Perhaps not.' Dominic's bluff was useless. 'Where's Phoebe? Where is Sir Philip? What have you done with them?'

'Don't you worry yourself about them.' Tristram's tone was smug. The room showed no evidence of a struggle.

'Where are they? What have you done with them?'

'There's no use in shouting,' Tristram told him.

'You can't imagine you'll get away with this.' As he spoke Dominic had the idea that he had often been given lines like this in his early days of television.

'Shut your face, Gallagher. Here are your car keys.' Tristram tossed them to his captive. 'We're going for a little trip.'

271

'You're too late, Tristram.' Dominic tried to sound calm. 'Your whole stinking crooked set-up is already exposed. It's in the hands of the police. You're finished. It doesn't matter what you do to me.'

'Perhaps not. But I can't tell you the pleasure it'll give me.' His lips drew back in their thin smile, his teeth were white as snow. 'We're going to take the lift down to the car park and then you're going to drive me out of town.'

Tristram took from his pocket a silencer and slowly screwed it to the barrel of his revolver.

'I shall be carrying this beside you at all times so don't try anything. None of your heroics, OK?'

Dominic nodded, he was fresh out of heroics.

Tristram draped his leather jacket over the gun. 'Let's go.'

If Dominic thought he looked haggard on the upward journey in the lift, it was nothing compared to the wide-eyed pallor he saw on the downward one. Tristram chewed his lip and watched him with narrow eyes as they walked across the underground car park to the Mercedes.

'Where are we going?' Dominic asked as they pulled into the street. Perhaps he was being taken to join Phoebe and Sir Philip in some sort of captivity.

'You'll see.'

Tristram was angled sideways in the passenger seat and gave instructions as they drove out of town.

The familiarity of his car was the only comfort Dominic had as his mind grappled with its new load. 'You're mad,' he said on impulse. 'You know that.'

'Shut up.'

'Raving. Barking. Howling mad.'

'Shut up.

'OK, OK. Just a bit dippy then. Let's talk it through, shall we?'

'Do as you please, you haven't got long.'

'To live or talk?'

'Either.' Tristram giggled.

Dominic had no wish to die at the hand of so worthless a human being. 'I imagine it all started when Austin died

272

leaving control of the theatres to Phoebe,' he said. 'You just wanted quick money . . . you and your father.'

'We wanted what was ours by rights.'

'You had already been operating the theatre ticket scam . . . Piece of Cake was all set up?'

Tristram nodded. 'A neat little business that. Nice little earner.' He could not resist the boast.

'And one that lent itself to your plan very well in terms of sopping up the shares. All those box office managers obediently following your instructions. But you needed a front man, didn't you? Someone to make the take-over bid look legit. So you got hold of Randal Morton . . . the perfect sucker to make the official running. He did quite well for you, didn't he?'

'He goofed up,' Tristram said, 'trying to put the squeeze on your Mrs . . . that was a mistake.' He did not seem to mind Dominic's curiosity, perhaps he was enjoying it.

'But what really stitched you up,' Dominic was driving along a motorway now, piecing together the story so far, 'was Peter Trevelyan meeting Leo Benson. He broke ranks, didn't he? He spilled the beans to Leo who made the mistake of calling your father to check it out.'

'Thought you were so fucking clever, didn't you?' Tristram lit a cigarette and blew the smoke into Dominic's left profile. 'Pressing the last digit recall and putting on a funny voice.'

So they knew it was him, Dominic pondered and then went on. 'You had to get rid of them, didn't you? A hit-and-run job for Peter Trevelyan but how did you manage Leo's suicide?'

Tristram grinned. 'Roger and Bruce.'

'Roger and Bruce.' Dominic repeated the names which hardly did them justice. 'The twins.'

'Yea. They sorted him out, silly old faggot, with the help of an oxygen mask . . .' Tristram's teeth flashed white as he giggled. 'And one of these.' He waved the gun.

'What about the suicide note?' Dominic asked.

'That was me. I knew the sonnet from school, I had to write it out as a punishment.' Again he giggled. '"When in disgrace with fortune and men's eyes" . . . I sent it with flowers, roses, a nice touch I thought, paid for on the phone by Leo's Barclaycard . . . a cinch.'

'Was the Major supposed to look like suicide too or do you only know the one sonnet?' Dominic regretted his sarcasm as his passenger's spit caught him on the cheek. They drove in silence for a while and Dominic's anger cooled.

'The silly old fart had it coming.' Tristram spoke with pride. 'He knew what was going on, of course. We had him on the payroll, but he went ape-shit when he found out about the development plan.'

'Project West Wind?' Dominic asked. 'He didn't know?'

'He thought it was a straightforward take-over bid, silly old bugger.' Tristram sounded angry at the memory. 'Said he was going to tell Phoebe everything, make a confession and all that.'

'So you had to get the hard disk out of his computer. It had all your names on.' Dominic remembered the Major hanging in the Stalls of the Brunswick with his grey flannels fouled. 'So you put a rope round his neck and stood him on the ladder, at gunpoint I presume?'

'No, arsehole, . . . I just asked him nicely, as a favour.'

'Then you kicked the ladder away and let him hang . . .'

'Yup.' Tristram grinned. 'Silly old bugger was blubbing and pleading. Said he wouldn't tell a soul, said he'd go to South America if I wanted. Silly old bugger.' Poor old Major Kendal.

'What about Randal Morton?' Dominic asked.

'He wasn't too pleased either when he found out what our game was. Very indignant about the Brunswick being developed, said it was blasphemy. Apparently it was you who told him, the toadying little son-in-law, the blue-eyed boy who never learnt when to shut up.'

'No,' Dominic said, 'not even when you took my dog.'

They had turned off the motorway and were driving now on a minor road south-east of the city. Either side of them rolling farmland was etched blue-green in the moonlight.

'Was it you who killed her, my dog?' Dominic asked quietly.

'The twins turned sissy. They wouldn't do it.'

'You shot her?'

'Yup.'

Tristram's monosyllabic reply was a turning point for

274

Dominic. No longer did he feel resigned to whatever lay in store, he wanted to survive and to be revenged. Even with his last breath, he would see the annihilation of this loathsome human being. He clenched the leather binding of the wheel and asked, 'Did she die at once?'

'Let me think now . . .' Tristram exaggerated his thinking. 'Actually I seem to remember she thrashed about a bit and sort of whimpered . . . *don't!*' he rammed the gun into Dominic's neck. He had seen the impulse in his left fist before it left the wheel. 'Don't move. Keep your hands on the wheel, Sunny Jim. You just do as I say. Understand?'

Dominic understood, the cool steel of the muzzle was quite explicit. 'OK, OK,' he apologised. This was not the moment to be foolhardy. 'What I was saying was – you hadn't reckoned on me sticking my nose in.'

'No, we hadn't.' Tristram was calmer now. 'You thought you were so fucking clever, didn't you? Giving out all that bullshit about the bearer shares.'

'Bullshit?' Dominic repeated the word dumbly while his mind raced with implications.

'It was just a heap of crap. Fake. A bluff . . . dreamed up by some wise-arse city pal of yours.'

Dominic felt icy cold. A new realisation was avalanching through his brain.

'We've got him marked out, don't worry,' Tristram went on. 'He seems to have done a bunk for the time being, but we'll get him, your old school pal, don't you worry. The twins'll sort him out. Only they won't screw up this time the way they did with your little friend on the *Sunday Globe*.'

How had he been so stupid, Dominic wondered? How had he managed to stay so resolutely one step behind? If Tristram and his father knew that the bearer share story in all its detail was a charade, there could be only one source of the information. With hindsight the betrayal looked so obvious, the signals had been flashing neon in the one direction he had chosen not to look.

'Sir Philip Sullivan.' He almost whispered the name. He remembered how without a second thought he had given himself away in every particular, how Sir Philip had listened with his air of urbane concern, had reassured him and quietly taken command. 'Leave it to me, dear boy, leave it to me.' The baronet could hardly have believed his luck.

'It's all him,' Dominic said. 'It's all him. Project West Wind . . . "Wild spirit which art moving everywhere. Destroyer and Preserver; hear, oh, hear."'

'But you didn't, did you?' Tristram was enjoying himself. 'You didn't hear, oh hear. You thought you had it all wrapped up, didn't you . . . You were so gullible we couldn't believe it. You stupid sucker . . . Fucker . . .' Tristram was giggling with his superiority.

Dominic couldn't argue, he *was* a sucker. He had been utterly gulled by Sir Philip, conned, cheated, betrayed. Like so many others he had been too readily dazzled by all that charm.

'Phoebe,' Dominic asked in a whisper, 'she doesn't know?'

'Of course not. Silly bitch.'

'She knows nothing? He hasn't told her . . . anything?'

Tristram laughed, treachery was his favourite joke.

Dominic went on. 'Sir Philip never went to the police . . . He has no friend at the serious crime squad? There is no Andy Naylor . . .?'

So Dominic found himself with no trick up his sleeve, no hope of rescue. He felt tired and stupid as he contemplated the backlog of his ignorance.

'What are you going to do with me?' he asked.

'You're going to be disappeared,' Tristram said as if it was obvious. 'Pull in here . . . Pull in,' he ordered.

Dominic slowed down and pulled on to the verge. Tristram turned on the light inside the car and took from his pocket the kit of his addiction. With the gun pressing into Dominic's neck, he unwrapped the cocaine single-handed, prepared it and shifted it into two lines on the flat surface of the dashboard.

'Don't try anything or I'll blow your head off.'

He put the two inch straw to his nose and sniffed in sharply, the left nostril and then the right with a glance at Dominic in between.

'You have to take that stuff to kill people, do you?' Dominic asked. 'Do you need the courage or does it just add to the pleasure?'

'It will in your case, Gallagher. Drive on.'

'Where are we going?'

'You'll see . . . I tell you it'll take more than a crummy piss-pot of an actor to screw up our plans. We're talking big business do you hear. Big. Bigger. Biggest. Do you hear?' Tristram shouted needlessly. 'Do you realise what they are worth, those theatres, in terms of development? Billions. Not just the Brunswick but the Royal at Marlow and the Princess in Manchester. Hundreds of millions. There's nobody, do you hear, nobody can stop us. There's nobody who can't be silenced or bought . . .' He giggled with the new feeling of power that had gone to his head so quickly via his nose. 'The world is a great big shit pile, a great stinking dung heap, do you hear? There's nobody who isn't bent, nobody who can't be bought, bribed, suckered . . . nobody who can stop us doing what we want. And that includes you. Arsehole.'

'You never tried to bribe me.'

'Screw you. Do you hear? You're going to die, die, die.'

Tristram let out a falsetto giggle that struck a new chord of alarm in Dominic. The boy was mad enough in his normal state without the cocaine fanning the flames of his insanity.

'Shall I tell you, Mr Gallagher, what is going to happen?'

'Please do.' The subject had been causing Dominic no small curiosity.

'In a few miles we're going to turn down a track at the end of which there is a long drive which leads to a farmhouse. Quite empty – the owners are on holiday . . . in Lanzarote.' Again he laughed and his teeth flashed phoney white in the darkness. 'It is . . . a pig farm. Hundreds and hundreds of hungry little pigs. Big pigs. Greedy pigs. And they are going to have a bit of a feast . . . a bedtime snack of raw actor, an interfering shit-arse actor, a piss artist, a know-all, a has-been . . . You. You see, Gallagher, they're not fussy, pigs. They'll eat anything.' He cackled again. 'It won't take them long. They're always hungry, pigs. Just think of it, the great Dominic Gallagher gobbled up and gone. *Voilà*. Vanished.'

With his father's funeral so imminent, Dominic had given

277

some thought to the question of burial or cremation. Neither
had appealed to him much but in the face of this alternative
they both looked quite rosy. What happens to the flesh when
its use is over is academic, he told himself. Dust to dust,
ashes to ashes, Gallagher to pigs. He shivered at the thought.

'What do you think of that?' Tristram roared.

'Not strictly kosher,' Dominic answered and received for
his joke a sharp jab in the ribs from the revolver.

'Shut the fuck up. You're going to die.' Tristram spoke
through clenched teeth.

Dominic drove in silence, reviewing his life on his way to
dying. It looked better than he remembered, like the trailer
for an old film worth seeing one more time. He wanted to see
Harriet again. He was on a tightrope that stretched from his
earliest memory into the future – he was only half way
between the two and didn't want to lose his balance; he
wanted to live.

'Turn right . . . Now take the track down there.'

Tristram gave his orders tersely. They were going down a
rough narrow driveway in a valley; on either side of them
were sloping fields with rows of shelters for the pigs like
metallic tombs in the moonlight.

Ahead of them in the beam of the headlamp were farm
buildings – oak-framed brick and flint barns clustered round
a yard. They were reaching a fork in the drive. Dominic
slowed down as Tristram looked about to see the place was
empty. Straight in front of them was a huge Dutch barn
which garaged an array of farm machinery that stood gleaming dully in the light. To the right a gravel drive led to the
front door of the Queen Anne house. Tristram seemed
undecided.

'Follow the drive,' he instructed.

On what impulse Dominic disobeyed he later had no
recollection. But by some instinct he knew that with every
second his chances of escape were narrowing. As he saw it,
his only weapon at the moment was the car; once out of it, in
the open, he would be powerless.

He did not follow the drive. Instead he drove ahead. He

pushed his foot flat on the accelerator. The Silver Strumpet surged forward, her tyres howling in the dirt track.

'What the fuck . . . Stop!' Tristram was shouting. 'Stop!'

Dominic was deaf to the command. He had mutinied and his eyes were focused ahead, peering at the contents of the cavernous barn in front of him. His headlamps revealed a great array of farm equipment, at the back a combine harvester and in front a row of tractors, loaders, bailers, spreaders, etc., like a cage full of neolithic monsters.

They were still gathering speed, charging forward. Tristram was screaming now, too panicked to pull the trigger. And there in front of them, just visible between the plough and the bailer, was the target Dominic had gambled on. Had he seen it at a distance or had he merely hoped to? Either way, there it was ideally placed, parked facing outwards, a JCB teleloader. A huge Massey Ferguson with its prong poised at waist level, a tapering spike, at its widest four inches in diameter and five feet long for the hoisting of four tonne bales. It was pointing straight at them like a great rhinoceros.

With twenty yards to go, Dominic swerved to adjust his aim. Even if Tristram pulled the trigger now he reckoned he would still be revenged. There were people he would rather die with, but what the hell. The car sped on. Ten yards; Tristram, both hands on the dashboard, was screaming wildly with fear. Five yards. Dominic braked. The car lurched a little and slid to the left. Dominic held the wheel firm against the skid and they glided forward dead on course. Tristram's screaming was more desperate now as he recoiled, held tight by the safety belt. Neither man could judge the speed of the impact that was racing towards them in the headlamps. Dominic pumped the brake as hard as he could and the Silver Strumpet shuddered with the rhythm. Both men, strapped firmly in their seats, were suddenly thrust forward by the force of gravity.

The great long spike gleamed darkly for a second before the windscreen exploded inwards. And then with a speed that did not seem excessive the great horn went home puncturing its target. As the Mercedes met the Massey Ferguson radiator to radiator, the sound of the collision served only to silence the final squealing of the man whose life was over.

With the impact Dominic was thrown forward and then back against the head rest. For a moment he sat stupefied like someone awakened from a dream. He was besieged with farm equipment and in the silence he could only hear the noise of metal groaning at its wounds.

Beside him there was no movement. He turned to look at Tristram. His face was frozen with the final moment of his life; there was disbelief in his open eyes and his mouth looked on the point of speaking. There would be no more giggling from him, no more anything. For him there was only the slow leakage of blood that was turning his blue shirt mauve.

Just below Tristram's Adam's apple, the great steel prong shone faintly in the light from the dashboard. He seemed almost disconnected from his body, hoisted and pinioned against the upholstery of the car. Dominic studied the picture, noted the clean penetration of the spike, the steel and the flesh seemed quite suited to one another. And he noted too the accuracy of his aim, for the wound was right in the middle of Tristram's upper chest.

Quite suddenly as if nudged by some unseen hand, Tristram's head fell forward with a thud against the metal that impaled him. Dominic scrambled for the handle of the door, threw it open, and fell gasping and vomiting to the ground. Eventually he rolled over on his back and lay staring at the stars and the great infinity that Tristram was now part of.

'I had no choice. I had no choice. I had no choice,' he whispered to the sky.

Some time later he staggered to his feet. He found a tap and soaked his head in cold water. An owl hooted and the moon cast long shadows across the lawn. He walked about shaking and muttering. He was a novice in these things, a first-time killer. He had no idea where to go, what to do, how to hide the body, and who to trust. In the corner of the nearest field some pigs disturbed from their slumber were rootling quietly, their backs an Aegean blue in the darkness. Dominic watched them, grateful not to be on their menu and pledged that they in turn would no longer be on his.

Steeling himself against another wave of nausea, Dominic got back into the car. He tried not to see the corpse beside him. He started the engine, no damage there at least, and with a trembling hand put the gear lever into reverse. Slowly he eased the car backwards from the teeth of the JCB.

The great steel proboscis slid slowly from its victim, an arm's length of tapering metal smeared with crimson. With this slow withdrawal Tristram's body was freed from its transfixion and fell forward against the safety belt. And as it did, the air forced from his chest made a gurgling sound somewhere in his gaping throat, a sound that somehow echoed the ghastly giggle he had used in life.

Margot Brunswick was not at all disturbed by her son's absence from the breakfast table. She saw him as a young Lothario and took a vicarious pride in the conquests he made. Opposite her Maxwell seemed not to share her peace of mind. Scowling at the *FT*, he seemed anxious and more irritable than usual.

'For goodness sake, Max, he's a big boy. He can look after himself,' she said.

Her husband grunted without looking at her.

'What's wrong?' Margot went on, her mouth full of prunes. 'He's a perfectly normal young man, he can look after himself. He's probably just been out painting the tiles red. And I know where he gets it from,' she nodded knowingly.

'Oh for God's sake woman.' Maxwell rose from his chair glowering at his wife in her turquoise housecoat. With her teeth black with prunes he found the sight of her vexatious. 'It's the town you paint red . . . not the tiles . . . You go out on the tiles. But you paint the town red . . . OK?'

'What?' Margot managed to look puzzled and indignant at the same time.

'There is no such thing, I'm telling you, as red tiles,' he shouted.

Margot knew he was wrong. She had seen them in Habitat, but she said nothing. Maxwell left the room as if he had made his point. Alone in his study he dialled a London number and when his sister-in-law answered he hung up. Phoebe was the last person he wanted to talk to.

'Name?'
'No name'
'We must have your name, sir, just for the record.'
'No name.'
The duty sergeant at Derby Police Station knew when he was beaten. 'Very well, sir,' he said, 'how can I help?'
'Listen carefully,' the caller told him. 'Three and a quarter miles exactly out of Ashbourne on the B5632 to Uttoxeter there is a farm, a pig farm called Three Gates Farm. OK?'
'Yes, sir.' The sergeant reckoned it was another animal rights issue. He had no time for such namby-pamby nonsense.
'In the corner of the furthermost stable under a horse blanket is a body.'
'A body?'
'A corpse.'
'One moment, sir . . .' The sergeant uncrossed his legs, leant forward with urgency. 'A corpse, you say?'
'Yes. It is the corpse of Tristram Brunswick. His parents live in Berkshire and their telephone number is Bagshot two-two-three-seven. Have you got that?'
'Yes sir . . . Yes sir.' The sergeant's pen had dried up, so too had his mouth. '. . . two-two-three-seven,' he repeated. 'And, er, can you tell me . . . did the gentleman die of natural causes?'
'No, he did not. As you will see . . . He was killed in self defence.'
'By you, sir?' the sergeant croaked.
'No name. That's all. Goodbye.'
Dominic hung up and lay back on the bed, pleased that he had decided in favour of the anonymous course of action. Had he confessed in person he would surely have been detained in custody – perhaps certified insane. His first priority was to protect Phoebe, a difficult task for her head was resting all too willingly in the lion's mouth. His second priority was to make sure that the tracks Sir Philip had so thoroughly
282

covered were exposed again, exposed beyond doubt for all to see.

For both these reasons Dominic knew he needed not just his liberty but a head start in taking the initiative. He was dealing with no common or garden crook, no simple belt and braces conman. Sir Philip was not an opportunist criminal, he was a shrewd and wily man who planned things meticulously in advance and left nothing to chance. He was the instigator of Project West Wind – "the wild spirit which art moving everywhere". Dominic loathed him most of all for having abused his trust. For this and all the rest he had a score to settle and he chose to settle it single-handed. There could be no more allies now, this was a revenge he had to manage alone.

All this he had worked out in the moonlit yard of Three Gates Farm. With the strength and purpose of his new resolve, he wrapped the still warm body of his enemy in a blanket and dragged it out of sight. He closed Tristram's eyelids with difficulty, and left the revolver fully loaded in his hand. (He'd see it again as Exhibit 'A' he didn't doubt.)

The Mercedes had lost a headlamp in her meeting with the JCB, her radiator was dented, and the windscreen, of course, was smashed, but for Dominic's purposes she was roadworthy. He had fetched water and a rag and wiped clean the passenger seat. He had even managed a makeshift repair on the punctured leather upholstery. With the night air blowing freely through his battered Silver Strumpet he left the farm and drove north. He was on the run, not just from the bad guys but also from the police. With the disadvantage of what the tabloids called 'a household name' and a face known to millions, he found his choice of bolt-hole was limited. So on impulse he called the hotel where he had spent the night before with Tessa.

The drive had taken him just over an hour. He parked the car in the furthest corner of the car park and took from the boot the only luggage he could lay hands on – his father's Gladstone bag. The same oblivious night porter led him to the self-same room and later brought him the same variety of sandwiches. The hot bath he took seemed quite different, and again it was dawn before he fell asleep, this time alone.

Dominic poured himself more coffee, picked up the telephone and dialled a London number. He heard it ringing only twice and then:

'Hello.' Sir Philip's voice was unmistakable; smooth and quiet with its impatience well hidden. 'Hello. Hello . . . Hello. Who is it? Who is it . . .? Hello.'

Dominic hung up. Some other way would have to be found of communicating with his mother-in-law. It was obviously in Sir Philip's interest to intercept her calls; her ignorance and trust were vital to him. He would no doubt be vigilant in his guarding of her, and subtle. For a while Dominic pretended to himself he didn't know the answer. From his window he watched his car being repaired – a new windscreen and headlamp; the dents would have to wait. He had no alternative, he told himself; he picked up the telephone and dialed his wife's Fulham number.

'Where the hell are you?' was the greeting she gave him. 'Everybody is going mad looking for you.'

'I'm in hiding,' he said.

'Where?'

'It doesn't matter.'

'Have you been on the booze?'

If anyone knew the symptoms she did.

'No,' he answered. 'Not a drop has touched my lips.'

The funnel had bypassed his mouth, the vodka had gone directly down his throat.

'Listen,' he said, 'I'm in trouble. I've killed a man . . .'

'What . . .?'

'I've killed Tristram.'

There was a pause. Dominic could picture her calmly digesting the information – could hear the soft exhalation of her breath.

'Tell me about it,' she said.

Dominic did so with as much detail as he thought necessary.

Harriet muttered, 'God Almighty,' from time to time and when he finished she said in disbelief, 'It can't be true . . .

284

You mean Sir Philip had planned it all . . . The whole thing is him?'

'Yes,' Dominic said.

'The bastard . . . The great, stinking, rotten bastard.' Harriet's invective carried with it all the vehemence that Dominic remembered so well. 'What about Mum?' she asked suddenly.

'That's why I rang. That's why I want your help.'

Dominic explained the need to get Phoebe away from under her lover's nose, out of earshot so that she could be told the truth about him. They both dreaded the pain this final betrayal would cause her.

'Oh dear . . . Poor Mum,' Harriet said. 'Poor, poor Mum. I think she rather loves him.'

'I'm sure she does,' Dominic said, 'but I think she's in danger, so you'd better find some way of getting her out of there.'

'OK . . . What about you?'

'I'm going to go to the police – I'll call you later . . . You will be careful, won't you?'

'Sure,' Harriet answered. She took for granted the concern that was not in his voice. 'You too.'

'These guys are bad . . . I mean wicked,' he said. 'If what's his name is there, I'd take him with you.'

'Greg,' she said. The faked amnesia about his name cut no ice with Harriet.

'Greg,' Dominic conceded. 'Take him with you.'

'He's gone,' she said.

'Gone?'

'Gone. Left. Departed. I've booted him out.We are no longer together . . . OK?'

'I'm sorry,' Dominic tried to sound it.

'No, you're not.'

'Yes, I am sorry for you . . . That's what I meant. I'm sorry if you're unhappy . . . That's all.'

'I'm not.'

'OK.' Dominic thought better of any further comment.

'Mum tells me you were great on Sunday night . . .'

'Yea . . . it seemed to be all right. Perhaps you'll come to the first night.' It wasn't an invitation, just a remark.

'Perhaps I will,' she replied.

'I'll call you later then . . .'

'Yea . . .'

'Be careful . . .'

'You too.'

'Bye.'

'Bye.' She hung up.

Dominic stared at the telephone as he tried to recall which Terence Rattigan play had been described by Kenneth Tynan as 'the failure of two people to agree on a definition of love'. It was time for him to be going, to turn himself in. It was time to go south.

Before leaving he used a razor and a toothbrush from his father's Gladstone bag. All his things from the theatre had been neatly packed on Sir Philip's instruction. As Dominic went to replace them he was reminded of the love letters that he had not had a chance to finish reading. There they were, still neatly bound in two piles. Dominic took them out and sat in the armchair by the window. As with the pile he had read at the theatre, the letters were all addressed to Griffith Gallagher, the first had been sent to the Theatre Royal Newcastle. There had evidently been a lapse in the communication for it was dated some six years later. It read:

'Dearest Griff. What a perfectly marvellous afternoon we had. I can think of no more perfect introduction to the theatre for a small boy than a trip to see Peter Pan and then to have tea backstage with the ferocious Captain Hook. You were splendid by the way, as ever – terrifying as Hook and adorable as Mr Darling . . . Poor little Pip, he's something of a lost boy himself I'm afraid, as I think you realised. At any rate he is a dreamer. It wasn't easy for me watching you take him by the hand and show him round. Horror of horrors, on the way home he said he wished his daddy was an actor . . . But seriously though, dear Griff, we must not meet again – it was my mistake and I'm sorry. On reflection I have decided that it would be crazy to meet for lunch next week for we both know that one lunch leads to another and my resolve is as always only paper thin . . . Oh why can't you be married or dead or abroad or somehow beyond my reach, out of temptation . . . Life with Archie doesn't get any easier, not that I deserve a bed of roses. Sometimes I think he actually hates me, of course though he dotes on his son and heir . . . Dear Griff, we must be strong, mustn't we? Thank you again for a magical afternoon in Never-Never Land. With much love as always, Charlotte. P.S. Against my better judgement I am enclosing a photograph of Pip as requested. It was taken at Glencoe last Christmas. Hasn't he got your smile? Yrs. C.'

Dominic held the small black and white photograph to the light. There was snow on the ground and the little boy with no front teeth was squinting at the camera with his head on one side. He wore a duffel coat, hunting cap and plus fours and in the foreground hunched towards him was the shadow of a proud parent with a box Brownie.

Dominic stared long and hard at the not quite focused face. Charlotte was wrong, he could see no likeness of his father's smile. He looked at the photograph of this grinning changeling halfway up Glencoe and could feel no fraternity, no jealousy, no sibling kinship. It was for quite a different recognition that Dominic peered at the picture of little Pip . . . Pip . . . Philip. Like it or not, there was no mistaking that the photograph shaking in his hand was of Sir Philip Sullivan, Bart, his older brother.

There were three more letters from Charlotte to Griffith; they were written some years later and sent to different addresses in West London. Dominic read them carefully, whispering their contents out loud so that his ears could confirm what his eyes saw. His heart was pounding in his chest. He read them again and again and then sat shivering in the sunlight as their full meaning fell into place.

21

Phoebe paced about smoking while Sir Philip sat in a chair with studied tranquillity. From time to time he tried to reassure her but she was filled with foreboding.

'I'll take it, my dear,' Sir Philip said as yet again the telephone rang. 'Hello.'

'Philip, it's me, Maxwell. I've got to talk to you,' said an anxious voice.

The baronet answered with his usual urbane courtesy, 'I think you must have a wrong number. I'm sorry,' and hung up. When it rang again he answered it more tersely.

'Hi, Sir Philip, is my mum there?' Harriet asked.

'Of course. I'll pass you to her,' he said and handed Phoebe the receiver.

'Hello, my darling – no news?' she asked. 'You haven't heard from him?'

'No, I'm afraid not,' Harriet answered. 'Mum, I need to see you . . . I've got something I want to tell you. It's urgent.'

'Why don't you come round here for lunch with us?' Phoebe offered.

'I want to see you alone, Mum. I want to talk to you.'

'Are you all right?'

'I'm fine.' Harriet was forced to play her trump card. 'The thing is, I think you're going to be a granny.'

'A granny . . . You're going to have a baby? Oh my darling, my darling . . . Congratulations. When? Oh my darling . . .' Tears were running down her cheeks. 'I'm coming right away. Don't move . . . I'll be there before you can say knife.'

She hung up and in five minutes was on her way to Fulham. Alone.

As Harriet had reckoned, Sir Philip made no attempt to stop her or accompany her – this was women's business, a

288

special time for mother and daughter to be together. He offered her the use of his chauffeur and kissed her goodbye with his usual affection. He smiled at her, holding her face between his hands. 'You a granny,' he said with a parody of disbelief.

When Phoebe had gone the telephone rang again and he snatched at it, this time with an open show of tension and no smile on his face.

'Yes.'

'Just to let you know,' his caller whispered down the line, 'that the Derbyshire police have found the body of Tristram Brunswick at Three Gates Farm.'

'Tristram,' he said, suppressing the shock perfectly. 'I see.' And then the line went dead.

For some time he sat back in his chair with his hands folded and his eyes closed like a man in a trance. It had to be faced, the writing was on the wall. He ignored the telephone when it rang again. With a slow deliberation he poured himself a drink, wrote a short letter addressed to Phoebe Brunswick which he left on the mantelpiece, took a set of keys from her desk and then quietly made his exit.

Dominic had not driven south. Instead he had spent the afternoon heading north to Scotland, the M6 to Carlisle, the M74 to Glasgow. The roads were busy with holiday traffic, but he made good time. By late afternoon he was on the A82 skirting the western side of Loch Lomond. The water looked dark and listless in the heat, not a day for fishing. He telephoned ahead to the editor of the *Oban Herald* and arrived at the office in time to spend an hour in the library going through all the cuttings he required.

Lady Sullivan was still alive, he found, long since widowed and in her early eighties. She lived alone with a skeleton staff in the family home, Brachameda, on the northern edge of Glenochy Forest. The estate was poorly managed and the life she led was by and large reclusive. In 1981 she had been diagnosed as suffering from Parkinson's disease and now required full-time nursing. According to the reports she was seldom visited by her only son, the business tycoon Sir Philip Sullivan, and she no longer took part in local matters.

The most recent photographs of Lady Sullivan were twenty-five years old. They were taken at all kinds of functions: cattle shows, the launching of life boats, children's fêtes, and hospital visits. They showed a delicate, smiling woman in her middle years, always in a headscarf or a hat – a kind face that was probably more beautiful in repose; a face that gave no hint of all the sadness in her most private life. Beside her in some of the early pictures was a portly tweeded figure with a handlebar moustache – Sir Archibald Sullivan, Bart.

Dominic dialled the number of the family seat some thirty miles away. It rang for a long time before a voice announced 'Brachameda' in the deep and fruity tone of a retainer.

With the utmost deference and tact Dominic explained who he was. 'I'm in Oban at the moment and if it were possible I would be most grateful if Lady Sullivan could see me.'

'You wish to call on Her Ladyship?'

'Yes, right away if possible.'

'This evening?' The butler's disbelief was manifest.

'Yes, it's on a matter of some urgency.' Dominic sensed his persuasion was lost.

'Mr Gallagher, I have to tell you that Lady Sullivan has not received a visitor for over . . .'

'If you could mention,' Dominic interrupted, 'that I am the son of the late Griffith Gallagher . . . I would be most grateful.' His tone implied that his gratitude might have a monetary endorsement.

'Yes, very well, sir,' came the reply. 'If you'll hold the line . . .'

And hold the line he did, for quite some time. Dominic stared out of the window of the editor's office. The fishing boats were chugging slowly up the Firth of Lorn, their colours vivid against the flatness of the sea. Dominic watched and envied them the commonplace pleasure of returning home in the evening. He was so far beyond reality it seemed unimaginable.

'Lady Sullivan,' he was told, 'will see you at seven-thirty, sir. We shall be expecting you.' His tone carried all the warmth of an invitation to the House of Usher.

An hour later Dominic was driving through the wrought iron gates of the house. What the sign lacked in ornamental detail, it made up for in solid weight: 'BRACHAMEDA – STRICTLY PRIVATE. KEEP OUT.' He followed the drive over several cattle grids and upwards through dense pine trees. He crossed a burn with its brown water tumbling brightly to his right and pulled into the forecourt of the house itself. Brachameda was a steeply gabled building of plain granite situated on a shelf cut into the hill side. The garden in front of the house was terraced down to the edge of the Loch and showed no signs of husbandry. The flower beds were full of unruly delphiniums and the lawn had been conquered by dandelion and thistle.

In the open doorway was the figure of a large man in a morning coat. 'Mr Gallagher?' the butler asked in his deep Celtic tone.

'Yes.' Dominic felt ridiculously underdressed in Professor Higgins's trousers and the new shirt he had bought at a filling station.

'Welcome to Brachameda, sir. Please come in.'

He led the way into the hall. It was dimly lit and the dank air carried a vague aroma of gun oil and old leather. The floors were flagstone and the walls panelled. In the distance Dominic could hear the title music of *Coronation Street* to add to the surrealism.

'Follow me. Milady wishes to see you directly.' From his tone it was clear that the family retainer found such an idea quite extraordinary, if not repugnant. 'As you may be aware, sir, Milady is not in good health. She is quite infirm at present and her speech is not always that easy to understand.'

Dominic followed him down a dark corridor lined with hunting trophies – a gauntlet of glass-eyed stags with dust gathering on their antlers. The drawing room was long and narrow with three huge mullioned windows overlooking the loch and the hills beyond. It was a thoroughly cluttered room, the walls were crammed with paintings, watercolours all askew and shelves piled with bric-à-brac, china objects (dogs mostly) and magazines. Everywhere there were vases of

291

flowers – gladioli, sweet peas, lilies, blood-red roses. Some had shed their petals and their scent was past its prime. The sound of the television blared out from behind a screen at the other end of the room.

'Mr Gallagher, Your Ladyship,' the butler shouted over the noise of the Rover's Return.

Dominic advanced down the length of the room into the old lady's line of vision. Lady Charlotte was lying in a hospital bed, propped up by a great bank of pillows – a frail, quivering figure with consternation in her deep-set eyes.

'Ah . . . Ah . . . Nice . . . Nice . . .' she greeted him. Her voice like the hand she waved in his direction, was distorted with her ailment. 'How do you, how do you – how do you do . . .? Gideon,' she turned to the butler. 'Fetch him . . . Fetch him whisky . . . or gin . . . it's not quite dark is it . . .?'

'A cup of tea, please,' Dominic said.

'Tea?' she screeched over the sound of the soap opera. 'Tea, Gideon, tea . . . Have you eaten? Food . . . Gideon. Things to eat. Fetch. Perhaps he'll stay for, for, for . . . the weekend. It's not the week, week, weekend, is it? Make . . . make up a bed . . . Yes, yes . . . And tell Phyllis to make soup, Gideon . . . And make the nurse come, come, come to see me . . . Go, go on.'

'Very good, Your Ladyship.' Gideon nodded, quite undisturbed by the vagaries of her speech and left the room.

'Well, well, well,' she said when Gideon had left. Her whole body was shaking to some gentle motor out of sight. Only in her eyes was there any stillness. 'Don't worry about strange sp . . . sp . . . speaking voice. Horrid, yes?' Her mouth jerked into a smile as she waved him to a wing chair. She fumbled with the remote control and stabbed the television to silence. Her disease was like being in quicksand she told him. 'Who cares about dying?' she said, waving a puppet's hand in the air.

When Dominic told her that his father had died she whispered his name to herself again and again and then touched her lips to remind herself of the silence she had kept so long. 'Very like him. You.' She pointed at Dominic with the agitated finger of a dowser.

292

Dominic took the bundles of love letters from his pocket and gave them to her. She held them in her quivering hands for some time without looking at them. 'So you know,' she said quietly.

Dominic nodded. Yes he knew, not much. He was thinking of the cruel way time leaves its mark on people. Not long ago this trembling old woman and his father had been smooth-skinned and agile together.

'Oh we had some wonderful times.' She put out her hand for him to hold. 'He was a love . . . love . . . lovely man.' Her blue eyes flooded with tears that hung heavily in her lashes before rolling down her face. Her hand between Dominic's was like a small animal in spasm. 'Oh dear oh dear oh dear,' was all she could say. Nostalgia and her wretched ailment were rendering her quite incoherent now. She pointed at the bottle of champagne beside her bed and then at the plastic cup, a beaker for one-year-olds with a special mouthpiece. Her meaning was clear, Dominic poured her drink and helped her hold it to her lips. She smelt of roses musty and sweet the way they are in the evening. She dribbled a little then belched.

'You want . . . want . . . want to know something . . . Yes, yes, yes.' Her voice was pitiful. Dominic was in despair for there was no way she could possibly release whatever secrets she held.

'Yes.' Was his mission that transparent? 'I want to know something.'

'It's . . . Ph . . . Phil . . . Philip, isn't it? Little Pip,' she croaked.

'Yes,' he answered, 'it's about your son.'

Charlotte rang for the nurse and demanded extra medicine. 'My w . . . w . . . wonder dr . . . drug . . . stop me w . . . w . . . wobbling for . . . a . . . while. Make . . . make sense,' she explained. In her hands she was still clutching the letters she had written sixty years ago.

'Dear oh dear,' she said. 'Little Pip . . . Bad boy.' She was gurgling, her mouth full of unwanted saliva. 'A n . . . n . . . naughty . . . boy.'

Dominic was in no doubt about it as he went upstairs to have his bath.

Sir Philip's answering machine had repeated many times that afternoon that he was unavailable. Under pressure, his manservant announced that he did not expect Sir Philip home for a few days and his private secretary said she had the impression he had gone abroad. For those who sought him he had vanished.

The Nova Hotel was ideal for banquets, weddings, conferences and seminars. It was situated just outside Derby's ring road; it had 'plentiful parking', a health and fitness club, a Greek Taverna in the basement and multilingual presentation technology. But it offered no facility for bereavement; it couldn't help with grief and had no comfort of that kind to offer.

Maxwell and Margot Brunswick had been escorted there and checked in by Detective Superintendent Merrick, the man in charge of the investigation of their son's murder. He was a softly spoken man who had done his best to make things as painless as possible for them.

'Please don't hesitate to call me – at no matter what time, if there's anything I can do for you,' he had said. 'And also, of course, if there is anything you can think of that we should know.'

Even under a heavy dosage of sedative Margot was beyond consoling. She lay on the bed clutching her stomach. 'My baby,' she wailed, 'my baby.'

Maxwell sat for a long time staring out of the window at the double-glazed gardens; he, too, ached with the sadness of his loss, not just the loss of his son and heir but of his partner in crime. Tristram had been their golden boy. Maxwell had tried again and again to reach Sir Philip without success. He sat with his head in his hands and searched his mind. He was blind with misery and confusion and the idea that he had been abandoned or betrayed. His ambition was gone now, he had nothing to lose. So perhaps the time had come to cut his losses.

294

'Why oh why oh why?' Margot moaned from the bed like someone in delirium.

Maxwell shook his head in silence, he knew the answer to her question. Yes, the time was coming to set the record straight. He poured himself another whisky and drank it undiluted. He dialled the number of the local CID.

'I want to speak to Detective Superintendent Merrick,' he said and when he answered, 'I've got something I want to tell you.'

The time had come.

The martini that Harriet had mixed for her mother was intended to sooth and to celebrate. It was for the soothing of a heart not so much broken as badly bruised by the ending of a love affair, and for the celebration of a new life still eight months away.

Phoebe had reverted to her native tongue to express her revised feeling for Sir Philip Sullivan. When Harriet told her the full details of his treachery, she cried a little and cursed a lot, not at the loss of a lover but rather at her own folly, her own misjudgement of his character. Later though she changed to the opinion that she had suspected him all along.

'I'll tear the balls off him. I'll see him hanged. He'll rot in hell.'

On the subject of her grandchild though she was ecstatic. 'It's the most wonderful news I have had in ages. You clever clever darling girl.' She hugged her daughter. 'And to think I thought you and Dom were not even on speaking terms.'

'I told you, Mum, we had lunch together.'

'Lunch?' Phoebe echoed. It was not a biological query. She knew about lunch. 'And you haven't told him yet?'

'Mother,' she used the formal title to silence Phoebe, 'you keep your nose out of it. I don't want him back on those terms. OK?'

'OK,' she answered and they sat in silence for a while waiting for the man in question to arrive or call. Sir Philip made no effort to contact them and they saw no sign of the dreaded twins.

On the *Six O'Clock News* it was announced that the body

of Tristram Brunswick had been found on a farm in Derbyshire. There were no details but the police confirmed they were treating the case as a murder enquiry. The photograph the BBC displayed of the deceased was not that recent and showed the face of a young boy smiling but already acquisitive.

'He was never right, that boy,' Phoebe said, 'a conniving little charlatan, rotten to the core, like his father.' She blew out smoke towards the screen and added, 'Poor Margot . . . Poor, dear, silly Margot. It'll break her heart.'

The detective sergeant who called to see them was of the old school, deferential and slow-witted. He stood awkwardly in Harriet's sitting room while her cat brushed itself repeatedly against his leg. 'No thanks, Madam,' he would have no tea, no martini either. It seemed he was making enquiries into the death of Tristram Brunswick and the disappearance of Sir Philip Sullivan.

'Sir Philip?' Mother and daughter showed their surprise.

'Have either of you seen the gentleman?'

'No,' Phoebe answered, 'not since this morning. Why?'

The policeman changed his mind about just one small glass of beer. 'Well it seems,' he revealed, 'that subsequent to an extensive interview with Maxwell Brunswick, the father of the deceased, the detectives on the case are now extremely keen to talk to Sir Philip Sullivan. He's in it up to here apparently.' He indicated a depth that came to his prolific eyebrows. 'And as far as we can make out, he's done what you call a bunk.'

'I see,' said Phoebe. 'Well I hope you catch him . . . Do you think he's left the country?'

'Possibly, Madam – there's no saying what he might be planning. He's not what you'd call your average criminal, is he?'

'No . . . he's not that,' Phoebe said. Nor an average man either.

'And we are, of course, still looking for your husband, Mrs Gallagher, in connection with the case.' The policeman seemed ill at ease.

'Oh really?'

'Yes. You haven't heard from him by any chance?'

'Not for a while,' Harriet looked down. 'Actually we're separated, you see.'

'They didn't tell me, Madam, I'm sorry,' he said. The cat was still weaving in and out between his legs.

The telephone rang at Harriet's elbow and she had no choice but answer.

'Hello,' she said rather fiercely.

'Hi, it's me, Dom,' came the reply.

'Oh, Beryl, hello,' said Harriet cosily. 'How are you? I was on the point of calling you, dear Beryl.'

'You can't talk, right?'

'Exactly. Yes, isn't it gorgeous?'

'Look, I shan't be home tonight, something's cropped up. I'll be in London tomorrow. I'm sorry I can't explain . . .'

'Never mind,' Harriet giggled.

'Have you got your mother with you?' he asked.

'Yes, yes. Absolutely.'

'Brilliant. Well done. How did you manage it?'

'You know – girl's talk.'

'How is she?' he asked.

'Oh fine, fine . . . Not too bad,' Harriet looked across at her mother, 'considering.'

'What about Sir Philip?' Dominic asked.

Harriet thought for a moment then let out a light-hearted laugh. 'Completely disappeared.'

'Disappeared?'

'Completely. It's wonderful stuff, I'll send you some,' she said.

'Oh I see. He's done a runner?'

'Yes . . . I should think so.'

'Look, for God's sake be careful, won't you,' Dominic whispered.

'You too, Beryl,' she said and then went on in the tone of a gossip. 'I say, did you see the news? Apparently Tristram Brunswick has been murdered . . .'

'Christ,' said Dominic.

'Exactly,' said Harriet. 'And guess what? I've had the police round here looking for Dominic . . .'

'Me?'

'You know – my old man. They're here now actually.' She wrinkled her nose at the sergeant.

'Christ Almighty.'

'No, not bigamy this time, my dear,' she giggled. 'They want to question him about the murder. Apparently Maxwell ... that's the boy's father, has been spilling some very interesting beans ...'

Harriet looked at the sergeant who was shaking his head at her indiscretion.

'Oh really?' Dominic was saying.

'Yes. Actually you'd better keep it under your hat ...'

'I will. I will,' Dominic said. 'Look I'll call back later if I can.'

'Yes,' said Harriet. 'That'd be nice. Where from?'

'I can't tell you. Look ... With Sir Philip on the loose, perhaps it would be better if you both went down to the cottage. It might be safer there ... Who knows what kind of maniac we're dealing with? Or what he might do.'

'Goodness me, yes,' Harriet answered in a scandalised tone, 'That might be the answer ... Look I must fly. Take care, poppet.'

'You too, for God's sake.'

'Bye bye, Beryl. Speak soon.'

Harriet hung up. Not for nothing had she won prizes at drama school for improvisation.

On his way back to Headquarters Detective Sergeant Pool came to the conclusion that he'd given out more information than he had taken in, and later he spent some time with sticky tape removing cat's hair from his trousers.

Mother and daughter packed up their things and left for Sussex. Harriet drove and Phoebe kept a lookout – not a twin in sight.

'Come and sit down and have your soup while it's hot.'

Charlotte's voice was fluent and clear, slightly like someone on the verge of tears. Dominic was unable to hide his amazement.

'My wonder pill ... Lerodopa, isn't it brilliant? I'm a

complete junky,' she giggled. 'It eases the dyskinesia, that's all the shaking – mouth, head, hands, etc., but the thing is it's not good for my dodgy old heart so the dosage is rather limited. Nurse Pasco is usually very strict but I made her give me an extra pill . . . I can go without in the morning. We'd better be quick, though. I'm afraid they don't last long.' She gave a little laugh that was almost girlish and waved him to a chair.

A table for one had been laid beside Charlotte's bed and candles had been lit. Dominic sat down as bidden, he was determined to put from his mind all the news he had just garnered from his wife. If Charlotte was in the mood to talk, had dosed herself especially for the purpose, he would be foolish not to listen.

Gideon had shown him upstairs to a guest room that stank of disuse, the *Horse and Hound* beside his bed was six years out of date and his tepid bath water was the colour of brandy. The telephone he had been allowed to use was in the gun-room off the hall. Surrounded by hunting miscellany, he had spoken to his wife and heard of the day's developments, it was a conversation that seemed to have not even a foothold in reality. He realised full well that his place was with them in Fulham. He should be there to protect his wife and her mother, not in the Highlands unravelling his father's past.

It was a relief, of course, to know that Maxwell had made a full confession but the idea that Sir Philip had now taken flight filled him with alarm. It struck him in passing as ironic that both the sons of Griffith Gallagher were officially on the run. He had hung up with a feeling of deep unease – a very worried Beryl.

'Champagne?' Charlotte offered, she was holding hers in a glass now.

'No thanks,' Dominic answered.

Darkness was creeping up the hills opposite and the loch had already taken on the patina of the moon from behind the house.

'You're very like him, your father, better looking actually.'

She studied him with her head on one side. 'He must have been very proud of you.'

A pride that was never shown. 'In his own way I suppose he was,' Dominic said.

'I still dream about him from time to time . . . when I'm lucky.'

She smiled and Dominic could see the beauty in her face. Her skin was like crumpled silk that sagged a little under her chin and her lips were puckered with eighty years' use. The powder blue of her eyes was undiminished either side of a fine nose. Free from the ghastly tremors of her disease, it was a face that held its beauty well.

'Oh it was a madcap, wonderful affair . . . he was so gentle and funny and oh dear me . . . he quite turned my head.'

Dominic remembered the indecision in her letters – the strength and the weakness side by side, and the pathetic quote from Dowson. Her days of wine and roses were long gone now.

'I was quite torn in two . . . Archie was a moderately kind man . . . dull and drunken but dependable. And he *was* my husband. And Griff . . . your Dad was . . . too . . . I don't know . . . spectacular. I loved him too much . . . the kind of love that has you on the rack.' She was sitting upright in her bed among a bank of pillows, reliving the old pain. 'I hadn't really got the courage to be what they called 'a bolter' – Archie wanted an heir and the baby needed a future . . . so . . . What do you do?'

It was a rhetorical question as old as man.

'But you kept in touch with Dad?' Dominic asked.

'It wasn't easy . . . of course I followed his career in the papers . . . I saw the photographs of him and your mother at their wedding . . . And you, when you were born . . . it wasn't easy.'

Dominic could see from her face that it couldn't have been. She sipped her champagne and let the focus of her memory slip back half a century.

'He was a funny child, little Pip,' she said. 'I never quite knew how to handle him . . . a strange boy.'

'In what way?' Dominic asked gently, for no matter how vile the chick the mother hen needs careful handling.

Charlotte sighed. 'Perhaps it would have been different if he had had a brother or sister. He was a solitary sort of boy . . . serious. Sullen really. And he had this wicked temper . . . oh the tantrums . . . I couldn't cope with them at all. He was very affectionate of course. He loved to sit on my lap. I used to read to him and he'd stroke my hair . . .

She paused at the memory, and then went on. 'Archie was marvellous with him . . . but oh, you've no idea of the guilt I used to feel watching the two of them together fishing or playing chess or whatever.

Again she paused and Dominic drank his soup in silence – he did not want to spoil her train of thought; with breathing space secrets came out of their own accord.

'He was very fond of his father but it was me he loved . . . you understand. At least he did then before . . . before he found out . . .'

'How did that happen? How did he find out?'

'By chance of course . . . His father died when Pip was fifteen and a couple of years later he had to have a blood test or something. The doctors thought he might have picked up hepatitis or whatever and for some reason he got it into his head to check his blood grouping against his father . . . And of course it didn't match . . . Oh it was dreadful, he just went for me, shouting and screaming. I thought he was going to throttle me . . . Sometimes I wish he had. It's funny, I remember thinking, if this is a love child, God help us.'

Dominic had read the details of the incident in one of her letters to his father . . .

'Oh my dear Griff, you have no notion of how petrified I was. I'm afraid he demanded to know your name and I was unable to refuse him. I am so sorry. Please God he will recover his senses soon but at the moment I fear his curiosity might drive him to paying you a visit. I realise of course that this must be the last thing you want at the moment with your son barely a year old and I

hate the idea of compromising things between
you and your wife.'

'And did he?'

'What?' Charlotte seemed distracted.

'Did he visit Dad?'

'Oh . . . no. Not straight away . . .'

'What was it that brought him and Griff together then?'
Dominic asked. 'You wrote in one letter about a meeting . . .
a favour he had done or something . . .'

Charlotte looked at him with her great pale eyes the colour
of faded mosaic, she studied him for a while without
expression.

'Must you know?'

Dominic nodded. 'Yes.'

He had to know. The worst, darkest dread of his imagin-
ation had to be put beyond all doubt. True or false, he had
come too far to go back empty-handed. He had finished eating
now and sat forward waiting for her to speak. She patted his
hand and sighed.

'I don't really know what the truth is or was.'

She looked deathly forlorn in the candlelight.

'It's so often irrelevant, don't you think, the truth? It's just
a choice you make . . . the lesser of two evils. Who cares about
the truth if some kind of falsehood is easier to live with.' She
sounded quite vehement in this justification of her credo. 'All
right then,' she said after a brief pause. 'Philip was eighteen,
handsome, you know, clean cut, athletic, quite intelligent.
But he had this serious, sort of inscrutable side to him.' She
lifted her glass and drank, then drew the crocheted shawl
tighter round her shoulders and went on. 'I remember the
telephone ringing in the middle of the night. It was Philip
calling from London somewhere; he was in a terrible state
. . . He said he was in some kind of trouble . . . a misunder-
standing to do with a girl . . . Some dancer he had picked up.
God knows what had gone on but he said the police were
after him. And he said he didn't want them making trouble
for the family and so forth . . . As if he really gave a damn.
Anyway, he said he needed someone to help him out . . . I

302

suggested he call the family solicitors and he said not to be bloody stupid, this was serious. And then he seemed to hit upon the idea of Griffith . . . said it was his responsibility to help protect his little bastard and wasn't it all his fault anyway.' Charlotte frowned with an old puzzlement. 'He sounded rather desperate and impatient, I didn't really understand . . . anyway I gave him Griffith's address. What could I do up here . . .? I had no choice.'

Her voice carried a plea for understanding. For a moment she seemed to have lost her drift, waylaid by, some other reflection.

'Go on,' Dominic urged gently. His heart was pounding with a kind of vertigo, he was on the brink of what he feared.

'Oh yes,' Charlotte collected herself. 'Well, the two of them got together. I don't know the ins and outs of it but I gather Griff sorted it all out . . . There was some talk about an identity parade . . . and this girl pressing charges or something and Griff managed to persuade her not to . . . not to do it. To let it drop . . . So the police had no case. That's it.'

It was clear to see that she wished it was as simple as that.

'What was the charge?' Dominic could not let go now.

'I can't remember . . . it was something to do with bodily harm I think.' Charlotte gave an imperceptible shiver. 'The girl's name was Rita.'

Dominic could see that the old lady was reluctant to revisit the memory any further. He asked as softly as he could, 'What had he done to her?'

'Does it matter?' she whispered.

'Yes.'

'Of course.' Charlotte stared into the candle that was flickering beside her bed. 'That's why you're here, isn't it?'

Dominic nodded. 'Yes it is.'

'Oh God,' she murmured, then took a breath. 'Well . . . according to your father, Philip was supposed to have somehow drugged this girl, this Rita, and while she was . . . unconscious . . .' Charlotte faltered with shame on her son's behalf, 'he apparently . . .'

'What?'

'Shaved her,' the words were barely audible, '. . . all over. And when she woke up . . .'

Dominic noticed that she had begun to shake again and wondered cruelly how much longer her coherence would hold out against the rapacious Parkinson's.

'When she woke up . . . what?' he prompted.

'When she woke up . . . she found that he was trying to do something . . .' she took a breath to whisper, 'surgical.' She covered her mouth with her hands.

Dominic looked away to avoid seeing her anguish. 'He was trying to sew her up between the legs?'

Charlotte nodded. 'That's what Griffith said . . . I mean who's to believe her, she was only a dancer . . . I mean she wasn't hurt. It was probably just a game or a fetish or . . . something.' And then she wailed out loud, 'I don't know, I tell you, I don't know.'

But she did know. She knew it was no game and more than just a fetish.

'So she was paid off?'

'Well, yes . . . eventually. Philip had no problem raising the money from his inheritance . . . but your father had second thoughts. He said he was worried he was doing the wrong thing . . . and for Philip's sake we should maybe tell the police so that he would be taken care of or given treatment . . . He wrote to me that he couldn't take the responsibility.'

Dominic could remember now reading Charlotte's reply and how she had phrased it forty years ago.

> 'Of course I understand your reservations about this unfortunate business, but I fail to see the point in getting too much holier than thou about it. Philip may be a little unconventional in his appetites – don't we all have our little foibles . . .?'

Dominic pondered briefly the definition of foible, surely it didn't embrace infibulation. The letter went on:

'Surely you can see that a man in his position really does not want a scandal round his neck. And no more do you, dear Griff, for it would hardly be to your credit to start muck-raking in the midst of such an acrimonious divorce. I hardly think you would succeed in gaining custody of Dominic, a mere toddler, if it were to get out that you had been attempting to pervert the course of justice by the bribing of a witness. For old times' sake, for the sake of that Burns night on the Isle of Mull, dear Griff, please, please leave it alone. Leave well alone. The enclosed is for your pleasure or for your son . . . I know I can trust you. Yours as ever, Charlotte.'

And that's what Griffith had done, he had left well alone, at least until last week. Dominic recalled the frantic message arranged in the Scrabble letters next to the photograph of Norma Kingston. Redhead. Stitched. He moved over to the open window, the stars seemed low and dense suspending their reflection in the loch, the air was warm and scented with peat and heather. He wanted there to be some doubt in his mind about what Sir Philip was and what he did. But there was none. As if to confirm it he could feel in his pocket the five other letters his father had put down. MY SON. How foolish he had been to interpret them as a token of paternal pride. Rather it had been a desperate deathbed effort to point a finger

'Your letter mentioned something about the enclosed being for my father's pleasure or for his son, me . . . What was it?' Dominic asked.

'A little cheque.' Charlotte shrugged an apology.

'For fifty thousand pounds?'

She nodded.

So that explained his father's untouched wealth, it was Charlotte's payment for his silence that had lain ignored for nearly forty years compounding interest at the bank.

'He never spent it you know,' he said, 'not a penny.'

'He was a stubborn man,' she said.

'But he didn't go to the police.'

'No, he didn't,' she answered. 'But it was always on his mind. I remember several years ago he sent me a newspaper cutting about some chorus girl in Melbourne, I think it was. She'd been murdered or raped or something. He had some theory about it being Philip . . . I took no notice. I expect he was rather gaga was he – recently?'

Dominic said nothing. He could see that this old lady whom his father had loved was holding firm to her definition of the truth, the truth she chose to live with. She was simply a mother, blind to the idea that her 'difficult child' was now a man of nearly sixty and something more than difficult.

Time was running out. Charlotte needed both hands again now to drink her champagne and still there was spillage. Her head too had begun to tremble once more and soon her lips and tongue would no longer be lucid.

'Do you know,' he asked, 'what she looked like, this Rita?'

'It was nearly forty years ago,' she answered, 'and how would, would, would I know any . . . anyway.'

'Did she have red hair?'

After a silence she conceded, 'Yes . . . I think, think so.'

There was no doubt left in Dominic's mind as he watched the mother of his brother begin again to dribble, the moment of remission borrowed from tomorrow was nearly at an end. Neither of them spoke for some time, they both knew the interview was at an end.

'I, I, I don't know why you came here . . . I don't want, want to know.' Her mouth was brimming again with unwarranted spittle. 'I don't think we'll meet, meet, meet again, you and I . . . I've told you what I know . . . and feel better for it . . . Those things have been a long . . . long time, time on my chest . . . Perhaps he is a bad man my little Pip . . . Perhaps . . .' She shook her hands in the air. 'I don't want to know . . . too old. It's maybe all my fault . . . a pun . . . pun . . . punishment for our sin . . . Griff and mine . . . the days of wine and roses.'

Huge tears were coursing down the grooves in her skin unstopped. 'Oh dear Griff. Dear Griff. My dear, my dear.'

She beckoned to Dominic in her confusion. With her vision

blurred with tears, it was suddenly the father not the son who was bending over her.

Dominic kissed her on the forehead and briefly felt the soft tremor as her illness reclaimed her.

'Go, go,' she said faintly. 'It's over . . . damn shakes back.'

From the doorway Dominic turned and looked back at the frail figure in her bed, the mother of a 'very bad boy'.

At the far end of the landing Dominic paused on his way to bed and found himself staring at the portrait of a most striking young woman in her twenties. It was not a great painting but in its likeness it carried an explanation that was simple and chilling. It was the wistful face of Lady Charlotte Sullivan in the year of her wedding.

Having spent the last two hours studying the residual beauty of the woman, Dominic was well able to imagine her in the full bloom of youth. He could have guessed at the striking blueness of her eyes; he could have reckoned on the delicate whiteness of her skin, but he had not allowed for the vivid redness of her hair.

*

Wednesday – Dear stupid blank page. What can I tell you? All you need to know is, it was all very nice, thank you . . . Isn't it funny, last week I would have given anything to have him and now I'd pay double to have him again. He is too distracted with all this incredible carry-on . . . It was all on the news last night, Tristram Brunswick has been murdered and his father Maxwell is now under arrest. Thank God he's got Sir Philip on his side. At least he's one of the good guys . . . Oh diary, why hasn't he rung – please Dominic call . . . Who am I kidding? It's his wife he wants . . . I think he nearly even said her name . . . I hate the cow. Why can't he ring . . . If my mother asks if anything is wrong once more, I'll throttle her . . . Actually in case I get run over by a bus or mugged to death and she reads this . . . I love you, Mum. You're fantastic . . . Please take no notice of all this drivel . . . Just make D.G. ring me . . . That's all, more tomorrow. Promise.

22

The dawn of a long day was reaching up the glen in front of him as Dominic had begun his journey south again. Without breakfast or a shave he had left Brachameda before anyone was awake. The roads were empty and above the lochs there hung a mist like chiffon. He drove fast and in silence, this was one appointment he would not be late for. His mind was numbed with a kind of gloom as he sped down the entire length of England. He did not feel like a wanted man. He made good time and reached his rendezvous in the late afternoon with a quarter of an hour in hand. He had stopped to buy a jacket and a tie and had shaved in a service station. He didn't look smart but it was the best he could do for his father's funeral.

The chapel at the crematorium had no adornment; parquet floor and strip lighting; inter-denominational as if anybody cared. The coffin was already in place and so too was the only other mourner – Sister Pearson stooped in prayer. Dominic had made no announcement of the time or place and was especially glad now to be alone. This was not the where or when for him to begin helping the police with their enquiries.

The tone of the chaplain was more DSS than C of E. It lacked poetry, conviction or even intelligence . . . not so much a funeral as a civil service. Dominic was grateful, for this was not the moment for his private grieving, he stood instead wondering what it all meant . . . 'Man that is born of woman hath but a short time to live, and is full of misery.' He watched dry-eyed as the coffin and all its lilies rolled forward on its mechanism out of sight. He bowed his head, not wishing to see this final exit . . . 'For the means of grace, and the hope of glory . . .' Goodbye, Dad.

308

Outside he thanked Sister Pearson for coming and for all her kindness.

'I told the police the service was tomorrow to give you breathing space,' she said. 'But if you want my advice the sooner you get everything straightened out the better, get it all off your chest. Stop doing everything alone. It's time, if you ask me, for you to be getting on with your proper life. Settle down . . . There's nothing wrong with the humdrum life, you know. The humdrum life would not do you any harm.' She patted his arm affectionately. 'And good luck with the show. Don't forget you promised me a ticket.' She smiled before getting into her Fiat Panda and driving back to west Worthing.

Dominic was stiff from his drive and tired. He stared round at the graveyard, the neat dormitory of departed souls, their names and dates tidily marked. He watched a hearse move slowly out of view and saw, or thought he saw, the figure of a girl some way off.

Under a sycamore tree half way down the central pathway she was standing in a pale cream dress. Her hair was fair and her arms were filled with roses, her face though was not quite visible for the wide-brimmed hat she wore. Dominic looked away and then turned back. She was a trick of the light, an optical illusion. He half closed his eyes to see her better. She stood quite still in the shade and let the breeze blow the dress against her body and her thighs. Any moment she would dematerialise the way ghosts do.

Dominic began to walk towards her as one does to disperse a mirage. He approached her slowly, his feet crunching loudly in the gravel. She remained intact, still studying him from under the brim of her hat. With the length of a wicket between them Dominic stopped.

'What are you doing here?' he asked.

'I brought some flowers,' she answered.

'I didn't expect youd' to be here,' he said.

'I'm sorry.'

'No . . . I mean I wasn't expecting anyone. It was . . .'

'Private,' she said. 'I know, that's why I waited outside.'

'Yes. I'm sorry.'

'I was really very fond of him, you know,' she said. 'After all he was my father-in-law.'

At first he wanted to turn away so that she couldn't see him crying but he didn't move. He didn't even raise his hand, he stood quite still and let the tears roll down his face, and to his surprise it did not feel like weakness at all. For some minutes he returned her gaze in silence and neither of them moved. He felt above all relieved – released of his past or was it his personality? He had not planned to speak but could not stop himself.

'You've never looked more beautiful.' He cleared his throat. 'Not even when we were married ... or when we went to the Oscars or when you played Beatrice or when we went to Tobago, do you remember the days on that deserted beach?'

She nodded. She remembered the days on that deserted beach. She didn't speak. She wanted him to go on. He did.

'Hattie, I miss you ... I've missed you so much. I think about you all the time ... every day all day ... I can't live without you, I mean I can but I can't be happy ... The whole world seems to stink and be ghastly and full of greed and crime and shit ... and I can't face any of it without you ... Now that I'm better ... dried out I mean ... off the bottle, I can't see any point in any of it, any tiny bit of it without you ... I don't care about anything else. I just want you.'

Dominic was flying solo, speaking unscripted and from the heart – he felt reckless and incoherent. He had lost the fear of falling or being rebuffed or misunderstood. From now on he would make his meaning clear the way his father never had.

'The point is,' he went on, 'I think ... I'm sure ... I know that we should try again ... Please let me show you ... Shall we? That's all.'

He had finished. It was her turn to speak. They faced each other, each laid bare for inspection. Time passed.

'I'm going to have a baby,' she said.

A small airplane flew low overhead. The sound of it cut through the silence between them. Harriet watched his face for any sign of registration. It showed none, but Dominic

310

understood it all at once, he took in every facet – the surprise, the pleasure, the honour, the doubt, the jealousy, the commitment, the worry, the fear, the excitement. He moved slowly forward towards his wife and took her in his arms, roses and hat and all. He held her close and said, 'That's wonderful . . . that's absolutely wonderful.'

'Dom, Dom, the point is . . .'

'It doesn't matter,' he said.

'Dom, will you listen . . .'

'I don't care . . .'

'Dom,' she pulled back so that she could see his face, 'the point is I'm not . . .'

'As I said,' he interrupted, 'I don't care . . . It doesn't matter. It doesn't matter to me. I am going to be the father of this baby. You are my wife. He or she will be our baby.'

He spoke slowly with the solemnity due to such an edict.

Harriet was crying now, she took his face in her hands and kissed him again and again. 'Oh Domo, Domo, Domo,' she said. And they hugged each other, man and wife, under a sycamore tree in the graveyard. Perhaps this was what Sister Pearson had meant; the humdrum life would not do him any harm.

The first run-through on a new stage is a technical exercise and is normally on the dismal side. The actors use the time to check the acoustics and their props. They will decorate their dressing rooms and complain about the power point for their shaver or rollers. The atmosphere backstage at the Brunswick was tense and sombre, the rumours that were going around were beyond even the black humour of the chorus. Tristram Brunswick had been murdered and everyone from the third electrician to the second trombonist had a theory to put forward. Apparently half a dozen box office managers from neighbouring theatres had been arrested and further speculation was incurred by Dominic's absence from the rehearsal.

'He's been unavoidably detained,' Phoebe announced. 'It's nothing to worry about, my darlings, everything is going to be fine. It'll all be made clear in due course . . . Have a good rehearsal and . . . Welcome to the Brunswick at last.'

The cast could see the strain in her face, she looked pale and suddenly older and they reckoned that she clearly needed Sir Philip by her side at such a time to comfort her.

With the understudy in the central role and the scenery not quite ready, the actors were told not to bother with wigs and costumes. The principals wore their microphones hardly concealed and carried the transmitters in the pockets of their street clothes. It was not so much a run-through as a stroll.

Tessa in particular gave only a casual energy to her role. Her voice reached out effortlessly through the auditorium but she left the big notes unsung. She was not wasting them on all those empty seats. Dominic's absence annoyed her, it denied her the chance of showing him how cool she could be. She wanted to blame him but couldn't. She found herself trapped by her own preconditions, had she really sat in the bath with him and promised, 'I won't get heavy or start sobbing or anything?' He could at least have rung her; she hadn't hoped for flowers, not much, but he could have telephoned. She sang more vehemently at the thought:

> 'Just you wait Henry Higgins
>   Just you wait.
> You'll be sorry but your tears
>   will be too late.'

At the end of the first act she went up to her dressing room. 'Screw you, Dominic Gallagher,' she said to herself. At all costs she would put a brave face on the one that looked pinched with love-sickness in the mirror. She would give an impression of nonchalance. She would be a party girl for him to hear about. 'Screw you,' she said again.

She had brought a change of clothes in case he (damn him again) asked her to dinner; she'd wear it anyway. She put on the lightweight suit, coarse linen rose pink with a jade green camisole. 'You're not the only pebble on the beach, Dominic Gallagher.' She fixed her new earrings, huge double clefs of silver plate. 'I don't give a flying toss for you, Dominic

312

Gallagher.' She painted her toenails and put on her silver sandals. She wasn't going to let the world see her with her pants down, the doleful virgin who had made a fool of herself with the leading man. 'No sir.' She rubbed on lip gloss and gave herself a final squirt of Opium ... All part of the charade.

In the wings the actor playing the hairy hound from Budapest helped her transfer her microphone. 'You got a date?' he asked. 'Or what?'

Or what? 'Maybe,' she answered.

'Well you look a million dollars,' he said.

She felt like only a dime. 'Thanks.'

'I wonder who the lucky fellow is,' the ruder pest enquired.

'Wouldn't you like to know?' she answered. And at the time she thought she was bluffing.

Phoebe did not stay to see the second half of the rehearsal, her head ached with tension and unhappiness. She was in no mood to play the jovial impresario – it would be known soon enough to what extent she had been swindled and jilted. She needed to lick her wounds before they went on show. For the second night, she was going to stay with her daughter whom she had not seen all day.

It had been decided to keep the hunt for Sir Philip under-cover. The media, it was thought, would not at this point enhance the search. Sea and air ports had been checked and flight lists carefully gone through. So far no trace of the baronet had been found. It hardly seemed likely that he would return to Phoebe's mews house but she found the police there on duty just in case.

'I'm only popping by to pick up some things,' she explained and let herself into the house. She poured herself a drink and repacked. It was only as she was on the point of leaving that she saw the envelope on the mantelpiece. The sight of it set her heart thudding for she knew her lover's handwriting – neat and upright, perfectly balanced.

My dear Phoebe, It seems the cat is out of the
bag so I'm afraid I must be off. I have never felt

313

any obligation to explain myself to the world or
to apologise for my behaviour – the former is
superfluous and the latter hypocrisy but in your
case I make the exception. I am sorry. And by
way of explanation I must revert again to Latin,
for as Virgil has it: *Flectere si nequeo superos
Acheronta movebo* . . . Yours Philip.

Phoebe felt a wave of new anger at the man who had duped
her – his cold, pompous note enraged her. It patronised her
and it puzzled her. She dialled the incident room where the
hunt for Sir Philip was being co-ordinated. She read them his
letter in its entirety. They, too, were puzzled and the Latin
was beyond them, there was apparently 'not much call for it
these days'. The feeling at Headquarters was that Sir Philip
must be out of the country, in Europe at least by now but
more likely in the States or beyond. The theory did nothing
to relieve the unease that Phoebe felt.

In ten minutes the police called back with a translation of
the Latin. 'According to our sources it translates as
follows – ' he had a crisp Glaswegian accent. 'If I cannot bend
the gods I will let hell loose.'

Dominic always wondered why it was that the old euphemism
of 'helping the police with their enquiries' took so long, the
reason was, he realised, that they ask all their questions
twice, the answers are double-checked and laboriously tran-
scribed. Then after a vile cup of tea it's all gone through
again.

He had come directly from his father's funeral and his
mind was full of the reunion with Harriet and the prospect of
fatherhood. Tristram's death already seemed long ago and
his conscience had no wish to go through the memory of it,
let alone repeat the details again and again. The horror of it
would be his for life but for the moment it was a mere
question of definition: self-defence, unlawful killing, man-
slaughter, murder. Misadventure sounded crazy, as if anyone
thought life was a bowl of cherries any more. It was a process
of negotiation more than confession.

Across the table Detective Superintendent Cameron nodded a lot while Dominic spoke. He was a large patient man who had the courtesy to blow his cigarette smoke out sideways or over Dominic's head. 'Crime doesn't pay' said the poster on the wall, a message too late for anyone in that room. There were two other policemen, one in and one out of uniform, and Dominic's solicitor Harrison Crockstead.

For the most part the police were understanding. They could accept the crime but not Dominic's delay in reporting it. He chose not to pass on the details of his findings at Brachameda for the moment. Sir Philip would soon be in police custody on a list of charges already long enough. Harrison Crockstead cleared his throat and suggested that Dominic had been 'in a state of shock and utter panic' at 'the terrible accident when his car had collided with the . . . er . . . tractor.'

Everyone nodded.

Through the frosted glass window Dominic saw the dusk deepening, a blurred sunset then darkness. 'Would it be possible,' he asked, 'to keep Tessa Neal's name out of all this?' It didn't seem fair for her to be exposed on his account, he felt bad enough already. The detective said he would do his best.

Hearing his statement read back to him, Dominic felt ludicrously tired and giddy at the narrowness of his escape. In the bland staccato language of police-speak it sounded even crazier than the reality. He signed it with a shaking hand as accurate.

Yes, he fully understood the terms of the police bail. Yes he would let them know all his movements, and, of course, anything else he thought of. Yes, of course they could keep his car for forensic tests. Yes, he would send a signed photograph for the sergeant's daughter . . . Would they all like seats to *My Fair Lady*? Yes. 'Another cup of tea before you go, sir?' No thank you.

Tessa wasted no time at the rehearsal. The director had not much to say and all the cast were anxious to get home.

'Good night, everyone. Good night, all,' she called out on the way to her dressing room. 'See you tomorrow.'

The backstage area of the Brunswick was a warren of corridors and staircases and Tessa's allotted room was at the end of a long passage on the second floor. She hummed brightly as she passed the others, the hum of a carefree girl who doesn't give a fig for her leading man.

The true prospect that faced Tessa was less appealing than that advertised – solitary scrambled eggs at home with an old video. Such is the price of putting on a brave face. She took out the key to her dressing room but found the door unlocked. Her visitor turned to greet her as she entered. He smiled at her surprise.

'Goodness you look lovely,' he said. 'I hope the rehearsal went well.'

She said it had.

'I hope you're not cross at finding me here.'

She said she wasn't.

'I wonder if you'd care to join me for a glass of champagne and maybe a bite to eat?'

She said she wasn't sure.

'We won't be alone,' he assured her, 'I'm expecting someone else.'

She asked who and when he told her she said, 'Why not then? I'd be delighted.'

He smiled. 'I thought we'd go upstairs to Phoebe's flat above the office. Are you ready?'

Tessa nodded and took Sir Philip's arm.

Dominic stood across the street from the Brunswick and stared up at the enormous *My Fair Lady* logo – the famous grinning puppeteer holding the strings of the flower girl beneath. There was his name in huge unlit neon, he shuddered at the thought of justifying its being there . . . Dominic Gallagher. Gallagher . . . His father's name and his child's too. He was filled with contradictions in his head: elation and sadness, optimism and dread, terror and confidence, he was exhausted and yet he had energy. He thought of his father, whose name had never been in lights, and he thought of the baby he was fathering. What sex would it be, he wondered, and what kind of person? He was impatient for its arrival, already making plans for a happy childhood, the one he had missed out on. He would do his best to give the child a sun-filled morning to his life. It did not matter whether this unborn baby was the progeny of his blood or just of his good will. Either way it was a love child to whom he would give all the benefits he had lacked. He or she would grow up carefree, would inhabit a proper child's world with two parents and no phobia of being abandoned. The love would be on hand without a premium. This was all part of the pledge that Dominic was making, a promise to a foetus five weeks old in the body of his wife but only five hours in his head.

His son or daughter would grow up articulate in the language of what he felt and would have no need for the licence of alcohol or acting to speak freely. The only memory of real embrace with his or her father would not be with a corpse in a nursing home. Oh yes, he was going to love this baby, feed and sooth and teach and carry. He would read to this baby and sing, he would listen to this baby and encourage. So many good intentions were teaming through him. Oh Harriet, my darling, my for-better-or-worse love, be patient with me, I've got some growing up to do myself in the next few months.

Dominic tried to put from his mind the uncomfortable thought of Tessa and the gift she had made him of herself. Certainly he felt a little ashamed, the guilt that goes with the memory of unnegotiated pleasure. In truth he realised he had simply used her as a litmus test of another love. But there had been no commitment, he told himself, no promises had been made. They were ships that had passed each other in the night, collided gently and gone their separate ways, they had no claim on one another – it was a knock for knock arrangement. He had been her first love, she his last. It wasn't unfair.

Quite suddenly the icy finger of foreboding was poking him in the eye. All was not resolved. Sir Philip was still at large somewhere in the world. Sir Philip, the bad boy who had gone so far beyond the boundaries of his mother's worst dread. Sir Philip, the psychotic changeling who had been wreaking revenge on hapless dancers across the world. Redheads. Stitched. Sir Philip, the financier and philanthropist who, without a backward glance, had pillaged the trust of everyone around him, poor Phoebe in particular. Sir Philip, the half-brother who had betrayed him. Dominic wondered where he was, this fellow product of his father's loins. Somewhere Sir Philip was still in existence. Dominic stared up at the great dark edifice of the Brunswick Theatre, that warehouse where the giant lives, and thought about the man. And as he did he felt a ghastly hatred for him, not just for his malignity but for the pain he had caused Griffith in his life, and the shame he would bring on him now in death. Soon it would all have to come out, all the appalling secrets that his father had so nearly taken to the grave. He stared up at the Brunswick in front of him and wondered where Sir Philip had found to run to. He wished him dead in hell and shuddered again without knowing why.

In Phoebe's apartment above the Brunswick, Tessa stared out at the roofs of Bloomsbury and beyond. Had she looked down across the street she might have seen the figure of the man she ached for staring up at where she stood. The room seemed too hot. With its windows double glazed against the elements and the city sounds the air seemed heavy inside. Sir Philip poured them both champagne and they toasted each other respectfully. Their conversation too seemed weighed down with courtesy. They shook their heads at the atrocious events that had been occurring and they moved around the room exchanging platitudes about the death of Tristram.

'And as for those dirty great bastards,' Tessa was saying, 'the twins who turned up in Dominic's dressing room before the gala . . .'

Sir Philip cocked his smooth groomed head. 'Really? What happened?' His curiosity was camouflaged with good manners.

Tessa told him everything, reliving the details as she did.

Sir Philip listened well, he nodded and shook his head on cue. 'A shocking business.' He was the ally of her lover after all and Tessa enjoyed the comfort of confiding in him. They were a team of three. She did not go into the details of her time in refuge with Dominic, she bypassed the memory of her pleasure, the picnic in the bath and all the rest.

'I mean,' she said, 'he was just so glad to have you on his side, there was no one else he could turn to, you see.'

Sir Philip nodded in appreciation. 'Yes,' he said, 'so when did you last see him then?'

'I dropped him outside your hotel in Manchester,' she said.

'Yes, of course,' he murmured. 'Poor chap, he was in quite a state. And you haven't heard from him since?'

Tessa shook her head as if to show it did not matter. 'Thank God it's all over.'

Sir Philip filled her glass. 'Yes indeed,' he said. 'Thank God it's all over.'

'Cheers,' she said.

'Your very good health,' he answered with a smile.

With reality still not coming home to roost Dominic was too tired or was it too elated to go home yet. Perhaps he simply wanted to prolong the happy ending. He wandered into the Brunswick through the stage door. A solitary scene painter was still at work remarbling the pillars of Professor Higgins's study and in the stalls Ron-Ron was rigging up his sound system.

Dominic stood centre stage and as he peered up the central aisle, the pathway that divides the giant in two, he struggled to put from his mind the memory of Major Kendal hanging suspended on a rope twenty feet from where he was standing. Poor Major Kendal with his polished toecaps and his eyes fixed for ever on the Royal Box. Poor Major Kendal who had known too much.

Dominic walked up the auditorium to join the sound engineer. 'I didn't get a chance the other night to thank you for your help . . . before the gala. You were terrific. Thank you.'

'No trouble, mate – what a bunch of bastards.' Ron-Ron

grinned, his mouth full of chocolate. 'Do you want some?' He offered Dominic his Toblerone.

'Thanks.' Dominic took it for friendship more than appetite. He sat and watched Ron-Ron at work, he took in the ethos of the Brunswick, ghostless and quiet under its rococo dome. There was no reason he could find for the adrenalin to be pumping in his veins, and his heart was thudding with an intangible fear, something worse than stage fright.

'Of course Dominic was marvellous,' Sir Philip conceded, 'but for my money, my dear, the evening was yours . . . You were quite superb. Excellent. I think come next week and the opening you'll be a star.' His lips spread into a smile that never reached his eyes.

The flattery made Tessa uneasy. 'It's a great show to do,' she said.

'Relax,' he said.

The silence between them was a weapon he had the use of. Tessa crossed her legs the other way and ran a hand through her hair. The conversation between them was no balloon bouncing back and forth. It was a medicine ball.

'It must have been marvellous for Phoebe having you around to support her through all this ghastliness,' she said.

'Yes, I hope I've been of some use to her.' He sipped his champagne. 'She certainly has been to me.'

'Oh good.'

'And what about Dominic?' Sir Philip asked.

'What about him?'

'Has he been any *use* to you?' He asked the question quizzically.

'How do you mean?'

'Are you not infatuated with him, my dear?' Sir Philip raised his eyebrows.

'I can't see that it's any of your . . .'

'Any of my business. Quite right.'

He gave her a half smile, in the dim light his skin was the colour of cheddar cheese.

'I was worried for you, that's all, being the way you are.'

320

What did he mean, she wondered, what knowledge of her did he have? She said nothing.

'In any case he's married, isn't he, at the end of the day . . .?' His malice had the precision of a scalpel. 'Everything will be fine and dandy between them now, what with the baby . . .'

'Baby?' Tessa felt giddy for a moment with stupidity and pain.

'Didn't you know?' he asked. 'They're having a baby. Harriet is pregnant.'

'No, why should I? It's none of my business,' she said too lightly.

'He's a dear boy.'

Sir Philip was studying her with the steady gaze of a predator.

'You said he was coming here,' she said. 'I wonder where he's got to?'

'He's probably been held up.' Sir Philip looked at his watch. 'Shall we eat a little something? I've prepared a light supper. I thought you might be hungry.'

Tessa felt trapped rather than invited. 'Perhaps we had better wait for him.'

'No need – we'll carry on,' he said, and as Sir Philip lit the candles the flame of his Dunhill was steady as a rock.

Tessa felt suddenly chill as she saw the table was laid for two.

'Dominic,' Ron-Ron called from the orchestra pit, 'could you do us a favour?'

Dominic was sprawling by the sound console drinking a Diet Coke. He was almost too tired to go home and his thoughts were fragments.

'Sure,' he answered.

'Push up one or two of the faders for me will you. They're there in front of you marked one to thirty. I want to test what I've got down here . . . Can you give us twenty-two.'

Dominic slid the button forward and on the speakers round the auditorium he heard Ron-Ron tapping the microphone in question.

'How now brown cow . . .' His voice rang out. 'That's OK. Try twenty-five.'

Dominic did. Again he heard the sound engineer amplified. 'Terrific. Twenty-six, please.'

Twenty-six was not so good, the crackle of its loose connection was an explosion in stereo round the theatre.

'Whoops,' Ron-Ron called out. 'I'd better check that one out.'

While Ron-Ron sorted out the problem, Dominic studied the massive panels in front of him, the rows of knobs and dials and faders. He tried to tell himself that the apprehension fizzing slowly deep inside him was merely an aftermath, a residue of the last days. It was time to go home, time to begin the new chapter. Roll the end credits.

Tessa hardly dare pick up the coffee cup in front of her for fear that it would spill in her shaking hands.

'You seem to know an awful lot about me.' She tried to sound casual but her mouth was dry as chalk. 'I mean, I can't see what possible interest it is to you to know that I had chicken pox in nineteen seventy-four or that I won the three-legged race with Deidre Simons . . . I mean what's the point?'

'Indeed, my dear, what is the point?' Sir Philip sipped his coffee from the demitasse with a steady hand. 'I'm afraid it's one of my little quirks. I take pleasure in knowing the details of . . . the people I admire. Shall I go on?'

'Yes.'

She was unsure if she answered from good manners or fear. There was nothing to stop her leaving and, she told herself, there was no chilling menace in the steel grey eyes of her host. None at all. The room could not be getting hotter, she told herself, or the music louder, Verdi's *Macbeth*. She must stay calm, keep cool.

'Yes, please go on,' she said.

Sir Philip inclined his head to acknowledge the boon.

'You had your tonsils out in the autumn of seventy-five and took the part of Joseph in the school nativity play at Christmas. You moved house the following year, a semi-detached Victorian house in Teddington, eleven Crawford

322

Road. You passed your singing grades with distinction and for your tenth birthday you were given a bicycle. Yes . . .?'

Sir Philip needed no confirmation of his facts.

'Your younger brother kept white mice and his best friend was a bully called Trevor . . .'

Sir Philip's tone had the smooth monotony of information learnt by heart. As the catalogue of her childhood secrets went on, Tessa could feel cold beads of sweat running slowly down her back. There was nothing healthy in this encounter. It was time to go. Casually she stood up, her knees were unsteady. She tried to give the impression of nonchalance as she moved about the room. And all the time she could feel herself under the relentless scrutiny of her host.

'Relax,' Sir Philip was saying. 'You look worried, my dear. Is it perhaps the memory of the white mice that has unnerved you? Or are you frightened perhaps that I might mention what happened with Uncle Ted on March fifth, nineteen seventy-six . . .'

'No,' she shouted. 'Stop, stop it. That is enough.'

Her heart was thudding against her ribs, her legs were stiff like stilts as she paced about behind the sofa.

'I can't imagine how it is that you have found out all this about me.' She spoke quietly with an effort to stay in control. 'I mean the trouble you must have been to. It's . . . it's . . .' She was going to say mad but realised in time the accuracy of it. '. . . it's not nice. It's not right . . . It's private. My past is none of your business . . . and I really think it's time I went home . . . I mean it's . . .'

'Sit down.' Sir Philip's interruption was quiet in its command.

'I'll just call for a taxi.'

Tessa picked up the telephone and let out a gasp at the silence that she heard. 'It's dead.'

Sir Philip nodded at the bereavement.

'You must not be alarmed, Tessa. Please don't be alarmed. I'm your friend.' He was advancing across the room towards her. Gently he took the lifeless receiver from her hands and replaced it. The sound of the West End traffic outside was so

323

faint that it only served as a reminder of their isolation. She was out of reach and out of earshot.

'Dominic isn't coming, is he?' she asked.

'I don't think so,' Sir Philip smiled. 'Sit down.'

She turned halfway towards the door. 'It's locked, I suppose.'

Sir Philip nodded as if the deed had not been his.

'Have a brandy.'

'No,' Tessa answered shrilly. 'No thank you.' She felt doomed.

'Oh, my dear girl.' Sir Philip's voice was soothing. 'You're all of a jitter. I'm so sorry that you're apprehensive, it's most remiss of me. It spoils everything . . . I'm a silly fellow.' He raised his hands in a hollow gesture of submission. 'Sorry.'

Tessa was no longer in the shadowy territory of undefined foreboding – there was no mistaking that she was in trouble. There was no ambiguity about what was going on, she had seen it all before and smelt it too, the same subverted maleness that her Uncle Ted had been possessed with all those years ago. For here on the face of this otherwise genial man was the same sly look of purpose, a leer like the one that had made her feel unclean as a child of eleven. She had sensed then that the fault was somehow hers and the guilt had taken many hours with her psychiatrist to expunge. She was not going through that again. This situation was not of her making, she was blameless now as she had been then, a cypher in someone else's fantasy.

'Do sit down, Tessa, my dear.' He gestured to a chair. 'I haven't finished.'

With all the resolution to stay calm that she could manage, Tessa sat as she was told. She wrapped her jacket close round her for comfort rather than for warmth, and felt in the pocket the rectangular shape of her transmitter. Had she really been so keen to accept Sir Philip's invitation that she had not waited to be unwired? The microphone, too, was still in place on the inside of her lapel, although it had been disconnected at the end of the rehearsal. Perhaps she was not so out of reach, not quite out of earshot.

'I've changed my mind,' she said gaily. 'I'll have a brandy

324

'... I'm being silly ... all of a dither.' She let out a feeble laugh to prove her point, and Sir Philip studied her for a moment, puzzled by her change of mood.

'There's nothing to be afraid of, the last thing I want to do is frighten you, my dear.' Sir Philip went to the drinks tray to pour her a drink.

'Oh, of course not. I'm just a bit, you know, tired.'

While his back was turned Tessa fumbled frantically to reconnect the microphone wire to the transmitter in her pocket. Just as Sir Philip returned with her brandy, she felt the faint click as the join was made good. It was only an outside chance she realised, there would be no one to hear her or the battery would be flat, but the thought of it made time worth playing for.

'Cheers,' she smiled.

Ron-Ron was still in the orchestra pit fixing the microphones for the string section. Dominic was sitting at the sound console gathering the energy to stand up and leave. Distractedly he slid the paddles up and down, appreciating their mechanical fluency – his mind quite blurred with fatigue.

He looked up at the stage for that was where the girl's voice came from. No one there. It was only a moment later that he realised that he was in fact controlling what he heard with the fader on channel 3. He pushed it up to full volume and listened to the disembodied speech:

'... I just can't think how you found out all those things. I mean all that detail ... I don't understand why you should bother. It's very flattering but what's the point ...? Tell me about you ...'

The voice had more edge to it than he remembered as he conjured up a picture of its owner, Tessa Neal. Was this a recording or what?

'Ron,' Dominic called, 'Who's that on channel three?'

Ron-Ron leant on the rail of the orchestra pit. 'It's Tessa.'

'Live? I mean here and now?'

'Yea it's live all right. Couldn't be anything else. Silly cow must have gone off with her mike on.'

'Where is she?' Dominic asked.

'In her dressing room maybe.' Ron-Ron shrugged. 'She's usually pretty good about disconnecting or switching off . . . it saves the batteries you see and then I let her keep them.'

The two men were standing side by side in front of the sound desk. Ron-Ron adjusted the controls. There was silence now on channel 3. With the volume up to maximum all they could hear was a faint rumble in the background, an indistinct male voice some distance from the microphone. And then Tessa was speaking again.

'No more brandy, thank you. Actually what with the first preview tomorrow, I really ought to get to bed . . . My voice is a bit croaky anyway. I'd better go home . . .'

'What do you think Ron-Ron?' Dominic asked. 'Does she sound OK?'

'Yea . . . She's with some bloke somewhere backstage. She's a bit of tease is our Tess I'm told. All the lads have been trying to get among her knickers.'

'How long since the rehearsal ended?' Dominic interrupted.

Ron-Ron looked at his fake Rolex. 'Three hours,' he said.

'Three hours? Wouldn't the batteries be flat then?'

'Yea . . .' Ron-Ron lit a cigarette, 'Unless she . . .'

'Exactly, unless she had disconnected it and then reconnected. Why should she do that?'

'I don't know.' Ron-Ron blew out a funnel of smoke. 'To be heard . . .'

'Wait here,' Dominic interrupted, 'I'm going to see if she's in her dressing room.'

There was nobody backstage now and everywhere there was evidence of tasks abandoned until morning. It was hard to believe that from all this disorder the first preview would emerge polished and precise. In the stage door cubby-hole a fireman on night duty was struggling with the *Evening Standard* crossword.

'No, squire, I haven't seen no one.' He shook his head to emphasise the double negative. 'Her dressing room,' he referred to a list, 'is number three at the end of the corridor on the second floor.'

Unlike his own, Dominic found that Tessa's room was already decorated with cards and mementoes. Her make-up neatly laid out on a tray-cloth embroidered with flowers. There was a photograph of her parents, not old at all like the parents of girlfriends years ago, they were wearing jeans for God's sake. Dominic held the photograph for a moment and studied it. Perhaps they were younger than him, standing there by a lake in their Reeboks.

Perhaps he, too, would be the father of a daughter soon, a girl whose virtue some shiftless actor might one day take too casually. Poor Tessa. He wanted to apologise or make amends, he owed her a little kindness to make up for the shortfall in his commitment.

'Tessa,' he called out down the corridor. Upstairs he checked the other dressing rooms and heard nothing except the echo of his own voice. He ran downstairs again.

'Is there anyone else in the building?' he asked the fireman.

'There's one or two electricians down in the crew room I think,' he answered.

'Where's that?'

'Two floors down under the stage,' he answered slowly.

Dominic found the two electricians asleep on the floor of the crew room, around them the empty cans of export lager told the story of how their overtime was earned.

'Sorry to disturb you,' Dominic said.

'No trouble, Dom, no trouble.'

On the dartboard was a pin-up photograph of a comely blond still smiling with her breasts all perforated.

Back on stage Dominic called out to Ron-Ron, 'Any more?'

'Not much,' the sound man was standing at the console holding an earphone to his head. 'All I can hear is a faint mumbling in the background, a man's voice . . . they can't be that close together or we'd pick him up on her mike.'

'What's the range of those things?' Dominic asked.

'It's difficult to say, it varies . . . About a quarter of a mile maximum . . . Hang on . . .'

Ron-Ron switched the sound back to the amplifiers so that Dominic could hear.

'Well it really is quite late,' Tessa was saying. 'Couldn't I do it another time . . .? Of course I don't mind doing it . . . maybe tomorrow . . . The truth is I'm rather tired . . .'

Dominic could hear the strain in her voice. Perhaps it was none of his business. Who was he to imagine she needed his help? Two questions, though, were in his mind: Where was she? And with whom? If he knew the answers he could maybe leave well alone. He was quite unprepared for the shock reversal of this idea when next she spoke.

'All right, if you insist,' Tessa said. 'But then I really must go home, Sir Philip.'

Sir Philip Sullivan, Bart. Sir Philip Sullivan, Griffith's other son, Pip to his mother. Sir Philip not on the run, not abroad or lying low. Sir Philip not in the guise of elegant philanthropist as the world knew him. Sir Philip not the ruthless asset-stripper that the City had come to know. Sir Philip not in the role of criminal mastermind as the police now knew him. This was Sir Philip, the psychopathic murderer whose secret Dominic had withheld and was holding still. This was his half-brother who mutilated women in the effigy of his mother, a man who spent his life revenging his bastard state. This was the maniac that Tessa was in the company of.

'Christ,' he whispered. 'Christ Almighty.'

'What? What is it?' Ron-Ron could see the urgency in the ghastly pallor of Dominic's face.

'It's Sir Philip . . . He's going to kill her. He's going to kill Tessa.'

He was standing centre stage like someone in a trance, he was dizzy with terror and blame. What options did he have? How could he save her? How could he find her? All he knew was that she was within a radius of a quarter of a mile, somewhere between Trafalgar Square and Oxford Street, Covent Garden and Mayfair. He also guessed that she was only a short distance from her death.

'It's one of my favourite poems,' Sir Philip was saying. 'My mother used to read it to me, you know, in the nursery . . . She knew it by heart and the way she recited was quite magical . . . She had a lovely voice. Lovely. Soft and pure . . .' For a moment he seemed lost in the remembrance. Then he repeated the word 'pure'. This time it rasped in his throat.

Tessa was sitting on the sofa wondering how best to handle

328

him now. Was this a mother fixation? And if so what was the antidote? How should she play it? She was as accustomed as the next girl to maladroit advances from unlikely sources; she had learnt to cope with the fumbling hands and the fevered breathing – the smell of urgent masculinity and the glazed eagerness in the eye. But it was the coldness of her host that unnerved her now, his unblinking stare and his well-cut suit. His interest in her had the detached curiosity of a collector, a lepidopterist perhaps. She was in his collecting jar, she knew that, a trapped butterfly.

Sir Philip handed her the leather-bound book of verse that he had taken from Phoebe's house. He gave it to her with both hands as if it were a sacrament.

'Page seventy-three, my dear,' he said. His lips had their quizzical smile of unkindness. 'Read it nice and slowly.'

He was standing over her so that she was in his shadow and could smell the cologne of him . . . Eau Sauvage.

'Like your mother?' she suggested.

She'd play anyone's game for a quiet life.

He stared down at her without speaking. The smile had left his face. He turned and moved to the fireplace gliding like a ghost. He stood with his back to her.

'Begin,' he said quietly.

The room was airless, sealed off from hope of rescue. Tessa struggled not to tremble. Her throat was dry like the bark of a tree and her palms were wet. She shifted her lapel to bring the microphone nearer to her mouth. Let someone hear me . . . Please God let someone somewhere hear me. She took a breath and read:

> 'Tyger Tyger burning bright
> In the forest of the night
> What immortal hand or eye
> Could frame they fearful symmetry.'

Tessa's voice echoed shakily round the auditorium. Dominic had no idea what this recital could betoken, he held his head in his hands desperate for inspiration.

'In what distant deeps or skies
Burnt the fire of thine eyes
On what wings dare he aspire
What the hand dare seize the fire.'

'Upstairs,' Dominic said, then shouted, 'The penthouse.
That's where they are. Phoebe's flat.'

In his mind it was a certainty, or a hunch, rather, masquerading as a possibility. He ran down the central aisle towards
Ron-Ron. 'Call the police . . . Call Phoebe, I'm going upstairs.'

He snatched up the torch on the console and ran out
through the double doors at the back of the stalls, and then
up the great sweeping staircase to ground level and on up to
the Royal Circle.

The door to the offices was locked, locked solid. Two floors
above him Tessa could not hear him shout her name. How
many doors separated him from Phoebe's private rooms above
the office? Three perhaps – all locked. Time was against him,
he knew that; how many verses were there in Blake's poem?
Not enough.

In the darkness Dominic had to concentrate as his feet
raced into the wavering pool of light from the torch as he ran
downstairs again. He stood at the back of the Stalls his mind
tumbling with a thousand combinations. The answer wasn't
far away. Think. Remember . . . Come on. Come on . . . How
had they entered the apartment on that evening of the storm,
of the Major's gormless death. Yes, yes, the spiral stairs . . .
of course, the escape route of absconding impresarios. That
was it. The spiral stairs with their side entrance in the street.
And from the huge amplifiers resounded:

'And what shoulder, and what art,
Could twist the sinews of thy heart
And when thy heart began to beat
What dread hand? And what dread feet?'

What dread hand? Tessa's voice was a slow, dry whisper now.
She was aware that Sir Philip had turned to face her. She
glanced up and against her will was caught in the full force
330

of his gaze, the intense cruel scrutiny of a cat. Tyger Tyger. Yet he seemed abstracted too, in some other darker world in which she was subordinate. He brought both hands up to the collar of his shirt and with long fingers he began to loosen his tie, cerulean blue silk with a motif of red fleurs-de-lys. Slowly he slid the knot free and unbuttoned his shirt. He inhaled deeply through his nose.

'Go on.'

He was moving towards her now, unhurried and spectral as if there was a book on his head. Tessa could feel his gaze still on her, relentless in its inspection. She was lost, spinning in outer space, without a hope. Her heart was pounding with a pneumatic thud and her brain was frozen with the idea that no rescue would come. Her cry for help was going untransmitted. Her batteries must be flat, she reckoned, and if they weren't, who could there possibly be to hear her?

'Go on,' Sir Philip said again and his voice had a soft urgency.

'Give me another microphone,' Dominic called to Ron-Ron as he ran down the Stalls, 'so I can tell you where I am. Stay here.'

Ron-Ron handed him a transmitter then helped him uncoil the microphone and attach it. 'It's on,' he said, as Dominic ran off again, this time towards the stage.

'Thanks,' he shouted and already the sound was amplified in the stalls. 'Get the electricians up from the crew room, we may need them.'

'The police will be here in a minute,' Ron-Ron told him, 'and Phoebe too I should think . . .'

'Thanks, Ron,' he said. If nothing else she might have the key to the flat upstairs, Dominic thought.

Ron-Ron buzzed the electricians on the house telephone lowering the volume on the speakers as he did. Tessa's voice was hardly audible:

'What the hammer? What the chain?
In what furnace was thy brain

331

What the anvil? What dread grasp
Dare its deadly terrors clasp.'

'There's no key to that door,' the fireman shook his head at
Dominic. 'It's private the flat is. Not our responsi –'
  'I want it open! Now! Open it!' There was no doubting that
Dominic meant what he said and the hold he had on the
man's lapels carried a certain persuasion.
  'All right, all right.' He was a man who knew better than
to reason why, the crossword and his cup of tea could wait.
'An axe. We need an axe.'

  'When the stars threw down their spears
  And water'd heaven with their tears.
  Did he smile his work to see?
  Did he who made the Lamb make thee?'

Tessa was reading more slowly now, stretching the poem for
dear life. Sir Philip was standing behind the sofa, his shadow
unflinching on the carpet in front of her. As she paused she
could hear the slow, earnest inhalation of his breath. She
held the leather-bound copy of the collected works of William
Blake in two hands that pressed against her knees to stop
them from trembling.
  She felt utterly dominated, as if by some effort of will he
was draining the life-force from her. It is a dangerous
business, the playing out of other people's fantasies, there is
no turning of the tables – Tessa knew that if you're cast as
victim, that's your lot. She took a deep breath for the last
verse. Oh someone, somewhere, somehow hear me.

  'Tyger! Tyger! burning bright,
  In the forests of the night,
  What immortal hand or eye,
  Dare frame they fearful symmetry?'

Tessa almost whispered the final line for her throat was dry
as a bone. 'Fearful symmetry.' What did it mean? The
atmosphere in the room was reverential as though a
ceremony was under way. For some time Sir Philip did not

move, even standing behind her he had the power to transfix her. She was the rabbit caught in his headlights.

'So,' he said, 'that's it then.' He sounded almost wistful.

'Shall I read it again? Or something else?' she offered. She would read the sonnets till dawn.

'No. No more poetry,' he said.

'Well . . . I really must be going, if . . .'

'No.' Sir Philip spoke the word quietly. It was inevitable. Of course she wasn't leaving. They both knew that.

Tessa sensed that she was in the very eye of the storm, she must stay still. A cascade of cold sweat ran down her back. Don't move she told herself. With soundless steps Sir Philip walked around her. His eyes never left her and his hands played gently with the tie. When she smiled at him he seemed not to see her. He stopped behind her again.

'Oh Tessa. Tessa. Tessa,' he said.

'What?' she asked. Surely she was not impatient for her fate.

Suddenly there was movement in the air, a blur of colour looping her head. With a shudder she felt the cool weight of the silk band round her neck. Sir Philip was leaning towards her from behind the sofa, his breath had the fetid warmth of a dance partner.

'Oh Tessa. Tessa. Tessa,' he whispered and there was melancholy in his voice.

She was tethered to him only loosely but she dared not move. There was no pressure on the silk at her throat but she knew his sanity was waning.

'You should have red hair, proper lovely long red hair . . . Red hair, Tessa, red, red, red . . . the colour of burnished copper . . . or autumn, that's the colour you should be. That's the real you, not this artificial dark,' he spoke reasonably.

'I'll change it,' she whispered. 'I'll change it tomorrow.'

'Too late. It doesn't matter anyway.' He rested his head on her shoulder. 'Oh yes. At least you have the smell . . . the smell of a redhead.'

'I'm sorry.'

'No,' he declared. 'The smell is good.'

'You like red hair?' she asked.

'It's wicked, do you understand, it's a wickedness . . . it's vile.' He growled, 'Dirty damn bitches . . . bitch. Bitch. Redhaired filthy bitches. Wicked. Wicked. Wicked, filthy, dirty bitch. Bitch. Bitch.'

He was sobbing, choking beside her so that she could smell the wine and fish on his breath. Frantically she wondered what had caused this awful wound that was now exposed. And as if in answer, Sir Philip sucked in air and roared out the one pitiful word that explained his madness: 'MUMMY'

Tessa didn't move, couldn't move, still anchored to the troubled man whose tears and spittle were dribbling on her shoulder. Did his ghastly cry of pain represent perhaps the culmination of the ordeal? Was it over? Was the boil now lanced? They were crucial, these minutes as they passed and Tessa knew not to force the pace.

'Look . . .' she said. The tenderness in her voice was a bid to survive. 'Look . . . Philip . . . I don't know how I can help you . . . but I really think . . . I ought to be going now.'

Her suggestion was misjudged. She felt the silk tighten at her neck. 'Oh no,' he said, 'you can't leave. Oh dear me, no, not now. You're not leaving.' Sir Philip was in control again. 'It's too late.'

'What do you mean?' she didn't want to know the answer.

'Too late, I'm sorry.'

'For what?' she said. 'Too late for what? What is going to happen?'

'Death.' He spoke the word with clarity. 'Death is going to happen.'

It was the confirmation of what she already knew but the shock of hearing it numbed her.

'You are going to kill me? I'm going to die?'

'Oh yes,' he replied, 'we both are. It's all over, I'm afraid. Red hair or not, heaven or hell, it doesn't matter. I should never have been born, you see, never allowed to grow up and run amok . . . It's all over now. It's time for a little peace and quiet inside my head, you see.'

In what furnace was his brain?

'You could get help,' she said, and felt no pity.

'No.' He was beyond helping.

'There's so much to live for.'

With his blue silk tie at her throat she knew the option was not hers. She was part and parcel of someone else's suicide pact – not fair at all.

'For you perhaps. Not for me. It's time.'

'Please let me go.'

'I'm sorry,' he said as if he meant it.

Tessa could feel his tie being pulled gently back and forth across her throat, a lulling sensation before the storm. And in the silence Tessa thought she heard the distant sound of something breaking.

The door was built of thick teak, no doubt to protect disreputable theatrical producers from the wrath of creditors or husbands. Dominic swung the axe heavily into the wood and wrenched it free, struck again. Behind him across the street a group of late night revellers looked on unconcerned which side of the law he was acting for. The wood began to splinter, its dense flesh screeching as it was torn apart. Beside Dominic the fireman was muttering about the advisability of breaking in. 'We have no authority . . .'

'SHUT UP!' Dominic swung the axe again. The panel parted from the jamb and then with another blow the door gave up its purpose.

Dominic took the torch from the protesting fireman and manoeuvred himself into the dark chamber at the foot of the spiral staircase.

'OK Ron,' he said for the benefit of the microphone on his lapel. 'I'm in and I'm going on up. Christ knows what we do if she's not there.'

'Tyger Tyger' would be running out on them.

He took the steps two at a time, the deep and narrow tread was turning him clockwise and upwards, so that he felt breathless and giddy. He stumbled and dropped the torch. In the darkness he groped and found it broken. In the distance he heard the wail of police sirens.

'Ron, they're coming, the police. Tell them to cover the front entrance to the office.'

With outstretched hands fumbling along the walls he

335

climbed on up the spiral stairs. The air was foul and the ascent endless, but the sirens were getting louder. The police were closing in.

In the stalls Ron-Ron was a helpless spectator observing the chase by sound not sight. From his console he had two channels amplified. On 3 he listened to Tessa pleading to be allowed to leave, to go home, to live. On 22 he had Dominic who for the moment could only be heard panting and cursing as he stumbled up the spiral stairs.

Ron-Ron was staring at the empty stage; but from all the frantic sound he clearly got the picture – in stereo. There was nothing he could do. He stood and listened praying that Dominic's hunch was right and that any minute 22 and 3 would converge.

When Tessa's red-raw scream resounded through the theatre, all poor Ron-Ron could do was turn the volume down a bit. Hurry up 22.

Sir Philip had suddenly seen that the time for talking was over, that it had merely been a ploy Tessa was using, the standard appeal for pity or fair play. He had seen it all before but this was his finale. If he could not bend the heavens, not now, not ever, he would let hell loose. The civil war inside his head would soon be over and he did not want reason or compassion fouling up his mission.

With a savage strength he had soon cut off the yelling of his guest. They were struggling now on the floor. He had grown to like this bit. The way these girls resisted! Why couldn't they take their punishment properly, these harlots, these vile cheating, red-haired bitches, these low, stinking animals with their polluted shameless bodies ... these wicked, lax and greedy women with their red hair and stench ... with their lecherous bodies that sucked in men between their legs and spat out bastards. It was his job, his duty to capture them, unsex them, to purge and obliterate them.

'Die, you bitch,' he growled.

Their two strengths were well matched – his to kill, hers to live. Tessa had her hands wedged beneath his tie to protect her throat, choking and spluttering they rolled about the floor. By turn they felt each other's weight and took each other's odour, the sweat of fear and loathing. Their ears were so full of the sound of each other's struggle they neither of them heard the police sirens.

'DIE. DIE. DIE,' Sir Philip roared, his face shiny and deranged. And in the midst of all this hurly-burly poor Tessa was tormented by a fleeting glimpse of something familiar in this face above her twisted in its ecstasy. She must be delirious, for it was Dominic she saw on top of her – his eyes for a moment and his smile of pleasure. Her head was bursting with a red hot fizzing of the blood, her lungs and chest were fathoms deep in an oily sea. This was no time to be hallucinating. And all the time Sir Philip's tie was burning into her throat. She could hardly breath and her tongue felt swollen in her mouth.

The two of them fought for purchase, scrabbling with their feet: Sir Philip in order to throttle his eighth victim and scourge again his mother's sin, Tessa merely to breathe. With one hand she tried to fend off the pressure on her throat, the other she used to punch at him and pull his hair to no effect. Her own knuckle was being forced into her windpipe. Frantically she groped for the heavy instrument that comes to the hand of those intended to survive. It didn't come. She was not intended to survive.

Phoebe and her daughter had not taken long to reach the West End. Straight after the telephone call from Ron-Ron they had set out. Harriet decided that she was nearer to sobriety than her mother and took the wheel. She drove too fast along the Mall, round Trafalgar Square and on up the Charing Cross Road. They neither of them spoke, wrapped up as they were in different priorities and fears.

As they approached the Brunswick they found the air thick with the flashing of blue lights, the police were out in force. The roads were blocked with patrol cars and there was much earnest consultation going on. Uniformed men had taken up positions in the doorways of strip joints and plain clothes officers in jeans and bomber jackets crouched among the rubbish bags. The man in charge had a megaphone in his hand but could think of nothing to shout for the moment. Another officer was talking to the fireman from the Brunswick stage door.

'There's a maniac in the penthouse,' he explained with a show of breathlessness, 'And he's about to murder this girl you see, Tessa what's her name. And Dominic Gallagher and I came to her rescue. I chopped down the door to the side entrance . . .'

The front of the theatre was in darkness, it was too late in the night for the neon to be on. Huge spotlights were being moved into position. Phoebe and Harriet were being held back behind a cordon despite the protest that it was their building.

'It seems, ladies,' a young constable explained, 'that there is a psychopath up there somewhere with some film star.'

Mother and daughter stood where they were told and watched in silence; the lover of the psychopath and the wife of the film star holding hands and shivering in the street.

From six floors above, Ron-Ron could hear the frenzied struggle of a man and woman. They were both of them close to the microphone now causing distortion on channel 3. In a voice rasping and breathless Sir Philip was shouting. 'Die. Die for God's sake, woman, die.' Tessa could only manage a feeble whimper, her resistance was going fast.

On channel 22, Ron-Ron could hear only Dominic's stertorous breathing as he stumbled on upwards. 'These fucking stairs are endless,' he gasped. 'Thank God . . . here we are . . .'

Dominic staggered up against the door at last, fumbled wildly for a handle, a bolt, a lock. He thumped with both fists and shouted with what breath he had, 'Tessa. Tessa. I'm here. I'm here.'

Tessa was floating now, flying free between life and death. She was a rag doll. There was a searing heat inside her skull and a crushing weight on her chest. Was this the fearful symmetry that she dared not frame? Was this William Blake or the feeling of death? She didn't care. She was just a rag doll.

Yet somewhere in the whirlpool of her dying – or was it

living? – her name was being shouted, 'Tessa. Tessa. Tessa.' She could hear it clearly. Was it God calling her? Oh no, not yet. Or Dominic, was it him? Impossible. What would either of them want with a lapsed Catholic in such a mess? Her head was rolling down a steep hill towards a cliff. She could feel Sir Philip's breath, rapid and putrid with his exertion. His face was out of focus in front of her, and muttering unintelligibly, sour nothings in her ear.

Then suddenly all movement stopped. Frozen for a second, the two of them lay sweating and locked together like a couple caught *in flagrante*. Even Sir Philip's breathing was suspended as they listened and heard Dominic's voice muffled calling out, 'Tessa, Tessa. I'm here. Open the door. Open the door.'

On the ceiling Tessa saw faint blue lights were flashing – was she in heaven or a discotheque? Her own name was ringing in her ears with the sound of the sea. The weight on top of her was gone, the smell and the pain and the menace too. She was giddy now as blood and air regained access to her brain and chest.

'Tessa. Tessa. Tessa.' The voice was calling and there was a thudding noise not now from within her ribs.

Tessa had no voice to answer, she could only groan a little as she crawled through broken glass and china towards the man who called her name. It couldn't be Dominic, she had dreamt it, all of it, their pleasure together and all the rest, the longing and the remorse. She had died a virgin after all. She wanted to answer his call, 'I'm coming, I'm coming,' but her throat was swollen beyond speech.

On all fours she reached the door, pulled back the curtain that concealed it and with fingers that weren't hers she fumbled for the locks. Swaying with dizziness she opened them and then collapsed. She was rolling now, unencumbered down the cliff, over the edge and falling endlessly towards the sea.

From the puce red contusions on Tessa's neck Dominic slid off Sir Philip's tie. He laid her on her back limp as a child. And then from some distant memory of what to do with people drowning, he turned her on her side. Her breathing was steadier now. She groaned and coughed and then vomited a sickly bile. Her eyes flickered and then blinked. She sucked in air and let it out, wavering between consciousness and oblivion. She blinked again and looked up at the mirage of her lover. There was Dominic gently wiping her face and telling her everything was OK.

'You're going to be all right,' Dominic said. 'Everything is going to be OK.'

She heard his voice through a fog of near wakefulness. And so too did Ron-Ron six floors below in the auditorium, for Dominic's voice was on both channels now, his own and Tessa's, 3 and 22 together at last.

'Tessa . . . Tessa,' he was saying. 'Tessa, where is he? Where has Sir Philip gone?'

She could feel pain now inside her head and chest but mostly in her throat which did not yet feel free from restriction.

'Dominic,' she croaked, 'Dominic.'

'Where did he go?' he asked again.

She shook her head and rasped, 'I don't know.'

Dominic went to the main door of the apartment. It was locked. In the kitchen, there was no way out, no window open. On the table was a plastic shopping bag. Dominic emptied the contents: scalpel, scissors, razor, needle and nylon thread – all new and unused, rubber gloves too.

He ran to the bathroom and knew as he entered that it was from here that Sir Philip had escaped. He felt a draught of cool night air. Above the bath the skylight window had been pushed open to reveal a rectangle of orange sky flashing with electric blue. Without hesitation Dominic went to follow in Sir Philip's footsteps. Standing on the edge of the bath, he reached up and took hold of the window ledge.

'Ron-Ron, if you can hear me,' he said, 'I'm going up to the roof after the bastard. Can you get someone up here to look after Tessa. She's OK but needs help.'

Ron-Ron heard the message loud and clear in the auditorium. So too did the group of policemen that had just burst in.

With an effort he would have thought quite beyond his

340

half-brother, Dominic levered himself up to the skylight. Unlike Sir Philip he didn't have the strength that insanity brings with it, and it took him several attempts to raise himself.

On the roof he found himself in the central gulley between a high double gable. Either side of him was a steeply angled roof which ran the entire length of the building. At either end was a V-shaped view of London north and south. No sign of life, no fugitive maniacs, only a row of sullen pigeons. Logically, Dominic reckoned, the bright light to the south would send a hunted man the other way, north, to the back of the theatre.

Dominic made his way along the thin wooden walkway which covered the bottom of the narrow gulley. He stood on the northern edge looking out over Soho and then down into the street, sealed off with police cars. His head reeled with vertigo as the ground tried to come towards him. Steady, steady. He looked to his right and left and saw no silhouette or shadow untoward.

'Shit,' he said, not knowing that it echoed in the Stalls two hundred and fifty feet beneath him. 'Shitting hell,' rang out for the police to hear in stereophonic sound.

Dominic turned to go the other way and was suddenly gripped with the fear that he had been duped. Without a second thought he had followed the obvious trail out through the bathroom window. Had he been tricked through, was it a dummy he'd been sold. An open skylight is proof of nothing. Maybe Sir Philip had hidden in the flat and was even now returning to his business. Hurrying forward as best he could along the duckboards, Dominic lay full length on the roof and called into the bathroom below, 'Tessa. Tessa . . . Are you all right?'

No reply. And then a moment later, half crawling, half stumbling, Tessa came into the bathroom. She looked up at Dominic framed against the darkness. 'I'm fine,' she croaked, '. . . fine . . . What are you doing?'

'I'm going to get the bastard,' Dominic said. Tessa was shaking visibly, her face was pale and bruised, blood and mascara were smeared down her cheeks.

341

'Ron-Ron, I hope you can hear me,' he went on. 'Get someone up here quick. Tessa needs attention.

Tessa looked up at him, the effort of it nearly overbalancing her. She went to speak and couldn't, was suddenly gripped again with a terror that took her speech away. She just stood quivering, quite unable to transmit the warning that was screaming silently inside her head.

From where she stood she could see the apex of the roof behind Dominic. And on it clearly silhouetted against the orange blackness of the sky was the crouching figure of Sir Philip. She watched in horror as he began to inch his way down the pitch of the roof.

'It's OK.' Dominic was blind to the danger behind him. 'It's OK,' he said, for beneath him Tessa just knelt trembling and croaking. 'It's all OK. No one is going to hurt you, it's all over. The police are on their way . . .'

Tessa's eyes were wide with alarm and their focus had gone astray somewhere behind him. She croaked again and raised her shaking hand to point over his shoulder.

Dominic turned in time to see Sir Philip sliding silently towards him down the roof. He had taken off his jacket and shoes and just for once his grey hair was out of place. His eyes glinted with malice and his mouth was set in the grin of a death mask. He was gathering speed as he tobogganed downwards and Dominic had no time to take evasive action, he could only brace himself for the collision.

The impact knocked Dominic flat against the angle of the opposite roof. He was pinioned to the slates by the weight of Sir Philip and the fierce grasp of his hands. Fleetingly, he smelt, as Tessa had done, the urgent fetid breath of the maniac and knew that death was his intention.

Both Sir Philip's hands were locked in an iron grip around Dominic's throat, his entire musculature was rigid like someone in spasm and all the time he was muttering incoherently a desperate guttural sound. Dominic was utterly immobilised with terror and the power of his assailant but in amongst the fear was a white hot hatred for this man whom he had trusted, this man who had taken so many lives and ruined

342

his father's, this man who deserved not the slightest benefit of any further doubt.

There they were, the two sons of Griffith Gallagher, face to face on the roof of the Brunswick Theatre. As their eyes met there was nothing between them but loathing – not a mere sibling antagonism but a hatred pure and simple. They were their father's blue and brown-eyed boys.

Dominic was unable to move and could feel his throat being squeezed in the vicious grip of his brother, could see the madness clearly in his eyes and knew that all the veneer of charm and sophistication had gone for good. On an impulse that came from desperation, Dominic took a breath and in the best voice he could manage began:

> 'Tyger Tyger burning bright
> In the forest of the night
> What immortal hand or eye. . .'

Sir Philip interrupted his recital with a bellowing scream of anger and pain, a cry that could be heard in the street below, a cry that tore the throat and swelled the sinews of his neck. It was the cry of man whose mind has blown its final fuse.

Dominic could feel his head being taken now between two hands, being clenched and brought forward nose to nose with the twisted sweating face of Sir Philip. He was held there for a moment, while another mighty roar blasted the air. The last sound he heard though before the silence of concussion was the sound of his head being thrust back with a sickening crash against the slates.

Only briefly was Dominic allowed to visit the state of muffled giddy blackness. Voices were all round him, near and far away. From below through the skylight window of the bathroom he could hear people attending to Tessa, shouting questions at her and she answering in croaky gibberish. Above this came a booming clear-cut voice echoing up from the street. With the power that a megaphone gives, it rang out among the roofs.

'Sir Philip Sullivan,' it said, 'this is Chief Superintendent

343

Cameron of the Metropolitan Police speaking ... This is to inform you that you are under arrest. The building is surrounded. You cannot escape ... Give yourself up. I repeat, give yourself up.'

Dominic looked about him at the blurred night and could see no sign of anyone. He stood up and staggered along the duckboards to the front of the building. He felt unsteady and his head was aching. The street two hundred feet below was filled with police cars. A crowd had gathered and been cordoned off. To either side of Dominic there was still no movement. He lay flat along the gulley and peered directly over the side of the building. At first he could see nothing for the top tiers of the theatre's façade were in the deep shadow thrown up by the police searchlights below.

Peering into the darkness he could at last discern the white head and shirt of a figure cowering on a ledge beneath him and perhaps twenty feet to the left. And as he watched, Sir Philip began to edge his way sideways. He moved slowly and with stealth towards the enormous network of iron trellising on which the front of house lights are fixed. When illuminated the gigantic letters would emblazon in red neon the name of the theatre and its star attraction. Now they were in darkness, and Sir Philip was sidling slowly towards what shelter they might provide.

Dominic did not have the strength or courage or desperation to follow his quarry. He lay flat on his stomach instead quite still and watched. He remembered for a moment Sir Philip's mother shaking pitifully on her pillow. Her son *was* a very naughty boy. The word 'stitched' flashed into his mind. He saw, too, for an instant his father's face racked with pain. He thought of his dog cold and dead, and of the terror he had just seen on Tessa's face. This wasn't a moment of hesitation, it was one of decision.

Dominic checked the microphone on his lapel and then spoke clearly into it. 'Ron-Ron, I hope you can still hear me. If you can, tell someone to turn on all the lights, all the outside ones front of house. The whole bloody lot ... Full up ... OK?'

Ron-Ron was flanked by a large group of policemen in the

Stalls. 'Shall I?' he asked them. 'There's an electrician on stand-by.'

The police saw no objection, they were tired of being impotent onlookers to this radio play. 'Yea, turn them on.'

Ron-Ron picked up the house phone. 'Fred – turn on the marquee lights on the front of the theatre. Full up. Immediately, OK.'

Fred obeyed.

And suddenly for Phoebe and Harriet and all the crowd around them, the theatre was lit up. The front of the Brunswick Theatre was framed in red neon with the famous puppeteer and his flower girl in the middle. Dominic's name was on two lines above the title, *My Fair Lady* and the other credits underneath. Again the police megaphone boomed out.

'Sir Philip Sullivan, give yourself up. Come down quietly. You are under arrest.'

From the ground there was no sign of the fugitive, but Dominic, dazzled by the sudden brightness of the lights below could still see Sir Philip through half closed eyes. He watched without moving as the desperate man clung like a bat to the wall, saw him turn, blinded and bewildered, and reach out for a handhold.

Sir Philip was sandwiched between the meshed trelliswork and the brick wall of the theatre, balancing on the narrow ledge of the architrave. He reached out for a handhold that wasn't there and for a moment he wavered like an anti-magnet, dancing with gravity. In slow motion Dominic watched him teeter, grasp out, his hands flaying desperately for support, skew his body round and begin to tumble.

From across the street the first that Phoebe and Harriet could distinguish of Sir Philip's crisis was the soft explosion of one of the neon letters high up in front of them. Sparks flew out from the vast hoarding and the 'M' in Dominic went out. Something seemed to be crashing through the letters. Or was it someone?

Dominic looked down and saw the figure of Sir Philip etched in electricity avalanching through the network of wires and filaments. He was grappling in a frenzy, screaming for help that didn't come to hand. Sparks spun off him like

345

fireflies as he tumbled through the giant letters. When at last he came to rest Dominic could see his body quivering with high voltage before stillness came to it.

'Kill the lights,' Dominic whispered into his microphone. He felt nothing except relief and vertigo.

From across the street the marquee's lighting now read:

```
D O    I N I C
G A   A G H E R
        Y
    F   I R
      A D Y
```

And in the simulated flower basket of Eliza Doolittle was the spreadeagled corpse of a man in a tailored shirt and well-made trousers. His hair was hanging from his head, charred like so much tinsel on a doll.

Even at this distance there was, for Phoebe, no mistaking that it was the man she had loved and trusted – Sir Philip Sullivan.

> And did he smile his work to see
> Did he who made the Lamb make thee.